Dear Reader:

The more you go back in time and history, the more magical the possibilities become. Just the word "medieval" conjures up visions of knights and ladies, candles and castles, unicorns and dragons. It was a time when the shape of the world was unknown, the universe was unknowable, and man held the night at bay only by torchlight.

Every time I read about the twelfth century in the British Isles, I couldn't help wondering what it would be like to be a Saxon woman married off to a conquering Norman lord for the English king's convenience—especially if the woman in question had a mystical connection to her Saxon land and people. How would such a woman balance her duties to her heritage with her own yearning for a life that had more warmth than duty gave, and more fire even than the flames in the hearth?

The men who earned the English king's favor in the First Crusade came back to the English islands with wealth and bleak memories of war. Some of those men were satisfied with money and power alone. A few had the vision and determination to achieve more.

What would happen if an unusual Norman lord met up with the Saxon lady of my imagination? What if each wanted something from the other . . . something that was believed to be impossible?

Untamed is the answer to my questions about what an unusual Saxon lady and a determined Norman lord might make of a marriage decreed by a distant English king.

Elizabeth Lowell

Further Titles by Elizabeth Lowell from Severn House

ENCHANTED

FORBIDDEN

FORGET ME NOT

A WOMAN WITHOUT LIES

UNTAMED

Elizabeth Lowell

This title first published in Great Britain 2006 by
SEVERN HOUSE PUBLISHERS LTD of
9–15 High Street, Sutton, Surrey SM1 1DF.
This first hardcover edition published in the USA 2006 by
SEVERN HOUSE PUBLISHERS INC of
595 Madison Avenue, New York, N.Y. 10022.
by arrangement with Avon Books, and Two of a Kind, Inc.

British Library Cataloguing in Publication Data

Lowell, Elizabeth, 1944-
    Untamed
    1.   Scotland - History - 1057-1603 - Fiction
    2.   Love stories
    I.   Title
    813.5'4 [F]

    ISBN-13: 9780-7278-6356-0
    ISBN-10: 0-7278-6356-8

Printed and bound in Great Britain by
MPG Books Ltd., Bodmin, Cornwall.

For
Denis Farina
White Knight, Magician, Champion

1

Spring in the Reign of King Henry I
Northern England

THE SOUND OF A WAR HORN sliced through the day, announcing the coming of Blackthorne Keep's new lord.

As though summoned, a dark shape condensed out of the mist . . . a knight in full armor riding a huge stallion. Horse and man seemed one, indivisible, fierce with the male power singing in their blood like a storm.

"They say he is a devil, m'lady," the widow Eadith muttered.

"They say that of all Norman knights," Meg said to her handmaiden with desperate calm, "yet among them surely there must be men of kind and generous hearts."

Eadith made a sound that could have been a throttled laugh.

"Nay, mistress. 'Tis fitting that your bridegroom wears chain mail and rides a savage destrier. There is whispering of war."

"There will be no war," Meg said firmly. "That is why I will wed—to end the bloodletting."

"Do not mislead yourself. War is more likely to be waged than a wedding," Eadith announced with savage satisfaction. "Death to the Norman invaders!"

"Silence," Meg said softly. "I will hear no talk of war."

Eadith's mouth thinned, but she spoke no more of war.

Standing at a high window of the keep, shielded from view by a partly closed shutter, Meg searched the land for the riding household that must have accompanied the warrior who would soon become her husband.

Nothing moved behind the war-horse but silver mist twisting above the fields. The horn had been sounded by someone hidden within the forest that lay beyond the keep's cultivated land.

Horse and chain mail–clad knight loomed larger with every moment, riding openly up to the keep, fearing nothing. No retainers hurried behind the knight. No squires appeared leading war-horses or pack animals burdened with the shining metal tools of war.

Against all custom, Dominic le Sabre approached the Saxon keep with nothing but the war horn's deep cry attending him.

"This one is truly the Devil wearing man's flesh," Eadith said, crossing herself. "I would never wed him."

"Quite true. 'Tis my hand to be given, not yours."

"May God save you," Eadith muttered. "I tremble for you, my lady, since you have not the wit to tremble for yourself!"

"I am the last of an ancient and proud line," Meg said in a husky voice. "What is a nameless Norman bastard to make a daughter of Glendruid tremble?"

Yet even as Meg spoke, fear washed coolly down her spine. The closer Dominic le Sabre rode, the more she feared her handmaiden was right.

"God be with you, m'lady, for 'tis certain the Devil will be!"

As Eadith spoke, she crossed herself again.

With outward composure Meg watched the proud warrior ride closer. This was the man who would claim her as bride, and with her, the vast domain that she would inherit upon the imminent death of her father.

That was the lure that had brought a famous Norman knight from Jerusalem to the northern marches of King Henry's realm. Her father's estates had always been the lure for the Scots lords whose families had asked Meg's hand for their sons. But first William II and then Henry I had refused to condone a marriage for Lady Margaret of Blackthorne.

Until now.

The knight on his war stallion approached closer, telling Meg that her future husband was unusual in more than that he rode alone.

Like an outcast knight, he wears no lord's colors, yet certainly he is favored by the English king. When he becomes my husband, he will control more land than any but the greatest of the king's barons.

Puzzled, Meg watched the Norman knight who had become a great English lord. He rode under no banner and wore no man's emblem on his teardrop-shaped shield. His helm was fashioned of a strange, blackened metal, the same color as the war-horse that bore him. The long cloak that mantled his mail-clad body and that of his horse was dark, rich, and swirled heavily with the stallion's powerful movements.

Proud as Lucifer, both of them. And as strong.

Meg watched the dark lord's approach, willing herself to show no fear.

"He's uncommon large," Eadith said.

Meg said nothing.

"Does he not appear fearsome to you?" the hand-maiden asked.

The dark knight did indeed look formidable, but there was no purpose to having every servant in the keep gossiping about how their mistress trembled at the approach of her future husband.

"No, he doesn't appear fearsome to me," Meg said. "He looks like what he is, a man in chain mail riding a horse. A common enough sight, sure-ly."

"To think," Eadith said in a bitter voice, "one moment he was a bastard knight and the next moment he was one of the king's favorites. Though the Sword has no land of his own, men speak of him as a great lord."

"Lord Dominic, called le Sabre, the Sword," Meg murmured. "Bastard or noble, he saved a great bar-on's son from the Saracen. 'Tis said without him Robert's crusade would have ended badly. A wise king rewards such a fine warrior."

"With Saxon land," Eadith retorted.

" 'Tis the king's right."

"You act as though you don't care."

"I care only that the killing ends."

Did you learn pity in the Holy Land, Dominic le Sabre? Will the hope in my heart be answered by generosity in yours?

Or are you like the chain mail you wear, glittering with harsh possibilities rather than future hopes?

Eadith looked sideways at the delicate features of her lady. Nothing showed of whatever Meg's inner thoughts might be. The handmaiden looked again at the Norman knight who was approaching the gates of a keep he had taken by promise of marriage rather than by honorable battle.

"They say he fought with the coolness of ice and

the savagery of a northern barbarian," Eadith offered into the silence.

"It will do him no good with me. I am neither ice nor warrior."

"Glendruid," Eadith whispered so softly that her lady couldn't hear.

But Meg did.

"Do you think he knows?" Eadith asked after a few moments.

"What?"

"That he'll never have heirs of you."

Meg's clear green eyes fastened on the Saxon widow her father had insisted Meg take as handmaiden.

"Do you often trade gossip with the cotters, villeins, and peasants?" Meg asked crisply.

"Will he?" Eadith persisted. "Will he have sons of you?"

"What odd questions." Meg forced herself to smile. "Am I a seer to know the sex of my unborn children?"

" 'Tis said you are a Glendruid witch," Eadith said bluntly.

"Glendruids aren't witches."

"That's not what the people say."

"The people say many fanciful things," Meg retorted. "After a year at Blackthorne Keep, surely you know that."

Eadith looked sideways at her mistress. "The people also speak the truth."

"Do they? No rocks burst into bloom for me, nor do trees bend to whisper in my ear. What nonsense."

"You have a fine hand with falcons and herbs," Eadith pointed out.

"I am no more a witch than you are. Don't speak of such things to me. Some slow-witted soul might take it for the truth."

" 'Tis true enough," Eadith said, shrugging. "The common folk fear your mother, make no mistake of it."

Meg bit back a sharp remark. Eadith could be quite tiresome on the subject of Lady Anna. The tales surrounding Anna's death fascinated the handmaiden.

"My mother is dead," Meg said.

"That's not what the shepard's widow said. She saw the ghost of Lady Anna at moonrise out toward that pagan burial place."

"The good widow is overly fond of ale," Meg retorted. "It quite turns her wits. Wasn't it she who swore that fairies danced on her milk saucer and that ghosts drank the ale she owed in payment for a piglet?"

Eadith started to speak.

With a sharp gesture, Meg demanded silence. She wanted to concentrate only on the warrior who was riding alone toward Blackthorne Keep.

Dominic le Sabre seemed so certain of his own prowess that his retinue rode well behind, just now emerging from the mists, too far to be of any aid to him if an ambush had been laid. Nor was the thought of such attack unreasonable. Her father's fury at hearing that he must wed his only heir to a Norman bastard had been so great that Lord John had nearly burst the heart within his body, a body once renowned for its size and brawn.

But even at the height of his youth and strength, John had been a full hand shorter than the Norman knight who rode so disdainfully into the keep's yard.

Proud warrior, Meg thought silently. *But if legend be true, only an equal prowess in seduction might earn you female offspring from the body of your Glendruid bride.*

With clear eyes, Meg measured the man who wore

chain mail over black leather, his hair hidden beneath a steel helm, his war stallion as dark and savage as Satan's dreams.

As for sons, my black lord . . .

Never.

That is the curse of Glendruid. In a thousand years no one has lifted that curse.

Seeing you, I fear that it will never be lifted.

As though sensing Meg's intense stare, the knight suddenly pulled his stallion to a halt. The horse half reared, as though facing an attack. Balanced on his muscular hindquarters, the charger lashed out with his forelegs, sending his hooves slicing through the air. Had a foot soldier been attacking, he would have died under the war-horse's hooves.

Dominic le Sabre rode the rearing animal effort-lessly, never taking his eyes from the window high in the keep where shutters were partly opened. Though he could see no one through the opening, he knew Lady Margaret of Blackthorne stood within the stone walls, watching her future husband ride up to the keep.

He wondered if she was like her father, still fighting a battle that had been lost in 1066, when William the Conqueror had taken England from its Saxon nobility.

Saxon lady, will you accept my seed without a battle? Will you give me the sons I hunger for the way a thirsty man hungers for drink?

A knight broke from Dominic's retinue and ap-proached at a canter. Dominic's horse reared again, calling out a challenge. Casually he curbed his war stallion as the knight came to a plunging halt a few feet away.

The second knight was in armor and also rode a charger. It was a breach of custom and common sense to use a valuable war-horse for ordinary travel, but no one had been certain if John of Cumbriland, Lord of Blackthorne Keep, had planned a wedding or a war.

"Still thyself, Crusader," Dominic said calmly to his horse. "There is no hint of treachery."

"Yet," said the other knight bluntly, coming up alongside.

Dominic looked at his brother. Simon's clear black eyes were watching everything, missing nothing. Simon, called the Loyal, was the most valued knight in Dominic's retinue. Without him, Dominic doubted he would have managed the feats of battle that had won him the prize of a Saxon bride whose wealth in land was enough to make the English king envious.

But not greedy. The Norman kings had learned to their cost that the fractious Saxons of the northern marches were too troublesome to be fought outright. Weddings rather than wars were to be employed.

"Have you seen anything amiss?" Dominic asked.

"Sven came to me in the woods," Simon said.

"And?"

"He did as you asked."

"A true knight," Dominic said sardonically, for what he had asked was that Sven go ahead to Blackthorne Keep disguised as a returning pilgrim and seduce one of the household maids.

"The wench was willing," Simon said, shrugging.

Dominic grunted.

"Sven learned that Duncan of Maxwell is in the keep," Simon said succinctly.

Dominic's stallion half reared again, responding to the surge of anger in his rider.

"And the lady Margaret?" he asked coldly.

"She is in the keep as well."

"A tryst?"

"No one caught them together."

Dominic grunted. "That could mean only that they are clever, not virtuous. What about the Reevers? Are they here, too?"

"No. They're with Duncan's cousin north of here, at Carlysle, one of Lord John's manor houses. Or rather, one of *your* manors."

"Not yet. Not until I wed the daughter and the father dies."

"Two days until the wedding. I doubt John will survive the feast that follows."

Dominic turned from his brother to Blackthorne Keep, looming above the green hill where it dominated the landscape. Lord John had spent himself into poverty building the four-story keep with its thick stone walls and blunt corner turrets.

No expense had been spared to make the place into a military stronghold that would be all but immune to attack. Surrounding the keep at a distance of thirty yards was a half-finished stone wall. Completed, the wall would have been twice the height of a mounted man. But stone gave way to wooden palisades whose weaknesses Dominic's keen glance catalogued in a single moment.

At least John had the sense to dig a wide, deep moat to slow attackers. Even so, the keep is too vulnerable. A few buckets of Greek fire against the palisades and the outer wall would be breached. The keep itself would last no longer than the knights' ability to endure thirst.

Unless there is a well within the keep itself. . . . If not, I will see to that lack immediately.

Dominic looked again at the looming stone structure astride the hill that was struggling to turn green. A gatehouse had been set into the partially completed outer wall. The bridge over the moat had yet to be lowered.

"Where is the gatekeeper?" Simon demanded. "Are we expected to lay siege?"

"Patience, brother," Dominic said sardonically. "John deserves our pity more than our anger."

"I'd rather put my gauntlet in his Saxon face."

"You may get the chance."

"Do I have your vow on that, my liege?" Simon retorted.

Dominic's laughter was as hard as the metal of his helm.

"Poor John of Cumbriland," Dominic said. "His father and grandfather couldn't hold back the Norman tide. Nor could he. Now he is dying of a wasting disease and has only a female for an heir. What a pitiable state. One might almost think him cursed."

"He is."

"What?"

Before Simon could answer, a slow grating of chain and cogs announced the lowering of the drawbridge.

"Ah," Dominic said with savage satisfaction. "Our sullen Saxon has decided to bow to his Norman peers. Tell the rest of my knights to come forward quickly."

"On their war-horses?"

"Yes. Intimidation now could save us bloodshed later."

Dominic's cool assessment of tactics came as no surprise to Simon. Despite Dominic's courage and skill in battle, he had none of the blood lust that some knights did. Rather, Dominic was as cold as a Norse winter when he fought. It was the secret of his success, and quite unsettling to knights who had never encountered such discipline.

Just as Simon turned his horse toward the forest, Dominic called out to him.

"What is this about John not outlasting the wedding feast?" Dominic asked.

"He's far more ill than we knew."

There was silence followed by the sound of a mailed fist meeting a mailed thigh.

"Then hurry, brother," Dominic said sharply. "I want no funeral to interfere with my marriage."

"I wonder if Lady Margaret is as eager to wed as you?"

"Eager or dragging feet like a donkey, it matters not. My heir will be born by Easter next."

ALONE IN HER ROOM ON THE
fourth floor of the keep, Meg unlaced her overtunic
and tossed the worn russet wool cloth onto her
bed. Her floor-length inner tunic quickly followed.
The cross she wore around her neck gleamed like
liquid silver in the candlelight. With each step she
took, dried rushes, herbs, and last summer's flowers
rustled underfoot. Hurriedly she pulled on the
simple tunic and coat of a commoner's daughter.

A woman's laughter floated up from the great hall
on the floor below. Meg held her breath and prayed
that Eadith was too busy flirting with Duncan to
bother about asking after her mistress's needs.
Eadith's constant chatter about Lord Dominic's
brutal strength and cold demeanor had worn Meg's
nerves.

She didn't want to hear any more. She wouldn't
even be presented to her future husband until the
wedding tomorrow because her father said he was
too weak to leave his bed. Meg didn't know if that
was true. She did know that she would be married
tomorrow to a man whom she had seen for the first
time only yesterday.

The wedding was being rushed too much for

Meg's peace of mind. The vision of Dominic le Sabre condensing out of the mist astride a savage battle stallion had haunted her sleep. She had no desire to lie in pain beneath a cold warrior while he planted his seed within her infertile body.

And she had no doubt it would be an infertile, painful mating. Denying the harsh knight any children would be small recompense for a future spent being harrowed by a harsh Norman plow.

Chills coursed through Meg's blood at the thought of it. For many years she had known what had driven her Glendruid mother to walk into the forest and never return, abandoning her daughter to John's harsh hand. Meg would rather not have known, for it was like seeing into her own future.

Perhaps the legends are right. Perhaps there is another, more gentle world just beneath ours, and its entrance lies somewhere within the ancient burial mound. Perhaps Mother is there, whistling to the falcon on her wrist while her great striped cat sleeps in her lap and sunlight pours around her. . . .

A woman's laughter spiraled upward, interrupting Meg's thoughts. She frowned. The laugh was new. Rich and sultry, like a summer wind. It must belong to the Norman woman Meg had spied from her room. Even at a distance, the woman's black hair and red lips had been enough to turn any man's head.

What do I care that Lord Dominic's leman is a beauty? Meg told herself impatiently. *More important that I get free of the keep before Eadith comes trotting to me with the latest tale of Norman brutality. Whether true or not—and I often wonder!—Eadith's tales are unnerving.*

With flying fingers Meg stripped away the embroidered ribbon that was twisted through her long braids. Impatiently she braided her long hair again and tied the ends with leather strings. A simple headcloth with a twisted leather circlet completed her costume.

Meg hurried from the room and down the winding interior stone stairs to the second floor of the keep. By the time she reached the bottom, one of her braids was half undone. Like a fall of fire, her bright, red-gold hair spilled down the neutral gray wool of her short coat.

Servants bowed quickly as Meg passed through to the attached forebuilding that guarded the keep's entrance. No one thought her common clothing odd, for she had been running free at the keep since she was thirteen and her marriage to Duncan of Maxwell had been refused by the king. At nineteen, an age when most women of her station had a husband and a handful of babes, Meg was an old maid whose father despaired of heirs.

Nodding to the servant who opened the door, Meg stepped out of the forebuilding onto the steep stone stairs that stretched down to the cobblestone-covered ground of the bailey. Her soft leather slippers made no noise while she descended the mist-slicked steps. As surefooted as a cat, she glided down the stairs to the open bailey where the wind searched through granary and kitchen alike, ruffling the feathers of fowl trussed and waiting for the hatchet.

Overhead the gray sky was streaked with tendrils of light blue. The incandescent circle of the sun burned palely through veils of mist. The fragile, silver light of spring fell around Meg like a bene-diction, lifting her spirits. To her left came the liquid call of birds within the dovecotes. To her right came the high, keening cry of a gyrfalcon being taken from the mews to be weathered on a block of wood in the yard.

Before Meg had taken two steps toward the gate-house, a black cat with three white feet and startling green eyes trotted toward her, yeowing happily, fluffy tail held high. Meg bent down and held out her arms just as the animal leaped lightly, confident that he would be caught and held.

"Good morning to you, too, Black Tom," Meg said, smiling.

The cat purred and rubbed its head against her shoulder and chin. His long white eyebrows and whiskers made a startling contrast to his black face.

"Ah, you have such soft fur. Better than the white weasels on the king's cloak, I allow."

Black Tom purred his agreement and watched his mistress with unblinking, green eyes. Talking to him quietly, Meg carried the cat to the gatehouse.

"Fair morning to you, m'lady," said the gateman, touching his forehead in respect.

"And to you, Harry. Is your son better?"

"Aye, thanks be to God and your medicine. He's lively as a pup and curious as a kitten again."

Meg smiled. "That's wonderful."

"Will you be going to see the priest's falcon after you've seen to your herbs?"

Emerald eyes searched Harry's face as she asked, "Is the small huntress still refusing food?"

"Aye."

"I will see her."

Harry limped toward the huge double doors that opened onto the keep's outer yard when the bridge was lowered over the moat. A smaller portal was set within the massive timber of one door. He threw open the portal, allowing a rectangle of misty daylight into the dark gatehouse. As Meg walked through, Harry bent forward and spoke quietly.

"Sir Duncan has been asking after you."

Meg turned quickly toward the gateman. "Is he ill?"

"That one?" Harry scoffed. "He's strong as an oak. He wondered if *you* were ill. You weren't in chapel this morning."

"Dear Duncan. It was kind of him to notice."

Harry cleared his throat. Not many men would have described Duncan of Maxwell as kind. But then, the mistress was a Glendruid witch. She had a way about her that soothed the most savage creatures.

"He wasn't the only one to notice, I hear," Harry said. "The Norman lord was fair put out not to see you."

"Tell Duncan that I am well," Meg said, hurrying through the door.

" 'Tis certain you'll see him before I do."

Meg shook her head. Her unraveled braid shimmered in waves of fire as she hurried forward, speaking over her shoulder.

"My father has asked that I not attend his sickbed after chapel. As Duncan rarely leaves Father's side these days . . ." She shrugged.

"What shall I tell Lord Dominic if he asks?" Harry said, giving his mistress a shrewd look.

"If he asks—which I doubt—tell him the truth. You saw no well-dressed lady leave the bailey this morning."

The gateman looked at the simple clothes Meg was wearing and laughed. Then his smile faded and he shook his head sadly.

"You are your mother's daughter, always wanting to be outside stone walls. Like a falcon she was, crying to be free."

"She is free, now."

"I pray you're right, mistress. God rest her poor soul."

Meg looked away from Harry's wise, faded blue eyes. The pity he felt for her was all too clear in his expression. She was Glendruid, daughter of a Glendruid woman; and like her mother, she wouldn't be free short of death.

Just beyond the fish pond a kingfisher waited hopefully for a meal to disturb the still surface of the water. In the reeds at the edge of the pond, motionless as a statue, a heron gleamed ghostly gray. Ravens called hoarsely from the battlements at the top of the keep. As though answering, one of the gardeners berated his helper for stepping on a tender new plant.

For a moment it was as though nothing had changed, as though Meg was still a child and her mother was singing softly of love lost while Old Gwyn embroidered runes on Meg's undertunic, where they could be felt but not seen; as though no arrogant Norman knight had ridden up to the keep, demanding a wife, an estate, and heirs to stretch into a future no one could see.

Meg breathed in deeply, drawing the clean air into her body, savoring its chill spring scents. Her skirts swirled in a gust of wind. The cold bite of the air on her legs warned of an uncertain spring, riven by the death throes of the hard winter past.

The cry of a wild hawk keened over the meadow where green shoots pushed through the last year's hay stubble. Nearby a sparrow hawk fluttered above the meadow, seeking the first meal of the day. A few days past, the priest's falcon had hovered just like that, then stooped to the kill. But the kill had been contested by an untamed falcon thrice her size. Before the priest could intervene, the gallant little bird had been sorely wounded.

Abruptly Meg turned and went back to the gatehouse. Her seedlings could wait. The falcon could not.

As though expecting her, Harry opened the door

before she had taken three steps, allowing her to hurry back through into the bailey. When she set Black Tom down on the damp cobbles, he gave her a look of green-eyed disbelief.

"You can't come with me just yet. I'm going to the mews first," she explained.

The cat blinked, then calmly began grooming himself as if he had never expected to be taken for a romp through the catnip in Meg's herb garden.

As soon as Meg came in sight of the wooden buildings that housed Blackthorne Keep's array of hunting birds, the falconer came forward, relief clear on his face.

"Thank you, mistress," William said, touching his forehead. "I was afraid you would be too busy with the wedding preparations to see the wee falcon."

"Never," Meg said softly. "Life would be so much poorer without the fierce little creatures. Have you my gauntlet?"

William handed over a leather gauntlet that he had made years ago for Meg's mother. It fit the daughter as well. Scarred and scored with long use, the leather was silent testimony to the razor talons of the hunting birds.

Meg went to the mews that housed the wounded bird. She had to bend slightly to enter, but once inside she could stand freely. After a moment her eyes adjusted to the semidarkness. She spotted the sparrow hawk on a perch in the darkest part of the mews.

When Meg went over and offered her forearm as a new perch, the bird refused. Meg whistled softly. The sparrow hawk stood on first one foot and then the other. Finally, with stiff, slow movements and a dragging wing, the bird was coaxed onto her forearm.

Meg walked to the door of the mews and held

the little hawk in the wash of daylight. Eyes that should have been clear were cloudy. Plumage that should have been luminous with subtle shifts of color from gray-blue to buff looked chalky. The grip of the bird's talons was uncertain on the gauntlet.

"Ah, little one," she whispered sadly, "soon you will be flying skies no man has ever seen. God speed you from your pain."

Gently Meg replaced the sparrow hawk on its perch. For long minutes she whistled and murmured softly to the bird. Slowly its clouded eyes closed. As soon as she was certain movement wouldn't disturb the falcon, she turned to go.

When Meg emerged from the mews, Dominic le Sabre was standing behind the falconer.

Her steps faltered as she looked up into bleak gray eyes and a face drawn in clean, harsh angles. Where other men wore long beards or none at all, this warrior had closely clipped his black beard and mustache. Nor did he have long locks of flowing hair to gentle the planes of this warrior's face; his thick, black hair had been cut short to fit beneath a battle helm.

Tall, powerful, motionless, Dominic le Sabre engulfed Meg's senses for the space of one breath, two, three. Then as certainly as she had sensed the death unfolding in the sparrow hawk, she sensed Dominic's rigid self-control, a fierce dominion over himself that permitted no emotion, no softness, nothing but the icy calculations of power and progeny.

At first Meg thought Dominic's self-control was as seamless and icy as winter itself. Then she realized that deep beneath the warrior's cold restraint there was an echo of suffering harshly contained. The discovery was as unexpected and poignant as hearing a meadowlark sing in the midst of night.

Dear God, what has this man borne that caused him to deny all but a faint echo of human emotion?

On the heels of that thought came another, more disturbing one. Despite everything, there was a savage masculine fire in Dominic that called to Meg on a level of her being she had never known she had.

And something within her was stirring, stretching, answering.

It frightened her. She, who had walked in fear of nothing, not even the most ferocious beasts of the forest.

"Mis—" began William, perplexed by her stillness.

Meg cut across his words before he could give away her identity.

"Good day to you, lord," she said to Dominic.

In front of William's surprised eyes, Meg touched her forehead, saluting Dominic as though she were a cotter's wench rather than the lady of the keep.

"The priest's small falcon soon will be free," Meg said to William in a low voice.

"Ach," he said. "The good father will mourn her keenly. He loved to go hunting with her. Said it lifted his soul like nothing but a fine mass."

"Is one of the birds ill?" Dominic asked.

"Father Millerson's falcon," William explained.

"Disease?" Dominic asked sharply.

William looked to Meg.

"Nay," she said in a husky voice. "It is a battle wound won from a wild hawk, not a plague to empty the mews or dovecotes of their birds."

When Meg touched her forehead again and turned to leave, Dominic said, "Hold."

He found he was intensely curious about the young woman who had emerged from the mews like flame from darkness, her eyes as green as sunstruck emeralds. Those magnificent eyes told much of her thoughts; sadness as she left behind the dying bird, surprise at seeing Dominic in the mews, and . . . fear? Yes, fear.

He frightened her.

Then as Dominic watched, the girl's eyes changed in the manner of the sea going from day to night. Now nothing moved to give away her thoughts.

What an extraordinary wench.

Dominic stroked his closely clipped mustache and black beard as he studied her.

That hair. Gold and red and russet. It makes her skin look like particularly fine cream. I wonder whom I must pay to have her in my bed. Father, brother, uncle?

Or husband . . .

Dominic frowned. The thought of the wench being married didn't appeal. The last thing he wanted to do was give the Norman-hating vassals of Blackthorne Keep an excuse to cry off the bargain King Henry had forced. The Scots thanes and minor Saxon nobility might mount all the local wenches at will, married or no; but let a Norman touch a local woman against her husband's desire and the complaints would be heard all the way to London.

Is the wench married? That is the question.

Yet instead of asking about marriage, Dominic asked after the queen of falcons that had been King Henry's gift to his newest great baron.

"Did my peregrine arrive safely?"

"Aye, lord," William said quickly.

"How is she?" Dominic asked.

But it was the girl he spoke to, not the falconer.

"Fierce," Meg said.

Then she smiled as she realized Dominic had taken her for what she appeared to be, a common maid. Relief, amusement, and a curiosity about the dark knight made Meg decide to stay rather than flee as she had first thought to do.

"Life pours through her like a torrent of fire," Meg said. "She will repay well the man who takes the time to gentle her."

A shaft of desire went through Dominic, startling him. He wasn't a boy to harden at a girl's smile and double-edged words. Yet he had done just that, undeniably. Were it not for the fall of his side-fastened cape, his instant response would be visible for all to see.

"Stay by me while I visit her," Dominic commanded.

There was naked demand rather than polite request in his voice. Meg barely stifled her instant irritation and the unease that grew greater with each moment she was in Dominic's potent presence.

Dominic saw Meg's mixed reactions and was again intrigued. Most girls of her station would have been delighted at any sign of a lord's attention. Yet he sensed quite clearly that she was getting ready to run from the mews.

"A man's first moments with a new falcon are critical," Dominic said. "I want her to accept me without hurting herself by trying to flee when no flight is necessary."

"Or possible," Meg muttered beneath her breath.

"Exactly."

Dominic noted the tiny tightening of Meg's mouth and the slight widening of her eyes in surprise at being overheard. He read other people with the ease of a farmer reading the seasons or a priest reading the Bible. The smile he gave her would have been taken by most people as a sign of reassurance.

But Meg saw through Dominic's gentle smile to the calculation beneath.

"Have no fear," she said crisply. "The falcon is

hooded. A sightless falcon flies nowhere. She awaits your gentling."

"Will you help me, lady falconer?"

"I am . . . Meg."

"Lord Dominic le Sabre," he said.

"I suspected as much."

Again, Dominic smiled slightly, enjoying the wry edge of the maiden's tongue.

Meg tried not to smile in return. She failed. It was impossible not to soften, for his flash of amusement had been real rather than calculated.

Dominic's smile widened as he read Meg's answer in the relaxation of her body. No longer was she poised to flee.

"Then come with me, maid Meg. William will see to your honor. Or have you a husband to stand for you?"

The falconer began coughing fit to choke. Meg whacked him soundly between the shoulder blades and prayed that he wouldn't give away the game. She suspected that her future husband would be more relaxed with a cotter's wench than he would be with his unwilling Saxon bride.

"There, William. Are you better or should I thump some more?" As Meg bent solicitously to the falconer, she whispered, "Enough, William! If you can't keep me secret, I'll go to the peregrine without you!"

The falconer cleared his throat heartily and pulled his mouth into a flat line as though he would never smile again. Instantly the line fractured into laughter. He clapped his hand over his mouth and made strangling sounds.

"I think we should leave the poor fellow to it," Dominic said smoothly. "Stay here, falconer. You're coughing fit to frighten a stone, much less a falcon newly come to your mews."

Meg glanced sideways. Her heart lurched when she saw Dominic watching her. There was a masculine calculation in his eyes that was different from his previous self-control. It was hot rather than cold.

He wanted to be alone with her.

"Which mews?" Dominic asked.

"I—er, there," she said, pointing.

"Show me the way."

Common sense told Meg to refuse. Curiosity made her accept. She could learn much about a man from the way he handled a fierce, captive falcon.

Warily Meg led Dominic to the mews housing the new peregrine. The room was three times the size given to the priest's falcon. An opening set high in the wall admitted fresh air and light. Only the air was appreciated by the peregrine, for she was hooded. It was a way of keeping the bird from dashing herself uselessly against the walls in search of freedom or exhausting herself by thrashing at the end of her leather leash.

Small bells chimed when the falcon moved restlessly on her perch, sensing people within her mews. As Dominic and Meg entered, the bird spread her powerful wings and turned her head from side to side, listening intently. Despite the hood, she could hear quite well.

Meg whistled an intricate five-note call, one she used only for this bird. Recognizing the call, the peregrine calmed, folding her wings. The small chiming of bells faded into silence.

"She is magnificent," Dominic said in a low voice.

"A bird for princes or great barons," Meg agreed.

"Does she come to the wrist yet?"

"Mine, aye. She is wary yet of men."

"Wise," Dominic said. "At this moment she knows us only as her captor, not as the partner in the hunt we will become."

The peregrine shifted restively at the sound of Dominic's voice. Bells chimed at the end of the leather jesses that trailed from each leg. Her hooked beak opened and her wings spread as though to attack or defend.

Dominic whistled, exactly duplicating the five-note call Meg had used. Startled, Meg turned and stared. Even the falconer had difficulty making his whistle sound like hers.

The falcon cocked her head quickly, orienting on the familiar whistle. When it was repeated again and again until it made a soothing rill of sound, the peregrine edged across her perch, getting closer to the source of the music. When a leather gauntlet nudged gently against her talons, she stepped forward onto Dominic's wrist.

"Touch her as you normally would," he said in a low voice.

Meg would have to stand very close to Dominic to reach the falcon as she normally would. She hesitated, divided between wariness and curiosity at what it would be like to stand within this man's reach as the falcon did, breathing his scent, hearing the soft rush of his breath.

Bells spoke, signaling the peregrine's increasing restlessness.

"Go on," Dominic murmured. "She grows nervous of your silence."

Speaking quietly, praising the proud falcon's strength and beauty, Meg stroked her fingertips over the peregrine's head, her wings, her breast, her cool legs, blowing gently into the falcon's face all the while.

"Indeed, you are the most perfect falcon in all the realm," Meg said softly. "Your wings are swift as a storm wind, your talons strike like lightning, and your courage is greater than thunder filling the land.

You will never turn aside from the hunt. The death you bring will be clean and certain."

The temporary blindness of the hood had heightened the peregrine's response to messages from her other senses. Surrounded by the scent, touch, and sounds that had comforted her since she had arrived in the strange mews, the peregrine became calm yet alert, focused entirely on the woman who touched and spoke to her so kindly.

Meg turned toward Dominic, a silent question in her eyes. The answer came as he began stroking the falcon as she had, head and breast and wings, his touches both gentle and certain. Unhurried, as though there were no more demands on him than those placed by the need to reassure the beautiful captive falcon, he stroked her and whistled her five-note call.

Fascinated, Meg watched. When the bird became restive at the strange breath bathing her, Dominic showed no impatience. Long minutes passed as he began the ritual all over again and yet again, touching the falcon as Meg had. Slowly the bird calmed, accepting him.

Only then did Dominic speak to the peregrine, praising her fine beak and the proud curve of her head. Bells jangled as the falcon moved restlessly, unused to Dominic's voice. Again, he showed no impatience. He simply began all over again, repeating the calming ritual until the falcon accepted his touch, his voice, his breath bathing her.

Meg let out a sigh she hadn't been aware of holding in. Smiling with pleasure, she watched Dominic finish gentling the falcon. He had a fine touch, light and yet firm. Even when he turned the bird to the light to see her better, she accepted him without restlessness.

"You are very gentle with her," Meg said softly.

"Falcons respond best to gentleness."

"And if they responded best to beating?"

"I would beat them," he murmured matter-of-factly.

There was silence while Meg measured anew the dismaying extent of Dominic's self-control. Had she not sensed the pain buried so deeply within him, she would have thought him an utterly cold man.

"Again, Meg," whispered Dominic. "Let me see your hands gentling her."

But this time it wasn't the peregrine on his wrist Dominic watched. It was Meg's graceful hands, her slightly parted lips, and her breasts rising beneath her open coat. His nostrils flared slightly as he drank in the scent of spices that rose from Meg's body like heat from a candle flame.

Desire surged powerfully, making Dominic uneasy. A warrior who wasn't in complete control of himself made mistakes. Fatal mistakes.

With the ease of long experience, he reined in his impatience to bed the wench. He couldn't control his body's hard response, but he could control what he did about that arousal.

"It might be worth captivity to be touched so sweetly," Dominic said after a moment. "Do you caress your lovers with your breath and fingertips, maid Meg?"

Startled, she turned toward him. He was very close, and he watched her with a falcon's intensity. In the half-light of the mews, his eyes gleamed like quicksilver.

"I—I know not such things," Meg said.

"Is your husband so ungenerous, then?"

"I'm not married."

"Excellent," Dominic said, blowing gently over the peregrine. "I would be loath to sever that which was melded together with God's blessing, yet I find

I want you as my leman. Do you have a father or an uncle who will receive your price?"

Spine straight, chin raised, Meg said coldly, "You overreach yourself, lord."

The clear tone of outrage in her voice amused Dominic.

"How so?" he asked.

"You are to be wed on the morrow!"

"Ah, that."

Dominic turned aside long enough to replace the peregrine on its perch.

"Marriage is for land and heirs," he said.

With no warning, Dominic turned and pulled Meg against his body, testing her response to a direct approach. When he lowered his head as though to kiss her, he felt the refusal in her stiff body and saw it in the fierce glitter of her eyes. The wench was as proud and aloof as any peregrine. And like a hunting bird, she would have to be taken by stealth rather than force in order to achieve the desired result.

God's teeth, why couldn't it be a willing wench who tugged at my loins?

But it wasn't. Not yet.

With a mental curse at being forced to go through the prolonged formalities of physical seduction with a simple cotter's wench, Dominic tipped Meg's stiff chin up with his cupped hand. If she were as cold as her voice, no seduction was possible; and that, too, had to be determined.

"Small falcon," Dominic said, "marriage has nothing to do with *this*."

The tender sensuality of Dominic's tongue as he traced Meg's lower lip was completely unexpected to her. She went still while strange sensations shivered through her body, making her feel as fragile as flame, as valuable as a dream come true.

How can so ruthless a man be so gentle with me? Meg asked herself wonderingly.

Inside Meg, as deeply held as Dominic's cry of pain, Glendruid hope lifted its careworn head. Perhaps now, after one thousand years, perhaps now the waiting would finally be at an end. . . .

Then Meg saw the cool patience in Dominic's eyes and remembered what he had said about the falcon: if beating the bird would have taught it trust, he would have beaten it.

He is using tenderness on me as surely as he used it on the peregrine. But Glendruid eyes see more clearly than even a falcon!

Meg wrenched free of Dominic's grasp so quickly that the peregrine spread her wings and called in sharp distress.

"Be still," Dominic said. "You frighten my falcon."

Though soft, the icy command in his voice was as unmistakable as the jangling bells on the falcon's jesses.

"Soothe her," Dominic said.

"Soothe her yourself," Meg retorted softly. "She is your captive. I, sir, am *not*."

STANDING JUST INSIDE THE DOOR-
way of the bath on the keep's fourth floor, Simon
watched his older brother warily. Dominic had been
in uncertain temper since he had been to the mews
that morning. Discovering that his future wife wasn't
going to break bread with him until the wedding
feast tomorrow had done nothing to improve Dominic's mood.

"The women's hall," Dominic said in disgust.

Black cape flung back, fists on his hips, Dominic
looked around the bare stone room. The draft from
the gutter that emptied into the moat was severe. The
wall hangings and wooden screens that might have
tempered the chill were absent. The bathing tub was
more suited to a woman's size than to a man's.

The water, at least, was hot. It breathed a warm
mist into the chill room.

"Why in the name of all the Angels of Judgment
would a man put the only bath—such as it is—in
the women's quarters?" Dominic demanded.

"John has never been beyond Cumbriland," Simon
said calmly. "He never had a chance to learn—and
enjoy—Saracen ways. He probably thinks bathing
will endanger his manhood."

"God's eyes, was the man good for no more than sowing crops of bastards over the countryside while his wife still lived?"

Wisely, Simon said nothing.

"The bailey wall is more wood than stone," Dominic snarled, "the armory is a rust closet, the fields are barely plowed, the cisterns are like sieves, the pasture is eaten down to rock, the fish ponds are more weed than water, the dovecotes are a shambles, and there isn't even a rabbit warren to put meat on the table in winter!"

"The gardens are excellent," Simon pointed out.

Dominic grunted.

"And the mews are clean," Simon continued.

Mentioning the mews was a mistake. Dominic's expression flattened into savage lines.

"God rot a lazy lord," he snarled. "To be given so much and to use it so badly!"

Simon glanced aside at Dominic's squire, who was looking very unhappy. Simon didn't blame the boy. Few men had seen Dominic in a temper. None had enjoyed the experience.

"Is everything at hand for your lord's bath?" Simon asked.

The squire nodded quickly.

"Then see to your lord's supper. A mug of ale, perhaps. Several, actually. Cold meat. Cheese. Has the kitchen managed a decent pudding yet?"

"I don't know, sir."

"Find out."

"And while you're about it," Dominic cut in, "find where my betrothed is hiding!"

The boy left the room with unseemly speed, forgetting to pull the drapery into place behind him.

"He has fought Turks with less fear," Simon said as he straightened the drapery so that it cut off all drafts from the doorway. "You frighten the child."

The sound Dominic made was more growl than answer.

"Is your peregrine ill?" Simon asked.

"No."

"Were the mews badly kept?"

"No."

"Should I find a handmaiden to attend your bath?"

"God's blood, no!" Dominic said. "I need no whey-faced wenches sniveling over my scars."

When Simon spoke again, his voice was as flinty as his older brother's.

"Then perhaps you would like some practice with sword and shield?" Simon suggested softly. "I will be delighted to do the honors."

Dominic spun toward his brother and gave him a measuring glance.

For a few taut moments, Simon thought he would get the fight he had suggested.

Abruptly Dominic let out an explosive breath.

"You sound irritated, Simon."

"Just following your lead."

"Um. I see." Beneath Dominic's beard, the corner of his mouth kicked up slightly. "Will you attend my bath, brother? I trust no one else at my back in this keep."

"I was going to suggest that very thing. I like it not that your betrothed evades you and your host is 'too ill' to greet you in a proper manner."

"Aye," Dominic said grimly. Dominic unfastened the big Norse pin holding his cape in place and tossed the fur-trimmed cloth over the trestle table standing near the door.

The cape settled over the small chest Simon had brought into the room and set the candle flames to shivering in their holders. Also on the table was a pot of soft soap.

Simon lifted the lid and sniffed.

"Spice. And a bit of rose, I believe." He looked at Dominic, blandly, trying not to show his amusement.

"God save me," Dominic said without heat. "I'll smell like a sultan's harem."

Simon's black eyes danced. He snickered behind his blond beard, but was careful not to laugh out loud.

With quick motions, Dominic laid aside the rest of his clothes, completing the burial of the small chest. In the wavering light, the long scar that cut diagonally across his muscular arm and torso had the nacreous shine of a pearl.

Dominic stepped into the bath and sat, threatening to send water overflowing out onto the floor. He made a sound of pleasure as the hot water lapped to his chin, easing the ache that came from his old injury when he was particularly tired.

"Soap?" Simon asked blandly.

Dominic held out his hand. A glob of soap plopped onto his palm. A fragrance that was almost familiar drifted up to his nostrils. Frowning, trying to remember where he had smelled that scent before, Dominic began working the soap into his hair and beard.

"Now," he said through the lather, "explain this nonsense about the lord of Blackthorne Keep being cursed."

"His wife was a witch."

"The same could be said of many wives."

Simon laughed curtly. "Aye, but Lady Anna was Glendruid."

Dominic's hands paused in their scrubbing of beard and hair. "Glendruid . . . Have I heard that name?"

"They're a Celtic clan," Simon explained. "A kind of matriarchy, from what I can discover."

"Hell's teeth, what foolishness," Dominic muttered.

With that, he lowered himself completely beneath the water, rinsing out the fragrant lather. Moments later he emerged with a force that sent water flying. Cursing, Simon jumped aside.

"Go on," Dominic said.

Shaking water from his tunic with one hand, Simon used the other to slap soap onto Dominic's palm with enough force to draw a hard look.

"A man who takes a Glendruid wife will have fields that prosper," Simon said, "lush pastures, ewes that give twins, industrious and obedient vassals, brimming fish ponds, and—"

"A staff like a war stallion and eternal life," Dominic interrupted, impatient with the superstitious nonsense.

"Oh, has Sven talked to you already?"

Dominic gave his younger brother a glittering gray glance.

Simon grinned widely and his black eyes danced with amusement.

"Where is this benighted Glendruid place?" Dominic asked dryly. "To the south where the Celts run amok?"

"Some say so." Simon shrugged. "Others say to the north. A few say east."

"Or west? The sea, perhaps?"

"They are people, not fish," retorted Simon.

"Ah, that is a relief. It would be arduous indeed to bed the daughter of a flounder. A man wouldn't know how to grip the creature. Or precisely *where*."

Laughing, Simon held out a large drying cloth to his brother. As Dominic stood, water ran off his big body in cascades, splashing and gathering until it reached the gutter and dropped unheard into the moat far below.

"This Glendruid nonsense will end within the year," Dominic said, "when my son is born."

Simon smiled slightly. He knew well his brother's determination to found a dynasty. Simon had the same determination himself.

"Until your heir is born," Simon said, "take care what you say in public about the Glendruid tale. It is a superstition dearly held by the local people."

"In public I will believe. But the bedchamber is a private place. I will have my heirs."

" 'Tis a good thing the sultan's harem nursed you back to health," Simon said. "Your wife won't have cause to complain of her treatment when it is time to make heirs. The harem girls were admirably trained."

For an instant, Dominic thought of getting Meg in his bedchamber, of fanning her hair like soft fire across the pillows before he opened her thighs and sheathed himself in another kind of soft fire. His blood ignited like dry grass at the image.

"The trick is to get a girl into the bedchamber," Dominic said irritably, trying to cool the heat in his blood.

"I doubt there is a female in this keep who wouldn't be delighted to take your staff in hand."

"There's one," Dominic said dryly.

"The elusive Margaret."

Lady Margaret hadn't been the woman Dominic had been thinking of at that moment, but he said nothing. Instead, he began drying himself vigorously.

"The lady will come to heel soon enough," Simon said after a moment. "She is noble born. She may not like her duty, but she will do it. As for the rest, there are always the wenches around the keep. Or the gifted Marie."

"A pretty whore, but a whore nonetheless. I

brought her and her like for my knights, not for myself. I don't want trouble with my vassals over their daughters."

"I know. I'm the only one who believes it, however."

Dominic grunted and continued rubbing himself dry rather forcefully. The thought of one of his knights catching the maid from the mews alone made cold rage uncoil in Dominic's gut.

"I had better warn my knights once again," he said flatly. "They will neither harry nor harrow unwilling girls. Particularly none with hair the color of fire, skin like fine cream, and eyes to equal a sultan's most prized emeralds."

Simon lifted his eyebrows in silent surprise. "I thought you didn't care for 'whey-faced wenches.' "

"There is a difference between cream and whey," Dominic retorted.

"You sound quite taken with the wench. That is unlike you."

Dominic shrugged. "She is an unusual maid. Cleaner by far than the average country lass, graceful of limb, and with delicate hands."

"You always preferred the ripe and willing type, a rose full-blown and eager for the bee's sweet sting."

"Aye."

"Is she willing?"

The smile Dominic gave his brother made Simon laugh.

"She will be," Dominic said. "She was taken with me, though she was nervous of it. Ah, what a joy she will be to seduce. She was made for spring, the season of desire. There will be no winter for the man who sleeps within her warm sheath. She will—"

Abruptly Dominic stopped speaking and turned toward the sound of hurrying footsteps.

"Lord Dominic," called the squire from beyond the drapery.

"What is it?" Dominic asked impatiently. "Have you found her?"

"Lady Margaret's handmaiden wishes to speak with you. Most urgent it is, lord."

"God's blood," muttered Dominic.

He wrapped the drying cloth around his hips, grabbed his cape, and whirled it around his shoulders to ward off the chilly drafts.

"Why is it the only women you can find are the ones you don't wish to see at all?" he grumbled.

Simon opened his mouth to speak, but Dominic wasn't finished.

"Whey-faced whelp of a temple whore . . ." he said beneath his breath. "God's eyes, but she is a tiresome female."

"Is that a yea or a nay to Eadith's request for an audience?" Simon asked.

"Send the good widow in," Dominic said in a normal tone.

Eadith must have been listening closely. The drapery shifted and she walked in. When she realized how little Dominic was wearing, her eyes widened into a stare.

"Speak," he said irritably. "Where is your mistress?"

"Lady Margaret begs your understanding. She is indisposed," Eadith said hurriedly.

Yet despite her unease, Simon noted that the widow's pale blue eyes fairly ate every bit of the lord who stood unconcerned before her, fresh from his bath.

Dominic glanced at the handmaiden's pale features, flaxen hair, and thin lips, and wished himself once more back among the Saracen women. Their darkly golden skin had been as seductive as the sideways glances from lustrous black eyes. Next to them, the women of the northern marches seemed as pale and uninteresting as cotter's cheese.

Except for one green-eyed girl, and she had fled him as quickly as her shapely legs could take her. The memory of it still angered Dominic.

God's blood! Since when does a gentle caress send a wench running?

"Indisposed, is it?" Dominic said silkily. "Nothing serious, I trust."

"Her father is ill. Surely that is serious?"

"I am her future husband." Dominic's teeth showed in a thin curve of white against his black beard. "Surely that is serious?"

The cold white gleam of his teeth made Eadith shift her feet uneasily. The motion sent ripples through the worn woolen folds of her tunic.

"Of course, lord."

"Take my greetings to Lady Margaret, and my most urgent wish to meet my future wife," Dominic said distinctly. "Simon, the gift."

His brother hesitated.

Dominic raised his left eyebrow in a silent warning.

Simon nodded curtly, scooped aside Dominic's discarded clothes, and opened the small chest. He picked out a piece of jewelry that rested on top of the gleaming heap, Dominic's choice as a gift for his reluctant bride.

"Take that to her," Dominic said. "A small token of my regard for my betrothed."

At Dominic's careless gesture, Simon stepped forward and dropped a brooch into Eadith's hand. She gasped audibly as she felt the weight of the gold and saw the fine green gem that was larger than her thumbnail.

"Why, 'tis the exact color of Lady Margaret's eyes!"

Instantly Dominic thought of the maid in the mews. His eyes narrowed in sudden speculation. Meg had been too proud and quick-spoken for a cotter's child. He would have realized it sooner had he not been blinded by the sensuous curves of her lips and breasts.

"Is that common among Blackthorne vassals?" Dominic asked idly.

"Nay, lord. None but she and her mother before her had such green eyes. 'Tis the mark of Glendruid blood."

Dominic's eyes narrowed even more.

Simon watched his brother uneasily. He had seen that look of cold assessment many times before, in the instants before a battle was joined. Yet there were no armed enemies here, no war horns calling knights to defend God's city.

"So heavy, my lord," Eadith said. " 'Tis a fine gift any lady would be proud to wear."

The handmaiden's fingers caressed the brooch with an envy she couldn't quite conceal.

Dominic looked to Simon and nodded slightly.

Without a word Simon turned and went to the chest once more. For a moment or two he fished about in the contents. The faint, unmistakable sound of gold coins and chains rubbing over one another whispered musically in the silence.

Simon grunted as he found what he sought. He turned toward his brother and held up another brooch.

Impatiently Dominic nodded.

Simon stepped forward, took Eadith's empty hand, and dropped the bit of jewelry onto her palm. There was no gemstone in this brooch, but its weight testified to its value. Startled, she looked up and met Dominic's cold silver eyes.

"For you," Dominic said.

Eadith's jaw dropped.

"Plain enough to see that the keep and its people have not been blessed with plenty of late," Dominic said as kindly as he could manage to the girl whose pale eyes and thin smile he had disliked on sight. "The widow of a brave knight should have a few bright bits of jewelry to please her vanity."

Eadith closed her hand around her brooch so fiercely that one edge cut visibly into her flesh.

"Thank you, Lord Dominic."

"It is nothing."

He saw the direction of Eadith's eyes as she bowed her head to him. Her pale blue glance was drawn to the chest like iron to a lodestone. Simon noticed too. He shut the chest with a casual gesture even as he gave his brother a hooded look of disapproval.

"Will there be anything else you require?" Eadith asked.

"No. Just take the brooch to Lady Margaret with my greetings. And send my squire in with supper."

Simon watched the handmaiden hurry through the doorway as though afraid of being called back and forced to give up the brooch. When he was certain he couldn't be overheard, Simon turned back to his brother.

"Now the whole countryside will know what was in those chests they watched being carried into the keep," Simon said neutrally.

"It's a good thing for vassals to know their new lord isn't so poor he will have to wring blood from them to keep his knights well fed and better armed."

"And for future brides?" Simon said. "Is it also a good thing for them to know?"

"Particularly for future brides," Dominic said with harsh satisfaction. "I've yet to see a female whose eyes didn't brighten at the sight of golden trinkets."

"Always the tactician."

Dominic smiled rather grimly as he thought of the emerald-eyed wench who had neatly outmaneuvered him in the mews.

"Not always, Simon. But I learn from my mistakes."

A CRISP WIND BLEW THROUGH THE bailey, lifting skirts and short coats and sending smoke from the kitchen fires leaping up toward the gray sky. Although Meg usually enjoyed a brisk spring breeze scented by the first rush of growing plants, at the moment she was too irritated to notice anything but the gamekeeper who stood uneasily before her.

"What do you mean, there will be no venison?" Meg asked, her voice unusually sharp.

The gamekeeper looked away and twisted his hands nervously. "The pale, m'lady. 'Tis so fallen down in places a hare could leap it, much less a stag. The deer . . . they're fled."

"How long has the deer park been in such a state?"

Looking only at his feet, the gamekeeper mumbled something.

"Speak up," she said. "And look at me while you speak."

Meg rarely took such a tone with the keep's vassals; but then, she was rarely lied to by them.

That wasn't the case now. The gamekeeper's falsehoods were so great they were sticking in his throat like chicken bones.

"I . . . the winds . . . uh . . ." he said.

Pale blue eyes beseeched Meg, stirring unwilling compassion in her.

"Good man, who told you to lie to me?" she asked gently.

Hands roughened by bowstrings, snares, and skinning knives pleaded silently for Meg's kindness.

"The laird," whispered the gamekeeper finally.

"He's too weak to leave his bed. Have you been to his chamber, then, to receive your orders to lie to the mistress of the keep?"

The gamekeeper shook his head so hard his oily hair lifted. "Sir Duncan, mistress. He told me."

Stillness came over Meg. "What did Duncan tell you?"

"No venison for the Norman."

"I see."

And she did.

It chilled Meg. She had been glad to see Duncan return from the Crusade, for his cousin Rufus wasn't interested in keeping peace with Henry. No matter how little she liked the idea of being pawned to a strange Norman knight in order to keep peace in the northern marches, Meg liked the thought of bloodshed less. The constant chivvying and thrusting against the English king—and among ambitious Saxons while leaders such as Duncan were off pursuing a holy Crusade—had worn out Blackthorne Keep's people, its fields, and its hope of a better future.

The vassals blamed their ill fortune on their lord and on the revenge of a Glendruid witch mated to the wrong man. Meg blamed the ruined fields on the inattention of her father, a man obsessed with stopping the advance of the English by marrying his daughter to a thane known as Duncan of Maxwell, the Scots Hammer.

Ah, Duncan. Don't succumb to my father's lures. They will lead to plague and starvation, bloody meadows and an early grave.

"M'lady?"

The gamekeeper's voice was uncertain. The lord's daughter looked pinched and drawn, far too old for even an unmarried maid of nineteen.

"You may go," Meg said tightly. "Thank you for the truth, though it nearly came too late. Make plans to kill a stag. There will be venison at this wedding feast, even though it will be tough for want of hanging."

The gamekeeper's dirty fingers touched his forelock, but he didn't leave.

"Is there more?" she asked.

"Duncan," he said simply.

"He is not the lord of Blackthorne Keep. Nor will he be. I, however, am the lady. *And I will remain so.*"

The gamekeeper took one look at the narrowed green eyes watching him and decided to let the lords and ladies fight it out among themselves. He was going hunting.

"Aye, m'lady."

Meg watched the gamekeeper trot across the bailey to the gatehouse with gratifying speed. But the gratification, like the man's speed, was short-lived.

This fighting must end, Meg told herself silently. *There will be no one left to bury the dead, nor any food for the living. One more year of meager crops will be the end of Blackthorne Keep.*

A sliding, changing pressure at Meg's ankles distracted her. When she glanced down, Black Tom looked back up at her with feline intensity.

"Not yet, cat. First I must see Duncan."

Black Tom stropped himself once more and walked off in the direction of the granary. Meg wished him luck. She doubted there was enough grain inside the structure to lure a mouse from the meadow stubble's skimpy food.

Holding her simple head cloth and leather circlet against the searching wind, Meg started for the keep.

"THE church will agree to your marriage," Lord John said hoarsely. "All you have to do is take the Norman's gold. And his life with it!"

A savage smile transformed Duncan's face, revealing the Viking ancestry that ran through Scots blood like lightning through a storm.

"Done," he said.

And then Duncan laughed.

John's pale lips shifted in a smile that was colder than the stones of the keep. His bastard son was much like him in ways that went beyond hazel eyes and hair the color of freshly turned loam; both men were warriors who gave no quarter and asked for none.

"Send word to the Reevers," John said. "Have them blend with the wedding guests in the chapel. Then—"

Abruptly words became a fit of coughing that wracked John's frail body.

Duncan went to the bed and slipped his arm around his father, helping him upright until the coughing passed. He held a cup of ale against the old man's dry lips until most of the ale had been drunk.

"You should rest," Duncan said.

"*Nay*. Listen to me. Whether I live or die, you must let the wedding go forward before more Normans come! You must! Only then will—"

Coughing took away words and the will to say them. When John was once again quiet, Duncan gave him more ale to drink; but this time he added two drops of the medicine Meg had made to alleviate John's pain.

"Ease yourself," Duncan said. "I'm listening. What have you planned?"

With a surprisingly gentle hand, Duncan brushed back the forelock that had gone gray between one winter and the next as disease ate John's strength.

"Get Meg," John said hoarsely. "I can say it only once."

"I'll send for—" Duncan began.

"There is no need," Meg said from the doorway. "I am here."

No longer was she dressed in the clothes of a cotter's child. She wore a long inner tunic of soft rose wool and an outer tunic of forest green that was trimmed with a heavily embroidered strip of cloth. Unlike the tunics many women wore, Meg's were closely fitted, for she had no patience with flapping cloth. Her narrow waist was wrapped about with a sash that crossed in back around her hips as well before being tied in front, further keeping folds of cloth from getting in her way when she worked in the herbal. The sleeves of the outer tunic were long and narrow, hemmed with more embroidery.

"What did you want of me?" Meg asked.

Her intense green eyes looked from Duncan's muscular good health to the withered shadow that was her father. She noted the stopper out of the small medicine bottle and looked quickly at Duncan.

"Two drops only," he said, knowing her concern.

Her mouth flattened. "He had that much before mass."

Everyone in the room knew that the potion was very strong. Six drops sent a patient into dreamless sleep. Three times that could kill the average man.

A person as frail as her father had to be given the medicine with great care.

"No matter," John rasped. "If I die sooner, so be it. Listen well, daughter of Anna of Glendruid. You will be wed on the morrow, before the feast."

"What feast?" Meg said tightly. "Duncan forbade the gamekeeper to—"

"Silence!" John coughed, but only weakly. "When the priest asks if you agree to the marriage, you will say no."

"But—"

John talked right over Meg, his voice as dry and withered as his body; and like his eyes, his voice burned with the intense flame of an obsession that was little short of madness.

"There will be confusion among the Normans when you refuse the match," John said. "Duncan will strike and the Normans will die. Then you will marry Duncan before blood dries in the aisle."

"You cannot mean that," whispered Meg.

Stricken, she looked at Duncan. His hazel eyes were as hard as agates. There would be no help from that quarter.

"The Church refused our marriage six years ago," she said urgently. "For good reason, Duncan. You are my half brother!"

For a long time there was only silence barely disturbed by the quick, frail breaths of a man who clung to life.

Duncan looked at John.

"Tell her," the old man said.

Reluctantly, Duncan turned back to confront the intense green eyes of the woman who had little real blood relationship to the men in the room.

"At most, sweet Meggie, I'm your stepcousin."

"Nonsense," she retorted. "You are John of Blackthorne's bastard. Anyone with eyes to see knows it."

"Aye. I am his son. *But you are not his daughter.*"

Meg took a step backward before she controlled her shock. She straightened her spine and stood proudly.

"What are you saying?" she asked.

Before Duncan could speak, John did.

"Your mother was breeding when we married," he said bluntly. "You might be my stepbrother's bastard. And you might be a groom's spawn, for all I know. The bitch is dead and it matters not to me, for I will die soon."

"I don't believe you," Meg said tightly. "You may be able to blind priests with lies and offers of gold, and lure Duncan with promises you can't keep, but not me. I am the daughter of Blackthorne Keep. I know it the way I know plants will lift their faces to the sun!"

John struggled to sit up, but had to be content with turning onto his side to confront the girl whose birth had been the greatest affront ever suffered by the proud Saxon thane.

"Look at me, Glendruid witch," he said roughly. "Know my dying truth. You aren't of my blood. Duncan is. Despite the meddling of English kings and the perfidy of Glendruid women, *my son shall inherit my land.*"

Meg sensed that Lord John wasn't lying.

For a moment she couldn't breathe. She fought the ice condensing just beneath her skin, chilling her until she shuddered. She had always known that her father could barely suffer the sight of her.

Now she knew why.

"Your son will inherit only death," Meg said in a low, clear voice.

"I'll nae listen to your curses, witch!" John hissed.

"Curses? What nonsense," Meg said harshly. " 'Tis only common sense."

She turned to Duncan, who was watching her unhappily.

"I'm sorry, lass," he said. "I didn't mean for you to find out this way."

"My bastardy or lack of it matters not one bit right now. Listen to me, for John is too far into death's embrace to care what happens to the living."

"Meggie—"

She put her hands on her hips and interrupted sharply.

"Don't you 'Meggie' me, Duncan of Maxwell. I vow we must be close in blood, for I am immune to your Scots charm!"

A crooked smile crossed Duncan's face. "That you are. 'Tis why I like you so well. We will do nicely as man and wife."

"God blind me," Meg said through her teeth, shocking both men. "John has the excuse of grave illness to explain his lack of wit. What is your excuse, Duncan? Does ambition cloud your mind as much as death clouds his?"

Duncan opened his mouth to answer, but Meg kept on talking, her voice both angry and pleading.

"King Henry won't accept the treacherous murder of his knights," Meg said. "The great barons will also—"

"They are busy with the Celts in the south," Duncan interrupted curtly, "when they aren't fighting among themselves or plotting against the king. They have tried to take the northern marches. They failed."

"They had no reason to succeed. There is easier land to the south."

"Exactly. They won't—"

"They *will*!" she interrupted passionately. "You will give them the reason!"

"No more than they had before. It wasn't enough then."

"Tell me, Duncan," Meg said in a scathing tone, "if your right arm were cut off by a bandit, would you notice its loss and seek vengeance?"

"Aye, but I'm not the English king."

"Ah, you've noticed that, have you? 'Tis a thing to keep in mind whilst planning the death of Norman nobles."

"Meggie—"

"Norman barons quarrel among themselves because there is no better game to play," Meg continued without pausing. "Slay Dominic le Sabre and you will provide the barons with the best game of all. *War.*"

Duncan shrugged. "It is a game we shall win."

"You will not win! If I can see that, why can't you?"

"You are a girl with a tender heart and no understanding of war." Duncan smiled. " 'Tis another of your graces, Meggie."

"Save the oil for the serving wenches," she said acidly. "I'm not so easily tricked. Neither is the king of England. When word of the slaughter reaches London, the king and his barons will unite and deliver such a harrowing to the marches as will still be whispered of a thousand years hence! You have but twelve knights—"

"Sixteen."

"—and a rabble of brutes good for little more than butchering women and children."

"Enough!" Duncan demanded.

"Nay! 'Tis not enough until you understand that you can't win!"

Duncan's hands wrapped around Meg's shoulders, holding her still while his words hammered at her like stone.

"Understand this," he said flatly. "If you marry that Norman bastard, I will have to watch my birthright—"

"Nay!" she raged. "Bastards have no birthright!"

"—pass into the hands of another man," Duncan continued relentlessly, "and with it the green-eyed Glendruid witch whom the vassals of Blackthorne Keep love more than they love anything but God. That, as much as the English king, is why John hasn't disinherited you. The vassals would have set aside their plows and walked from the land as from a cursed place."

Pale, trembling invisibly, Meg tried to get free of Duncan's grip. He barely noticed her struggles.

"Know this, Lady Margaret. I will have land and a noble wife to bear my children. If I must kill ten Norman nights or ten thousand, *I will have land.*"

Shaken, Meg wrenched free of Duncan's grip. Torn between understanding of her childhood friend's need for a place in a society that made no place for bastards, and her certainty that his plan would be the ruin of the land and the vassals she loved, Meg watched Duncan with tears overflowing her eyes.

"You're asking me to throw Blackthorne Keep into war," she whispered.

"I'm asking you not to marry a brutal Norman lord. Is that such a grand favor to seek from you?"

Meg's only answer was her tears.

"Ask not for favors of a Glendruid witch," John rasped fiercely. "I'm commanding you, Margaret. I am lord of this keep and you are as much my chattel as a pig rooting in my forest. You will obey me or you will rue the day of your birth as often and as deeply as I do!"

"Dinna worry, Meggie," Duncan said softly, tugging on one of her long braids. "I'll see that you come to no harm in the church."

Meg closed her eyes and struggled not to scream out her anger at the ambitions of the men around her. To have her life and her body used as pawns in the name of the English king's peace was an expected, if harsh, duty of a noblewoman.

To have her life and her body used to start a war could not be borne.

"I cannot," she said.

"You shall," hissed John. "You may be Duncan's wife or you may be a whore for his Reevers, it matters not to me."

"Lord John—" Duncan began unhappily.

"Silence! Far better you have any other wife than the green-eyed spawn of Glendruid! At your urging, I agreed to ask the witch for her alliance. She refused it. Go you now and tell your Reevers to rise up and slay the—"

"Nay!" Meg said. "Father—"

"I am not your father."

Meg's breath came in harshly as she looked for a way out of the trap Duncan and John had sprung around her.

No way came. Meg interlaced her fingers and gripped so harshly that she drove blood from her hands and feeling from her fingers.

"I—" she began, but her voice cracked into silence.

The two men watched her with hazel eyes so alike and yet so subtly different. In John's there was a hatred as old as her mother's betrayal. In Duncan's there was a hope as old as his understanding of who his father really was.

"Meggie?" Duncan asked quietly.

She bowed her head.

"I shall do what I must," Meg whispered.

5

MEG LEFT HER FATHER'S ROOM
so quickly that her wool mantle lifted and swirled
behind her. She had much to do before she fled the
castle. First she must prepare a quantity of medicines
for the vassals who depended on her aid. Then she
must sneak enough food and blankets from the castle
to last her a fortnight.

And then what? she asked herself.

There was no answer except the obvious one: anything was better than being the stone upon which
her beloved Blackthorne was broken.

Candle flames bowed and whipped as Meg hurried by on flying feet, descending the tight spiral staircase at reckless speed. No sooner had she
reached the great hall than Eadith spotted her and
moved to intercept despite Meg's obvious hurry.

"My lady—"

"Not now," Meg interrupted.

"But Lord Dominic wants—"

"Later. I have medicines to prepare."

Startled by Meg's curt manner, Eadith was for
once speechless as she watched her mistress's rapidly vanishing form.

As though afraid Eadith would pursue, Meg

redoubled her speed. Once below the level of the great hall, she met no one on the ground floor but servants. She slowed to a more reasonable pace. Even so, her mantle still rippled and stirred behind her.

Small, dark rooms—more like stalls than true rooms—opened on either side of Meg as she hurried down the aisle. Smells of piled roots and ale casks permeated the gloom, as did the odors of salted or smoked fish and eels in their barrels, and fowl hanging by their cool, faintly scaled feet. Beneath all the food smells was the arid, complex scent of the herbal that had been created by Lady Anna for the drying of her plants and the preparation of her medicines.

Meg's memories of her mother were vivid. Many of them involved standing in the herbal or in the garden with Anna, listening to her musical voice describing each plant and its properties for healing or soothing the small aches and great pains of the vassals' lives. The herbal, the gardens, and the bath had been constructed according to Anna's exacting requirements, for each was important to the rituals and well-being of someone raised in Glendruid traditions.

Close to the entrance to the herbal were two tables for the crushing, chopping, and powdering of leaves, stems, flowers, roots, and bark; all of which were used in Meg's medicines. Small chests, pots, bowls, mortars and pestles, knives and spoons were arrayed neatly at the back of the tables.

Twelve paces into the hillside, supported by stone rather than wood, there was rack after rack of things drying or stored beyond the reach of light. Basins waited to be filled with the fresh springwater that welled to the surface in the center of the keep, for water was at the heart of many Glendruid rituals.

Meg breathed deeply, letting the familiar mixture of scents fill her, driving out the malodorous air of the sickroom. After a few more breaths her hands stopped trembling and the ice in her stomach began to melt. Meg loved the serenity and generosity of the herbal, with its silent promise of aches eased and ills healed.

But nothing in this room will cure war or the famine and bloodshed that attends it.

The unhappy thought made ice condense once more in Meg's stomach.

"I can't send my people into that bloody maw," she whispered, looking around the herbal with eyes that saw only catastrophe. "And for what? For nothing! Duncan can't win. Dearest God, make him see that!"

But even as the prayer left her lips, Meg knew it wouldn't change what was planned. Duncan would have Blackthorne Keep or he would have an early grave.

"Oh, Duncan," she whispered, putting her face in her hands. "I would not see you dead. Of all the people of my childhood, only you, Mother, and Old Gwyn ever truly cared for me.

"What will I do?"

As though Anna were still alive, words came to Meg. *Do that which you can, daughter. Leave the rest to God.*

After a moment Meg straightened, wiped away her tears, and tried to concentrate on the tasks that had always soothed her in the past. One of her favorite jobs was to create the fragrant bouquets of herbs that both pleased the senses and kept vermin from hiding within mattresses and sleeping pallets. Harry's wife was bedridden with a difficult pregnancy, and in special need of anything to ease her days.

Everything Meg needed was in front of her, for she had been preparing sachets for the wedding mattress that was even now being made up from fresh straw; the mattress upon which she would have lain down a virgin and arisen the next morning a maid no longer.

Unbidden came the image of Dominic's fingertips soothing the falcon so sweetly that the fierce bird calmed. Meg had wondered then what it would feel like to be so carefully touched. There had been little of gentleness in her life from the man who was her father in name only.

And, even though she sensed that Dominic's restraint had been a tactician's cool calculation of the quickest way to victory, his caress had raised a hunger within Meg to be gentled like that again.

If we had married, would Dominic have treated me like a falcon or like an opponent to be vanquished?

Meg remembered the tip of Dominic's tongue gliding warmly over her lower lip, a tasting as light as a breath, a caress so sweet and unexpected that remembering it made her shiver. The tactile memory sent odd frissons shimmering through her. She had felt nothing like Dominic's caress in her life. She had imagined nothing like it in her dreams.

If that is what marriage offers, 'tis no surprise that women settle to it after a time.

Then came the memory of Dominic's words to the young mews girl he so casually had offered to buy.

Small falcon, marriage has nothing to do with this.

For Dominic, marriage was a matter of cold calculation. It had nothing to do with Glendruid hope, much less affection between a man and a woman.

A pot tilted and dried leaves leaped from Meg's suddenly uncertain hands. The herbal bouquet came

apart like a flock of ducks at the shadow of a peregrine flying overhead.

"Keep that up, girl, and I'll have you out weeding
the garden as though you were six once more."

Gwyn's familiar voice made Meg jump. More
herbs scattered.

"Are you ill?" the old woman asked, her voice
suddenly earnest rather than wry.

"No. Just . . ." Meg's voice died.

"Just what?"

"Clumsy."

"Pah. Better to accuse Blackthorne's cats of barking than to accuse you of clumsiness."

Smiling, Meg turned around and hugged the old
woman with a need that went deeper than words.
Old Gwyn's seamed face, white hair, and faded
green eyes were as familiar to Meg as her own
hands.

"What is it, child?" Gwyn asked finally.

"My father . . ."

Meg's voice faded as she remembered John's flat
denial that he was her father.

At the mention of John, followed by silence, Old
Gwyn's pale green eyes went to the shelf where a
second vial of his medicine was kept in reserve for
future need. The shelf was empty.

"Is he worse?" Gwyn asked.

"Not really."

"Oh. With the last of his medicine used up, I
assumed he was failing."

"Medicine?" Meg looked over her shoulder. Her
breath came in swiftly. "It's gone!"

"You didn't take it to him?"

"No."

Uneasily Meg went to the table and searched
among the pots. She found only leaves and dried
flowers. The shelves yielded nothing unexpected

when she went through them quickly, shifting the contents in her pursuit of the missing medicine vial.

"That's odd," Meg said finally.

Frowning, she stepped into the outside aisle, grabbed a fat candle from its holder, and went back into the herbal. Gwyn watched through narrowed eyes as Meg rummaged efficiently through the nooks and shelves, bins and basins of the room.

When Meg finally gave up, the fear she had felt in Lord John's room returned redoubled.

"Gone?" Gwyn asked.

"Yes. And the antidote with it. Perhaps Duncan fetched both. John was beset by coughing and I was in the mews."

The old woman said something in an ancient language. Whether it was a curse or a prayer, Meg didn't know, for she couldn't hear the words clearly enough.

"I like this not," Gwyn muttered finally. She looked at Meg. "Say nothing of it to anyone. We need no more trouble."

Meg nodded. "Yes."

"Can you make more?" Gwyn asked.

"Of the medicine itself, yes. I have an ample supply of the seeds. The antidote will be much more difficult to replace. The plant grows only in undisturbed ground. This year we plowed up everything in hope of a good crop."

With a grunt, Gwyn rubbed her sore knuckles.

"The wet wind bothers you," Meg said softly. "Have you taken the medicine I made for you?"

The old woman seemed not to hear.

"Gwyn?"

"My dreams have been disturbed, but not by chilblains," she whispered.

A cold breath of unease slid down Meg's spine. Saying nothing, she waited to hear whatever the old

Glendruid woman had gleaned from the world that was visited only in sleep.

"What was written in the past shall become in the future. No one, neither lord nor vassal, escapes. The winds of change are blowing, bringing the call of the war horn and the howl of the wolf."

Gwyn blinked as the vision passed, saw the expression on Meg's face, and sighed.

"Tell me about your father," Gwyn said in a low voice.

"He denies being my father."

Strangely, Gwyn smiled. There was little of warmth or humor in the curve of her lips. Even at her advanced age, the old Glendruid had a full set of hard white teeth. They gleamed as a wolf's teeth gleam, in warning.

"Did he threaten to set you aside and put Duncan in your place?" Gwyn demanded.

"Only if I don't marry Duncan."

"What of Dominic le Sabre?"

"He is to be slain even as we stand before the priest," Meg said bluntly.

Gwyn's breath came out in a low hiss. "The Church will not abide that."

"The Church will receive an abbey."

"A small price for a large betrayal."

"Not really," Meg said grimly. "The Church has been seeking ways to lessen Henry's power. Duncan will be beholden to Church rather than to king. No cry of excommunication will be raised. If I can see that, surely John can as well."

"By Hell's deepest reaches, John is a clever man," Gwyn muttered. "Would that he were compassionate, too."

"There is nothing in him now but a burning need to see his son inherit his lands."

Gwyn hissed again, shaking her head. "What of

you, Glendruid daughter? Will you take Duncan as your husband?"

"I refused."

"Good."

"Then John ordered Duncan to begin the slaughter immediately. . . ."

The old woman cocked her head as though listening. "I hear nothing from the bailey but wenches calling to one another about their sweethearts."

Meg took a deep breath and spread her hands. "I told him I would do what I must."

There was a silence so deep that the tiny sounds of flame eating into candle wax could be heard. After a long time Gwyn sighed.

"Is it true?" Meg asked finally.

"That you aren't John's daughter?"

"Yes."

" 'Tis true," Gwyn said casually. "He is not your father. His stepbrother was a man full of laughter and smiles. Anna went to him two fortnights before her wedding."

"Why?" Meg asked, shocked.

"She had no love of John, but knew the heir to the Glendruid Wolf must somehow be born."

"The heir to the Glendruid Wolf?" Meg asked. "What are you talking about?"

"A man who would be wise enough to bring peace to our lands."

"Ahhh, the fabled Glendruid *male*. Instead, I was born. Female. A disappointment to all."

Old Gwyn smiled and touched Meg's cheek with a hand as soft and dry as candle flame.

"You were a boon to your mother, Meg. She enjoyed John's stepbrother, but she didn't love him. She felt neither passion nor love for John. But you she loved. For you, she endured John until the vassals had learned to love you, too."

"And then she walked out to the haunted place and never returned."

"Yes," Gwyn said simply. "It was a blessing for her, Meg. Hell had nothing to teach her after living with Lord John."

Turning away, Gwyn looked at the herbal without seeing any of it.

"Would that we would be blessed now," Gwyn whispered after a few moments. "But I fear that by the time a man is born who can wear the Glendruid Wolf, there will be nothing left to inherit but the wind."

"What is the Glendruid Wolf?" Meg asked, perplexed. "I've heard vassals whisper of it occasionally, but they fall silent when they realize I'm listening."

" 'Tis a pin. A pin that was old a thousand years ago."

"What does it look like?"

"A wolf's head cast in silver with eyes made of colorless gems so hard not even steel can scratch them," Gwyn said. "The pin is the size of a man's hand."

"You never mentioned this to me before."

"There was no purpose. There was nothing to be done."

"And now?" Meg asked.

"Change comes. A wise woman hopes for the best and prepares for the worst."

"What is the worst?"

"War. Famine. Disease. Death."

Meg barely suppressed a shudder at hearing her worst fears spoken aloud by Old Gwyn.

"And the best?" she whispered.

"That the man who wears the Glendruid Wolf will bring peace with him."

A thrill of hope coursed through Meg at the

thought of a land no longer riven by strife. The feeling was not unlike what she had known while she watched Dominic handle the peregrine with such exquisite tenderness.

"Tell me everything you know about the pin," Meg demanded.

" 'Tis little enough."

" 'Tis better than nothing," retorted Meg.

Gwyn smiled slightly. The smile faded as she spoke.

"The Glendruid Wolf was worn by our headmen back to the dawn of memory. As long as it was worn, peace reigned and we prospered."

"What happened?"

"A brother's envy. A woman seduced. A love betrayed."

Grimly Meg smiled. "The story has a familiar sound to it."

"Glendruids are but human. The headman was slain from ambush. The pin was taken from his cloak."

Meg waited.

Gwyn said nothing more.

"What happened then?" Meg asked.

"From that day forth, strife reigned. And from that day forth Glendruid women conceived few babes, for there was little of pleasure in their lives; and without pleasure, no Glendruid female will quicken with a man's seed."

"Didn't our people look for the talisman if it meant that much to them?"

The old woman shrugged. "They searched. They found only their own greed. The pin was never seen again. 'Tis said it is hidden within one of the ancient mounds between here and the mountain, guarded by the ghost of the adulteress."

Meg had an odd sense that there was more to the

story. Yet even as she started to ask, she looked into the old Glendruid's eyes and knew that no more would be said.

"I wish that I had the pin in my hand right now," Meg said finally.

"Don't wish that."

"Why?"

"Whether you gave the talisman now to Dominic le Sabre or Duncan of Maxwell, blood would run through Blackthorne's meadows rather than clear water."

Meg made a low sound of distress. "I fear you're right. My poor people. When the land is at war, nobles might win or lose, but the simple folk always lose."

"Aye," Gwyn whispered. "Always."

"Why can't men see that the land needs healing rather than more hurting?" Meg demanded.

"They aren't Glendruid to understand the ways of water and growing things. They know only the ways of fire."

"John's plan will be the ruin of Blackthorne Keep and its people," Meg said. "If we sow blood instead of seed this spring, the survivors will live only long enough to die of famine in the next winter."

"Aye. If King Henry doesn't kill them first. If John follows his plan, the king and his great barons won't leave one stone standing upon another in all of Blackthorne."

Meg closed her eyes. She had only until tomorrow to find a way to save the land and the people she loved more than she loved anything in her life.

"What will you do, Meg?"

She stared at Gwyn, wondering if the old woman had somehow seen into her mind.

"Will you warn the Norman lord?" Gwyn asked.

"To what purpose? It would be kinder—and

quicker—to slay Duncan with poison. I cannot bear to see him hanged. Or worse. No. I cannot."

Meg's mouth thinned as she continued. "In any case, Duncan's death would change nothing. The Reevers would slaughter the Normans in reprisal and Blackthorne would be lost."

Gwyn nodded. "You are your mother's daughter, Margaret. Shrewd and kind at once. What will you do? Flee into the forest and the haunted place?"

"How did you know?"

"It was what your mother did. But it won't help you. Duncan is as shrewd as you."

"What do you mean?" Meg asked.

"He has stationed one of his men at the gatehouse. You are a prisoner, and the keep is your jail."

6

DOMINIC LOOKED UP AS HIS brother strode into the high keep room where the squire Jameson was helping Dominic dress. At the moment, all he wore was a cape for warmth and water from his recent bout with a razor. His hair was neatly cut to lie close to his head underneath a helmet and his beard was gone. The effect was to make him more formidable, rather than less. Without the softening effect of the beard, there was nothing to mute the angular lines of his cheekbones or the stark, inverted V of his black eyebrows.

"Are the preparations complete?" Dominic asked as he dried his face.

"The chapel is ready," Simon said, "your knights wait to stand with you in front of God and the Saxon rabble, and the men-at-arms are looking forward to the wassail and wenches."

"What of the bride?" Dominic asked. "Has anyone seen her?"

"Not in the flesh. Her handmaiden is everywhere, running about like a chicken with its head cut off, shrilling at the laundress for a garment still damp or at the seamstress for a poorly sewn hem or at the tanner for shoes too harsh for noble feet."

Dominic grunted and rubbed the drying cloth over his powerful body.

"It sounds like I won't have to go and drag Lady Margaret from her rooms," he said.

"I hope the lady dresses grandly," Simon said after a few moments.

"No matter. 'Tis not her clothes I'll be marrying."

"Yes, but the bride is supposed to be the best-dressed of all the maids at the wedding, is she not?"

Dominic raised one black eyebrow at his brother in silent demand.

"Marie is wearing the scarlet silk you gave her," continued Simon slyly, "and around her forehead is the golden circlet with its fine rubies that was your present after Jerusalem fell."

"If Lady Margaret wishes such baubles to wear, she will have to be more civil to her husband," Dominic said under his breath. He threw the drying cloth with emphasis onto the table. "A great deal more civil!"

Simon snickered. "Perhaps you should send her to Marie for instruction."

Dominic ignored his brother in favor of Jameson.

"No," he told the squire, "I'll need heavier undergarments than that. Dress me for battle."

The squire looked surprised. "Sire?"

"The hauberk," Dominic said impatiently.

Jameson looked shocked. "For your *marriage*?"

The look on Dominic's face sent a surge of red up the squire's smooth cheeks. Hurriedly the boy retrieved his lord's soft leather undergarments from the wardrobe. Next came the chausses, whose metal bands would protect Dominic's shins from blows during a battle.

A curt movement of Dominic's head refused the chausses. Relieved, Jameson went to the wardrobe for the chain mail tunic. The garment was slit in front and back for riding and quite heavy. With every movement, the metal rings on the hauberk sang quietly of battle and death.

"God's teeth," Simon muttered as he watched Dominic's squire fasten the flexible metal tunic into place. "I've never known a bridegroom to go to his wedding wearing a hauberk."

"Perhaps I'll start a new fashion."

"Or bury an old one?" his brother asked silkily.

Dominic's smile was like a drawn sword. "See that you follow my fashion, brother."

"Will you wear it to the bedchamber?"

"When you handle a brancher," Dominic said dryly, "caution saves many regrets."

Simon laughed aloud at Dominic's comparison of his future bride to a young, recently captured falcon that had never known man's touch.

"She is hardly a fledgling snatched fresh from the branch," Simon said. "She has barely a handful of years less than you."

"True. What you forget is that we fly females rather than tiercels in the hunt because the female is not only larger than the male falcon, she is far more fierce."

Dominic settled his hauberk into place with a muscular shrug that spoke of a decade's experience at war. The heavy hood lay on his shoulders in gleaming, sliding folds of chain mail.

"Sven has heard nothing to suggest that Lady Margaret is so redoubtable," Simon pointed out. "Rather the opposite. The vassals love her greatly for her kindness."

"Falcons are always kind to their own."

"Your helm, sire," the boy said neutrally.

"I think not," Dominic said. "The hauberk's hood will have to serve."

The squire set aside the bleak metal helm with visible relief.

"Will John be attending the ceremony?" Simon asked.

"I heard something about a pallet being readied in the church," Dominic said indifferently.

"Your sword, sire," Jameson said, holding out the heavy sword with both hands.

The squire's expression plainly stated that he hoped his lord would refuse the weapon as he had the helm and chausses.

Jameson was to be disappointed. Dominic buckled the sword in place with a few swift movements. Its grim weight at his left side was as familiar to him as darkness was to the night.

"My mantle," he said.

Within moments Jameson appeared at Dominic's side with a richly embroidered damask mantle. Gemstones and pearls winked and shimmered within the elaborate weave, suggesting laughter buried in the luxurious folds. It was a mantle fit for a sultan. Indeed, it had been a sultan's gift to the knight who had prevented his men from defiling the sultan's five wives after the palace had fallen.

"Not that one," Dominic said. "The black one. It lies more easily over chain mail and sword."

With a sigh, Jameson traded the fine cape for the heavy black wool. In its own almost secret way, the cape was just as costly, for it had a deep border of sable from a forest a thousand miles distant.

Dominic swirled the cape into place with a deft motion. Wool and fur settled luxuriantly around his body, concealing all but the occasional glint of chain mail and the gleaming length of Dominic's heavy sword. Jameson fastened the cape in place with the simple iron pin Dominic wore into battle.

Watching, Simon shook his head in a combination of amusement and rue. Even naked, Dominic was a formidable man; dressed as he was now, he was a blunt warning to the people of the realm that a new lord had come.

A lord who meant to be obeyed.

"You'll have the maiden fainting with fear at the sight of you," Simon said.

"That would be a refreshing change," Dominic muttered.

But he didn't say it loudly enough to be overheard. He had told no one about his brush with the lady of the keep dressed as a cotter's child. The ease with which she had fooled him still rankled his pride.

Bells pealed from the church across the meadow, telling the people of Blackthorne Keep that it was time to gather for the nuptials. Before the last bell was rung, Dominic had walked from his rooms and was mounting a horse in the bailey.

The bride was not nearly so eager for the wedding to begin.

"Eadith, do quit hovering like a sparrow hawk questing for a meal," Meg said.

Despite the words, Meg's voice was gentle. For once she enjoyed the handmaiden's chatter and constant motion; it kept Meg's mind from what lay ahead.

Duncan, be as clever as you are brave. See what must be. Accept it.

Forgive me.

"You heard the bells," Eadith said. " 'Tis time. Hurry, mistress."

Meg glanced at her mother's water clock. The hammered silver bowl with its ebony support and catch basin had been handed down from mother to daughter for years without name or number. With the bowl had come the knowledge of how to use it in marking off the proper time for medicines to steep.

It seemed to Meg but a moment ago that she had filled the keeper to its utmost, water brimming and shining like primeval moonlight in the sunless room. Yet less than a finger's width of water remained in the upper bowl.

"Not quite," Meg said. "There is more water, see?"

"You and your Glendruid ways," Eadith said, shaking her head. "I will mark the passage of the sun with the church's bells."

As though to emphasize the handmaiden's words, the bells pealed again. Meg bowed her head and touched the silver cross that lay between her bare breasts.

"M'lady?"

Eadith waited for Meg's attention. The handmaiden's arms were overflowing with the unusual silver garment that Old Gwyn had brought out the day the king had decreed that Lady Margaret of Blackthorne would marry Dominic le Sabre. The dress wasn't new. Lady Anna had been married in it, and Anna's mother as well. Like the water remaining within the silver Glendruid bowl, the cloth shimmered subtly, as though infused with ancient moonlight.

Meg looked at the dress and remembered what Gwyn had said: *May you give birth to a son.*

Now Meg wondered if the wedding dress, like the clock, had been passed down from mother to daughter through all the years, and if each daughter had donned it hoping that she would be the one to give birth to a Glendruid son.

Dearest God, grant us peace.

"Lady Margaret, we really must hurry."

Reluctantly Meg turned from watching the measured dripping of water from silver bowl to ebony basin.

"The priest is always slow," she said absently. "He dresses more carefully than any bride."

"More carefully than you, 'tis certain!"

"Dominic le Sabre is marrying Blackthorne Keep, not me. He would marry me if I arrived wearing sackcloth and ashes."

"Even so, you must look finer than that Norman whore."

Meg tore her mind away from the remorseless glide of water from silver to black, drops sliding into darkness as surely as Blackthorne Keep into war.

"What?" she asked.

"La Marie," Eadith muttered, giving the woman the nickname she had earned from the servants who were constantly attending her needs. "The men can't look away from her, whether they be Norman swine or Saxon nobles."

"If the men are like crows, captivated by all that flashes brightly, then let them go to the leman's well."

"They are dogs, not crows," Eadith said bitterly. "A red-lipped smile, a wink, perfumed breath, a leg shown and then hidden as she climbs a stair . . . they follow her like dogs after a bitch in heat. And Duncan is at the head of the pack."

"If he sickens from her much-used well," Meg said calmly, "I have a tonic that will put him right once more."

Eadith said nothing.

When Meg saw the unhappiness in her hand-maiden's face, she realized how deeply Eadith had counted on attracting Duncan's eye.

" 'Tis for the best," Meg said, touching her hand-maiden's arm. "Your father was a thane. So was your husband. You deserve better in life than to be Duncan's leman."

The sour curve of Eadith's lips said she disagreed. With quick, strong hands she shook out the silver cloth.

"Were it not for Duncan's ambition, I would have been his *wife*," Eadith said bitterly. "But he was ever longing for land and I have neither wealth nor land to give him. So I will be a poor man's wife. Pah. Better to be a rich man's leman!"

"Better to be an untamed falcon, free of men and wealth alike."

"Easy for you to say," Eadith retorted. "In yonder church stands a knight whose wealth in gems and gold is thrice your weight when you stand fully dressed. Before the bells ring the end of day, you will be one of the richest wives in all of England."

" 'Tis the first kind word I've heard leave your lips about Dominic le Sabre."

"If one must be a Norman swine, then one should at least be a rich Norman swine. Then the priests will be well paid for the lies they will intone over Dominic le Sabre's corpse. May it be an early grave and as deep as Hell itself."

The hate in Eadith's voice made Meg flinch. Eadith had never forgiven the Normans who had slain her husband, father, brothers, and uncles, and taken their estates.

Into the uncomfortable silence came the slow dripping of water. The sound made gooseflesh rise on Meg's arms. She found herself holding her breath, counting, wanting to stem the relentless drops.

Silence came.

The silver bowl was dry.

"Quickly," Meg said, holding out her arms. "Let us get it done with."

Within moments Meg was wearing folds of cloth that fooled the eye like moonlight on a river. Eadith pulled laces at the back, making the fabric snug against Meg's body. As light as mist, the garment clung and swirled in silver stirrings that outlined the supple feminine form beneath.

When Eadith was finished, Meg turned a full circle. The cloth lifted and then flowed into place as though made for her rather than for her mother before her.

"Are you certain you won't wear the brooch Lord Dominic sent you?" Eadith asked.

"Before her marriage, a Glendruid girl wears only silver. After it, she wears only gold. I will wear the brooch soon enough."

If I live.

"Foolishness," Eadith muttered. "You will look a drab creature next to the Norman whore."

Eadith held out a very long, intricately made chain of silver and clear crystal. Like the clock, the chain had been passed down through generations. No wider than Meg's smallest finger, almost as flexible as water itself, the chain circled her waist, crossed behind at her hips, and returned to her front in a shining girdle.

The ends of the chain reached to the hem like silent, slender waterfalls. And like water, the crystals in the chain transformed light into elusive flashes of color, fragments of rainbows caught and held for an instant of time.

Meg lifted hands naked of rings and pulled the combs from the hair piled on her head. Her hair tumbled down around her shoulders, over her breasts, falling to her hips and beyond. Against the ethereal silver of the dress, her hair burned with all the passions she had never felt.

"Well," Eadith said grudgingly, "it does make your hair look bright."

The handmaiden held out the plain silver circlet that was all Meg would wear to hold her hair from her face. Incised on the inside of the band were ancient runes.

"I could fasten the brooch to—" Eadith began, only to be cut off.

"No."

Meg gathered her hair into a single long fall down her back. Without a word she held out her hand for the hooded silver mantle that fastened to the dress at the back of her shoulders with two silver clasps. The fluid weight of the cloth swept down her back to the floor and beyond in a rippling silver train.

A quick motion of Meg's hands lifted the hood into place, covering her hair. Eadith put the circlet on her mistress and looked disapprovingly at the results.

"You'll not outshine the whore," she said bluntly.

"Still your tongue," Old Gwyn said from the doorway. "You know nothing of what is at risk today."

When Meg spun toward the door, subtle currents of silver ran the length of her dress and crystals flashed fragments of rainbows, but it was her eyes that drew Gwyn's attention. Within the silver cloud of Meg's mantle, her eyes burned like green flames.

Gwyn's breath came in with an audible hiss. She touched her forehead in silent obeisance to the Glendruid girl who smoldered before her, wrapped in rituals and hopes as old as time.

Before Gwyn could speak, church bells rang, summoning Meg to marriage.

And war.

INCENSE AND PERFUME PERMEATED the wooden building's sacred hush. Pews shone with recently applied beeswax. Myriad tongues of light rose from massed candles. Costly brooches, necklaces, circlets, girdles, and rings flashed like distant stars throughout the church, reflecting the dance of candle flames.

Scots thanes, Saxon nobles, Norman aristocracy, and knights of all kinds mixed together with the wariness of wild animals forced into unaccustomed closeness by a spring flood.

Dominic's wintry gray eyes catalogued the gathering. As he had expected, there was an abundance of swords evident beneath the men's mantles. Some of the sword hilts were set with gems, signifying that the weapon was intended for ceremonial rather than military purposes. Other swords were like Dominic's, gleaming with war's steel blush rather than with decorative silver.

Despite the crush of people in the church, no one stood close to Dominic, including the black-haired woman whose flowing scarlet dress and costly jewels had drawn many glances. Not even the dark-eyed temptress dared approach Dominic now. There was the look of an eagle about him, a predatory readiness that radiated as surely from him as heat from fire.

Only Simon had the courage to approach his brother. Only Simon knew that intelligence held sway over Dominic's passions rather than vice versa.

"All is ready, save for the bride," Simon murmured, stepping up close behind Dominic so that no one could overhear.

Dominic nodded. "Did the priest object?"

"He complained of crowding in the choir. I pointed out that there was little choice. I could hardly seat my men with the nobility, could I?"

Simon's bland summation made Dominic smile.

"Duncan's men are armed to the teeth," Simon said.

"Yes."

"That's all you have to say?"

"The Reevers are a ragged lot."

"Their steel is well cared for," Simon retorted.

Dominic grunted. "When Duncan appears, stay very near him. Be like his heartbeat. Close."

"What of John?" Simon objected, looking at the first pew, where the lord of Blackthorne lay wrapped in costly robes. "Any trouble would begin with him."

"He has the will to cleave me in two with a sword, but not the strength," Dominic said dryly. "Duncan has both. He was once betrothed to Lady Margaret."

Simon's dark eyes narrowed. He said something under his breath that would have made the priest flinch, had the good man heard it.

"You will do penance for that," Dominic said, smiling slightly. "But I find myself in agreement with your sentiments concerning a man who would marry his daughter to his bastard son."

"Perhaps she isn't his daughter?"

"Then why hasn't he set her aside and named Duncan his heir?" Dominic countered. "No man wants to see his lands pass to his daughter's husband while his own name and line dies for want of sons."

A stir went through the church, for the bride had just appeared in the wide doorway. In the shifting illumination of the church, Meg appeared to be wrapped in silver mist from head to heels, a girl as ethereal as moonlight. A large man loomed behind her, all but blocking out the light from the cloudy day.

"Go," Dominic said softly.

Without another word, Simon eased back into the throng clustered around the first pews.

Because the heir to Blackthorne had no male blood relatives capable of standing with her and giving her shoe to Dominic as a symbol of passage from her father's domain to her husband's, Duncan of Maxwell accompanied Lady Margaret in John's place.

The sight of the Scots thane walking with Meg clinging to his arm made something very like rage turn deep within Dominic. Its ferocity surprised him, for he had never been a possessive man. Yet he knew deep in his soul that he must be the only man standing close to Meg, breathing in the faint spicy fragrance of her breath and skin, feeling her warmth so near, touching him even as he touched her.

Then Dominic saw Meg's eyes and forgot Duncan's presence, forgot the priest waiting, forgot the swords buried in their sheaths, waiting for a word that might or might not be spoken. Dominic could only watch his future wife approach, beginning to understand why the common people of Blackthorne Keep looked to their mistress with expressions of agonized hope transforming their weathered faces.

If spring wore flesh and walked among mortals at winter's end, she would have eyes that color; and they would burn just like that, twin green flames radiant with the hope all men lay at spring's feet.

Silence followed Meg's slow progress down the aisle. She didn't notice it. Her glance had fallen on the foreign woman whose lush body and costly clothing announced how well Dominic had paid to lie with her. Marie didn't notice the look she got from Meg, for the leman was watching Dominic hungrily.

The bride followed the leman's eyes. Meg's breath came in and stayed. Dominic was watching her approach, his body at ease yet obviously powerful. Motionless, he waited at the front of the church, following her progress with the intense stare of an eagle or a god. He was clothed like night, and like night there came from his darkness small splinters of light as chain mail glittered in place of stars.

With a distant sense of shock, Meg realized that Dominic wore a hauberk beneath his black cloak. The tension that radiated up through Duncan's arm where her hand rested told her that he, too, had noted Dominic's unusual wedding attire.

A wedding or a war, Meg thought. *Which will it be?*

The question consumed her so that she could barely follow the ceremony. As though in a dream, she moved through the kneeling and rising and kneeling, letting the plainsong chants of the concealed choir wash through her until the priest looked at her sharply.

"I say again, Lady Margaret," the priest intoned, "it is your right to refuse this marriage if you so desire, for wedlock is a holy state entered into freely. Do you accept Dominic le Sabre as your true husband in the eyes of God and man?"

Meg swallowed dryly, trying to force a word past the constriction in her throat.

Behind her rose an agitation that began with Duncan and rippled through the crowd. In its wake were muted whisperings as though of steel being drawn. She turned and looked at the dark Norman knight who was watching her as though his will alone could force agreement from her lips.

But he could not. Nothing could.

Dominic knew it as well as Meg did. This was the one time in a woman's life when her desires could make or break the plans of men.

Marriage or war?

Suddenly it was easy for Meg to speak.

"Yes," she said huskily. "I accept this man as my husband in the eyes of God and man."

A surprised cry from Duncan was cut short.

Her father's cry of outrage was not. But before he could speak coherently, one of Simon's men materialized by John's side. Only one person saw the knife in the knight's hand, but that one person was John. He made no more objection to the progress of the ceremony.

Nor did Duncan. He had felt cold steel slide through the back slit in his hauberk to lie between his legs, pressing in silent threat against a man's most vulnerable flesh. Clammy sweat broke over his body. To die in honorable battle was one thing; to be castrated like a capon was quite another.

"Don't move," Simon said very softly to Duncan.

Duncan didn't move.

"Unless you wish to disappoint Marie tonight," Simon continued, "and every night hereafter, you will say nothing. Nod your head if you understand me."

Duncan nodded his head very carefully.

"Hand Lady Margaret's shoe to my brother as tradition requires," Simon ordered. "*Slowly.*"

With great care, Duncan gave Dominic a delicate shoe embroidered in silver thread. Afterward Duncan didn't move again, not even to check on the odd sounds issuing from the gathering behind him. He suspected that his men were having the same difficulty he was, and for the same reason— a knife between their thighs.

Thirty men-at-arms stepped out from behind the partition that had set apart the men who chanted the wedding mass. Though not one of the men raised the crossbow he carried, it was clear that the weapons were fully wound and ready to fire.

Meg looked at Dominic's men, sensed the currents of stifled rage and fear that swirled through the room, and knew that Dominic had foreseen the possibility of an ambush in the church.

Foreseen and countered.

Ice condensed beneath her skin as she waited in dread for the bloodletting that would surely follow such treachery. Trembling with fear for her people, she watched Dominic with haunted eyes.

Dominic's cold gaze swept over the church like a winter wind. No one moved. Many of the Saxons and Scots stood stiffly, as though afraid that any motion might be their last. And it would have been, for Norman steel lay against their vulnerable flesh.

"Well done, Simon," Dominic said.

"It was my pleasure."

"I don't doubt it."

Then Dominic turned his back on everyone and looked only at Meg.

"As my betrothal gift of gold didn't please you," Dominic said coolly, "I offer a different kind of gift today: I will slay no man for his part in this treachery. Do you accept this gift?"

Unable to speak, Meg nodded.

"A wise man will understand that his lord is merciful rather than weak," Dominic continued. "A foolish man will try my patience again. *And die.*"

Though Dominic raised his voice not at all, his words carried clearly to every part of the church. There was a murmuring of relief as Duncan's men understood that they would not be taken out and summarily hanged for their stillborn rebellion.

Meg wanted to thank Dominic for his unexpected mercy, but her own relief that carnage had been prevented was so great she became light-headed. The church began to revolve slowly around her while light from the candles dimmed as though someone had drawn a veil over her face. The floor shifted beneath her feet.

With a soft sound of dismay, Meg reached for Dominic to steady herself.

Dominic heard Meg's low cry, saw the color run from her cheeks, and caught her up in his arms before she fell. Silver swirled and seethed against black before flowing into place, soft Glendruid cloth matching each fold of Dominic's war cape as though cut for that sole purpose.

The steady beating of Meg's heart against his hand told Dominic that relief rather than anything more sinister had temporarily taken her strength. He looked from her to the priest.

The man's face was as pale as a death lily, his guilt clear to see in the sweat standing on his brow.

"Finish it," Dominic said coolly.

"I c-cannot."

"Lady Margaret has done her part. Do yours or die."

The priest began talking, his voice shaking so much that the words were all but unintelligible. He completed the ceremony with unseemly haste.

Meg heard the words as though at a great distance. Nothing was real to her but the knowledge that she had betrayed John and Duncan; and in doing so had saved Blackthorne Keep and its people from destruction.

Gradually the power of the man who was holding her sank into Meg's senses, giving her something tangible to cling to in a world that still seemed very insubstantial. She looked up at Dominic's face, trying to gauge the fate to which she had agreed, wife of the dark Norman lord.

Candlelight didn't soften Dominic's features. It brought them into bold relief, laying black shadows beneath his cheekbones and along the hard line of his jaw. His eyes were as clear and colorless as the eyes of the fabled Glendruid Wolf. And surrounding all was the grim winking of chain mail lying just beneath the flowing, midnight cape.

The church whirled around Meg again, but this time it wasn't the rushing of her own blood that caused it. The ceremony was complete. Dominic had turned and was striding down the aisle, carrying his wife in his arms as though she weighed no more than the mist her dress resembled.

Just before Dominic reached the doorway of the church, he stopped in the shadows to assess the reaction of the people of Blackthorne Keep. He didn't know if they, like the priest, had wished Duncan of Maxwell to be their new lord.

An uncertain sound went through the tenants when they saw their lady being held inside the church by the grim Norman warrior as though he had sacked a city and taken her as a prize. Seeing the harsh planes of Dominic's face, Meg could well understand the hesitation in her people. She herself could hardly believe Dominic had withheld the death that Duncan and her father had earned.

Yet Dominic had shown mercy. Duncan and her father still lived. Dominic had taken advantage of the shock caused by her acceptance of marriage and used those precious instants not to slay, but to force a peace.

Hidden within the shadows in the church doorway, Meg touched Dominic's cheek just above the cold chain mail, reassuring herself that he was indeed flesh rather than steel, and that she herself was alive to feel his warmth.

Dominic looked down into eyes that were the clear, burning green of spring itself.

"Thank you for not killing them," Meg said.

"It wasn't done from the softness of my heart," Dominic said bluntly. "Much as I would enjoy hanging the men who would have forced war upon me and incest upon you, I have no wish to be lord of a ruined keep."

Chilled, Meg removed her fingers. "John is not my father."

"Then why didn't he disinherit you?"

As Dominic spoke, he stepped forward, carrying Meg into the tenuous, silver-white light of day. Again, an uneasy murmuring ran through the gathered vassals.

"The people," Meg said simply. "They are why."

"What?"

"This."

Again Meg touched Dominic.

This time the people of Blackthorne Keep saw their mistress's fingertips resting on the knight's cheek where flesh rose above chain mail. It was a touch freely given by their lady to her new husband.

If she was his captive, she was a willing one.

A great shout went up from the people as they understood that this spring they would sow crops for the living rather than dig graves for the dead;

and in their joy it was Meg's name the people called, not that of their new lord.

As the waves of jubilation broke over Dominic, he knew why John had never disavowed the girl who was not his daughter.

8

THE FEAST SPREAD IN THE BAILEY before the vassals of Blackthorne Keep was a luxury beyond their imagining. Scents both familiar and exotic filled the cool air. Potent ale and even more potent mead waited in barrels that had just been broached. There was fish both fresh and salted, fowl both fresh and smoked, pigs roasted whole and doves lying on beds of fresh greens, breads both traditional and flavored with imported spices so costly they had never before been tasted by the keep's servants. It was a feast fit for nobles, and it was being given to the commoners of Blackthorne Keep.

As they approached the laden trestle tables, a shallow bowl was given to each person. In the bottom of the bowl was a silver coin and a piece of candied citrus. Cries of wonder and pleasure rippled through the crowd. No one could say which was more pleasing, the money or the sweet. Most common people lived and died without holding either in their palm.

Grimly Duncan watched as Dominic and Meg strolled among the people of the keep, accepting their good wishes. For each vassal Meg had a question or a compliment. With Dominic the people were reserved and respectful; with Meg they were both reverent and joyous.

Whatever hope the Scots Hammer might have had of the vassals refusing to serve their new lord died as Duncan watched Dominic bask in the reflected glow of the people's love for Meg. Yet even as Duncan watched, he could not help but admire both the intelligence of Blackthorne Keep's new lord and the ruthlessness Dominic kept as carefully sheathed as his sword; but like his sword, able to be drawn and used in an instant.

"Saying fare thee well to your ambitions?" a voice asked sardonically.

Duncan didn't have to turn to see who was digging spurs into his pride. Simon hadn't been more than a hand's reach—or a knife's—from Duncan since the beginning of the wedding ceremony.

"Your brother is a clever man," Duncan said evenly. "He did the one thing that might win Blackthorne's people to his side."

"Spared John's life?"

Duncan shook his head. "No."

"The feast?"

Smiling slightly, Duncan still shook his head. "It was shrewd, but not enough."

"The money?"

"Nay."

"What, then?"

"Somehow your brother convinced Meg that he was the only way to peace for her people. When did she come to you with John's plans? Last night?"

Simon gave Duncan an odd look. "Lady Margaret didn't come to us."

"God's blood, I'm not an entire fool! When did Meggie betray us?"

"You knew it as soon as we did," Simon retorted.

"As for betrayal, the only treachery today was on the part of John. And you, of course."

"I am a Scots thane," Duncan said coldly. "I bend the knee to none but my own king. Henry is not that king!"

"Aren't you grateful that your life was spared?"

"It was spared for Lord Dominic's purposes, not mine."

Simon shrugged. "Of course. He made a present of your life to Lady Margaret. I hope he doesn't rue his generosity."

For a moment Duncan measured the brother of the man who had defeated him so handily. Duncan had seen men such as Simon and Dominic in the Holy Land, knights who had little to bring to life but their own wit and brawn.

Duncan was himself such a man.

Next time use the wit rather than the brawn, Duncan advised himself sardonically. *Dominic did, and see what it got him—Meggie's hand and all of Blackthorne Keep for his domain.*

"Am I permitted to see Lord John?" Duncan asked.

"Dominic wouldn't keep a son from seeing his dying father."

Duncan shot him a glance through narrowed eyes. "Do you listen much to scullery gossip?"

"A great deal," Simon assured him cheerfully. "It makes for less nasty surprises that way. You should be grateful that Dominic listens, too."

"Why?" Duncan asked curtly. "It lost me Blackthorne Keep."

"Nay. Dominic had laid his plans for the wedding before we ever rode up to the keep."

Duncan's eyes widened in a shock he didn't trouble to hide. "How did he know?"

"He didn't. He simply knew that if trouble were to come, the most unexpected place for it would be in the church itself. So he asked after the priest's parents, if his brothers were John's vassals, if his sisters were married to Saxons or Normans, if Lord John had paid for his education in the Church. We quickly discovered that the priest owed far more to Saxon and Scot than to King Henry."

Duncan turned and stared openly at Simon.

"Then," Simon continued, enjoying himself, "we heard talk of John's bastard, a knight of courage and quick temper, a fine warrior known as the Scots Hammer, and a man who had been betrothed to John's own daughter until the king squeezed the Church into refusing the match. The Church was quite reluctant, however. 'Tis appalling what some men of God do in God's name."

"Amen," Duncan said.

And meant it. Some of the things he had seen done by men of God to other men of God during the Holy War would haunt him until the day he died.

"I suspect," Simon said slowly, "that was when Dominic decided to kill John. The thought of a man marrying his bastard son to his own daughter sickened my brother. Dominic thought no better of the ambitious bastard who would marry his own half sister. Once the facts were known, King Henry would raise no objections to the hangings."

A soft whistle came from between Duncan's teeth as he understood how close to death he still was.

"Meggie isn't my sister."

It was Simon's turn to be surprised. And relieved. He admired the Scots Hammer's audacity and courage. Under other circumstances, they might have been friends.

"I am pleased to hear it," Simon said simply.

"See that your brother hears it as well."

Simon looked closely at Duncan and smiled thinly.

"You begin to understand," Simon said, nodding. "Dominic is as savage a man in battle as I have ever seen, because he considers war to be a failure of intelligence that must be hacked through as quickly as possible. 'Tis ever so much more useful to have peace, you see."

"No, I don't."

"Neither do I," Simon admitted.

The two men looked at each other and laughed.

Dominic turned at the sound of male laughter, saw Duncan and Simon, and shook his head.

"What is it?" Meg asked.

"My brother and the Scots Hammer."

Meg looked puzzled.

"They're laughing together like friends," Dominic explained, "yet they came within a single breath of trying to kill one another in the church."

"Perhaps that is why they are laughing. They are alive and it is spring and a feast awaits in the great hall. What more could they require of life at this moment?"

Gray eyes focused on Meg. Slowly Dominic nodded as he considered what she had said.

"You are very wise, for a maid."

She slanted him a green-eyed glance and said dryly, "Wiser than many a man, I assure you."

One corner of Dominic's mouth lifted in a smile. "I shall remember that."

Dominic and Meg continued across the bailey through the throng of vassals, making slow progress. It seemed that each tenant, cotter, freeholder, and serf must assure himself personally of Meg's well-being. Eadith waited rather impatiently at the edges of the crowd, plainly wishing access to her mistress.

"What is it, Eadith?" Meg asked finally. "Come forward."

The vassals parted for the handmaiden's progress. The light of day wasn't as kind to her clothing as it was to Meg's. Eadith's poverty—and that of the Blackthorne Keep itself—showed clearly in her mantle gone threadbare from much use.

"Lord John is feeling the strain of the day quite keenly," Eadith said. "He wishes to give the wedding toast soon."

Meg closed her eyes for an instant. She dreaded having to face John's wrath.

Dominic saw Meg's reluctance. He put his arm about her waist under her mantle. The warmth and resilience of her body beneath the silver fabric sent a shaft of heat through him.

"Tell John," Dominic said, "that we will join him shortly."

Startled, Eadith looked at Dominic. His expression told her she had better become accustomed to taking orders from him. She nodded hurriedly and pressed through the crowd. The pale orange of her dress and the shimmer of her long blond hair showed clearly against the keep's damp stone as she climbed the steps to the forebuilding.

Dominic looked down into Meg's shadowed eyes and guessed the reason for her unease.

"You are my wife. I protect what is mine. Your father's ambitions will trouble you no longer."

Long auburn lashes swept down for a moment, concealing Meg's eyes. She wondered if Dominic would feel the same way about protecting her when he realized that he had been trapped into a union with a Glendruid girl of doubtful fertility.

"But do not try to deceive me again as you did in the mews," he added coldly. "No trick works twice on me."

"You startled me. I wasn't dressed to receive my future husband. In any case, my father had forbidden our introduction until the wedding itself."

Though Meg wasn't looking at Dominic, she could sense him weighing her words as carefully as a miller weighed wheat to be ground into flour. Unease rippled through her. He was a very powerful man; should he choose to beat her, there was nothing she could do, no place to which she could flee. She was like her mother.

Trapped.

After a moment Meg put her hand on Dominic's arm and looked up, in control of her emotions once more. Her most important goal had been accomplished: Blackthorne Keep was safe from a ruinous war. For the remainder, she would simply take each difficulty as it came and pray that Dominic showed as much restraint in the rest of his life as he did in battle.

Together Dominic and Meg climbed the steep stone steps to the keep, then turned to acknowledge a final chorus of good wishes from the people. Once inside the forebuilding's dark interior, Meg turned hesitantly to Dominic.

"Will you go to our wedding feast in chain mail?" she asked.

"Yes."

When Meg would have spoken again, Dominic put his thumb lightly against her lips. Startled, she stood very still, watching him with eyes that were luminous even in the half darkness of the keep's forebuilding. Her dress shimmered with light, as though mist and moonlight and stars had been woven into the fey cloth.

"Fear not, bride," Dominic said deeply. "I won't wear hauberk and sword in the bedchamber."

Meg's breath went out in a rush of warmth across Dominic's thumb. An odd smile changed his face, making it both handsome and compelling.

"Well, perhaps a sword," he said huskily. "It will

be quite hard but it will have not one cutting edge. It will lie quite smoothly within your warm sheath."

So surprised was Meg by the transformation the sensual smile made in Dominic's face that it took a few moments for the meaning of his words to register. When she understood, heat rose in her face. He saw the blush and laughed softly.

"We shall do well with one another," Dominic said with obvious satisfaction. "I expected to do my duty by my wife, but I didn't expect to enjoy it overmuch. I see that I was wrong. Planting my seed within you will be a very pleasant duty indeed."

"Pleasant for whom, my lord?"

"Both of us."

"Ah, I see you want heirs."

"Of course I want heirs," he said. "There is no other reason to marry."

"Land and a keep?" Meg suggested with a cool smile. "Are they not worth a marriage?"

"Without heirs, land is a demanding burden and marriage a cruel hoax," Dominic said succinctly.

Before Meg could speak again, Simon and Duncan strode into the forebuilding. When Duncan saw Meg, he stopped abruptly. Simon looked at Dominic, who signaled his brother to go on into the keep alone. But when Duncan started to talk to Meg, Dominic spoke first.

"Before you berate my *wife*," Dominic said icily, "know that you enjoy life only by her sufferance."

Duncan gave the other man a long look, took a deep breath to cool his temper, and said, "Meggie had naught to do with any of our plans."

"Except as a pawn," she said before Dominic could speak.

The two men looked at Meg in surprise, for there had been an edge to her voice that was unusual for her. She continued talking in that same biting tone.

"My father—or is he my stepuncle, or perhaps no blood relation at all?—has spent much time planning ways to use me. Why should Duncan apologize for doing the same?"

The Scots Hammer moved uneasily. What Meg said was the truth, but it sounded quite unpleasant spoken aloud.

"Meggie," he said in a deep voice, "I wouldn't have you hurt. Surely you know that?"

"Is that why you planned to launch a war while she stood in the center of the battlefield?" Dominic asked sardonically.

"My men had their orders," Duncan retorted. "If one of them had so much as jostled Meggie, I would have killed him."

"And *my* men? What were your orders to them?" Dominic asked savagely. "How were you to prevent them from hacking through a treacherous female to get at my murderer?"

Duncan paled visibly.

"Meggie," he protested to her. "It wouldn't have happened that way. I would have protected you!"

"Why? Death would have been a blessing."

It took a moment for Meg's bitter words to penetrate the men's anger. When they did, both men stared at her.

"What are you saying, lass?" Duncan whispered, appalled.

"John has tried to use me to make war on the Normans since I was eight," Meg said. "If he had succeeded, I couldn't have borne knowing I was the cause of my people's suffering. I would have welcomed the blow that ended my life."

"You can't mean that, Meggie."

"I can. I do."

Dominic had no doubt Meg meant every word. He had seen the green fires of spring burning in her eyes and had felt the unleashed hope of the people of Blackthorne Keep focus on her. To live under that burden of expectation—and then to fail the people's trust—would have destroyed her.

Unsettled by Meg's words, Duncan raked a large hand through his dark brown hair, totally at a loss for words. When she saw his distress, she sighed and touched his arm with gentle fingers.

"I believe you didn't mean for me to be hurt," she said.

"Thank you," Duncan said in a low, strained voice. "I . . ." He shook his head and put his hand over hers. "I wouldn't want to lose you, Meggie. I never meant to put you at risk."

"I don't blame you," she said, smiling slightly. "You are very much a man. You are doing only what men have always done."

"And what is it that men have always done?" Dominic asked coldly, removing Meg's hand from the Scots Hammer's arm.

"Seek land and sons," she said.

Dominic shrugged. "That is like saying the sun rises and sets."

"Yes."

Oddly, Meg's agreement didn't please Dominic. He disliked being put in the same category as John, a man who had outraged Church and king alike in his quest to ensure that his bastard inherited Blackthorne Keep.

"Some things are beneath even ambitious men," Dominic said.

"Truly?" Meg retorted. "Name just one of them."

"Spare me the sharp edge of your tongue, wife. I've done nothing to earn it save grant mercy to the men who would have murdered me."

Meg lowered her eyelashes, screening herself from Dominic's icy gray stare.

"My apologies, husband. I fear the events of the day have unsettled me. I would never place you in the company of merely mortal men."

"Your apologies are sharper than your insults."

Duncan snickered, enjoying Dominic's discomfort. Meg's lips quirked in a smile she barely managed to stifle.

"If you will excuse me," Duncan said to Dominic, "I'll leave you to the business of getting acquainted with your new wife."

"I think not," Dominic said instantly.

Startled, Duncan turned back.

"You will go into the great hall with us," Dominic continued. "I would have all men see that you aren't being restrained by a knife held between your thighs."

Meg made a startled sound and stared at Duncan. Red tinged his cheeks. He looked distinctly uncomfortable at the memory.

"Give him your arm," Dominic said to Meg. "And then *never again touch him within my sight.*"

The suppressed violence in Dominic's voice made Meg turn quickly to look at him. What she saw in his eyes chilled her. Saying nothing, she rested her fingertips on Duncan's arm.

Not a word was spoken until the three of them entered the great hall, where fires burned and tapestries glowed in rich colors along the wall. Silver plate and goblets gleamed from every spot on the long trestle tables. Saxon and Norman were interspersed quite carefully along the lower tables. They were watched over by men standing along the walls with the servants. The men, however, weren't fetching and carrying; they were holding fully armed crossbows.

It had a dampening effect on the festivity.

John had been waiting for Meg and Dominic. A

weak yet imperious gesture summoned them to the dais on which the lord's table was elevated above the remainder of the great hall. Three plates of beaten gold gleamed at John's table. At his signal, a server leaped forward to pour wine into a jeweled goblet.

"A toast to the bride and groom," John said.

Despite his obvious frailty, when John spoke, he pitched his voice to carry throughout the room. Small conversations stilled as knights and their ladies turned toward the dais.

"Behold the great Norman lord," John said in a voice rich with contempt. "Behold the fool who trusted King Henry and was betrayed by him."

Gasps and uneasy murmurs rose from the tables.

Dominic smiled wolfishly. "You have great knowledge of betrayal, having practiced it all your life. Tell me, I pray thee, how King Henry betrayed his Sword."

"Why, 'tis simple, simpleton. Your king didn't love you enough to give you a noble Norman girl to wed."

Dominic slanted a sideways look at Meg. Her mouth was pale and drawn. He put his hand under her chin and turned her face toward his.

"Nay, my king loved me more," Dominic said clearly. "He gave me the fairest maiden in all his kingdom to wed."

"He gave you hell on earth!" John rasped.

"You're ill, old man. Make your toast and let us get on with the feasting."

John laughed. The sound of madness lying just beneath the laughter made Meg stir in silent protest.

"That I will," John said. "We shall drink to the king who hated you enough to give you a daughter of Glendruid to wed."

"No great burden," Dominic said dryly.

"Ha! You're as ignorant as a stone. It is the greatest curse a man could bear. *Like me, you will have no heirs.*"

The sardonic smile vanished from Dominic's face. "What are you saying? Is your daughter infertile?"

"She is a Glendruid witch," John spat. "If you take her without pleasing her, there will be no fruit."

Dominic shrugged. "The same is said of every girl."

"But in the case of the Glendruids, it is truth!"

Against his will, Dominic was drawn by the combination of madness, despair, and triumph that glittered in John's hazel eyes as he spoke.

"Within living memory, no sons have been born to a daughter of Glendruid," John said.

A quick glance at Duncan and Meg told Dominic that they accepted as truth what John was saying. So did the knights of the keep. They sat silently, watching Dominic with great interest, wondering what the husband of Lady Margaret would do when he realized how he had been fooled into accepting a marriage that was less than it had seemed.

"All Glendruid unions produced daughters, and precious few of them," John continued.

"If that is true, why were you so eager to marry your son to Lady Margaret?" Dominic countered.

"It was the only way to give Blackthorne Keep to Duncan. And . . ." John's voice faded.

Dominic waited.

John gave Meg and Duncan a hooded glance.

"There is affection between the two of them," John said finally. "There always has been."

The thought didn't please Dominic.

"So?" he asked in a clipped voice.

"So there was a chance of an heir," John said simply. "And if not, there are always wenches willing to bear a great man's bastards. One way or the other, the seed of my loins would have inherited my lands!"

Dominic's eyes narrowed to splinters of ice as he heard his own dream from the lips of a man who hated him.

"But," continued John, "no man can seduce a witch, for she has little passion in her; and if a rare witch does feel passion, it is for a man other than her husband. The fruit she bears is female, and comes not from her husband's loins!"

A rustling movement went through the room as people glanced carefully at Meg.

" 'Tis true," John said bitterly. "The witch Margaret didn't grow from my seed."

He turned and pointed a shaking hand at the silver-haired woman who was watching him from the side of the table.

"Tell the Norman bastard what awaits him," John said. *"Tell him now."*

Old Gwyn stepped up to the dais with a grace unexpected in a woman her age. She turned to Dominic, facing him unflinchingly despite the savage expression on his face.

"What John says is true," Gwyn said simply. "My lady was carrying another man's babe when she married."

Gwyn said no more.

"Tell him!" John shouted. "Tell him what will happen if he forces a Glendruid witch in order to get a babe of his own!"

Gwyn was silent.

"Old woman," Dominic said with fierce restraint, "it would be best if you told me freely."

"If you rape Meg in your haste to make heirs, your crops and flocks will fail and your vassals will sicken," Gwyn said.

Dominic's left eyebrow rose in a silent arch of disbelief.

"If you are skillful enough to give her great pleasure in the marriage bed, you might be granted a girl."

"Continue," Dominic said when the silence lengthened.

"It there is great love, there is a chance of a male heir."

A murmuring went through the gathered people, the same two words repeated over and over.

Glendruid Wolf. Glendruid Wolf. Glendruid Wolf.

"God rot all Glendruid witches!" John screamed suddenly. "They are as cold as a mountain grave! They never love!"

With the strength of madness, John dragged himself upright and held his goblet in Dominic's face.

"So I give you a toast, enemy mine," John said with savage satisfaction.

"I give you a life without sons.

"I give you a life in which you cannot beat obedience into your cold wife for fear of your crops and flocks.

"I give you a life in which you cannot set aside your infertile wife for fear that your vassals will quit the land.

"I give you a life in which you will live every minute knowing that your line dies with you.

"I give you Lady Margaret, witch of Glendruid!"

John drank swiftly, turned his goblet upside down, and slammed it onto the table. Abruptly he gasped, staggered, and sprawled forward, sending gold plate flying.

When Dominic reached him, John of Cumbriland, Lord of Blackthorne Keep was dead.

And he was smiling.

9

"**W**HAT ARE YOU GOING TO do?" Simon asked his brother.

Impassively Dominic looked at the wall hangings in the small room that opened off the great hall. Fire guttered in the brazier, warming stone walls still chilled by winter's cold. From the great hall came random noises, but no merriment. The tables had been empty of feasters for some time.

Now servants moved through the echoing hall, clearing away the trestle tables and benches, leaving only the lord's permanent table standing. The remains of the food were being dispersed among the poorest of the vassals. The scraps were being snarled over by Dominic's lean greyhounds.

He wished them good appetite. Certainly no one else had enjoyed the wedding feast.

At least no one had objected when Dominic had coolly decreed there would be no outward signs of mourning until the funeral ten days hence, for the joy of the marriage took precedence over grief at the death of a man long wracked by pain.

"Dominic?" Simon pressed.

"I'll give the whore's spawn a Christian burial, what else?" he said curtly.

100

"That isn't what I meant."

There was silence. Slowly Dominic's hand formed into a mail-covered fist. It descended to the table with a force that shook the solid wood.

"I regret not killing the Scots Hammer when I had the excuse," Dominic said through his teeth.

"Why?" Simon asked, startled. "He left without quarrel, taking his Reevers with him."

"I'll be forced by custom and courtesy to have him back for the funeral."

Dominic made a sound that was remarkably like one of his greyhounds.

"But by then your other knights and mercenaries will have arrived," Simon said. "The keep will be secure against anything but the king himself."

With an impatient movement Dominic turned away from his view of the great hall and confronted his brother.

"You heard John," Dominic said coldly. "There is 'affection' between my wife and that Scots spawn of the Devil. Sweet Jesus, she could be carrying his bastard right now!"

"Aye," Simon agreed reluctantly. "That is why I ask again: What will you do?"

"I will bide my time before I plant my seed within my fair Glendruid bride."

"I'd think you would hurry to it," Simon muttered. "Sounds as though it will be a tiresome process, getting the wench with child."

"When—or *if*—my wife's monthly bleeding commences," Dominic said distinctly, "I will know thereafter who is the father of any babe she carries."

Simon's eyes widened in comprehension.

"Until that first bleeding passes," Dominic continued, "I will reconnoiter the legendary walled fortress that is my Glendruid wife. I will discover her truths, ferret out her lies, find her secrets, weigh her weaknesses; and then I will lay siege as I have so many times before."

"Successfully."

"Yea and believe it," Dominic said flatly. "It will bring me great pleasure to have the Glendruid witch on her knees in front of me. *Affection between them.* God's blood!"

Simon smiled rather savagely, feeling better than he had since John had hurled his dying curse at Dominic.

"Almost I feel sorry for the maid," Simon said.

The lift of Dominic's black, angular eyebrow was the only question he asked, or needed to.

"She knows not what demon she has summoned by challenging you," Simon explained.

With a shrug, Dominic went back to staring out at the great hall where every knight in the keep had heard his new lord cursed by the old lord.

A dying curse. Not a thing to think upon with ease, even for a man as formidable as Dominic le Sabre.

"Dominic?"

He glanced aside at Simon.

"What if she is breeding Duncan's bastard?" Simon asked bluntly.

Dominic shrugged. "The babe will be fostered in Normandy. And then . . ."

Simon waited, watching his brother with hard black eyes.

"And then I will teach my wife that, Glendruid witch or no, she will be faithful to me henceforth. If I find otherwise, she will pray to God to release her from the living hell I will make of her life."

"But what of the Glendruid curse?"

"What of it?" Dominic retorted bitterly.

"The people believe in it, whether or not you do. If you mock her openly . . ." Simon's voice died.

"If the witch won't give me a son, I will lay waste to the crops and flocks with my own hand," Dominic said harshly. "Land and wealth serve only to mock a man who has no heirs to accept the fruits of his life's labor."

Again Dominic's fist descended on the table with a force that made the thick wood shudder.

"God's blood, but I have been savagely used. *To come so close to my dream and then to see it all turn to ashes!*"

In the taut silence that followed Dominic's words, the normal sounds of the keep seemed unnaturally loud. The creak of water being drawn from the well just below, the servants calling back and forth about the best place to store a bench or a platter, or who had neglected the hearth fire and the candles guttering sullenly in their holders. Surrounding all sounds were the thousand sighs of raindrops seeking the earth, a liquid whispering so familiar none noted it save when it stopped.

The fluid sighing reminded Dominic of Meg's breath flowing out at his touch.

Abruptly he straightened and strode away from the room. He took the winding, right-hand turning of the stairs two at a time, heading for Meg's quarters. As Dominic attacked the stairs, he spoke carefully chosen verses of Ecclesiastes to himself, reminding himself that other men had gone before him into life's small battles and large wars, and had emerged holding wisdom in both hands.

Repeating the verses had become a ritual that rarely failed to school the rage that boiled within Dominic. His self-control had been learned at cruel cost in a sultan's prison. The discipline was all that had kept him from going mad. He had learned to accept the cold directions of his intellect rather than the hot violence of the Viking blood that ran through him as surely as it did through Duncan of Maxwell.

But tonight, Ecclesiastes' stoic enumeration of man's failings and life's inevitable cycles barely controlled Dominic's impatience. Beneath an outward appearance of calm, the rage in him burned with a flame as primal as that which he had seen in Meg's Glendruid eyes.

The visual memory of Meg walking toward him wrapped in silver mist and hidden fire sent a flash of heat through Dominic's loins, hardening his body in a rush that dismayed him. He hadn't realized how thin his self-control was.

Nor had he understood quite how much he wanted the witch.

If Dominic hadn't seen the silent, fierce burning in Meg's eyes, he might have tried threats to bring her to bay—and to bed. But she would no more be dominated by fear than he. She had stood unflinchingly by his side and agreed to be his wife, and all the while she had expected to feel the bite of steel in her flesh no matter whom she betrayed in the church.

There were few men who could have done what Meg had without trembling. Dominic had never known a maid with that kind of courage.

The realization brought him to a halt just short of his wife's room.

Think, Dominic advised himself harshly. *Which will be more effective against her defenses, a surprise rush or a bitter siege?*

Neither, he told himself brutally. *She is too well defended to take without a cost that would turn brief victory into lifelong defeat.*

Then what? Think!

The best way to take a stronghold is by treachery from within.

The thought rang within Dominic's mind like thunder. As the last echoes of understanding faded,

the noose that had been tightening around Dominic's chest since the lord's dying curse began to
ease minutely.

Treachery.

From within.

Aye!

*I felt her startled breath and saw the color rise to her
cheeks. There is passion in the witch. I will use it for my
own ends.*

When Dominic took the remaining steps to Meg's
rooms, he was fully in control of himself once more.
He was going into battle, and he knew it. The taming and eventual seduction of his Glendruid witch
would be the most important and difficult victory
of his life.

But first he had to get through her door.

Unlike many of the other chambers opening off the
hall, Meg's room had a stout door as well as a curtain
that could be drawn across to cut drafts if the door
were left open. The door, however, was shut. From
the look of its heavy brass hinges, it would take a
battle-ax and a stout yeoman to open the door short
of the mistress's agreement.

The sound of Dominic's mail-encased fist striking
the wood of the door was loud in the empty hallway.
Grimacing, he knocked again, but more lightly.

"Who goes?" Eadith called.

"A husband looking for his bride," Dominic
retorted.

Inside the room, Meg flinched subtly, hearing the
echoes of buried rage in Dominic's voice.

"Open the door," Meg said. "Then leave us."

Eadith looked uncertain.

"It is a husband's right to be with his wife," Meg
said with a serenity she was far from feeling. "Go."

The handmaiden hesitated before she turned
away. She opened the door, nodded to Dominic,

and eased past him. The speed with which she retreated down the hall told Dominic that he wasn't wearing his most reassuring expression.

"Do I frighten your maid?" he asked neutrally, stepping into the room.

"Yes."

"But not you."

Meg's lips shaped an uncertain smile. Dressed in hauberk and sword, chain mail glittering as though alive with each movement of his powerful body, Dominic looked like a devil come to life. She glanced down at her hands. They rested with false calmness in her lap. The events of the day had almost numbed her ability to feel anything.

Almost, but not quite. She kept remembering Dominic's exquisite restraint with the peregrine, and the warmth that had made his gray eyes smoky when he had whispered to her of his sword lying within her sheath.

Caught between John's curse and Glendruid hope, the possibility of warmth in Dominic called irresistibly to Meg. She wanted him to seek that same warmth in her, to come to her without the calculation and cold self-control of a tactician planning a battle.

"Your guests have been seen to," Meg said.

She spoke formally, reporting to her new lord about the state of his keep as she had once reported to John.

"My guests?" Dominic asked silkily. "I wasn't the one who invited Reevers to my wedding."

"The purser will have accounts for you to check on the morrow," Meg continued, "unless you wish me to do it for you as I did for my fath—that is, for John."

Dominic grunted. "I see you've managed quite nicely to quell your grief at his death."

"There is little to grieve after. He has been in much pain since harvest. Now he is in pain no more."

"Blackthorne's people seem to feel as you do about their lord's departure. Only Duncan was truly saddened."

"Aye. Fath—John always was different with Duncan. More kind." Meg shrugged tightly. "Now I know why."

Dominic said nothing. For a few moments he simply watched his bride with the unflinching stare of an eagle.

Though Meg said nothing more, it was impossible for her to remain wholly still under her husband's cool regard. Without realizing it, she reached for one of the smooth river pebbles she kept in a dish by her table. The shape and texture and gentle weight of the stone soothed her.

Silently Meg waited for Dominic to speak. As she waited, she let the pebble glide lightly from her palm to her fingertips and back, leaving in its wake cool memories of the hours she had spent listening to the river Blackthorne run clean and bright from its lake in the fells. Through forest and glen to Blackthorne Keep's fields the water sang, and from there it ran on to the mysterious sea.

"What is the sea like, my lord?" Meg asked wistfully.

The unexpected question—and the poignancy of Meg's smile—surprised Dominic.

"Restless," he said simply. Then, remembering, "Wild. Beautiful. Dangerous."

Breath came out of Meg in a long sigh. For the first time since Dominic had come into the room, she met his glance.

And for the first time, Dominic realized that Meg was afraid of him despite her brave appearance. He wondered why. There was nothing he could do to her that wouldn't rebound doubly on himself, his dreams, his hopes. Like a wolf in a snare, no matter which way he turned, the snare only tightened more.

"Do you fear the Glendruid curse won't protect you?" Dominic asked.

The edge in his voice couldn't be entirely concealed.

"Protect me?"

"From rape," Dominic said bluntly. "From me."

Meg's hand clenched around the pebble. It was no longer cool and soothing. Slowly she forced her fingers to relax.

"I know my duty as a wife," she said in a low voice. "You'll not have to beat me until I can't run away."

"Is that what you expected?"

Again, Meg shrugged tightly. "Yes."

"Is that what John did to your mother?"

"Once."

"But no more."

"Aye. Just once."

"What happened?" Dominic asked smoothly. "Did lightning cleave the keep in twain?"

"She went into the woods. Shortly afterward, a storm came. Hail destroyed the crops in the field and the forage in the pasture. Because the sheep were hungry, they ate a deadly weed, sickened, and died."

Dominic grunted. "All because your mother had been soundly beaten for cuckholding her lord?"

Meg's face drew into tight, unreadable lines. "The priest found no stench of the Devil on the land. Never once, no matter how many times my father paid for exorcism!"

"The storm was mere coincidence, then."

"Some believe so."

"But the simple people of the keep . . . they believe their fate is bound up in that of their lady, the Glendruid witch."

"Aye," Meg said.

"Do you?" Dominic pressed, curious about the girl who was now his wife.

She shrugged and threw back the silver hood of her mantle, feeling stifled by the past, by the present, by the future; and most of all by the man looming over her like a storm on the savage edge of breaking.

"It matters not what I believe," she said tonelessly.

Dominic looked at the fiery cascade of Meg's hair against the silver fabric of her tunic. Without meaning to, he reached out to touch a silky lock.

Meg flinched away before she could control herself.

"Did he beat you, too?" Dominic asked.

She said nothing. She didn't have to. The tightness of her body as she waited for a blow to fall said all that was needed.

"God's teeth," Dominic muttered. " 'Tis just as well he is dead. It saves me the trouble of sending him to Hell with my own hands."

Silence expanded in the room while Dominic studied the girl who looked so fragile, and yet . . .

And yet, somehow this slender reed had managed to confound the hopes of a powerful Saxon lord. Though she had flinched at Dominic's unexpected movement toward her, she had quickly controlled herself. The witch was far from cowed. She sat with spine straight and head high, measuring him even as he measured her.

Reluctantly Dominic found himself admiring Meg's spirit, though he knew it would put him to much trouble as a husband.

This one will come willingly or not at all. God's teeth, what a trial for a man who wants only peace!

Then, almost secretly, came another thought. *I shall enjoy taming her even more than the peregrine. To hear soft cries of pleasure from her lips as I bathe every part of her in my breath, my touch . . .*

And to know with each cry that I will have sons of the witch!

Deliberately Dominic pulled off first one mailed gauntlet, then the other, and tossed them to the table. They thumped heavily into place between the bowl of river pebbles and a box that held bright, fragile twists of floss used for embroidery. A quick glance around the room told him that there was no substantial chair save the one Meg was using.

"That will have to be remedied," he muttered.

"I beg your pardon?"

Dominic looked at the wary green eyes that were watching him.

"There is no place for a man to sit," he said.

Gracefully, Meg got to her feet and gestured to the empty chair.

"I'm not such a churl as to take a lady's chair," Dominic said.

"I'd rather stand than sit whilst you loom over me with your fists on your hips."

Dominic's mouth formed a wry twist as he realized Meg was correct. His fists were indeed on his hips as though he were about to upbraid a knight for abusing a war-horse or a squire for not taking suitable care of his knight's armor.

"The day has been . . ." Dominic's voice faded.

"Trying?" offered Meg.

"Aye. That and more. 'Tis like having to fight again a battle you were certain was already won."

When Meg saw the soul-deep weariness beneath Dominic's discipline, her heart turned over with the same compassion for him that she had for the people of Blackthorne Keep; for he was one of them now.

"Your hauberk is heavy, husband. May I help you out of it?"

Dominic gave her a startled look and nodded.

The fastenings were unfamiliar to Meg. While she fussed and tugged, Dominic watched her bent head. Scents of spice and roses floated up to him from her hair, reminding him of the soap he had been using since he had come to the keep.

"You smell like a garden," Dominic said.

The change in his voice from weariness to velvet darkness startled Meg. She looked up so quickly that her hair shifted and shimmered like wind-blown flame.

" 'Tis my soap."

"Yes. Do I smell like a garden, too?" he asked.

The humor curling through Dominic's voice was as unexpected as his question. Meg smiled and ducked her head.

"You smell of battle," she said. "Chain mail and leather and urgency. And strength. That most of all."

"Next time I shall use more of your soap."

Meg looked up, curiosity plain in her green eyes. "More, lord?"

He made a rumbling sound of agreement. "When I bathe."

"Ah, 'tis you who has left the bath such a mess! Here I was blaming poor Duncan."

Beneath her hands, Dominic's body tightened until his muscles stood hard against his hauberk. She felt as much as sensed the sharp return of his rage at the mention of Duncan's name.

"Do you bathe often with the Scots Hammer?" Dominic asked.

The velvet seduction of Dominic's voice was gone

as though it had never existed. Meg's hands tightened and jerked, scraping her knuckles across a stubborn buckle. It gave way suddenly.

"There," she said. " 'Tis free."

She stood on tiptoe to peel one side of the hauberk from Dominic's body. He turned suddenly, shrugging off the rest of the garment. The weight of it sent Meg staggering. Instantly Dominic reached out and lifted the hauberk from her arms, using only one hand.

Meg looked from the armor to the man who held its weight with such careless ease. She had known Dominic was large and certainly strong, but until that moment she hadn't understood how much stronger he was than she. The muscular lines of his body were clear against the supple leather undergarments that were all he wore.

She felt an urge to test his strength with her fingertips, her nails . . . her teeth. The thought of it startled her even as it sent a curious frisson of heat shimmering through her core.

"Do you?" Dominic asked curtly.

"Do I?" Meg repeated, dragging her attention back to his words with an effort.

"Bathe with the Scots bastard."

She frowned. "Why would I do that? We both have attendants."

It was Dominic's turn to frown.

"Why?" he asked. "For the pleasure of it, of course."

Color climbed up Meg's cheeks.

"I'm neither a handmaiden nor a leman to attend Duncan's baths," she said distinctly.

" 'Tis not what I hear."

"Then you are listening under the wrong eaves!"

Dominic grunted. "They are the same eaves where talk of Glendruid witches is heard."

"The winter was long. There was little else to do but gossip and wait for the storms to pass."

"Have you lain with Duncan of Maxwell?" Dominic asked bluntly.

"What a low opinion you have of your wife."

"Your mother married when she was pregnant. You were betrothed to Duncan once. You knew Duncan's treacherous plans and made no outcry. What opinion should I have of you, *wife?*"

10

MEG DREW A SHARP BREATH that made the chain of Glendruid crystals she wore flash and sparkle in the candlelight.

"If you had Glendruid eyes, you would not see me so badly," she said.

"I have the eyes God gave me and they see quite clearly."

"If you think so little of me, why did you agree to the match?" The instant the words left her mouth, Meg knew the answer.

"Land and keep," she said before Dominic could.

"And heirs."

"Ah, yes. Heirs."

"Unlike John," Dominic said curtly, "I have no wish to raise another man's bastard, nor to scatter my own about the countryside like chaff on the wind."

Meg turned away with a speed that made the fey cloth of her dress lift and swirl like mist. Dominic's free hand shot out, catching her arm before she could get beyond reach.

"I ask you for a third time, wife. *Are you breeding Duncan's bastard?*"

Meg opened her mouth to speak but no answer

came. If she had been in Dominic's place, and had lacked Glendruid eyes, she would have been as suspicious as he. But it galled her just the same.

"Nay," Meg said, keeping her face turned away.

Her voice was low, trembling. The same tension vibrated through her.

When he remembered the rough treatment Meg had had at John's hands, Dominic's grip shifted subtly on her arm, becoming caressing, reassuring her even as his words did.

"Have no fear of me, small falcon," he said. "I've never abused a horse, a squire, or a woman."

Meg's head snapped up. A single look at the green blaze of her eyes told Dominic that it wasn't fear that had made her tremble.

It was fury.

"I am not a red-lipped leman to lie down on every man's command," Meg said through her teeth. "I stood beside you before God as pure as freshly fallen snow, yet I have heard nothing but insults from your lips."

One black eyebrow lifted. With a casual strength that told its own tale, Dominic flipped the hauberk one-handed onto the back of Meg's chair. Metal links flashed and rattled as the garment settled over the wood.

Then there was silence while Dominic studied his reluctant wife, a girl who stood close to him only because he held her arm within the iron grip of his right hand. His sword hand.

"You have heard nothing but truth from my lips, not insults," Dominic said in a clipped voice. "Was your mother pregnant when she married?"

"Aye, but—"

"Were you once betrothed to Duncan of Maxwell?"

"Aye, but—"

Relentlessly Dominic overrode Meg's words. "Did you warn me of the ambush in the church?"

A shudder ran the length of her slender body.

"No," she whispered.

"Why? Was the *affection* between you and that bastard so great you couldn't bring yourself to warn your betrothed of the murderous violence that had been planned?"

Meg's captive hand moved in a gesture of helplessness that was stilled almost as soon as it began.

"You would have hanged Duncan," she whispered.

"Aye, madam, from the stoutest oak in the forest!"

"I could not bear being the cause of his death."

Dominic's mouth hardened as he heard his fears confirmed: his wife did indeed have affection for Duncan of Maxwell.

"Hanging Duncan would have caused war," Meg said, "a war the people of Blackthorne Keep would not have survived."

Dominic grunted.

"My people . . ." Meg's voice faded.

A slight shudder ran the length of her body. She was like a thong tautly drawn and then drawn tighter still, trembling on the point of breaking.

"My people must have a time of peace in which to raise crops and children," Meg said, facing Dominic once more. "They simply must. Can you understand that?"

Silently Dominic looked at the uncanny green eyes of the girl who stood before him proudly pleading for her people's lives. Not for her own life. Not for Duncan's life.

For her people.

"Aye," Dominic said finally. "That I can understand. Anyone who has suffered war can understand the balm of peace. 'Tis why I came back to England. To raise crops and children. Peace, not war."

Air rushed out of Meg's lips in a long sigh.

"God be praised," she said. "When you touched the falcon so carefully, I felt hope ..."

Her voice faded into the soft whispering of flames in the hearth. With battle-hardened fingers, Dominic turned Meg's face up toward his.

"What did you hope?" he asked.

"That you were not the bloodthirsty devil gossip said you were. That there was kindness in you. That ..."

Meg's voice caught at the gliding pressure of Dominic's thumb over her lower lip.

"That what?" he asked.

"I can't think ... when you ..."

"Do this?"

Dominic repeated the slow caress.

She nodded slightly. Even that small motion was enough to shift his touch to her upper lip. Her eyes widened at the unexpected sensation. Without thinking, she pulled back, only to find that his other arm had come around her, holding her for his touch.

"Don't fight me, small falcon. I am your husband. Or does my touch displease you so much?"

"N-no. I just didn't expect to be treated kindly by you."

"Why?"

"You think badly of me," Meg said.

"I think like a husband who doesn't know his bride. If I am to change my thinking, then I will have to know you better, won't I?"

Meg's eyes widened. Dominic could almost see her turning his words over in her mind, testing them for truth or falsehood ... weighing him almost as carefully as he was weighing each of his own actions.

"You have the right of it," she admitted after a moment. "You must know me better. Then you will understand that you can trust me with your honor."

Dominic made a neutral sound and stroked his thumb over Meg's lips again. More sensations shimmered through her, unsettling her. She hadn't known that her body had silky threads of fire hidden within.

"So soft," Dominic said in a deep voice.

"You're not."

He raised his left eyebrow and the corner of his mouth in amused agreement. At the moment, there wasn't one part of his body that was soft. Being this close to his reluctant wife had a profound effect on him.

"Your hand," Meg explained, not understanding Dominic's rueful amusement. " 'Tis hardened by war. Yet careful. I feel rather like the peregrine."

"The thought occurred to me," Dominic admitted, smiling slowly.

Meg looked into gray eyes that burned with a clear masculine fire. The sight was so beguiling that she didn't look beyond, not wanting to see the warrior's calculations that lay beneath. She was fairly light-headed with relief; of all the things she had antici-pated on her wedding night, none had involved being gentled by Dominic's touch as though she were an untamed falcon newly brought to the mews.

"Are you still nervous of me?" Dominic asked.

"Aye," she whispered.

"You need to be accustomed to your new estate," he said. "Should I keep you in a darkened mews with eyelids carefully seeled, so that nothing is real to you but my voice, my touch, my very breath?"

When Meg would have answered, the back of Dominic's hand brushed over her lips as lightly as a sigh, scattering her thoughts before she could speak.

"Nay," he said, answering his own question. "Not even the finest seeling thread of silk would I permit to mar the beauty of your eyes."

The touch of Dominic's hand on Meg's throat drew a startled sound from her.

"I won't hurt you," he said soothingly. "Like my peregrine, you are much too fine and fragile and courageous to damage with careless handling. Close your Glendruid eyes and simply feel, wife. Let me touch you until you no longer fear my hand."

While Dominic spoke, he continued the caresses that were both reassuring and disturbing, sending glittering thrills coursing through Meg.

Slowly her eyelids closed, leaving her without a Glendruid woman's clear sight into a man's soul. For long moments there was only the whisper of flames and the soft rush of breath between lips parted in surprise. Meg had never known anything like Dominic's caresses, yet she kept feeling that she had. The familiarity haunted her.

"Why, 'tis like sunlight," Meg whispered at last, remembering when she had felt such undemanding warmth before.

"What is?"

"Your touch."

Dominic's smile wasn't nearly as gentle as his fingertips, but Meg's eyes weren't open to measure the difference.

" 'Tis only fair that my caresses be as soft as sunlight," he said, "for your skin is as tender as any rose petal I've ever known."

A smile changed Meg's lips. Then her mouth opened slightly on a swift intake of breath when

Dominic's fingertips skimmed from the hollow of her throat to trace the sparkling chain of Glendruid crystals that wrapped around her body just beneath her breasts.

"Gently, falcon," Dominic said in a low voice. "Soon you're going to trust yourself to my arm."

"Even your strength couldn't support me if I gave my whole weight to your wrist."

Dominic laughed and swooped like an eagle, lifting Meg in one arm. Her eyes opened in surprise.

"Will I have to make you go hooded?" Dominic asked. "Close your eyes and see as the newly caught falcon sees."

As Dominic spoke, he bent and touched Meg's eyelids with the tip of his tongue, closing her eyes.

The unexpected caresses stole Meg's breath. By the time she got it back, Dominic was sitting in the big chair that had once belonged to John's grandfather, and she was half reclining across her husband's lap, her legs draped over one arm of the chair. She stirred restively, only to be restrained by her husband's hands.

"You are a falcon, remember?" he asked. "This is how we will learn about one another."

Slowly the tension went out of Meg's body. Dominic shifted her hair free of its captivity, sending it cascading over the chair's arm and down to the floor, where it lay like embers waiting for fire.

A breathless sound came from Meg, nervous laughter or a tremulous sigh or both at once. The hushed intimacy and unexpected caresses kept taking her by surprise. They made her body feel both taut and languorous, flushed with heat. In the space of a few moments Dominic had given her more pleasure than she had ever expected from a man.

Yet Meg found she wanted more. As certainly as

she had sensed the pain beneath Dominic's ruthless self-control, she now sensed that there was a
seething, twisting, hungry fire at her own core. She
had never guessed such a thing existed within herself. It was like looking in the mirror and seeing a
stranger, unnerving and enthralling at once.

Without realizing it, Meg settled more deeply into
Dominic's grasp. The telltale softening of her body
against his sent both cold triumph and hot hunger
racing through him. He was heavy, full, hard, stirring with every rapid beat of his heart.

Meg smiled as though even through closed eyes
she could see the evidence of his arousal straining
against the supple leather of his undergarment.

"Are you peeking?" Dominic asked huskily.

"No, but I would like to."

The thought appealed to him as well.

Slowly, he cautioned himself. *I can't take her until
she bleeds, no matter how stoutly she denies having lain
with my enemy.*

*But it would be sweet indeed to be naked with her, to
have her touch me as she touched the peregrine.*

The thought of Meg's pale, slender hands stroking
him dragged a rough sound of hunger and anticipation from Dominic.

"Are you laughing?" she asked.

"Nay. Would I laugh at a fierce peregrine beguiled
by her master's touch?"

The pleasure curling through Dominic's voice
charmed Meg. She smiled again and leaned against
his chest. Heat radiated up from his body to her,
luring her as greatly as her own pleasure, for the
stones of the keep still held the chill of winter.
Without understanding why, Meg yielded still
more of her weight and herself to the man
who was weaving a calculated spell of delight
around her.

"You are like the sun in another way," Meg murmured.

Dominic looked down at Meg's long, dark auburn lashes, creamy skin, and strawberry lips softly parted. The girl was yielding to him with a sweet sensuality that was as unexpected as the fierce hunger she called from his body. Need raked him with razor talons that threatened to slice through his self-control.

He needed her the way fire needed to burn.

Ruthlessly Dominic fought the violent passion Meg had aroused in him so unexpectedly.

"How am I like the sun?" Dominic asked when he trusted his voice not to reveal his naked hunger.

"Heat, my lord. You are like fire."

"Do I burn you?"

"Not painfully. You warm me like sunlight after winter's long siege."

"Then come closer, small falcon. Lay your head against me. Learn my scent and taste and textures."

After a moment's hesitation, Meg gave in to the gentle pressure of his hand against her head. In silence she smoothed her cheek along Dominic's leather-clad chest. The texture of his garment was as fine and supple as a kid glove, and it fit him the way his own skin did. When she realized how clearly she could feel each ridge and swell of muscle, an odd tremor rippled through her.

"You're cold," Dominic said. "Let me warm you."

The thickening of his blood with passion made his voice low, almost rough. He feared it would make Meg wary. He didn't want that. Not when she was coming over to his side of the sensual battle without a fight, taken in ambush by the skilled caresses of a man from whom she had expected only blows.

The touch of Dominic's mouth against her own startled Meg. Her eyes flew open, only to be closed once more by tiny, quick kisses. In a hushed silence his lips roamed over her face as his fingertips had.

"You taste clean," Dominic whispered. "Like warm rain."

"Gwyn says I am a creature of water and growing things."

Glendruid.

Meg's breath caught, for Dominic had taken her lower lip between his teeth and licked his tongue across it. Almost as soon as the odd caress began, Dominic retreated, leaving no more than a beguiling hint of his taste. The tip of her tongue traced the place where his teeth and tongue had touched her.

Passion's talons clenched, hardening Dominic's whole body as he fought against a need that was rapidly becoming ungovernable. He had expected many things of his wife, but not an artless passion that set fire to him as no woman ever had.

"Did that hurt you?" he asked.

"Nay."

"You started."

"You have the most surprising way about you," Meg said simply. "I don't know what to expect next."

Dominic's smile was a fierce slash of victory; an opponent who was easily surprised was easily defeated.

"Did it displease you?" he asked.

She shook her head even as she slowly licked her lower lip again.

"You taste of the Holy Land," Meg said.

"Do I?" he said thickly. "How so?"

"Lemon infused with sweet."

" 'Tis only the Turkish candy."

"My candy didn't taste that good," she said.

"Next time, choose the one that is as yellow as the sun."

"Next time I shall have you taste it for me."

"And then you will taste me?" he asked.

The idea both startled and intrigued Meg. Her eyes opened. In the room's dim light, their color was a green so dark it was nearly black. She could see nothing of Dominic but the strength of his shoulders and jaw outlined against the dying fire.

"Is that . . . seemly?" she asked.

Dominic started to say that Duncan of Maxwell's courtship must have been a rather boorish affair, but bit back the comment just in time. The last thing Dominic wanted to do at the moment was ruffle the feathers he had so cautiously and patiently soothed. He wasn't certain that his self-control would be up to another round of gentling this night.

God's teeth, but I ache. Not since I was an apple-cheeked boy have I been this hard!

" 'Tis not only seemly," Dominic said as he shifted Meg discreetly on his lap, "there is great pleasure in it."

"How so?"

"Lick your lips."

She did. He watched with an intensity that did nothing to slow the savage beating of his blood.

"What did you feel?" he asked.

"Er . . ." Meg frowned and admitted, "Nothing, in truth. My lip was dry and then it became wet."

Dominic smiled darkly as he bent down to Meg.

"Now see how *this* feels," he whispered.

With great care Dominic ran the tip of his tongue around the rim of her mouth. He meant to do no more than that, but the startled sound she made, the parting of her lips, and the warm rush of her breath created a temptation too great to deny.

His tongue slid into her mouth more gently than he wanted and less gently than was wise at this stage in the seduction of his very special falcon.

The glide of Dominic's tongue startled Meg for a

moment. Then she realized that, though unexpected, the caress was rather pleasing. He tasted of exotic sweets and yet was familiar as well, heat and the faint savor of salt, as well as a complex flavor she couldn't define. In an attempt to taste more fully, she returned the soft stabbing of his tongue with her own.

Dominic's fingers speared through Meg's hair, pulling her head back, opening her mouth so that he could take it deeply, repeatedly.

At first she was too surprised to move, but the primal rhythm of the kiss and the sensuous penetration and retreat of his tongue soon sent cascades of shimmering, glittery sensations through her. Heat leaped deep within her, a fire both tender and fierce ignited by the sweet friction of tongue over tongue.

A low sound was torn from Dominic's throat. He wanted to put his hand beneath the silver fabric and feel the curves of Meg's breasts change to meet his touch, but the silver-and-crystal chain was too cunningly fastened for him to defeat without ending the kiss. And that he would not do.

Dominic's hand abandoned the frustrating Glendruid chain and instead sought the hem of Meg's dress. There was no hindrance there. He swept up the fey, filmy cloth and felt the living heat of his bride's flesh beneath his palm.

With the same patience Dominic had shown for the peregrine, he gentled his wife again and again, his touch retreating and returning, caresses that slid higher and higher up her legs while he watched with eyes that measured even as fire ate into his very bones.

Then Dominic lowered his head and seduced Meg's mouth with the slow, sure strokes that echoed those of his hand. Finally Meg began stirring with a different kind of restlessness beneath the deep kisses and warm caresses. The slow tremors that took her owed little to fear and much to the hushed sensuality of his hand stroking her while the kiss deepened into an elemental joining.

Even as Dominic told himself that he must stop very soon, that he should have stopped already, that the seducer was rapidly becoming the seduced, he couldn't deny himself one more gliding caress up the warmth of Meg's calf, across the hidden crease at the back of her knee, a slow caress up her silken inner thighs.

He knew he should stop there as he had before, but found the temptation to push farther irresistible. When he reached the apex of her thighs, he curled his hand around her, cupping her softest flesh in his broad palm. In the same motion he traced her secret warmth with his thumb.

Shocked by the intimacy of Dominic's hand between her thighs, Meg stiffened suddenly and tore her mouth free of Dominic's. He barely noticed her struggle, for she was a sultry mist against his palm. Violent triumph swept through his tensed body and a low groan of need was dragged from his lips.

Too soon. I must not take her.

Reluctantly Dominic released the lush fire he had so briefly touched and looked at his unexpectedly sensual wife.

Meg was staring at him with wide green eyes that still glowed with passion recently ignited. Her lips were red, glistening, parted with shock and pleasure combined. Her breasts rose and fell with each ragged breath she took.

Dominic longed to see Meg as she was now, sprawled across his lap, but without the dress concealing her hunger for his seed. Just the thought of seeing her naked in languid disarray was enough to bring him to the edge of bursting. Slowly he began drawing up the silver folds of her dress, wanting to see the moist yielding of her body to his touch, her flesh flushed and glistening, scented by passion.

"Dominic—"

"I am your husband," he said in a low voice. "You can't become accustomed to being my wife if you cover yourself and lock your legs together like the jaws of a sprung trap. Have I hurt you in any way?"

"N-no."

"Do you believe I am intent on hurting you tonight?"

"No," she whispered.

"Then yield to me what any other husband would simply take."

Slowly Meg's legs relaxed but for the trembling she was helpless to stop.

Again the silver cloth began its gliding retreat up Meg's body. The sweet foretaste of triumph brought husky laughter from Dominic as he looked at the graceful arch of Meg's foot, the feminine curve of her calf, the dimpled knee peeking from the silver cloud of her dress, the creamy thighs, and the lush thicket that was the color of fire.

She lay within his grasp; it all lay within his grasp, the land and the heirs and the dream of life that had kept him sane during the brutality of the Holy War.

"John's curse was in vain," Dominic said thickly. "I will have sons of you after all."

Sons.

Even as Meg's reason told her that it was her duty to bear her husband heirs if she could, her pride cried out at being nothing more than a vessel for Dominic's ambitions.

She had felt a wild, sweet fire burning in her soul. He had felt only triumph at seducing her.

"Nay!"

Meg didn't realize that she had moved until she saw her own hands yanking on her wedding dress, trying to push the wispy folds of cloth back down her legs.

"Don't be shy," Dominic said, laughing softly. "Let me see John's vengeance lying open, swollen with passion, pleading to know the sword within the softness."

"Count not your victories before you are through the gates!" Meg retorted.

The coldness of her voice brought Dominic's glance up to her eyes. For the space of one breath, two breaths, three, husband and angry bride measured one another.

'Tis just as well. I must not take her, he reminded himself. *Not yet. It's unlikely that such an ardent maid is untouched.*

One thing is certain. Her soft gate hasn't been often breached. So tightly closed . . .

Ah, God's teeth, it would be a foretaste of paradise to press into that silken sheath!

Desire hammered through Dominic's blood, threatening his control. The realization of how close he was to his own limits shocked him as nothing else could have. He dropped the silver cloth as though it burned his fingers.

"Now you know," he said savagely.

"That you want my body only to breed heirs? Aye, my cold Norman lord, I know that well!"

Dominic looked at Meg's furious face and had to stop himself from spreading her legs and taking what she plainly had been willing to give.

"Nay, my passionate witch," he said. "Now you know the magic of a certain kind of kiss."

"What is that?" she asked sarcastically.

His hand slid swiftly up beneath her dress once more, overpowering her struggles with casual ease.

"This," Dominic said through his teeth. "What was once dry is now wet!"

11

"**W**HAT ELSE DID SVEN HAVE to say?" Dominic demanded without rising from his bed. "Besides the obvious, of course."

Simon gave his brother a sideways look and barely managed to bite off a curt retort. Whatever had put Dominic in such temper likely had to do with the fact that on what should have been his wedding night, the groom was lying in John's hastily refurbished quarters . . . alone. His Glendruid bride presumably was sleeping in the solitude of her maiden quarters on the far side of Blackthorne Keep.

Presumably. It wasn't a topic Simon was foolish enough to bring into the open. He had been awakened in the night by the sound of his brother returning to the lord's quarters. Frustration had rung in the repeated sound of boot heel meeting wood floor.

Obviously the wedding night had been less than successful. It not only had ended early, it had left Dominic in a savage state of mind. Simon had listened to his brother pacing the floor for quite some time. Then there had been silence followed by the sound of something metallic hitting the wall with great force.

Finding it impossible to sleep himself, Simon had gone to report to Dominic on the mood of the keep's people and the progress of Duncan and his Reevers.

"While Duncan and some of his men will be missed by the people of the keep," Simon said, "most of the Reevers will not. They are little better than rogues and bandits."

"It took no great wit to discover that," Dominic retorted.

"Duncan and his followers will be at Carlysle Manor within the morrow."

Dominic was no kinder to the second offering of news than he had been to the first.

"God's teeth," he snapped. "Even the village fool could have told me that."

"Your leman grows restless," Simon said smoothly. "Perhaps you should see to her comfort?"

Dominic gave his brother a sideways look.

"Am I that obvious, Simon?" he asked with a rueful smile.

Simon gave a crack of laughter and gestured to the blanket that didn't quite cover his brother.

"I've seen stallions less imposing than you when they mount a mare," Simon said. "You must have frightened her to death. Go to the leman. Then you'll have more patience with—"

"I've no desire to harrow yet another of Duncan's fields," Dominic interrupted harshly.

"Another?" Simon's laughter vanished. " 'Tis true, then? Lady Margaret is Duncan's lover?"

A savage movement of Dominic's hand was his only answer.

"There's no way to be certain," he said after a moment. "She swears not."

Simon's grunt was unenthusiastic.

"Aye," Dominic agreed sardonically. "I would hardly expect my noble bride to entertain me with tales of her previous lovers."

"So you let her sleep alone?"

"Until she bleeds. That way I'll be certain I'm not like John, raising another man's get."

Simon grimaced. "I beg a favor from my liege."

Dominic's left eyebrow lifted in silent inquiry.

"Send me out into the forest to bring back a wild-cat in my bare hands," Simon said.

"Pardon?"

"It will be less taxing than walking on eggs around you for a fortnight or two while you wait," Simon explained.

Dominic scowled.

"Better yet," Simon continued, "go after Duncan and his Reevers. 'Tis certain they will give you the fight you desire."

"I would rather have my wife."

"The leman would be less troublesome."

A shrug of Dominic's broad shoulders dismissed Marie.

"Then one of the local wenches," Simon said.

"I don't need a procurer."

"You never have before," Simon agreed. "But—"

"Enough."

No one, not even a man who was both friend and brother, crossed wills with Dominic when he took that tone. Simon shut his mouth and waited.

"Is Sven with the Reevers?" Dominic asked after a time.

"Not yet. It will take time to get close to them. They are a clannish lot."

"Keep him here, then. Let him put an ear to the ground for any signs of unrest among John's few knights."

"I doubt they will trouble you. They are too old to trouble anyone, even their wives."

"Nonetheless, see that each knight gets a freehold

large enough to support himself and his family in a manner suitable to his station and years of service."

"As you wish. You've land enough and then some."

"Aye. See that each gets an ox and a plow, wood from my forests for building, four sheep, a cow, seed, fowl, and some rabbits as soon as the ones we brought from Normandy breed. It's foolish to lack for meat."

Simon listened as Dominic continued to list the necessities for setting up a small freehold. As always, his brother's command of detail fascinated Simon. Whether it was war or farming, Dominic made a thorough study of the matter, assembled what was required for success, and then attacked with breathtaking swiftness.

"Don't forget the cooking pots. They are more valuable than gold," Dominic concluded.

"Anything that keeps a wife contented is more valuable than gold."

Dominic threw his brother a sharp look. Simon's black eyes held both understanding and carefully shielded amusement.

"Was there more?" Simon asked.

"Aye. Tell Sven to keep an eye out for my wife. I want to be quite certain that she meets no one from beyond the keep."

"Do you really think she will try to go to Duncan after marrying you?"

"She is the key to everything I have ever wanted in life," Dominic said flatly. "Until I am certain she is breeding my heir, I will watch her as carefully as an eagle watches a foolish rabbit."

THE dream condensed slowly, relentlessly, eroding the peace of Meg's hard-won sleep.

Danger.

Meg whimpered and turned on her other side as though to escape something only she could see. But there was no escape, for the dream was caught within her mind and she was caught within the dream.

Bleak, colorless, cold, the nightmare engulfed her.

Death.

A silent scream froze in Meg's throat, tearing at her with claws of ice.

Disaster.

Wordlessly Meg clawed against the silence, asking what she must do.

The answer was equally wordless. Green welled up through the emptiness surrounding her. Shapes condensed from the void. Plants growing in secret, drinking raindrops, opening their leaves to an unseen sun. The plants were all the same color, the same shape, the same leaves, the same sense of silence and ancient, undisturbed ground.

Go.

Eyes still closed, Meg sat bolt upright, her heart hammering. Her head throbbed from the violence of the dream. A single certainty resonated through her mind and body.

Danger.

With a muffled cry, Meg opened her eyes, ran to the window and threw open the shutters.

Nothing greeted her but the eerie silence that comes just before dawn. In the next few moments a cock would crow the sun awake and then strut before his hens, arrogant with his prowess and with the certainty of future generations coursing through his loins. In the moments after the cock crowed, the cotters and serfs would stir, cooking fires would be lit, men would call across the bailey as they discussed chores to be done and maids to be wooed.

In the next few moments . . .

But not now. Now there was only a transcendent hush as the earth awaited the coming of the sun.

Breath held, Meg stared out the narrow window, straining toward the ghostly mist rising from mill-pond and fish pond, meadow and lake. No movement was visible. No sound of armor or bridle came through the silence, no hoofbeats, no muffled orders to men creeping through the dawn.

Yet danger existed. Meg knew it as surely as she knew her eyes were Glendruid green.

The certainty of peril was a knife in her heart. She had thought her marriage would end the danger of war. She had thought her marriage would ensure the safety of her people and the survival of Blackthorne Keep.

And now she was certain only that something was savagely wrong.

Death.

Meg shuddered.

Disaster.

She had not dreamed so vividly since the night her mother walked into the forest and did not return. Ever.

Are you calling to me, Mother? Will I finally know the secrets of the ancient mound?

As soon as the haunted place occurred to Meg, a certainty grew in her that she must go there. There, where the ground was undisturbed by man, where plants grew on ancient soil steeped in primeval secrets; there she would find the harvest that was all that stood between Blackthorne Keep and ruin.

She didn't know how she knew it.

She knew only that it was as true as death.

With a stifled sound Meg threw off her nightshirt and yanked on the cotter's clothes she wore while working in the herb garden or mews. Fingers stiff with cold and fear fumbled her hair into loose braids and bound them with leather thongs.

Simple head cloth and circlet in place, wool stockings pulled on, boots in hand, Meg slipped soundlessly through the keep's stone halls and down its winding stairways. Stopping only long enough to take some bread and cheese from the larder and push her feet into the boots, she went quickly to the forebuilding.

A fair-haired stranger kept the door there, allowing servants to come and go between keep and bailey as they set about their early morning chores. The man barely glanced at Meg as she rushed by.

Smoke from the kitchen shed rose in the bailey, blending with the misty dawn. The cobbles in the well-trod paths were slick and cold. Meg moved over them as though wearing wings. The gatehouse was cold and dark but for the torch burning near the guard's stool.

"Good morning to you," Harry said, getting stiffly to his feet. "You be up and about early."

"I've neglected my herbal and my garden," Meg said.

"Aye," Harry said gravely, "I heard the plants pleading most sweetly for their lady all of yesterday. I sent Black Tom to tell them you were busy with your duties as wife of the keep's new lord, but the rascal just rolled in the catnip and said not one word of comfort to the wee plants."

The twinkle in Harry's eyes was obvious even in the gloom of the gatehouse. Meg smiled at him despite the urgency driving her. She touched Harry's hand as he reached for the door.

"You brighten my day," she murmured.

"Nay, lady. 'Tis you who brighten our days. Not one of your people but doesn't have a tale of your kindness to tell."

Smiling, Meg shook her head in denial. "Not one of you hasn't done a kindness for me."

"Are you . . ."

Harry's voice died. A ruddiness that had nothing to do with torchlight appeared on his weathered cheeks. He cleared his throat roughly.

"Is all well with you, my lady?"

When Meg realized that Harry was asking about her new status as wife rather than maiden, she flushed to the roots of her hair.

"The people . . ." Harry cleared his throat and tried again. "Your mother was a stranger when she came here. We saw . . . That is, your father was a harsh man even when he wasn't in his cups. And when he was . . ."

"Aye," Meg whispered.

Harry shifted his feet uncomfortably.

"You're nae stranger to us, lassie," he said in a rush. "If that Norman bast—er, if the lord hurts you, we'll nae stand for it. Do you need us, send up a shout and we'll come running and let the devil take the hinder part. You've nae need to go to the forest like your mother to find your peace. Many accidents can befall a man while hunting. I promise you."

Tears shimmered in Meg's eyes, making them huge. She brushed a quick kiss over Harry's cheek, which flushed even more at the gesture of affection.

"Tell the people to be at ease," Meg said. "Lord Dominic has not been unkind to me in the way you fear."

Before Harry could speak, Meg was gone. She hurried out the portal and over the drawbridge like a fleeing wraith. Chills that had nothing to do with the cold morning chased over her body, shortening her breath. Indeed, Dominic had not forced his

Glendruid bride. He had simply let her sip paradise from his lips and then had told her that she was alone in that paradise; for he sought only heirs from her body.

Are you in Hell, John? Are you laughing at the hell you made for others on earth? Dominic wants only a son, an heir.

Futile dream. Dominic has no love within him, simply a burning need to found a dynasty and a shrewd tactician's understanding of the battle ahead.

The path led between low, dry–stone fences that marked off fields and pastures. The rich, deep brown of the furrows glistened with moisture. Parallel stripes of light green marked the first, fragile growth of a future harvest. Blackbirds hopped from ridge to ridge among the furrows, seeking seeds or insects. Like pale patches of mist, sheep hovered in the pasture while their clever black lips searched out new growth amid the straw of last year's grass.

Church bells rang through the hush, calling the hour and telling the people it was time to go out into the fields. The sound of the bells normally delighted Meg. This morning they simply goaded her, feeding the urgency that grew with each step she took away from the keep.

Danger.

12

"**S**HE'S GONE," SIMON SAID flatly.

Dominic looked up from the dull, battered lance he had just found in the Blackthorne armory.

"She?" he asked in an absent tone.

"Lady Margaret."

"God's holy *teeth!*" Dominic snarled.

He looked aside at the miserable steward whose day hadn't been enhanced thus far by Dominic's cutting comments about the deplorable state of the keep in general and the armory in particular.

"See that the servants sweep and scrub every floor in the keep," Dominic said curtly to the man. "Then have them put down fragrant herbs and fresh rushes until the whole place is as clean as Lady Margaret's quarters. Do you comprehend?"

"Aye, lord."

"Then go to it!"

The man obeyed with admirable speed. The sound of his footsteps echoing down the hall and up the spiral staircase in the corner tower was like a rapid drumbeat.

"When?" Dominic said, fastening an icy gray glance on his brother.

"I don't know."

"Where is her handmaiden?"

"Flirting with your knights."

Dominic's eyes narrowed as he absently toyed with the rusted lance.

"Who is the last person who saw Meg?" he asked.

"Harry. He let her out of the gatehouse just before dawn."

The fact that Meg hadn't slept well either was a small consolation to Dominic for his night spent roasting on the spit of unsatisfied desire.

"Who accompanied her?" Dominic asked.

"No one."

Dominic's small consolation vanished.

"She was alone?" he asked incredulously.

"Aye." Simon's voice was grim.

"What does Sven have to say for himself?"

" 'A man has to sleep sometimes, begging your pardon, lord.' He thought she would be lying abed late this morning of all mornings."

Simon's exact mimicry of Sven's voice drew a thin smile from Dominic.

"Harry," Simon offered, "assumed she had simply gone to see to her gardens, as she usually does."

"What is there to see?" Dominic shot back. "The fields are bare."

"Her gardens were planted well before John got his surly farmers to put plow and oxen in the lord's fields."

Dominic grunted. "Send someone to fetch Meg in from the gardens. With all the dispossessed Reevers about, it's not safe for a woman to be abroad alone."

Simon shot his brother a look of disbelief. "Do you think I'm so slack-brained I didn't send someone after her? I tell you, she is *gone!*"

"What about the cotters? Did she go to see to a woman who was giving birth?"

"Nay. None of the vassals have seen her since she disappeared into the mist this morning. Nor have the people of the settlements seen her."

Dominic threw the lance into a corner of the armory with a force that shook loose flakes of rust and stone alike.

"Get the dogs," Dominic said curtly. "Tell Harry to open the gates wide."

Before the words were out of Dominic's mouth, the excited yapping and howling of his greyhounds showed that Simon had foreseen his brother's desire. The hounds had been brought up by their handler and were waiting just outside, eager for the hunt.

"Crusader is saddled and ready for you," Simon said before Dominic could ask.

"Get your own war-horse," Dominic said.

"What about the keep? Who will be in charge?"

"Thomas the Strong will guard it for us. Tell him to call the vassals in from the fields and to draw up the bridge after we leave. This all may be a trick to take the keep."

"Surely you don't believe that your own wife—"

"I believe," Dominic interrupted savagely, "that my own wife could have been stolen in order to be ransomed at a price that would ruin all hope of building Blackthorne Keep into the stronghold it must be in order to survive."

Simon's black eyes narrowed.

"And that is precisely the word you will put out around the keep," Dominic concluded. "Do you understand me? There will be no hint of what I suspect is really afoot."

"And that is?"

"Duncan of Maxwell and my damned Glendruid wife!"

The silence resonated with all that Dominic had

not said, treachery and betrayal and the death of dreams.

"Do you want anyone else to come with us?" Simon asked after a moment.

"Nay. Not my squire. Not yours. Not even the master of the hounds. What is done today will go no further than us."

"You don't really believe—"

"I am a tactician, Simon. Treachery from within is the best way to take a keep. If I know it, surely the Scots Hammer does."

Simon looked into his brother's eyes and felt a chill of foreboding.

God help the maid if she is with Duncan when Dominic finds her, Simon thought uneasily.

God help us all.

A few minutes later Dominic strode out of the keep wearing chausses and hauberk, helm and sword. In one mailed fist was a crossbow. In the other was the nightshirt Meg had worn and then cast aside in her haste to leave.

The hounds danced and whined their impatience to be off the leash. Long-legged, lean-bodied, narrow-tongued, moving like fanged ghosts, the dogs seethed with eagerness as they waited to be given the scent they would course that day.

Dominic's squire held Crusader's bridle, quieting the restive stallion. Simon waited nearby, mounted on his own charger. If he had been in any doubt as to his brother's lethal temper, it vanished when Dominic literally leaped into the saddle, scorning the stirrup. The maneuver was one every well-trained knight could manage in full battle gear, but few did so when a squire stood nearby ready to give a hand up.

The dark stallion half reared, ears flat to his skull as he caught his rider's mood. Dominic rode the charger effortlessly, seeming not to notice the stallion's fiery temperament.

"Harry is at the gatehouse," Simon said.

Dominic nodded curtly and set off for the gatehouse across the bailey. The huge, muscular stallion crabbed sideways, snorting and prancing, caught between the vise of Dominic's mood and the iron bit restraining him. Huge hooves beat out a rhythm of throttled urgency as the chargers minced across the bailey's cobblestones.

Harry was waiting in front of the gatehouse. He touched his forehead and waited.

"When did you last see your lady?" Dominic asked bluntly.

"Before the sun broke over Blackthorne Crag."

"Did she speak to you?"

"Aye. She seemed to be heading for her herb gardens."

"*Seemed?*" Dominic asked sharply.

"Aye. But when the path split, she took the right-hand fork."

"The gardens are to the left," Simon said in a low voice.

Dominic grunted. "Why did you think she was going to her herb gardens?"

Harry looked uncomfortable.

"Speak to your lord," Simon said curtly. "Your lady might be in danger."

"Meg—Lady Margaret—often goes to her gardens when she is troubled."

The look Dominic gave the gatekeeper wasn't likely to make the man feel any more at ease.

"Troubled?" Dominic asked smoothly. "How so?"

Harry looked even more uncomfortable. Before he could choose words to speak, an old woman walked out of the gatehouse. In the late morning sunlight her hair was so white it was nearly transparent.

Dominic turned to Gwyn. For the first time he noticed that the woman's eyes, though faded by age, were of the same pure, spring green as Meg's.

"John," Gwyn said without preamble, "had a heavy hand when he was in his cups. Meg learned to stay out of his way."

"From the filthy state of the keep," Dominic said, "I would hazard that he was in his cups much of the time."

"Aye."

"I am not John."

"Aye," she agreed. "If you were, your horse's flanks would be scarred from your spurs and his mouth hardened by a cruel bit brutally used."

"You have a keen eye."

"So do you, Dominic le Sabre, Lord of Blackthorne Keep. Use it when you ride out. You will see that Meg is but collecting herbs as is her custom."

"Without her handmaiden?"

Gwyn sighed. "Eadith can be tiresome."

"Is Lady Margaret accustomed to running about the countryside without a companion?" Dominic asked in a sharp voice.

"Nay," Gwyn said grudgingly. "Eadith goes with her, or I do, or one of the men-at-arms."

Dominic looked at Harry. The gateman shook his head unhappily.

"She was alone," Harry said.

"Take the dogs to the fork in the trail," Dominic said to the handler.

The man went quickly across the bridge, towed by a rowdy turmoil of greyhounds. When Dominic moved to follow, Gwyn spoke quickly.

"Fear not. Neither man nor beast would harm a Glendruid girl."

The icy glitter of Dominic's eyes swept over the old woman.

"Lady Margaret is no longer a girl to run the fields like a cotter's wench," he said in a cold, precise voice. "She is the wife of a great lord and the mistress of a powerful keep. She is a prize that any man would be glad to take."

"There is danger," Gwyn admitted. Then, so softly that most men wouldn't have heard, she added, "But not to her. Not quite."

"What do you mean?"

The old woman looked up at Dominic for a long, silent moment.

"I sense danger," she said finally. "Meg must have sensed it as well. But the danger wasn't to her. It was to the keep. There are perilous times ahead, lord. The omens—"

Gwyn's words stopped abruptly when Crusader half reared and champed fiercely at the bit. Despite Dominic's coldly running rage, he curbed the stallion without cruelty. Crusader pranced in place, flexing his powerful neck and hindquarters.

"Spare me the Glendruid nonsense," Dominic said bitingly. "There are always perilous times. There are always omens. There are always betrayals. It is what a man makes of them that matters."

With that, Dominic released the stallion. The horse sprang forward as though shot from a catapult. Simon followed quickly. The clatter of hooves on cobblestone became a hollow thunder as the two big horses crossed the bridge. Sun struck lances of light from hauberks and helms, making them gleam coldly.

When Dominic reached the fork in the path, the hounds were waiting with an impatience that equalled his own. Like the man, the hounds were disciplined. Despite their whining, seething eagerness, they were well-behaved. They stood ready to respond to voice or horn.

"Give this to Leaper," Dominic said, handing over Meg's nightshirt.

The handler took the shirt and held it out to a silver-gray bitch. The hound sniffed, whined, and sniffed again. After a few more moments she lifted her head and whined eagerly.

"She has the scent, lord."

"Loose her and only her," Dominic ordered. "If she picks up the scent quickly, keep the others tied. I want no unnecessary noise arousing the countryside."

The handler took the leather leash from Leaper's collar. At his signal she bounded forward to cast about for the scent she had been given. It took her only a brief time to find it, for the ground was damp, ideal for holding spoor. The greyhound began tracking at a run.

Dominic and Simon followed at a hard canter, their chain mail glittering in the cloud-veiled light. Behind them the leashed hounds howled their disappointment.

SLOWLY Meg stood and stretched, trying to loosen the muscles of her back. She had spent the past few hours on her hands and knees, searching among the heaped rocks and at the base of the standing stones that ringed the haunted place. The small sack she used for gathering herbs was finally plump with the hard-won harvest. It bounced companionably against her hip as she headed out of the sacred oak grove.

It had taken Meg much longer than she had expected to harvest the new leaves and stems and a few of the bitter roots of the plant she called ghost slipper. She had even found a few other useful herbs and some seedlings to take to her gardens. There were others she could have taken, but it would have killed the plants to steal their leaves. The season was early for much foliage. Only the daffodils were fully grown, their yellow faces searching for the sun from every glade and streamside.

The haunted place was well behind Meg when the sun finally managed to pierce the spring overcast. A shaft of pale yellow light lanced down, setting scattered oaks and moss-grown rocks softly afire. Stone and bare branch gleamed darkly, as though freshly made. Far out at the tips of the oaks' spreading arms, the first green whisper of summer's leafy bounty swelled.

The silent promise of the buds and sun loosened the tension in Meg's body. As though the shaft of sunlight was a wild falcon to be tamed, she held up her hands and whistled sweetly, bathing herself in light.

From the crest of the hill, an answering whistle came.

Instants later a greyhound raced toward Meg at a fantastic pace, eating the ground with fleet, graceful motions. When the hound was only a few paces from her, a horn sliced the silence. The hound stopped, spun, and bounded back in the direction it had come.

Heart pounding, Meg shielded her eyes and looked across the mist-swathed vale where sunlight struck fire from drops of water. Two warhorses loomed at the crest of the hill. One of the horses had a rider. The other did not.

Just as Meg recognized that it was Dominic's battle stallion that was riderless, her husband's voice came from behind her.

"Where have you been, lady?"

She spun around. "You startled me."

"I shall do much more than that if you don't answer my question. *Where have you been?*"

"Collecting herbs."

Dominic looked at Meg's simple clothes. They were stained, rumpled, and showed every sign of having been ill used. They looked, in fact, as though they had been bedding for an illicit tryst.

"Collecting herbs," he said tonelessly. "Odd. Your clothes look as though you've been rolling around on the ground in them."

Meg glanced down, shrugged, and looked at Dominic again. Despite his carefully neutral voice, she sensed the icy fury in him. It was an avalanche looking for an excuse to come loose on her head.

"That is why I wear these rags," she said crisply. "It makes no sense to ruin the good tunic I have by grubbing about on my hands and knees in it."

Dominic made another neutral sound. He looked around the area. Except for the cheerful daffodils, there was a singular lack of growing green things. He turned back and fixed Meg with an assessing gaze.

"Did you collect here?"

"No."

"Then where?"

Meg was reluctant to discuss the ancient place. She knew that even the vassals who loved her thought the place was at best haunted—and at worst cursed.

"What does it matter?" Meg asked. "I have what I need."

The rage in Dominic almost slipped free. With great difficulty he kept it leashed.

"Do you?" he asked silkily. "And what was it you were lacking?"

Again, Meg was reluctant to explain. If she discussed the antidote, then she would have to discuss the missing medicine too. She had promised Gwyn not to do that.

Into the silence came the distant trills of birdsong and the much nearer sounds of the war-horses

approaching as Simon rode up, leading Dominic's
stallion. The greyhound danced attendance, its long,
narrow tongue hanging after the run.

"My lady," Dominic said in a clipped voice, "what
was it you lacked so urgently that you set off alone
into the countryside without telling anyone?"

"Seedlings," Meg said, looking away from his
eyes. "For my gardens."

"You lie rather badly."

"I am not lying. I collected seedlings for my garden."

"Show them to me."

"Not until I plant them. Handling them too much
makes them—"

Meg's words ended in a startled gasp as the harvest bag was ripped from her hands, upended, and
shaken thoroughly. Whole plants and dirt showered
onto the ground. Small leaves fluttered down like
green rain.

"No!" Meg said frantically.

She snatched the bag from Dominic, went to her
hands and knees, and began combing the ground
for the small leaves as though she were gathering
tiny gold coins.

Frowning, Dominic watched. He had doubted
Meg's words but he didn't doubt her sincerity
right now. She plainly valued the greenery in the
harvest bag.

"Simon."

"Yes, liege?"

"Backtrack her."

"Aye."

"It will do you no good," Meg muttered without
looking up.

"What Simon can't see, Leaper can scent."

"Not in the ancient place. No dog will go there,
nor horse."

"Why not?" demanded Dominic.

"I'm not a hound or a horse to answer that question," Meg retorted as she put leaves back into the bag. "I simply know 'tis true. Animals sense some things more clearly than men."

"The ancient place," Dominic repeated, a question in his tone if not in his words.

Meg muttered something and kept gathering leaves.

An instant later there was a mailed fist beneath her chin, raising it, forcing her to meet her husband's bleak eyes.

"You don't fear this place?" Dominic asked.

"Why should I? I'm no long-tongued hunting bitch."

Simon made a sound like coughing—or muffled laughter.

Without looking away from Meg's angry green eyes, Dominic gestured for his brother to get on with the backtracking.

"No, you're neither hound nor horse," Dominic said distinctly. "You're a Glendruid witch. What mischief have you been hatching here?"

"I am Glendruid, but I'm not a witch."

"Yet you come to a place the common folk consider cursed."

"It doesn't disturb the cross I wear," Meg said. "If the ancient place were the evil some people think it is, the cross would burn. It does not. It lies cool and quiet between my breasts."

Dominic looked at his wife while the sound of hoofbeats faded into a silence disturbed only by birdcalls and a rising wind. When he released Meg's chin, small marks reddened her creamy complexion where chain mail had met skin. He would have felt worse about even that fleeting hurt if the certainty that she had been with a lover were not lying in his gut like cold, undigested food.

No wonder my bride responded so quickly to the sensual lure last night. She is no nestling newly caught, but a falcon ready trained to a man's touch.

I will have heirs of her, that is certain. She can no more resist the wild flight in a man's arms than a falcon can resist the untamed sky. But whomever she belonged to in the past, she is mine now.

And mine she shall remain.

Grimly Dominic looked at the greenery scattered over the ground. Using her fingertips, Meg had gently raked up all but a few seedlings that were rapidly wilting. He was no herbalist, nor was he a gardener, but the seedlings looked common to him. He was certain he had seen their like growing far closer to the keep.

Expecting Meg to object, Dominic picked up several of the seedlings.

No protest came, not even when he carelessly stuffed the seedlings into a travel pouch tied to Crusader's saddle. Yet when he bent to help Meg gather the few remaining loose leaves, stems, and tiny roots, she pushed his hands forcefully away.

"Nay," Meg said. "Your gauntlets are too clumsy. If you bruise the leaves before the potion is prepared, it will be too weak to serve its purpose."

"Is that why you didn't bring Eadith or one of the men-at-arms?" Dominic asked smoothly. "They're too clumsy?"

Meg said nothing.

"Answer me, *wife*. Tell me why you came into the forest alone."

Meg's hands stilled. "I . . ."

Dominic waited with a growing certainty that whatever he heard next would be a lie.

What he heard was silence.

"How much farther up this way lies Carlysle Manor?" he asked in a carefully conversational tone.

Meg let out a breath of relief at the new topic. While she spoke, she began picking up the last of the tiny leaves.

"It's more than a hard day afoot," she said. "It would be moonrise long before you saw the manor from the Old Pass."

"Less, if you ride the path you just walked?"

"Aye, yet few do, though the way is a shortcut between cart roads," Meg said, talking quickly in her relief at having a safe topic. "The short way is arduous in places. Most people prefer the cart roads. Before John grew too weak, we traveled by road from the keep to the various manors several times a year."

"Are the cart roads in ill repair? Is that why you came this way?"

"Nay. Duncan has had men working on the roads since he returned."

Dominic's eyes narrowed. If Meg could have seen him, she would have forgotten the few remaining scraps of leaves and taken to her heels. But her attention was entirely on gathering up each precious bit of green.

"Do all the common folk prefer to go around these hills, walking the extra distance on the cart roads?" Dominic asked.

"Yes. They avoid the haunted places."

"How convenient."

The savagery of his tone was like a sword being drawn. Meg's hands fumbled and went still.

"Convenient?" she asked. "How so?"

"For trysts," Dominic said succinctly.

Meg looked up and met Dominic's eyes without flinching.

"So that is it," she said. "You think I've been out rolling in the meadow with some man."

"Not *some* man," Dominic said harshly, "but Duncan of Maxwell. Look at you—cheeks all flushed and eyes glowing, and your clothes hung with bits of forest litter."

"My cheeks are flushed and my clothes are dirty because I've been all but standing on my head gathering my plants!"

"Maybe. And maybe you are a maid recently tumbled."

"Nay!"

"Did Duncan think that once I'd had you, I wouldn't know if he had you as well? Does he hope to foist off a bastard on me as your mother did on John?" Dominic continued relentlessly.

Meg's head came up proudly. "I give you my vow, husband. I have been with no man."

"So you say, wife."

"Lie down with me," she said rashly. "Here and now, Dominic le Sabre. You will find you are the first."

The cold slash of her husband's smile didn't reassure Meg.

"Well played, Lady Margaret," he said softly.

"I'm not playing!"

"Neither am I. If I lie with you and find you're not a maid, and if you quicken, I wouldn't know who was the father, would I?"

Meg was too taken aback to respond.

"No, my clever little wife, I'll not lie with you until you have bled. Then I will keep you quite close. When you quicken, there will be no doubt as to whose son you bear."

Understanding came to Meg like a blow.

"You truly don't care if I'm maid or wanton," she whispered, appalled. "You care only that you have a son of me."

"Aye. But if you were a whore before this moment, your whoring days are at an end."

"I could be a liar, a cheat, a robber, a felon . . . none of it matters to you. One womb serves as well as another, so long as it comes with Blackthorne Keep."

Dominic's eyes narrowed to icy splinters.

"Believe me, madam, whatever you were in the past, I will expect you to set an example of great rectitude as my wife. You will sore regret any dishonor you bring to my name."

The stubborn tendril of hope that Meg had harbored in her soul slowly withered under the wintry reality of Dominic le Sabre. He was not the Norman devil Eadith had named him, nor was he the generous heart she had dreamed might live beneath his chain mail trappings. He wanted neither her laughter nor her tenderness. Nor was he curious about her hopes and her dreams and her hunger to build a better life for her people—and for herself, that she might not taste the same bitter dregs of marriage that her mother had.

Dominic le Sabre was simply a man, as John of Cumbriland had been a man. And when thwarted in his drive for dynasty, Dominic would sour as John had.

The bleak shadows she had sensed in Dominic's soul were as real as a winter night and far more lasting. They would freeze her life as surely as they had frozen him.

A silent cry of protest for what might have been twisted through Meg, but no sound escaped her lips.

When Dominic spoke her name again, sharply, Glendruid eyes looked right through him. Silently Meg measured the spring that was slowly overtaking the land in a celebration of life that she wouldn't share.

"Such an old face for such a young girl," Dominic said angrily. "Is it that much a hardship to give up your immoral ways?"

Meg said nothing. She had no heart to speak, much less to be mocked for her feelings by a man who had none.

"I will make you a bargain," he said in a frigid voice. "Give me two sons and I will send you to London. There you will certainly find entertainment that pleases your wanton tastes."

Barely withheld tears made Meg's eyes huge. "You know nothing of what pleases or displeases me."

"I know that last night you refused your husband what is his by right," Dominic retorted savagely.

"I have known all my life that it was my duty to marry whatever man was chosen for me," Meg said as though Dominic hadn't spoken. "I have known that I would be a loyal, dutiful wife. I have known that I would be capable of so much more if I was well matched in my husband. And now . . ."

Her voice faded into aching silence.

"And now?" Dominic said. "Speak."

"I know that it will never be," Meg whispered. "Spring has come, but there will be no spring for Glendruid or for me."

"Forget your pining after Duncan," Dominic said harshly.

"Duncan? What—"

"You are married to me," Dominic continued relentlessly, talking over her. "I am the only husband you will ever have."

"Aye. And I am your only wife. Until death do us part. Will you drive me to an untimely death in order that you might still be fertile when you wed again? Is that the danger that woke me cold and trembling?"

"What nonsense is this?" he demanded.

Abruptly Meg shuddered. The blood left her cheeks as chills coursed over her suddenly clammy skin.

"Do you hear that?" she whispered.

"What?"

"Laughter."

Dominic listened intently. "I hear naught."

" 'Tis John."

"What?"

"Laughing. He knows his curse will be more potent than ever he was." Shadowed green eyes fixed on Dominic. "You will die without sons."

Dominic's hands whipped out, gripping Meg's shoulders as though he thought she would flee him.

"I will have sons!"

"Nay," Meg whispered, ignoring the cool silver glide of tears down her face. "For a Glendruid son, love is required. There is no love in you, Dominic le Sabre."

 13

B Y THE TIME SIMON CAME BACK
to the keep, Dominic had changed out of his battle
clothes and was sitting at ease in the lord's solar off
the great hall. What once had been a sickbed had
been transformed just that morning into a couch for
Dominic when he wished to speak with someone in
a privacy the great hall didn't permit.

The topic at hand—what Simon had found along
Meg's back trail—definitely required such discre-
tion. Meg's pale, drawn face, haunted eyes, and
unbroken silence as she rode pillion with him back
to the keep had unsettled Dominic in ways he found
difficult to describe, much less to understand.

In addition to the privacy Dominic sought, the
lord's solar offered warmth to ease a chill that was
as much of the heart as of the body. The fire burned
brightly in the room's big hearth, driving back the
cold that was a combination of spring rain and building stones that still harbored the icy breath of winter. Even though the narrow, high windows were
shuttered against the afternoon rain, the solar somehow managed to be more airy and inviting than any
other room in the keep.

"You look like a wet hound," Dominic said quietly

157

as Simon walked in, trailing rivulets of rain.

"I feel like one."

"Warm yourself. We'll talk in a moment."

While Simon stripped off his gauntlets and wet mantle and went to the fire, Dominic turned to the servant who waited at the doorway for his lord's pleasure.

"Ale for my brother," Dominic said. "Bread and cheese, too. Something hot—a soup?"

"Aye," Simon said.

"And while you're about it, find out what is keeping Old Gwyn. I sent for her long ago."

"Yes, lord."

Sitting upright, Dominic waited, listening to the sound of retreating footsteps. As he waited for the servant to get beyond the point where he might overhear what was said, Dominic's hand went to the nearby trestle table where a gleaming heap of golden jewelry lay. Absently he stirred the baubles.

A sweet, pure chiming filled the air, as though from captive songbirds with throats of purest gold.

The delicate music came from chains of tiny golden bells that once had graced the wrists, ankles, hips, and waist of a sultan's particularly favored concubine. After Dominic took the city, the woman had been returned unharmed to her sultan. Her golden jewelry had not.

"How is the peregrine?" Simon asked, reminded of the falcon by the sound of bells.

In any case, Simon had no desire to raise the subject of Meg.

"The falcon progresses at uncanny speed," Dominic said absently. "I took off her hood after I came from the forest. The bird showed no fear or fluttering. She came to my arm and my whistle as though born to it. Tomorrow eve I'll take her into the bailey for a time. Soon I'll let her ride on my wrist throughout the keep. Then we will course the skies together."

"Excellent," Simon said, relieved that something was going well.

"Yes . . ."

Dominic closed his eyes as though to better hear the elegant golden bells.

"One would almost believe she had been previously trained," he said after a moment.

"Has she?" Simon asked.

"Possibly. I'm told she was taken in a net rather than from the nest. But the falconer assures me such cleverness is common for Blackthorne's birds . . . if the witch Meg handles them."

Simon made a neutral sound.

"What did you find when you backtracked her?" Dominic asked with almost no change of tone.

Almost, but not quite. The difference was enough to remind Simon just how deeply his brother cared about the reluctant wife with whom he was determined to found a dynasty that would outlast both the casual cruelty of nature and the calculated cruelties of man.

"I found nothing," Simon said bluntly. "Leaper lost the scent."

The sound of bells stilled. Dominic looked intently at Simon.

"Lost the scent?" Dominic said. "How curious. Leaper has the keenest nose of any hound I've ever coursed."

"Aye," Simon said.

"Were there any other tracks around?"

"There is a grand stag living back up from the creek that comes down to the Blackthorne River. A fox had taken a hare. An eagle and five ravens were arguing a kill."

Dominic grunted. "Any sign of horses?"

"Nary a one, even of the wild moorland breed."

"Oxen? Carts? Boot prints?" Dominic persisted.
"No."

"Where did you lose the scent?"

"Just where Lady Margaret said I would, at the standing stones surrounding a heathen burial place."

"And there was no sign of anyone else?"

"Not one whiff," Simon said succinctly. "If Duncan of Maxwell—or any other man—was there with your lady this morning, he came on an eagle's wings and left the same way."

Dominic grunted.

"Perhaps she was doing as she said, gathering plants," Simon offered.

"Perhaps. But the seedlings could have been gathered closer to home."

"What of the odd leaves?"

"The gardener had never seen their like," Dominic admitted.

That was why Dominic was in the solar and Meg was in her rooms; he needed time to think. The first skirmishes in the battle to secure sons had gone badly. Dominic was too good a tactician to repeat his errors.

And if he weren't, he would learn and learn quickly. Never had he joined a battle half so crucial to his future.

"I may have misjudged my wife," Dominic conceded slowly. "I certainly have mishandled her."

"How so? Any other husband would have beaten her soundly for setting off alone into the forest and telling no one where she went."

"How do you know I haven't done just that?" Dominic retorted without heat.

"After I dragged you out of that Turkish dungeon, you vowed you would never permit lash or cane to be used when you had your own domain. You are a man of your word."

Dominic suddenly came to his feet. The horror of the dungeon was so great he remembered it only in dreams. And he forgot those dreams upon waking.

He preferred it that way.

"Have I thanked you for that, Simon?"

"We've saved each other's lives too often to keep track," his brother said dryly.

"It wasn't my life you saved that time, it was my soul."

Bells sang, disturbed by the clenching of Dominic's fist amid the cool chains of gold.

"I have a new duty for you," Dominic said after a moment. "That of guard."

Simon turned swiftly from the fire. "Has Sven discovered more threats against you?"

" 'Tis not myself you'll be guarding, but my wife."

"God's teeth," Simon said in disgust.

"Who else can I trust not to seduce or to be seduced?" Dominic asked simply.

"Now I know why sultans use eunuch guards."

"I won't ask that final sacrifice of you."

" 'Tis just as well," Simon retorted, running a hand through his light hair. "I owe you much, brother, but not my manhood!"

Dominic's laughter blended with the quiet murmuring of the bells as he caressed them.

"It will be your task to see that no one goes into Meg's rooms except me," Dominic said.

"What of her handmaiden?"

"What of her?" Dominic said indifferently. "I can dress—and *undress*—my wife as needed."

Simon managed not to laugh out loud, but his amusement was plain on his handsome face.

"For a few days," Dominic said, "Meg will be as a falcon newly come to my mews. What she eats will come from my hand. What she drinks will come from my lips. When she sleeps, it will be beside me.

When she awakens, my breathing will be what she hears and my warmth will be how she herself is warmed."

Simon's eyebrows rose, but he said nothing.

"Meg said that I didn't know her," Dominic continued, thinking aloud as he often did with Simon. "She is correct. The error is mine. She seemed willing enough at first, but somehow she is better defended than any keep or city I've ever taken."

Silently Simon wondered just what had happened after he had left his brother and Meg alone in the forest. But Simon said nothing. He knew Dominic better than to interfere once he began planning how to take a fortified position.

Or a woman.

"By the time her monthly flux passes," Dominic said, "I will know her much better. But not as a husband knows his wife. It will be a different kind of knowledge."

"Have you told her that she is to be a captive in her own keep?" Simon asked neutrally.

"Aye."

"What did she say?"

Dominic's eyes narrowed. "Nothing. She hasn't spoken to me at all since she informed me I would die without sons."

"God's blood," Simon said, appalled.

Before Dominic could speak again, the servant returned. Gwyn was right behind him. The servant set food and ale on the table and withdrew. When Simon walked over and began to eat hungrily, Dominic motioned the old Glendruid woman to come stand nearer the fire.

"Have you supped?" he asked politely.

"Aye, lord. Thank you."

Dominic paused, wondering what was the best way to broach the subject of his Glendruid bride, of curses and hopes, of superstition and truth; and of the secret connections among them. Finally he shrugged and followed the example of the people of Blackthorne Keep. John and Meg had taken the issue head-on. The new lord would do no less.

"Tell me about Glendruid wives," Dominic said simply.

"They are women."

From behind Dominic came odd sounds as Simon smothered laughter or oaths or both at once.

"Indeed," Dominic said with outward calm. "I've noted that very thing about Meg. 'Tis quite reassuring, as I am a man."

Gwyn's faded eyes showed a glimmer of humor. "Was there anything else, lord?"

"Quite a lot," he shot back. "Tell me how Glendruid wives differ from the normal run of women."

"They have eyes of an unusual shade of green."

Dominic grunted. "Go on."

"They are quite talented with living things."

He waited.

So did Gwyn.

"God's blood," Dominic said, glancing imploringly at the ceiling. " 'Tis like pulling teeth. Speak!"

"It might be quicker if you were to tell me what you particularly wished to know," Gwyn said serenely. "However, the solar is quite cozy and my old bones savor the warmth. I'll be glad to begin with Lady Margaret's birth and work forward carefully to this very day."

Dominic put his fists on his hips and studied the old woman. She studied him in return, but less aggressively. Her arrogance, however, was quite equal to his.

"I've learned that Glendruid women are stubborn," Dominic said after a time.

"Aye."

"Fearless."

Gwyn tilted her head to the side as though considering the matter.

"We aren't cowards," she said after a few moments. She paused and then added, "There is a difference, lord."

"Aye," Dominic said, surprised at the old woman's shrewdness. "Among men it is called courage."

He reached over and stirred the golden bells absently, considering his next line of attack. The small chiming sounds made Gwyn turn her head to the exotic jewelry.

"If flowers could sing," she said in a pleased tone, "they would have voices like that."

Dominic glanced at her. "Again you have surprised me, madam."

" 'Tis hardly an achievement to surprise a man who fixes his attention on one thing only and ignores the rest of life."

"Are you perchance describing me?" Dominic asked dryly.

Gwyn nodded.

"What am I fixed upon?" he asked.

"A dynasty."

"No more so than other men."

"Nay," she said quickly. "Other men want many things. Some manage to want one after the other. Most want all at once."

"And so get none."

It was Gwyn's turn to be surprised.

"Aye," she said. " 'Tis so. But you are not as other men. You are obsessed with one thing and one thing alone. A son."

Dominic's eyes narrowed into splinters of clear ice.

"In any case," he said smoothly, "I find myself saddled with an infertile wife."

"Not so!"

There was no doubt in the old woman's voice.

"Then why is Meg so certain I will die without sons?" Dominic demanded.

Gwyn's eyes widened, then narrowed in consideration of the tall warrior who stood before her. For the first time she realized just how deep a rage he was concealing.

"Is that what she said to you?" Gwyn asked carefully.

"Aye."

"Precisely? Word by word, lord. I must be certain."

At first Dominic thought he would refuse. Yet there was something in the old woman's eyes that couldn't be denied.

"She said, 'For a Glendruid son, love is required. There is no love in you, Dominic le Sabre.' "

The sound that came from Gwyn could have been a sigh or a whispering sound of pain that was absorbed by the slight noises of the hearth fire. She rubbed her eyes as though inexpressibly weary. Then she looked at the man who wanted only one thing in life.

"It's not that Meg is infertile, Lord Dominic. It's that no Glendruid son will be conceived if there isn't love between the parents."

"How can that be, old woman?"

"I do not know," she said simply. "I know only that it has been thus since the loss of the Glendruid Wolf."

"And how long is that?"

"Long, long ago, lord. So long only God remembers and He has told no one."

"Come now, madam," Dominic said in a voice rich with sarcasm. "Are you asking me to believe that in such a great span of time, not one man has deceived a Glendruid lass into thinking he loved her?"

Gwyn shrugged. "It wouldn't matter what lies he told her to bed her. Ultimately the curse rests on the woman's love, not the man's. Many Glendruid women have wanted sons to bring peace to their world. Not one has managed the kind of love a son requires."

Dominic narrowed his eyes. Nothing of what Gwyn was saying pleased him. But then, he was never pleased to discover the traps and fortifications of a city he must take.

" 'Tis true, then, what Lord John said," Dominic murmured. "The witches are as cold as a mountain grave. They feel no passion."

Gwyn smiled oddly. "Do you believe John or do you believe the untouched Glendruid flesh that came to your call as a falcon to its master?"

Dominic's whole body tightened at the reminder of the desire he had indeed aroused in Meg, only to have her angrily withdraw at the thought of giving him heirs.

"Then why haven't the witches loved? Are they incapable of it?" he demanded tightly.

"Some, yes. The ability to love is rare in any clan or kin. But not in Meg. There is great love within her. Ask any of the people of the keep."

"What of the witches who could love?" Dominic persisted. "Did they marry brutes unworthy of them?"

"Brutes? Nay. They simply married men, lord. Just men."

"You speak in circles," he said impatiently.

"No. You simply choose not to understand. Could you give your soul in love to a woman if you were absolutely certain she wanted nothing but to use you in order to gain lands, wealth, and sons?"

"God's teeth, what foolishness is—"

"Could you," the old woman continued relentlessly, "allow yourself to love any woman? Could you share your tightly guarded soul with her?"

Dominic gave her a look of disbelief "Do I appear a fool, madam? I cede that kind of control over my destiny to no one, man or woman!"

Tears magnified the old woman's eyes, but they did not fall. She had had too many years on earth to believe that tears changed anything.

"Then you will have no sons and I will be doomed to watch yet another generation pray for release from the curse."

"I don't believe you," he snarled.

"Then believe this: Glendruid women see beneath the sensual lure of broad shoulders and handsome faces. They see a man's soul. Seeing that deeply makes love surpassingly difficult, for Glendruid women are also human.

"Understanding someone, *and loving him despite that understanding,* is a trait more often found in angels than in mankind. Meg is a woman, not an angel."

Dominic's eyes narrowed into splinters of ice, a reflection of the cold condensing in his gut as the old woman's certainty and grief rolled over him like a dark wave. Without warning, his fist slammed onto the table's surface. Bells leaped and jangled. After that brief, unmusical cry, silence came.

No one disturbed it.

Simon looked from the old woman to his brother. Dominic's eyes were narrowed. He had the air of a man thinking very rapidly.

Slowly the tension eased out of Simon. Once his brother concentrated on an objective, there had never been a keep, a city, or a wench that Dominic couldn't take by force or stealth.

Or treachery, if it came to that.

After long minutes of silence, Dominic focused once more on the old Glendruid woman. His eyes were like ice, hard and very cold. His voice was the same.

"Thank you, madam. You have clarified the problem of heirs for me."

It was a dismissal, and Gwyn knew it. She nodded slightly and withdrew as quietly as smoke.

Dominic turned to his brother and asked bluntly, "Do you believe the old witch?"

"I sense *she* believes her words are the truth."

"Aye," Dominic said bitterly. "I saw enough in the Holy War to know that kind of faith can pass miracles."

"Or call down curses?"

Dominic's fist hit the table once more, making bells cry in protest for the man who would allow no protest of his own to escape his rigid control.

"What will you do?" Simon said after a time. "Have the marriage annulled because she is infertile?"

"Nay," Dominic vowed. "Never."

The force of his instant reply surprised both men.

"We could hold the keep even if the thanes and vassals rebelled," Simon pointed out. "If the people refuse to work the land for you, our father has more peasants than his estates in Normandy need. The serfs would be glad to come here where each would get a garden of his own, and a pig."

"Aye."

Dominic said no more. The solution Simon offered was workable, but Dominic refused it out of hand. He couldn't precisely say why. He knew only that his instincts clamored against a solution that didn't involve the Glendruid witch who was his wife.

Frowning, Dominic looked at the delicate golden bells that shivered so musically with the least touch.

If flowers could sing . . .

If Glendruid witches could love . . .

"Aye!" Dominic said fiercely. "That is it!"

"What?"

"The solution, my brother, is simple. I must teach the witch to love me."

14

DOMINIC AND SIMON CROSSED through the great hall on the way to one of the corner stairways that wound up the inside of three of the keep's four towers. The soft music of the golden jewelry overflowing from Dominic's left hand was lost in the noise of servants raking and scraping the wooden floor of the hall.

As soon as the planks were bared, more servants with buckets of water, lye soap, and coarse brushes went to work. Heaps of soiled rushes were piled up along one wall, waiting to be burned. The fire in the huge hearth leaped high as it devoured all that it was fed.

The steward hurried from group to group of servants, urging that they work harder and faster in order to please Blackthorne Keep's new lord.

"At least the steward knows who his new master is," Dominic muttered.

"They all know who their new master is. Some of them just find it harder to swallow than others."

"They had best not take too long in the chewing," Dominic retorted as he began climbing stairs with long strides. "I have little patience for some things. Sloth is foremost among them."

Simon's laughter echoed in the twisting stone passageway.

"Your knights well know it, Dominic. I doubt that your wife will be long in learning."

"There will be no need of teaching in Lady Margaret's case. Her breath and body are as sweet as spring itself. The cleanliness of her rooms tells me that it was John, rather than she, who was at fault for the state of the rest of the keep."

Leather boots slapped rhythmically against stone as the brothers climbed the right-hand turning staircase. If they had been trying to take the keep by storm, they would have been hampered by the fact that all knights were trained to use their right hands in sword fighting. As a result, it was far easier to defend the stairs than it was to take them, for in fighting up the steps, the stone wall forever thwarted the thrust of the attackers' swords. The defenders, retreating up the stairs, were under no such handicap. They could cut and slash with a will, and their blades would find only the enemy rather than the stone walls of the tower itself.

Dominic took the final three stairs in a single leap and strode down the passageway that led to his wife's rooms. He ignored the two small rooms that opened along the way. Those were the quarters of the lady's maids. As only one was being used by Eadith, he had given the other to Marie.

The thought of seeing either woman didn't appeal to Dominic at the moment. He had decided Eadith was a greedy flirt with little to recommend her but her clean hands. Nor was Marie good company. She was sulky that no more gifts of gold and gems and been forthcoming from him since Jerusalem.

Rather wryly, Dominic realized that part of Meg's appeal for him was that she wasn't tripping over her own feet with eagerness to discover the contents of the small chests he had brought into the keep when he arrived. In fact, it seemed she wasn't eager for anything at all from him.

Except her cursed plants.

She had snatched them back from him with great speed. He still found it difficult to believe that she had gone on foot over fen and moor—and risked her husband's certain displeasure—simply to collect a few odd bits of greenery. But there appeared to be no other explanation for what had happened.

Dominic found himself curious to discover if a few hours of silence had made Meg more willing to talk to him. He also wondered if the golden jewelry in his hands would make her eyes light with welcome for him, despite her anger that he wasn't falling under her spell as all the other people of Blackthorne Keep manifestly had.

The door to Meg's room was closed. Dominic rapped on it impatiently.

"Open, madam," he said. "It is your husband."

No answer came.

Dominic knocked less gently. "Lady Margaret. Open the door."

No one spoke from within.

The force of Dominic's fist made the door shudder. "Open the cursed door or I'll have it off its hinges!"

The door swung open.

"Wife, you and I will reach an agreement on the basic courtesies I expect from . . ."

Dominic's voice died as he realized that the door had been opened by the force of his fist rather than by his wife's softer hands. He strode into the room.

It was empty.

"God's teeth," he snarled, throwing the jewelry onto his wife's bed. "The witch isn't here!"

Dominic strode through the room into what had once been the nursery. From the look of it, Meg spent time sitting there by the window, embroidering and listening to the sounds of servants in the bailey below.

"Empty," Dominic said before Simon could ask.

The two men quickly checked the ladies' quarters of the keep, the bath, and the latrine. All were empty.

As one, the brothers rushed back down the stairs to the forebuilding. The man on duty looked as bored as he undoubtedly was.

"Did Lady Margaret leave?" Dominic asked.

"Nay," the knight said, surprised. "You told me she wasn't to pass from the keep unless she was with you."

Dominic grunted.

"What of the lady's handmaiden?" Simon asked. "Has she gone from the keep?"

"No. Only serving wenches, and I looked at each of them quite carefully."

"I don't doubt it," Dominic said.

Both of them knew the knights were still smarting from the rough edge of Dominic's tongue for not having realized that the "serving wench" they had let out earlier that morning had been, in fact, Lady Margaret.

"What now?" Simon asked. "Shall we find Eadith?"

Dominic grimaced. As much as he disliked the wench with the covetous eyes, Eadith was more likely to know where Meg was than anyone else in the keep.

"Where to first?" Dominic asked unhappily. "The battlements or the garrison?"

"It's storming."

"The garrison, then," Dominic said. "Eadith has a taste for dalliance, but not in a cold rain."

"What wench does?" Simon retorted.

Dominic grunted.

In a silence that seethed with Dominic's frustration, the two men headed for the knights' quarters. Since Duncan and the Reevers had departed, Eadith had spent much time checking the battlements—and flirting with the knights on sentry duty.

If the weather was too blustery to enjoy being out in the open, she spent time around the wellhead, supposedly checking that the servants were careful in the water they drew. Actually, she was simply hanging about the garrison, which was located on the same level as the well.

The second floor was alive with the sounds of knights and squires from the garrison area, and servants chanting rhythmically as they hauled up water for the keep's use in a large wooden bucket. Among the masculine sounds, it was easy to pick out the teasing feminine laughter.

When Dominic and Simon emerged from the tower staircase into the garrison, the first thing they saw was Eadith standing close to Thomas the Strong. Just behind him was Marie. Both women appeared to be interested in capturing the knight's roving eyes—and hands.

"Perhaps you should have saved Marie's cost, and that of her like," Simon said.

Dominic said only, "Marie will be earning her keep as a seamstress, beginning this moment."

"And Eadith?"

"Some women are born to be whores."

Thomas heard the sound of Dominic's approach before either woman did. He turned, saw his lord's face, and knew he was in trouble.

"Sir Thomas," Dominic said without preamble, "the armory is a heap of rust. When you aren't drilling the men on leaping into the saddle and using the broadsword one-handed, you will oversee the armory's thorough cleaning."

"Aye, lord," Thomas said, reluctantly removing a ham-sized hand from Eadith's hip. "When shall I begin?"

"Now. Draw up a list of what you will need and present it to me tomorrow morning."

"Aye, lord."

Thomas fastened his mantle, which had come undone beneath Marie's clever fingers, winked at both women, and withdrew.

"Marie," Dominic said.

The dark-haired woman watched him with eyes as black as Simon's. She couldn't conceal her hope from Dominic as she walked gracefully to him.

"Aye, lord? Do you finally wish something from your faithful Marie?"

"You are quite skillful with clothing. You will attend to the lacks in my lady's wardrobe. You may draw freely upon the silks I brought from Jerusalem. There is the cloth from Normandy and London as well. If you lack for anything, see me immediately."

Marie's full mouth thinned, but all she said was, "Yes, lord."

"You will have little work," Eadith said to Marie as the Norman woman turned to leave. "Lady Margaret cares for nothing but her gardens and herbal."

"Marie," Dominic said.

He hadn't raised his voice, but Marie froze in the act of turning away from him.

"Use your clever little hands for sewing, and I will reward you with silk of your own," Dominic said.

Marie smiled with delight and said, "There is no silk finer than my lord's mouth upon my body."

He laughed. "Be gone, wench."

The look Marie gave Dominic was full of memories. She leaned close to him and spoke softly, but not so softly that the others couldn't hear.

"When you tire of your gardener-bride, come to me. My body will smell of passion rather than dirt. And if you like not my scent, you can bathe me in yours."

"Go," Dominic said, but his voice wasn't harsh.

Smiling slightly, he watched Marie walk from the garrison. The fine wool of her tunic was closely drawn about her body, revealing the ripe feminine shape beneath. With each step her hips swung in a silent, unmistakable invitation.

"As for you," Dominic said, turning to Eadith. "Where is your lady?"

"I don't know, lord," Eadith said carelessly. "Have you lost her again so quickly?"

Simon winced at the girl's foolishness. Just because Dominic was willing to treat his people well didn't mean that he could be taken lightly.

"Do you have any kin?" Dominic asked, his tone polite.

"At Blackthorne Keep?"

"Yes."

Eadith shook her head.

"Do you feel a calling to the Church?" he asked.

"Nay," she said, surprised.

"Then I suppose I must continue to pay for your keep as an act of Christian charity. Henceforth, wench, you will oversee the scullery and the kitchen."

Shock showed on Eadith's face. "Is that what Meg said I should do?"

"How would I know?" Dominic asked silkily. "I keep losing her, as you so kindly pointed out. But then, it doesn't matter what my wife said or didn't say. When it comes to the keep, I am absolute ruler."

Eadith's cheeks became as white as salt. Tears appeared in her eyes.

"I overstepped, m'lord. Forgive me. The past few days have been upsetting," she said in a rush, "what with Lord John's death and the wedding and Sir Duncan being banished and seeing Normans walk unhindered where . . ."

Eadith's voice died as she heard what she was saying.

"Having a Norman lord is difficult for you," Dominic said evenly, "for your father was killed by Normans."

"Aye, lord," she whispered. "My brothers and husband, too."

Eadith's fingers played with the gold brooch Dominic had given her.

"That war is over," Dominic said flatly. "If you wish to continue fighting it, you will have to go to another keep."

With a stricken cry, Eadith went to her knees and grabbed his hand.

"Nay, I beg you. Let me but stay until—" Her voice broke off.

"Until?" Dominic inquired.

"I know no other home. I want no other home. Please, lord. Let me stay. I will prove my worth to you in any way you ask."

Dominic's first impulse was to free his hand from the kisses Eadith was bestowing, for their intent was seductive rather than conciliatory. Even so, Dominic didn't withdraw, because he had learned that impulse was a poor way to order his life.

"In any way?" he repeated softly.

"Aye," she said without looking at him.

"Then stand and tell me where my wife's favorite places are."

Eadith remained kneeling, pressing Dominic's hand against her full breasts.

"The garden," she said, "the mews, the—"

"Inside the keep," Dominic interrupted, freeing his hand with barely concealed distaste.

"The herbal, the chapel, and the bath," Eadith said. Then she added, "Duncan and she used to enjoy the bath most particularly. 'Tis a very private place, and the lady's soap is as soft as swansdown."

Then Eadith saw the look on Dominic's face and knew she wasn't endearing herself to her new lord.

"Sorry, lord," she said hurriedly. "It was all quite innocent, I'm sure."

"Go to the chapel," Dominic said through his teeth to Simon. "Take Eadith with you."

Before either one of them could argue, Dominic spun on his heel and left the garrison. The stairs to the herbal were dark and cold, for it lay at the back of the keep, where the building itself merged with the stony hilltop. He snatched up a torch and held it to the candle that always was kept burning at the entrance to the lower reaches of the keep. The torch caught and burned with a sullen, orange glow that spoke of slovenly construction.

The air was cold, damp, and rich with smells of larder and herbal. Dominic walked quickly down the aisle, trying to control his rage at the thought of Meg and Duncan playing sensual games in the bath. He told himself it didn't matter what she had done before she became his wife.

He didn't believe it.

The realization shocked Dominic out of his anger. Meg had been betrothed to Duncan. The king had refused the marriage and all others that John had proposed. Given that, it was only natural she would seek what pleasure she could find with the man for whom she had "affection."

Dominic was not such a saint that he could fault his wife for following her sensual nature. Yet the thought of Meg lying abandoned across Duncan's lap while he plundered the feminine riches that lay open to him made a killing rage leap in Dominic.

To control it, he forced himself to note the state of the rooms that opened on either side of the aisle. These rooms were neatly kept, and had been even before his edict.

Meg's doing, I'll warrant, Dominic admitted silently. *She is as clean as a cat. Pity she's as independent as one, too. The most simple command is beyond her ability to obey.*

Dominic ducked beneath the low lintel of the herbal. No sooner had he straightened than Meg's voice came to him. Her back was turned as she worked over a mortar and pestle on a long stone table that looked as though it grew from the earth beneath her feet.

"Whoever it is," Meg said without turning around, "leave the torch outside. It fouls the air in the herbal. How many times must I remind the keep's people of that?"

"As many times as I must tell you to stay in your rooms, perhaps?" retorted Dominic.

Meg spun around. In the leaping torchlight her eyes were wide, startled. The light made her skin as golden as the jewelry Dominic had thrown in disgust on her bed upstairs.

"You!" she said. "What are you doing here? This is my place!"

"Nay, madam. The keep and everything in it is mine," Dominic said curtly. "It is a fact you would do well to remember."

Cloth swirled as Meg went back to working over the mortar. She cast a quick eye at the water keeper and picked up the pace of her strokes.

"I am speaking to you," Dominic said, holding on to his temper with an effort that thinned his lips.

"I am hearing you."

"Did you hear me when I said you were to remain in your quarters unless I was with you?"

Silence.

"Answer me," Dominic snapped.

"Yes, I heard you."

"Then why are you here?"

"The herbal is part of my quarters," Meg retorted.

"Don't try my patience."

"How could I?" she muttered. "You have none."

Dominic, who prided himself on his patience, discovered he was out of it. He crossed the room in three long strides and grabbed Meg's arm with one hand.

"Enough of this foolishness," he said curtly. "You stood before God and promised to obey your husband. And by God, you shall. To your room, madam."

"Soon," she said, "but the leaves must be worked for a little time yet."

Dominic didn't argue. He just turned to go, pulling Meg in his wake.

When Meg felt herself being dragged away from the table, she didn't try to argue, either. She didn't even think. The fear that had driven her since she had awakened exploded in a mindless black rush. She jerked her arm and twisted wildly from side to side in an attempt to break Dominic's hold.

"What in God's name . . ." he muttered.

Meg dropped the pestle and clawed at Dominic's hand, trying to force him to free her. His fingers didn't loosen at all, so she tried to pry them off one by one.

It was futile. He was far stronger than she was.

"Stop this thrashing about before you hurt yourself," Dominic said curtly.

"Let go of me!"

"Not until you're in your quarters."

"No," Meg said hoarsely. "I must finish what I started!"

Dominic shifted his grip with lightning speed. Between one instant and the next, Meg found herself hauled up off the ground, her feet flailing, as helpless as a bird in a net. Thinking only of the irreplaceable leaves that must be prepared immediately or ruined beyond use, she fought back with a fury that was all the more startling for its silence.

The torch dipped and arced frantically as Dominic sought to subdue Meg one-handed. The sullen flames came breathtakingly close to her eyes, her hair, her cheek. She didn't notice. Her head cloth and circlet came off, sending her hair cascading wildly about.

"God's teeth," Dominic hissed. "You little idiot, you'll burn yourself!"

Meg didn't seem to hear. The torch's flame careened against her unprotected wrist as she made a frantic grab for Dominic's face. With a savage oath, he dropped the torch and ground it out underfoot.

Once both hands were free, Dominic quickly finished the struggle. Before Meg knew what had happened, he had her flat against the wall, her wrists locked over her head in one of his hands, her chin in the other, and her knees clamped between his. No matter how hard she fought, she could do little more than breathe.

Dominic looked at the frantic face of his wife and wondered what had possessed her to attack him. He had expected Meg to argue or to plead, or perhaps to drag her feet and sulk the length of the keep when he insisted that she obey him. He hadn't expected her to turn on him like a cornered wildcat.

Slowly Meg's thrashing abated. She watched him with feral eyes as she fought to draw breath into her lungs despite the weight of his body pressing her into the wall.

"Are you finished?" Dominic asked with sardonic politeness.

Meg nodded her head.

"Then we will go to your rooms and—"

Dominic's words broke off as he felt the tension in Meg's body return.

"If I let go of you, you'll fight me again, won't you?" he asked.

Meg said nothing. She didn't have to. The fierce tautness of her body told its own story.

Perplexed, Dominic regarded his wife in the light of the sweetly scented, cleanly burning candles of the herbal. Meg was clearly defeated in this contest of strength, and she knew it as well as he. Just as clearly, she would continue to fight if he relaxed his grip.

There was a long, seething silence while Dominic considered Meg's watchful green eyes. Abruptly he remembered the initial cause of the problem.

"Are you, by chance, working with the leaves you gathered this morning?" Dominic asked curiously.

"Aye," she whispered. Then, in a tumble of hopeful words, "Please, let me finish. It's more important than you know. I must prepare them before they lose their potency."

"Why?"

"I don't know," Meg admitted. "I just know that I must do it or something fearful will happen to Blackthorne Keep."

Dominic cocked his head as though listening to an inner voice. What he heard was the faint slow dripping of water somewhere nearby. He turned and saw a silver bowl suspended above an ebony bowl. Water dripped down with measured speed.

"Is it a Glendruid matter?" he asked, turning back to the wife who was more an enigma to him with every hour.

"Aye."

"Old Gwyn mentioned danger this morning. Something she sensed. She said you had probably sensed it, too."

Meg nodded eagerly.

"What danger?" he asked.

"I don't know."

Dominic grunted. "It seems you know little, Glendruid witch. Or is it that you simply won't tell me?"

"I—I dreamed," she said in a low voice. "There was a danger I couldn't name. Then I saw the leaves of this plant. I knew I must gather them to avert disaster. Please, Lord Dominic. Allow me to finish what I began. I can't replace these leaves for at least one fortnight, perhaps two. *Please*."

Anxiously Meg watched Dominic, knowing that her well-being—and the future of Blackthorne Keep —depended on his being reasonable after she had tested him far beyond the limits of most men's patience.

Before Dominic spoke, Meg sensed his answer. The feel of his body changed subtly as it relaxed against her without freeing her in the least. His caging of her became sensual rather than enraged. Suddenly she became aware of the very masculine contours of his body pressed against the length of hers.

"Shall we bargain, then?" Dominic asked huskily. "What will you give me if I let you finish preparing your Glendruid potion?"

"All you want from me is a son," Meg said, trying to keep the bitterness of defeat from her voice. "That is beyond my power to give you."

His eyes narrowed in a mixture of anger, rueful humor, and speculation.

"There is more to man and maid than simply making babes," Dominic pointed out.

"Is there? You've not spoken of it to me."

"Aye," he said slowly. "I've erred in that."

"Lord?" Meg asked.

"My name is Dominic," he said as he brushed his lips across hers. "Let me hear you say it."

"Dominic . . ."

He absorbed the whispering warmth of the word against his lips.

"You do that very well, sweet witch."

Slowly, reluctantly, Dominic eased the pressure of his body from Meg.

"You owe me a favor of my choice at a time of my choice," he said thickly. "Agreed?"

"Aye."

"So quick? Aren't you worried what I might want?"

"Nay," Meg said anxiously, looking toward the table, where water dripped relentlessly into the keeper bowl. "I'm worried only about the leaves. If I don't finish the preparation soon, all will be for naught."

"A kiss to seal our bargain, then."

"Now?" she asked, dismayed.

"Why not?"

Meg explained in a rush, not knowing how much time she had. "By the time we finish kissing it will be too late and my mind will be a muddle and my fingers will be all thumbs. You kiss in a most distracting way."

When Dominic understood the meaning of the tumbled words, he smiled sensually. His thumb traced the faint trembling of Meg's lower lip.

"Does Duncan?" he murmured.

"Duncan?" Meg blinked, perplexed. "What in heaven does he have to do with kissing? He has never muddled my mind one bit."

"Do I?"

"You know you do," she said, exasperated. "I just told you so. And if you don't stop running your thumb over my lip I shall bite you!"

"Where? Here?"

As Dominic spoke, he drew one of Meg's captive hands to his mouth, bit the base of her thumb with great care, and was rewarded by the swift, sensual breaking of her breath.

"Oh, stop," she begged. "I must have steady hands."

Dominic tried not to show his pleasure at her response to him, but found it impossible. He freed Meg and laughed to make the stones ring.

"Finish your work, sweet witch. Then we'll go to your rooms and discuss the nature of your captivity."

Before Dominic finished speaking, Simon ducked beneath the lintel and stepped into the herbal.

"Is she here?" he asked.

"Aye," Dominic answered, his voice still rich with laughter. "Come, we'll wait outside. The torch you're carrying fouls the air of Meg's herbal."

Outside, Simon gave Dominic a curious look. "The maid must indeed be a witch."

Dominic made a questioning sound tnat was rather like a satisfied purr.

"I left you angry enough to flay her alive," Simon said, "and a short time later I find you laughing like a boy."

The smile Dominic gave Simon made him uneasy.

"It's a serious matter," Simon said.

"Why? Can't I laugh like other men?"

"She has bewitched you," Simon said bluntly, "just as Eadith said she would."

" 'Tis a sweet enchantment," Dominic said, smiling.

"God's blood, you are bewitched. Look to your soul, brother, or soon Duncan of Maxwell will have by treachery what he couldn't take by force!"

15

MEG CARRIED THE TIGHTLY STOP-pered bottle in both hands through the keep and up to her own rooms. Normally she would have left the potion to ripen in a dark area of the herbal, but she was afraid to let the bottle out of her sight.

With a mixture of irritation and amusement, Dominic watched Meg open a concealed panel in the wooden partition that divided her quarters into a bedchamber and a sitting room. She put the bottle in the secret niche, closed the panel, and let out a long sigh of relief.

"You won't tell anyone where the bottle is?" she asked anxiously, turning toward the silent man who had followed her every step of the way from the herbal.

Dominic shrugged and shut the door behind him. "Does it matter that much?"

"If anything happens to that bottle, I can't replace the medicine for at least a fortnight. By then, it might be too late."

"Why? What is it for?"

Meg thought quickly, wondering how much she could tell Dominic without breaking her word to Old Gwyn. After a brief hesitation, Meg spoke, choosing her truths carefully, for she disliked lying.

"Some of my medicines are quite strong. If given wrongly, they can kill. That," Meg gestured toward the hidden bottle, "is an antidote to one of my most powerful pain medicines. After John died, I made a new batch of the pain medicine, so it is only prudent to make the antidote as well."

"For whom?"

"I don't understand."

"John is dead. For whom are you preparing such risky medicines?"

The blunt question made Meg wince. Again, she chose her truths with great care.

"I've seen that your knights train most strenuously. Soon or late, your men will hurt one another. Now I will be prepared to help them."

For a long count of three, Dominic looked into the Glendruid eyes that were watching him with barely concealed anxiety. He suspected he wasn't being told the whole truth, and he knew there was no way to be certain.

"I'll tell no one except Simon," Dominic said finally, "and he already knows that you took the bottle to your rooms."

"See that he tells no one."

Dominic nodded. Then he smiled rather darkly.

"That is two boons you owe me, wife."

Meg's cheeks colored at the combination of sensuality and triumph in Dominic's smile.

"Aye."

Nervously, Meg turned to tend the fire. Dominic watched as she bent to the hearth to stir up the embers. The more he was with his wife, the more impatient he became for her monthly flux to come and go so that he could plant the seeds of dynasty within her soft body. The grace of her movements aroused him to the point of pain.

And the quick skill of her hands told him that tending the fire was a task she performed often.

"Eadith barely earns her keep," he said in a disgusted voice.

"What?"

"Your handmaiden seems to spend little time doing·her tasks."

" 'Tis easier to do some things than to send word for one of the servants. In any case, Eadith wouldn't have been a handmaiden if her father or husband had lived. She would have been a lady with a handmaiden of her own. I spare her pride where it is possible."

"What happened to her family's lands?" Dominic asked.

"The same thing that happened to all of England— William or his sons took the land and divided it among their Norman knights."

Dominic listened carefully, but discovered none of the hatred he had sensed in Eadith's voice when she talked of the Normans—a hatred more than a few of Blackthorne Keep's servants bore despite their love of Meg. Nor did Dominic hear the refusal to accept his position that had been obvious in Duncan's voice. Meg was as matter-of-fact as though she were describing the number of sheep in a fold. She didn't even look up from her rummaging in the beaten brass container that held wood for the fire.

"Don't you hate the Normans as many of the keep's folk do?" Dominic asked curiously.

"Some of them are brutal, bloodthirsty, and cruel," Meg said bluntly as she chose a length of oak.

"You could say that of men from Scotland, Normandy, or the Holy Land," Dominic pointed out.

"Aye," Meg agreed, watching broodingly as tiny flames sank their teeth into the wood she had just laid in the hearth. "Cruelty knows no clan boundaries."

Dominic went to the bed and picked up the long golden chains with their sweetly chiming bells. Meg turned toward him, charmed by the musical sounds.

"What is that?" she asked.

"A wedding gift for my bride."

Meg stood and came to him, called by the golden voices of the bells.

"Truly?" she asked, surprised.

"Will you wear them, or must I require it of you as one of my boons?"

"Whatever do you mean? They're beautiful. Of course I'll wear them."

"But you didn't wear the brooch I gave you," he pointed out.

"Glendruid maids wear only silver before they are married."

Pointedly, Dominic looked at Meg's long tunic. It was barren of any decoration.

"You are married now."

Meg unlaced enough of the outer tunic to show that the brooch was fastened to her inner tunic, below the hollow of her throat.

"Ah," Dominic said. "I see."

And he did. What he saw was the proud rise of Meg's breasts and the delicate hollow of her throat.

"I envy my gift," he said.

Puzzled, Meg looked at the stranger who was also her husband. "Envy, lord—er, Dominic. How so?"

"It is free to lie between your breasts."

Red bloomed along Meg's cheekbones. Rather clumsily she fastened her tunic again.

Dominic was watching, smiling in a way that made her breath catch. She cleared her throat and pointed to the long chains he held.

"How shall I wear those?" Meg asked.

"I'll show you."

With a muscular grace that pleased Meg, Dominic

sat on his heels in front of her.

"Put your foot on my thigh," he said.

Hesitantly, Meg obeyed. Beneath her tunic, warm, strong fingers closed gently around her ankle. She made a startled sound. Before she could withdraw her foot, Dominic's hand closed firmly. The grip both steadied and restrained her.

"Be easy," he said. "There is nothing to fear."

" 'Tis rather unsettling," she said.

"Being touched?"

"No. Realizing that a man I've known only a few days has the right to touch me however and whenever he wishes."

"Unsettling," Dominic repeated thoughtfully. "Do you fear me? Is that why you ran into the wood?"

"I expect to feel pain when I lie beneath you, but that isn't why I went to the wood."

"The tiny leaves for your potion?" he asked.

"Aye."

Bells rang discreetly as Dominic wrapped one chain around Meg's ankle and fastened the clasp. He tested the security of the clasp and then stroked his palm up Meg's calf. Her breath came in audibly. The subtle jerk of her body set the bells to whispering musically.

"Why do you expect to feel pain when you lie with me?" Dominic asked, stroking Meg slowly. "Is it that difficult for you to accept a man?"

"Accept? How so?"

"Into your body."

Meg's breath came in swiftly. "I don't know. Eadith has told me 'tis no pleasure."

Dominic's hand paused, then resumed its slow, gentle strokes.

"Yet she flirts so intently," he pointed out.

"That is work, not pleasure. She is casting for a husband. Just as you are casting for an heir."

Dominic was too much a tactician to deny the truth. He simply feinted in another direction, distracting his opponent, keeping her off balance.

"Do you like it when I touch you?" he asked, squeezing Meg's calf with sensual care.

"I . . ." Her breath caught as he stoked her calf again. "I think so. 'Tis strange."

"What is?"

"Your hand is very large and strong. You make me feel rather fragile by comparison. Yet I don't think of myself as delicate at all."

"Does that frighten you?" he asked.

"It should."

"Why? Do you think me brutal after all?" Dominic asked.

"I think I'm quite glad that you don't beat falcons."

He laughed, but he didn't cease the slow caress of his palm up Meg's calf to the back of her knee. Tender frissons of fire raced through her body.

"You were very angry when you came into the herbal," she said, trying not to be distracted.

"Yes."

"And you're quite strong."

"Yes," Dominic said, hiding his smile against Meg's tunic. "But you fought me anyway, small falcon."

Slowly he traced the sensitive crease at the back of her knee and felt the subtle, almost unwilling shiver of her body in response. Carefully he shifted her foot from his thigh to the floor.

"Now the other foot," Dominic said.

When Meg moved, bells chimed beneath her tunic. She waited in taut anticipation of more of the disturbing caresses while Dominic wrapped a second chain around her ankle and fastened the clasp. As unsettling as his touch was, she found she liked the shimmering sensations that came in the wake of his caress. It made her want to forget what she knew all too well—beneath her husband's careful seduction burned a warrior's cold ambition rather than a lover's hot passion for his mate.

Dominic straightened with a grace that reminded Meg of Black Tom. He stood so close to her that her breasts almost brushed against him with each breath she took.

"Now your wrists," he said.

His low voice ruffled Meg's nerve endings almost as much as his touch. She moved skittishly, making bells cry beneath her skirts. Tentatively she held out both hands.

In a silence that was somehow intensified by the muted stirring of golden bells, Dominic wrapped bracelets around each of Meg's slender wrists. When he was finished, he lifted first one of Meg's hands and then the other. Slowly, he kissed the center of each palm, then tasted her with a single touch of his tongue.

The sound Meg made was a combination of surprise and sensual discovery. It went to Dominic's head like winter wine. He wanted very much to pull her into his arms for a thorough kissing, but his body had hardened in a rush that boded ill for the careful, and unfinished, seduction he must conduct if he were to win the first skirmish in his war to seduce a Glendruid witch.

A man too impatient to train his falcon will lose her the first time he takes off the leash, Dominic reminded himself. *I have barely succeeded in putting my leash in place, much less in training her to fly at my command and for my pleasure.*

To take her now would be to lose the war for the sake of winning one sweet battle. Only a fool is ruled by his passion.

Cold determination banked the sensual fires burning within Dominic, leaving him in command of himself and of the seductive battle.

Releasing Meg's hands, Dominic turned her so that her back was to him. He removed the circlet and head cloth that she had hastily replaced after their battle. In the muted light of the room, her hair glowed richly. The temptation to sink his hands into its silky luxury was so great he almost succumbed. Instead, he smoothed her hair quickly into braids, wrapped a chain around each one, and left bells trailing down.

When Dominic finished, he had just one long chain remaining in his hands. He wrapped it around Meg's narrow waist, brought the gold around the fullness of her hips and tied the chain as she would have a girdle, allowing the long ends to trail almost to the floor.

Meg stood wrapped in delicate riches and muted music. With every breath she took, with each movement she made, bells chimed softly.

"You are like a falcon made of fire," Dominic said, looking at the play of candlelight through Meg's hair. "And you wear golden jesses as such a magical falcon should."

Deliberately he turned Meg until she was facing him. He looked down at her with eyes as clear and cold as springwater while he caught her face between his hands.

"Are you hungry, wife?"

"Aye," she said in a low voice. "I've eaten only a piece of bread and cheese since dawn."

With an odd smile, Dominic turned away and went to the door. He opened it and saw the cold supper he had requested that Simon bring.

"Breads, cheeses, fowl, mustard, ale . . ." Dominic said.

He picked up the tray and walked into the room, closing the door behind him with a casual movement of his foot.

" . . . figs, raisins, nutmeats, honeyed almonds," he continued, "and a pile of raw greens whose purpose eludes me. Was Simon expecting a rabbit to join us for supper?"

Meg smiled. " 'Tis Marta, the cook. She knows I have a fondness for fresh greens in the springtime."

"Indeed?"

A single black eyebrow lifted as Dominic looked skeptically at the small heap of greenery.

"Is it a Glendruid ritual?" he asked.

"Nay," Meg said, laughing and reaching for a piece of crisp green. "Even Gwyn teases me about grazing in my garden like a sheep."

Dominic turned aside, blocking Meg's hand with his body before she could take any food.

"Patience, small falcon. There are a few things that must be done before you eat."

Perplexed, Meg watched as Dominic set the tray on the table near her big chair and then calmly went about extinguishing every candle and oil lamp in the room. There were many to be put out, for she craved light with the same instinctive yearning she had for clean water and growing plants.

"What . . . ?" she asked, alarmed.

"The mews are kept in darkness. Or would you rather go hooded?"

"You can't be serious."

"I can. I am. Darkened mews or a silken hood for my small falcon. I leave the choice to you."

The cold steel beneath Dominic's matter-of-fact tone told Meg that she had pushed her husband too far. The words he had spoken in the church rang ominously in her ears: *A wise man will understand*

*that his lord is merciful rather than weak. A foolish man
will try my patience. And die.* She had already defied
him in front of vassals and keep. To do so again
would not be wise.

"Darkened mews," Meg said bleakly.

Dominic closed the shutters, as though expecting
one of the harsh winds of winter to pry at the wood.
Meg watched and bit back a cry of protest. In all but
the most savage weather, she kept the shutters open
a crack. She loved the radiant, silver-blue glory of
daylight spilling into her living quarters.

Seeing the room as it was now, with only a small
fire in the hearth, made her feel . . . caged.

When Dominic went to the fire as though to extin-
guish even that source of light, she couldn't stifle
her small sound of protest. He turned, looked at
her thoughtfully, and added a bit more wood to
the fire. She let out her breath in a long, almost
soundless sigh of relief.

Dominic heard it and smiled to himself, knowing
he had read his small falcon well. The first battle
was won; she had agreed to her captivity. Now they
would negotiate the terms of it.

He sat in the big chair and gestured to his lap.

"Sit. I will serve you."

Uncertainly, Meg stepped forward. Countless tiny
bells stirred and sang.

"Oh," she said, hesitating and then moving again,
listening. " 'Tis very beautiful."

"Like flowers singing?" Dominic asked.

"Aye," she said, smiling despite her unease, "or
butterflies laughing."

"I'm glad my gift pleases you."

"It does, lord—er, Dominic. It was very kind of
you."

"I'm glad you think me kind," he said with an
enigmatic smile.

Gingerly Meg lowered herself onto Dominic's knees. He picked her up and rearranged her across his lap until she was half reclining against his left arm. Meg wondered at the silver blaze of his eyes. In the dim light they glowed like clear crystals.

With his right hand, Dominic plucked a drumstick from the heaped platter. Meg reached for the food. He held it beyond her reach.

"Nay," he said. "I will feed you, small falcon."

She gave him a startled look. He smiled and stripped a bit of meat from the drumstick with teeth that were as white and clean as a young hound's. Then he plucked the morsel from between his teeth and held it out to her with his fingertips. When she reached to take the meat with her hand, the food was withdrawn once more.

"Nay," Dominic said softly. "Falcons have no fingers."

Meg's mouth opened in surprise. Deftly he slid the bit of meat between her lips.

"There," he murmured as though talking to his peregrine in the mews. "That wasn't such a difficult thing, was it?"

Chewing slowly, she shook her head. Bells at the end of her braids rang like a falcon's jesses.

"More?" Dominic asked.

She nodded.

He smiled darkly. "Some falcons—the special, magical ones—speak."

"About what?" Meg asked as Dominic stripped another bit of meat from the drumstick.

"Food, water, the hunt, the kill, the wildness of flight . . ."

"Freedom," she whispered.

"Aye," he said, holding out the morsel. "I suspect untamed falcons talk about that most of all."

Meg watched Dominic's eyes as she ate from his hand. There was an odd intimacy in the act. A bond as tenuous as a single silk thread stretched between them with each bit of food she accepted; and like silk thread, when one was laid next to another, and then another, and then another, the resulting strand strengthened until there would be no breaking it.

As the moments slipped by in a hush defined rather than broken by the tender chiming of bells, Meg understood in a way she never had before precisely why the best hunting hounds were fed only by their master and why babes learned closeness with their mother's milk.

And why falcons—the most free of God's creatures—were fed only from their lord's hands, rode only on his wrist, came only to his special call.

"Is the food not to your taste?" Dominic asked.

"It's very good."

"Then why have you stopped eating?"

"I was thinking of falcons and masters," Meg said.

"Falcons have no masters."

"They hunt only at their lord's pleasure."

"Falcons hunt at their own pleasure," Dominic countered, popping another bite of food between her lips. "Their lords simply provide an opportunity."

"Do all men see it thus?"

Dominic shrugged. "It matters not to me how other men see the bond between falcon and man. If foolish men wish to believe they fly the bird rather than vice versa, who am I to disturb their shallow understanding?"

Chewing thoughtfully, Meg considered what Dominic had said. As soon as she swallowed, bread and cheese appeared before her lips. She opened her mouth for the food, received it—and felt the distinct caress of his fingertip on her lower lip as he withdrew.

"But falcons are captive and men are not," she said.

"Have you ever freed a falcon?"

"Once."

"Why?" he asked.

"She never accepted her jesses."

"Aye. But all the other falcons did."

Meg nodded.

"And in doing so," Dominic continued, "your fierce sisters learned a different kind of freedom."

Green eyes asked a silent question.

"They learned the freedom of being cared for when ice covers the land," Dominic said, "of being fed when there is no game in forest or field, of living in comfort twice or thrice as long as their untamed kin. Who can say which freedom is superior?"

Meg started to speak, only to have a fig slipped between her lips by Dominic's deft fingers.

"It all depends on the falcon's acceptance of her new life," Dominic continued.

Meg chewed quickly, parted her lips to say something, and found herself with another mouthful of food. When she gave Dominic a sidelong look, she saw that he was smiling.

"Ale?" he asked innocently.

She swallowed and wisely nodded instead of trying to speak.

When Dominic picked up the mug of ale and drank, Meg expected him to hold the mug to her lips as though she were a child learning to drink from a bowl.

But instead of a cold mug, it was Dominic's warm lips that met hers. A stream of cool, potent ale poured over her tongue. Automatically she swallowed. Dominic bit her lips very gently, lifted his head, and drank again from the mug. Then he turned and let Meg drink the ale from him.

The elemental intimacy of the act made her tremble. Bells stirred almost secretly, a music more sensed than heard. He drank from the mug and she sipped from his lips until she felt light-headed.

"Enough," Meg whispered.

The words were spoken against Dominic's mouth. She was breathing the heady scent of ale on his breath, tasting his warmth, feeling the edges of his teeth as he delicately nibbled on her lower lip.

"Are you certain?" he asked, biting with exquisite care.

"I fear I have no head for ale. I'm quite dizzy."

Dominic's laugh was like his voice; low, velvet, very male.

" 'Tis not the small bit of ale you've drunk," he murmured against her lips, " 'tis the way you drank that is making you light-headed."

Meg didn't argue. She knew that ale had never gone to her head so quickly before.

"Maybe it's simple hunger," she said, looking longingly at the platter of food.

Laughing silently, Dominic resumed feeding Meg with his fingertips rather than with his lips. Her heartbeat settled as she became accustomed to the novel way of eating. Meat and figs, cheese and bread—and the crisp greens—vanished with surprising speed.

"You have taken nothing," Meg protested as Dominic held out another bit of fig for her to eat.

"I'm not a small falcon."

"Even eagles eat," she said dryly.

But she was smiling at him, her eyes sparkling as she watched him from beneath long, auburn eyelashes.

Dominic laughed aloud and stole a crumb of bread from the corner of Meg's smile. Then he continued feeding her one small bite at a time until she could eat no more.

Yet even then Meg was reluctant to stop. The man who was holding her so carefully, teasing her so gently, feeding her so intimately was a revelation to her. Her heart insisted that there must be more to the dark Norman knight than ambition and deadly skill with sword and lance.

The stubborn hope that had kept generations of Glendruid women alive stirred once more within Meg, whispering to her that a man who was capable of such tenderness and laughter might also be capable of love. She could not love a man who was too cold and self-controlled to love her in return, but if he could love her . . . if that were possible . . .

Then anything was possible.

Even a Glendruid son.

When Dominic offered Meg yet another bit of bread, she shook her head in refusal; but at the same time, she brushed a fleeting kiss over his fingertips. His eyes narrowed and his breathing quickened at the caress that had been given freely.

"Something sweet?" Dominic asked, his voice husky.

Meg looked at the tray and saw the selection of Turkish sweets that had been hidden beneath the bread. In the wavering light from the hearth, she couldn't tell which of the sweets would have the flavor she preferred.

"Which is the lemon?" she asked.

"We shall find out."

With deceptively lazy grace, Dominic picked up one of the sweets. He popped it in his mouth, rolled it around on his tongue, and then bent to Meg.

"Taste me, small falcon."

A delicate network of fire shivered over Meg's nerves as she looked at Dominic's cleanly defined lips. They appeared hard, as though cut from stone, yet she knew them to be wonderfully warm and yielding.

Dominic watched his bride, understanding her with the same ruthless clarity he did men, potential battle sites, and fortified towns. Each had its strengths, but it was the weaknesses that mattered to him. In weakness lay defeat.

Meg's weakness was her need to believe in love.

Come to me, Glendruid witch. See in me what you want to see. Betray your living fortress to me. Lie open and undefended for my taking.

Give me the son I must have.

Slowly Meg pressed her mouth over Dominic's. When he made no move, she touched the tip of his tongue with her own and quickly retreated to watch him with wide, wary eyes. He raised his eyebrow in silent question.

"Sweet, but not lemony," Meg said in a low voice.

"Ah. We'll have to try again, won't we?"

Dominic discarded the candy and selected another one. When the taste of the sweet filled his mouth, he looked expectantly at Meg. This time she came to him without hesitation, tasted him less warily, and withdrew with less speed.

"Better?" he asked.

"Yes . . ."

"But not what you sought?"

Slowly Meg shook her head.

"Then we'll just have to keep trying," he said.

She nodded, smiling slightly.

Dominic's smile was a trifle wolfish, but Meg didn't notice, for he had turned away to make his choice among the remaining sweets. In an increasingly taut silence, he selected another, offered it for her sampling, and felt the warm stirring of her tongue within his mouth.

The suspicion Meg had that Dominic knew quite well which candy was lemon-flavored strengthened with each sweet tried and discarded, but she didn't object. The honeyed kisses were addictive, and the sensual game was more delectable than any Turkish candy.

Finally only one sweet remained. Meg watched with languid eyes as Dominic put the candy between lips that were shining from the heat of their shared kisses. He didn't have to ask her to taste him. She lifted her face to him as eagerly as a falcon lifts her face to the sky.

The piquant taste of lemon spread through Meg, drawing a sound of pleasure from the back of her throat. Dominic moved his head a fraction.

"Is this the one?" Dominic asked against Meg's lips.

"Aye."

"Share it with me."

As Dominic spoke, he lowered his head. This time the kiss didn't stop until the last bit of sweet was melted and Meg didn't know whether she was kissing him or he was kissing her, for their mouths were so deeply joined that she couldn't have said where one ended and the other began.

When Dominic finally lifted his head, Meg was breathing quickly, lost to the kiss, her body flushed from the delicate network of fire that had bloomed beneath her skin. She opened eyes that were hungry, languid, sensuous; and she saw herself being watched by eyes as cold as she was warm.

"You have tasted my mercy and found it sweet," Dominic said distinctly. "But a wise man shows mercy only once to the same person."

Meg went still.

"Never fight me again, small falcon. That is the favor I ask of you."

16

WITH EACH PASSING DAY, MEG'S promise not to defy Dominic grew more difficult to honor.

"But my garden," she protested as Dominic stepped out her door. "I must—"

"Old Gwyn is tending it," Dominic said across Meg's words. As he spoke, he pulled the door to her room shut behind him. "I'll be back before the noon bells ring."

"But when will I be freed?" she cried to the sound of his retreating footsteps.

"When there can be no doubt that any babe of yours is also mine. I'll come back soon, small falcon. In the meantime, remember your promise to me."

Making a sound of frustration, Meg hit the door with her fist, setting her golden bells to jangling in distress.

" 'Remember your promise,' " she mimicked in disgust. "Pah! How can I forget it? I've had little else to think about these past three days!"

Like a new falcon in a mews, Meg had been kept alone in a twilight room. Unlike a falcon, she had a hearth fire to relieve the gloom and warm the stone walls. She could also pace, a comfort denied the hunting birds.

The lord of Blackthorne Keep was Meg's only contact with the world beyond her quarters. Upon his orders, no one came to her rooms, no one spoke to her through the door, no one brought either food or drink: only Dominic kept her company.

He was with her often throughout the day, coming in without announcement, bringing a flower freshly bloomed or a smooth river pebble to add to her collection. He stayed for a time to talk about his peregrine's rapid progress, the state of the fields, the refurbishing of the armory, the litter of kittens that looked just like Black Tom, and the progress of Meg's gardens.

If one of Dominic's visits occurred when it was time to eat, he held Meg and fed her with a patience that never varied no matter how she chaffed at confinement. When it was time to sleep, they shared her canopied bed in an intimacy that was unsettling to her, but had the unexpected benefit of keeping her warm.

And when it was time to bathe . . .

Meg shivered, remembering Dominic leaning against the doorway, watching her with glittering silver eyes as she washed herself in a ritual that was as old as her first initiation into Glendruid ways. Yet for all the smoky sensuality of her husband's gaze, for all his obvious potency when they slept in the same bed, his self-discipline never varied. He touched her only to feed her, to give her drink, to warm her in the cold of the night.

For the first time in her life, Meg wished she had a leman's skills. Then she would tempt her husband so greatly that his formidable self-control would burn up like dry straw in the torch of his passion. He would take her before she bled, and in doing so find out how baseless his distrust had been.

If she had a leman's skills . . . but she did not. She had only the certainty that each day of her captivity made the people of the keep more resentful of their new Norman lord. When Harry had spoken to her the morning after her wedding, he had spoken for all of Blackthorne's people.

If the lord hurts you we'll nae stand for it. . . . Many accidents can befall a man while hunting. I promise you.

Fear coursed through Meg as she remembered Harry's words. Such an act would be a catastrophe for the keep. Simon already distrusted Blackthorne's affection for Duncan of Maxwell. If Dominic were hurt by rebellious peasants, Simon's vengeance would be more swift and savage than any his brother might devise.

Bells chimed as Meg paced her living quarters wearing golden jesses, worrying about the future of her people. Finally sounds from the bailey below distracted her, men's voices raised in exuberant cries. Even through the closed shutters the clash and clang of sword on shield was clear.

Meg went to the window. She had discovered she could open the shutters a bare crack without it being visible from below. The opening wasn't large enough to admit sunlight, but she could put her eye to the slit and watch the bailey below.

Under Dominic's keen supervision, the knights were keeping their battle skills honed. Hauberk and helm, chausses and chain mail gauntlets protected the men while they hacked and chopped with weapons that had more weight than a battle sword and no edge to speak of.

That didn't mean the swords weren't dangerous. In the hands of a strong knight, even a blunt weapon could badly wound a careless, unskilled, or unlucky opponent.

Eadith poured ale and called out encouragement to her favorites. The black-eyed Marie moved among the fighters, serving frothing mugs of ale. Even from the height of Meg's rooms, the swing and sway of the Norman woman's hips was obvious.

With eyes like green ice, Meg watched the leman approach Dominic. She stood so close to him there was no daylight between, and tilted her face up as though to a god.

When Dominic laughed at something the leman said, Meg's hands became fists. All that prevented her from opening the shutters and hurling the contents of the chamber pot at Marie's head was the certainty that Dominic hadn't bedded his leman recently. There had been no opportunity; when he wasn't tending to the keep's affairs, he was with his wife.

If she was captive to Dominic, he was also captive to *her*. The thought gave Meg a certain fierce satisfaction.

Even so, she was glad when Dominic turned away from his leman to answer a question from Simon. A moment later Dominic nodded and signaled to his squire.

Soon both brothers were fully attired for battle. When they stepped into an open space in the bailey, the contests of the other knights slowed and then halted. Even the most battle-toughened knight learned something new when the two brothers tested each other's skill.

At an unseen signal, Dominic and Simon sprang forward, wielding their heavy blades with deceptive ease. Physically the brothers were well-matched. Both were taller than was common, broader of shoulder, stronger, and quicker. It was like watching a man fight himself.

The wicked whistle of steel slicing through air made Meg hold her breath. The blows the brothers rained upon one another would have quickly felled smaller men. At first it seemed that one of them must surely give way before the onslaught. Gradually it became clear that while Dominic had a slight edge in strength, Simon had a slight edge in quickness. The only question was which man would first put to use his superior gift in a telling way.

Again and again Meg bit back a cry as it seemed certain that Dominic would catch a savage blow to the ribs or head. Each time he lifted his shield at the last instant, absorbing the blow. Then his own sword would glitter savagely as it descended, only to have Simon slip much of the blow with a lithe movement of his body. Both brothers crouched, circled, feinted, and attacked again and again, until Meg thought one of them must surely lose strength or quickness, giving the battle to the other.

"Lady," called someone softly from the hall. "Are you there? 'Tis Marta."

"The lord has forbidden anyone to speak with me for a time," Meg said reluctantly. "Hurry away before you are seen and punished."

" 'Tis Harry's wife, lady. The baby has been trying to come for near two days now, but she is too weak to push it out."

"Where is Gwyn?"

"Over to the Dale settlement trading medicines with a wise woman from the south. You are sorely needed, my lady."

Meg began stripping off gold bells from her wrists. The jewelry would only get in the way of what was to come.

"I'm on my way, Marta. Leave before you're discovered."

"Aye, lady."

There was a pause, then, "Must you take the straight way out? 'Tis sure the Norman devil's guard—er, your husband's knight will see you."

"There is another way. Now go!"

"God love you, gentle lady. I am gone."

Meg grabbed a special smock from an oddly carved chest, took the bottle from the hidden niche, and opened the door to the hall. As she stepped through the doorway, Dominic's warning echoed in her head:

You have tasted my mercy and found it sweet. But a wise man shows mercy only once to the same person. Do not fight me again, wife.

Yet she had, and now she must once more.

Without hesitation, Meg closed the door behind her and rushed down the hall. There was no other choice for her to make. Harry's wife would surely die without aid, and the babe with her.

Ignoring the curious stares of the servants, who knew well what their lord's orders had been, Meg pelted down winding stairs in a wild flurry of her remaining golden bells. She ransacked the herbal, shoving packets of herbs and tightly stoppered potions into a basket along with the painkiller, the antidote, and the smock.

Instead of climbing back up the stairs to the fore-building and the stone doorway guarded by Dominic's blond mercenary, Meg lit a small candle and went into the deepest part of the herbal. Rack upon rack of herbs, bark, stems, seeds, and flowers were drying in a darkness that the single candle flame seemed to make greater rather than to lessen.

Behind the last rack, hidden in the utter darkness and closed off by a heavy wooden wheel, there was an opening barely large enough for a kneeling man to squeeze through. It was the keep's bolthole, the last escape for the lord and his family if the place ever was overrun by enemies.

Meg put her shoulder to the wheel, pushed it

aside, and dropped to her hands and knees. A light so faint it could have been imagined rather than real showed at the farthest reach of the tunnel. She pinched out the candle, put it in the basket, and began crawling forward, pushing the basket in front of her. She had come this way many times before, when her mother was alive and used the bolthole to escape John's fury at having married a woman who would not give him heirs.

The tunnel's floor was covered with woven mats of reeds that creaked and rustled and barely cushioned the rocky stretches. Where the tunnel passed beneath the moat, the walls and floor were dank with seepage. Meg crawled as quickly as she could, for she had never liked the tunnel's clammy embrace, though she no longer feared it as she had when a child.

Despite the need to hurry, Meg waited at the far end as she had been taught to do, breathing the clean outer air and listening for anyone nearby. Nothing came back to her but a silence disturbed only by the sound of wind toying with the emerging leaves of the thicket that guarded the bolthole's exit.

Meg pushed through the tangle of shrubs and looked around the pasture. At the far corner, ewes ate spring's bounty with single-minded intensity. Around them, lambs leaped and scattered like white flowers bobbing on a green sea. Neither shepherd nor dogs were in sight. The ewes barely lifted their heads when Meg emerged from the thicket.

She hurried through the gate. Harry's home lay just over the hill, amid fields whose shining dark earth showed a frosting of green. The lane leading to the cottage wound between waist-high dry–stone walls whose rocky faces were a patchwork of lichen and moss in shades of green, black, and a rich rust. In sunny places beyond the reach of sheep or plow, gorse bloomed in bright yellow profusion. In grassy areas daffodils burst from the earth like small children set free to play.

Normally Meg would have savored the pearly light and the elegant shapes of the oaks rising naked from steep green hills, the sharp scent of gorse and the silent laughter of flowers; but today she barely noticed the signs of spring's victory over winter. She had eyes only for any obstacle in the lane that might trip her and send her sprawling, scattering the precious medicines in her basket.

Harry's cottage was of stone and timber, for his father had been a favorite knight of John's. At fourteen, Harry had been a squire well on his way to becoming a knight, but he had been crippled in the same battle that had killed his father. Instead of becoming a knight, Harry had become Blackthorne's gatekeeper and a freeholder with a tiny bit of land to call his own.

The local midwife must have been watching from the window, for she rushed out while Meg was still in the lane.

"Thank you, my lady," she said, grabbing Meg's hand and kissing it in relief. "The poor woman is at the end of her strength."

"Is there ample water?"

"Aye," the midwife said.

Her emphatic tone said she well remembered the previous birthings she had attended when Meg had been called to aid. The midwife might not understand Glendruid water rituals, but she no longer questioned them.

Meg could barely walk beneath the lintel without ducking her head. Inside, the cottage showed evidence of Adela's difficult pregnancy—cold porridge spilled and left everywhere, scraps of food even the dogs disdained left on the floor, half-rotted turnips brought from the cellar and discarded, weeks of refuse piled about waiting to be removed. After the clean air outside, the smell was like a blow.

"She is sleeping lightly," the midwife said in a low voice.

Adela's pallet was against the far wall. The mattress was the only fresh-smelling thing in the cottage, for Meg had sent herbal sachets home with Harry every fortnight.

Though only three years older than Meg, Adela looked twice her age. She had married at thirteen and produced her first babe before she was fourteen. After nine years of marriage, she had six living children and three dead.

Meg went to the hearth, poured a basin of warm water and took it outside. There she added three herbs and some slivers of the soap she made herself. Chanting softly in the silence of her mind, Meg pulled off her outer tunic with its long, narrow sleeves and thrust her hands into the basin.

> Cast off the clothes of field and keep
> Bathe away old sins and sorrows deep
> Put on the smock of Glendruid reverence
> Touch sickness with hands of health.
> Ease where you must death's slow dance.
> Aid where you may life's wealth.
> God keeps all between heaven and earth
> 'Tis for love of Him we bear the pain of birth.
> Amen.

Meg touched the cross she wore, no longer silver but gold, her mother's cross, which had lain waiting in a carved box for the daughter finally to wed.

I wish you were with me, Mother. Your hands drew pain so quickly from those who suffered.

But there was no one to take the pain from you.

Shaking the last of the scented water drops from her fingers, Meg pulled on the Glendruid smock. It was freshly made, for a smock was used once and once only at birth or sickbed; then the garment was burned in a ritual as old as that of water, basin, and herbs.

"Where are the other children?" Meg asked softly.

"The two youngest are with her sister. The rest are in the fields."

"Has no one stayed with Adela?"

The midwife shrugged. "The girls are too young. The boys are needed elsewhere for plowing and planting, both the lord's domain and that of their father. There aren't enough hands to go around. As soon as the fields are taken care of, someone will rake this lot out and put down fresh rushes."

"It must be done now."

The midwife's mouth flattened but she didn't argue. She simply went into the yard to look for a rake.

As Meg knelt by the pallet, Adela's eyes opened.

"Ah, my lady," she whispered, distressed. "I told them not to send for you. Your lord will be sorely put out with you."

"That weighs little against your need. Tell me, how goes it with you?"

As Adela began speaking in a halting voice, Meg leaned closer, eased her hands beneath the bed covering, and began to touch the woman's swollen body with gentle hands.

"WELL fought, brother," Simon said, leaning against the stone wall of the keep and breathing hard.

"No so well as you," Dominic said ruefully. "My head rings like a bell."

"And my ribs are squealing like piglets," Simon retorted.

With a laugh, Dominic swept off his helm and held it out. His squire leaped forward to take it. Across the bailey, Thomas the Strong called to Eadith to broach another barrel of ale. At Dominic's signal, knights paired off once more. Soon the keep again rang with the sound of sword on shield and the shouts of men when they successfully gave or avoided a blow.

Dominic stretched and resettled the heavy hauberk with a shift of his muscular shoulders. As he did, he looked up at the top story of the keep. All the shutters were open save two. In Meg's rooms, sunlight's warm fingers were kept out by heavy wood.

"She hasn't even cracked them to watch me whack at you," Simon said, following his brother's glance. "How much longer will you keep her shut away? Until she bleeds?"

Dominic smiled strangely. "I haven't decided. I rather enjoy keeping my wife secluded like a concubine in a harem. Feeding her from my hand is unexpectedly sweet. Eating from her hand is even sweeter."

A slanting, searching look was Simon's only answer for a moment. Then he turned to face his brother.

"Marie is right," Simon said, worry clear in his voice. "The witch has enchanted you. You have no carnal knowledge of your wife, yet you seek none of other women."

"I'm too busy gentling my small falcon."

The masculine satisfaction—and anticipation—in Dominic's voice made Simon throw up his hands.

"I don't expect you to understand," Dominic said, "so I'll tell you something you can understand."

"I pray thee," Simon retorted, "do!"

"While my wife and I are secluded together—and when she is in seclusion alone—I don't have to worry about her being seduced by a hazel-eyed Saxon with a honeyed tongue and an eye toward killing me and taking my wife and my keep."

Simon grunted.

"You may like secluding her, but the people of the keep are getting restless," Simon said bluntly. "They whisper about Duncan of Maxwell and the rescue of their mistress."

"God's teeth!" Dominic said in disgust. "I haven't harmed one fiery hair on the maid's head. I've handled her as gently as the most prized falcon ever brought to the mews."

"Then show her to them so they may see her health for themselves. And do it soon."

Dominic gave his brother a look through narrowed eyes. Simon gave it back with the confidence of a man who knows his opinion is respected even when it isn't welcome.

"Is Duncan lurking about?" Dominic asked after a moment, wondering if that was what lay behind Simon's blunt advice.

"Someone is," Simon said. "The hounds found deer slain in the far park. Nothing remained but head and heels."

"Poachers are common enough."

"Riding war-horses?" Simon asked sardonically. "They also—"

Dominic held up his hand for silence as Eadith approached with two mugs of ale. When Simon reached for one, she danced back from his hand.

"Nay, sir. 'Tis for the lord to drink first," she said boldly. "He drank little when he had dinner with his wife."

Smiling at Dominic, Eadith held a mug out to him.

"Thank you," he said, returning her courtesy despite his dislike of her pale, covetous eyes.

Dominic drank, grimaced, and finished the mug quickly. Simon drank his own ale with equal dispatch.

"I've rarely tasted worse," Dominic muttered as he handed the mug back to Eadith. "Pah. Gall would taste better."

"Must have been a sour barrel," Simon agreed. He spat. "Bitter as a witch's envy."

"Shall I bring you some fresh?" Eadith asked hurriedly.

"Not for me," Dominic said.

Simon shook his head. He, too, had had enough of Blackthorne's bitter ale.

Eadith took the mugs and rushed back across the bailey. Other men called to her for drink. They had worked up a heavy thirst fighting while wearing nearly half their own weight in sword and armor.

"There are signs," Simon continued as though nothing had interrupted him, "that Duncan and his Reevers are setting up an illegal keep less than a half day from here. Rumor has it they're building a palisades and bailey."

Silently Dominic looked at the clouds flying above the dark stones of the keep.

"Dominic?" Simon asked.

"There is nothing I can do about Duncan until the rest of my knights arrive," Dominic said bluntly. "I have enough men to hold Blackthorne Keep against attack and not one more. If I let myself be lured from the keep's safety by a handful of slain deer and rumors of illegal keeps, I'll lose both the land and my life."

Simon wanted to argue, but didn't. When it came to tactics, he deferred to his brother's expertise.

"It is bitter to admit," Simon said after a moment.

"Aye," Dominic said flatly.

He started across the bailey.

"Where are you going?" Simon asked.

"To my small falcon. She will wash away the bitterness."

THE stimulant Meg had given Adela was strong, dangerously so, but there was no other course left. If the babe weren't born soon, neither mother nor child would survive the coming night.

"I am sorry," Meg said unhappily. "I must give you nothing for the pain but a simple salve."

"It doesn't—matter," Adela panted. "Strength—is all—I ask."

Between Adela's ragged breaths and subdued groans, Meg heard the distant sounds of horses galloping and men shouting. Then Adela's labor abruptly increased in intensity, requiring Meg's full attention. She knew nothing of what happened around her but the struggles of the exhausted woman to give birth.

"Well done!" Meg said after a time. Excitement made her voice rise. "The babe's head is out! Just a little more, brave woman. Just a little more effort and then you may rest."

The door of the cottage burst open behind Meg and the laboring Adela. Ignoring the strident protests of the midwife, Dominic ducked under the lintel and strode into the cottage with sword drawn. The honed edge of the blade shone malevolently.

His silver eyes searched the cottage's single room with the speed and precision of an eagle seeking prey, but it was his ears that found Meg first in the gloomy cottage. The muted chiming of her golden jesses gave her away. She was kneeling at a pallet wearing only an odd shift.

Fury lanced through Dominic at this proof that

gossip had been correct. Meg had escaped her luxurious captivity in order to lie with Duncan of Maxwell,
a man who had neither nobility nor land.

By God, lady, you will rue the—

A baby's first, tremulous cry cut off Dominic's
silent vow. He stood as though transfixed. Relief
drove the raging anger from his body, leaving him
feeling almost weak. For the first time he noticed
the bitter taste that coated his mouth.

He swallowed, then swallowed again, but his
mouth was too dry to wash away the taste of the
foul ale. He sheathed his sword with a fumbling
motion that would have surprised Simon had he
been there to see it.

"You have given Harry a fine new son," Meg said
to Adela as she finished clearing the baby's mouth
and nostrils. "Take him to your breast, though he
likely won't nurse. He is as weary as you."

"Thank you," Adela said raggedly. "Now go—
before your lord—discovers."

"Her lord has already discovered," Dominic said.

Meg's startled cry was lost beneath Simon's shout
from the yard.

"Dominic?" Simon cried again. "Is all well?"

"I have found her!" Dominic called over his shoulder.

Before he could add anything, Simon burst into
the cabin with his sword drawn.

"Stand down," Dominic said calmly. "All is well.
The falcon flew not to Duncan's wrist."

"Then why did she break her vow to you? Why
did she—"

Whatever questions Simon had were answered by
the baby's trembling cry.

"By God," Simon said, sheathing his sword in a
single smooth stroke. " 'Tis a new babe."

The midwife pushed past Simon into the room

with total disregard for his superior strength, status, and weaponry.

"Nay," she said angrily. " 'Tis a miracle. The poor woman labored in vain for two days. Only when I told her the babe would die before supper—and she with it!—did she allow me to send for your lady."

Dominic's eyes narrowed as he turned to Meg. "Is that true? Has she had a long labor?"

Adela moaned softly.

"Yes," Meg said as she turned again to Adela. "Now leave, husband, and take your brother with you. This poor woman's work is not yet finished. And it is *woman's* work."

Under the hostile eyes of the midwife, Dominic and Simon retreated from the cottage. The light outside hit Dominic like a blow.

"God's teeth," he muttered, shielding his face. "Not since Jerusalem have I seen such blinding sunlight."

Simon gave his brother an odd look. "You must have drunk too much ale. The light is no different from any other cloudy day in Cumbriland."

When Dominic squeezed his eyes shut to close out the painful light, dizziness and a strange languor crept through him, stealing his power. Distantly he realized that his strength was draining away one heartbeat at a time. Taking a step was difficult.

He stumbled and barely righted himself.

"Dominic?" Simon said in disbelief.

Again Dominic staggered. This time he almost didn't catch his balance before he fell.

"God's blood, man," Simon said, appalled. "Are you in your cups?"

"Nay," Dominic said thickly.

Trying to dispel the maddening slowness of his thoughts and tongue, he shook his head fiercely.

Instead of helping him, the movement increased his dizziness.

"Simon, I . . ."

This time it was only his brother's strong arms that prevented Dominic from going to his knees.

"Is it your skull?" Simon asked urgently. "Did I truly hit you that hard?"

Dominic shook his head. It was a mistake. He made a thick sound and sagged against his brother.

"Can you walk?" Simon asked.

"Yes . . ." Dominic said in a hoarse voice.

"Then do so," Simon commanded. *"Now."*

With a great effort, Dominic forced himself to walk toward the war stallions that waited a hundred feet beyond the cottage yard. Mounting Crusader was almost impossible, but finally it was accomplished with the help of Simon's strength.

Once in the saddle, Dominic reeled as though he were on the deck of a storm-lashed ship instead of sitting on the back of a motionless horse. While Simon watched in growing fear, his brother's left foot slipped from the stirrup.

Dominic was fast losing his senses. There was no way he would be able to ride even the short distance to the keep.

"Hold, Crusader," Simon commanded as he caught up the charger's single rein.

Without ado, Simon vaulted on behind his brother. Crusader's ears half flattened at the double load, but the stallion made no further protest. All battle horses were trained to accept double and even triple riders if it came to that, for survivors carried off their injured friends even in the heat of battle. Dominic had once borne Simon to safety on Crusader's back.

"Hang on," Simon said.

"Wait . . ." Dominic mumbled. "Meg."

The words were so slurred it took Simon a moment to understand. When he did, his lips flattened into a silent snarl.

"I'll see to the witch later," Simon said.

"Not . . . safe."

Ignoring his brother, Simon turned Crusader quickly toward the keep. Within three strides, the charger was covering ground at a fast canter. A shrill whistle brought Simon's own well-trained mount cantering behind.

"Meg," Dominic said urgently.

"Burn the witch!" Simon snarled. "Now you know why it was so important for her to go to the cursed place to gather leaves."

"Meg . . . ?" Dominic groaned.

"Aye, brother. Meg. Somehow the hell-witch poisoned you."

Simon's spurs goaded Crusader, sending the stallion into a hard gallop.

By the time they reached the keep, Dominic was lost to an unnatural sleep.

 17

"**W**HAT DO YOU MEAN, I MAY not enter?" Meg demanded. "He is my husband!"

"Aye," Simon said bitterly. "A husband you didn't want. You have done every evil thing within your power to defeat Dominic."

"That's not true!"

Golden bells sang with the controlled fierceness of Meg's movements as she spun aside to get around Simon. He moved very quickly, blocking her entrance to Dominic's quarters. She feinted to the other side, then darted forward. Mail-clad gauntlets closed painfully around her wrists. The handle of the basket she carried cut into her palm.

"Don't try my patience, witch," Simon said savagely. "I know what use you had for the plants you gathered in that cursed place. It was sickness and death you sought, not life and health."

Meg's eyes widened into startled pools of green. "What are you saying?"

"Poison, you cursed witch. You poisoned my brother!"

"Nay! Never! Do you hear me? *Never!*"

"Save your lies for your lover, Duncan of Maxwell," Simon spat.

Meg bit her lip against a cry of pain. The force of Simon's fingers closing around her wrists was like being caught between stones. Her breaths came deep and hard, for she had run the entire way from Harry's cottage, driven by a fear such as she had never felt outside of her dreams.

"I went to your room," Simon continued relentlessly. "I checked the niche. The potion you fought my brother to make is gone."

"I took it with me," Meg said quickly. "I knew Adela would be weak. I was afraid the midwife might have given her too much medicine to kill the pain and thereby slowed the birth. The potion would have countered such weakness, not created it."

Simon looked at Meg's clear, anxious eyes and wanted to crush the Glendruid witch between his hands like an empty eggshell. Only the certainty that Dominic—if he lived—would never forgive the loss of his wife stayed Simon's fury.

"You lie very well," he said through his teeth.

"I lie very badly," she retorted. "Ask anyone. Now let me by. If Dominic is ill, I can ease him."

"Nay. You'll not get close to him while I draw breath."

Meg bit back the desire to scream at Simon, for she knew it would accomplish nothing but to release the rage that burned so visibly within him. Several deep breaths went by before she trusted herself to speak calmly despite the wild urgency clawing deep in her mind.

"All Harry said was that you came galloping up to the keep as though the devil were a step behind," Meg said carefully.

"We left the devil at Harry's cottage."

She kept talking as though Simon had said nothing.

"Dominic could neither talk nor sit his horse," Meg continued. "You and Thomas the Strong carried him to the lord's quarters. That was all Harry knew."

Simon said nothing.

"Please," Meg whispered. "I beg of you. I sensed danger and I ran here and was told Dominic had been felled by a blow to the head from your sword."

Simon fought to control his temper. "Watch your tongue, vile witch."

Vile.

Witch.

Meg realized Simon wouldn't let her go to Dominic no matter how carefully she pleaded. A wild anger swept through her.

"Why should I watch my tongue?" she demanded. "Does the truth hurt so much? Or are you hoping to inherit the keep if Dominic dies and thus don't want me to tend him?"

The accusation was so unexpected that Simon was struck speechless. Meg suffered no such handicap. She wrested her hands free of his grasp and continued flaying him with her tongue.

"If that is so, my brave knight," she said with fierce disdain, "hear me now. I will tear down Blackthorne Keep stone by stone with my own hands and poison the well before I let you profit by your brother's untimely death!"

"Hell-witch," Simon whispered. "I would slay a man for even suggesting that I was such a cowardly villain."

Simon's voice reminded Meg of Dominic at his most coldly furious. At any other time she would have bowed to the male anger and withdrawn, but not now. Dominic was dying. Next to that, nothing mattered.

Hell-witch.

Meg's free hand came up and ripped the frail Glendruid smock from neck to waist, revealing the fine, creamy skin and the smooth swell of her breasts. Between them shone the golden cross that had once been her mother's.

"Could a true witch wear God's cross?" Meg demanded. "Could she?"

For three long breaths there was silence.

"No," Simon admitted finally.

With one gauntleted hand he carefully pulled the smock's edges together, covering Meg's breasts completely.

Meg waited, but still Simon made no move to step aside.

"Let me by, Simon the Loyal. Use your brains instead of your brawny arms to aid your brother. Who else in this keep can help Dominic but me?"

There was a taut silence while Simon stared at the girl with the uncanny green eyes. Ever since he had come to Blackthorne Keep, the vassals had told anyone who would listen what a magic touch Meg had with the sick or the wounded. They called her Glendruid witch.

White witch.

A cross lay cool between her breasts. Dominic lay ill unto death.

Never had Simon been more frightened for his brother, not even when Dominic had ransomed twelve knights by turning himself over to a sultan whose cruelty to Christians had to be endured to be believed.

"If my brother dies," Simon vowed quietly, "you will die by my hands an instant after Dominic draws his last breath. I swear this before God."

"So be it," Meg agreed, sealing the vow.

Surprise showed in the fierce lines of Simon's face.

He had expected many things from his brother's witch-wife, but not such unflinching acceptance of danger to herself. Whatever else might be said of her, she didn't lack courage.

Simon stepped away from the door. Before he could turn around, Meg was in the room and leaning over Dominic's canopied bed. A huge fire burned in the hearth, making the room hot.

"He barely breathes," Meg said in a low voice.

She touched Dominic's skin. Her breath caught in the vise of her clenched throat.

"Dear God . . . 'tis cool as water."

Bending low over Dominic, she breathed in deeply of the air he had just exhaled. A stillness came over her body. She forced air from her lungs, then breathed in deeply again.

Simon stood without moving, listening to the small golden bells Meg wore shiver and murmur among themselves as though mourning for their dying lord.

Slowly Meg straightened, pushing aside hair that had come free during the wild run from Harry's cottage. A golden cascade of music trembled in the silence from the long chains of bells still tied around her half-unraveled braids.

"Lady?" called Eadith from beyond the door. "Here is the water and smock you requested."

"Get it from her," Meg said in a low voice. "Do not let her in. She has a taste for gossip. If the Reevers were to hear that Dominic was ill . . ."

Simon was turning away before Meg finished her sentence. The door shut quite rudely on Eadith's anxious questions.

"Put bowl and smock by the hearth," Meg said quickly. "Then turn your back while I prepare myself."

Without waiting to see whether Simon watched

or turned away, Meg ripped off the used smock and threw it into the fire, whispering the old chant beneath her breath. She threw a mixture of soap and herbs into the basin and bathed herself hurriedly, chanting so quickly that the words ran together like a waterfall. When nothing remained on her skin but the astringent scent of herbs, she pulled the new smock into place and turned around.

Simon's back was to her.

"I'm finished. Now tell me what happened," Meg said. "Think carefully but quickly. Dominic's life hangs by a very thin thread. If I give him the wrong medicine he will certainly die. If I give him the right medicine, he could very well die anyway. When did you first notice he was unwell?"

Simon turned to face Meg. His breath came in as though at a blow. It wasn't Meg's words that surprised him; it was the slow, soundless fall of her tears down her cheeks.

"When he came out of Harry's cottage," Simon said simply. "Dominic said the light was as bright as Jerusalem, but it wasn't. It was the same as it had been when we entered the cottage."

Meg's lips thinned, but she said nothing, only listened as though Dominic's very life depended upon it.

"Then he stumbled and began talking as though drunk," Simon continued.

A sharp movement of Meg's hand dismissed that possibility. She knew Dominic well enough to know he would never yield his self-control to ale.

"He staggered, righted himself, and then would have fallen if I hadn't caught him," Simon said. "His eyes looked very strange."

"How so?" Meg asked sharply.

"Their centers were so wide his eyes looked as black as mine."

"Did he eat or drink anything in your presence?"

"Food? No. He ate with you. We had a mug of ale." Simon grimaced as he remembered the taste. "It was a bitter brew."

"Did you share the same mug?"

"No."

"Then what happened?"

"Dominic said he was going to his small falcon to take the bitter taste from his mouth. But when he got to your room, you were gone."

"You say your ale was bitter, too?"

"Yes."

"But you felt no dizziness or languor, no need to hide your eyes from light?"

"I'm tired and somewhat slow for such a mild workout with sword and shield. And . . ." Simon frowned. "Odd, but my ribs don't hurt as they should. 'Tis rather pleasant, actually."

Meg's eyes closed against the fear that was clenching her heart. There had been enough pain medicine in the missing bottle to kill many knights. Obviously Simon hadn't drunk enough to be in danger. The same couldn't be said for Dominic.

"Send to the garrison quickly," Meg said. "Find if any other knight is ill. I fear the ale was poisoned."

Simon stuck his head out the door. Dominic's squire hadn't moved from the place he had found earlier, when he had been thrown out of the room. Jameson sat on the floor at the end of the hall, his head in his hands and fear plain on his young face.

While Simon gave clipped orders, Meg pulled the antidote from her basket, eased the stopper from the bottle, and tipped a scant amount into a bowl of water that sat near Dominic's bed. As she started to stopper the bottle once more, she hesitated. Her husband was an uncommonly large man. She added a few more drops of the bright amber potion, and then a few more after that, before she set the bowl on the table and concentrated on the man who lay so still upon the bed.

"Dominic," Meg said in a clear, commanding voice. "Arise. Your brother is in danger!"

There was no response from Dominic. He lay pale and slack, his breath slow and shallow.

"Am I in danger?" Simon asked calmly from behind Meg.

"No. But of all that Dominic holds dear, you are the dearest. If danger to anything would rouse him, it would be danger to you."

Simon was too surprised by Meg's insight to respond. He simply watched as she bent over his brother and shook him to no effect.

Without warning her hand lifted. The sound of the slap seemed as loud as a thunderclap in the room. Simon caught himself even as he started forward to prevent Meg's hand from slapping Dominic's other cheek. Much as he disliked seeing his helpless brother pummeled, he had no better idea of how to rouse him.

"Dominic," she said loudly, slapping him again. "Hear me. You must awaken! Simon has his back to the wall! He needs you!"

For a moment Meg thought Dominic might have responded, but the motion was too small for her to be certain. With tears running down her face, she raised her hand and slapped him soundly once more.

"Lord! Your brother is wounded! The keep is under siege! Awaken now or you will never have a son!"

Dominic's hand twitched as though reaching for a sword, but after that single, futile movement, he lay motionless. Holding her breath, Meg waited for any further sign of response.

There was none.

" 'Tis no use," she whispered. "He is too deep for mere words to reach him."

Simon hissed a blasphemous phrase.

"Quickly," Meg ordered without looking away from Dominic. "Lift him so that he might drink."

Simon pulled his brother upright. Meg held the bowl to his lips and tipped it. Liquid ran from the corners of Dominic's mouth. His head lolled to one side, further wasting the precious medicine. Desperately, Meg tried again, but to no better effect. The metal bowl clanged against Dominic's teeth.

"No more," Simon said roughly, easing his brother back onto the bed. "He's as slack as a dead eel."

Meg didn't bother to answer. She put her fingertip between Dominic's lips, slid along his teeth to the corner of his mouth, and from there behind his molars as though she were getting a horse to accept a bit.

Dominic's mouth opened slightly. Meg tipped in a bit of the potion, but more ran out the corner of his mouth than went behind his teeth.

"He swallowed!" Simon said eagerly.

"Yes, but too much is wasted. I haven't enough to do him any good if so much is lost each time."

"How long will it take to make more?"

"A fortnight. The plants must grow. I left only enough leaves to keep the roots alive."

"God's eyes," Simon hissed. "Are you certain?"

Meg's only answer was the slow, relentless glide of tears down her cheeks. Beneath her outward calm, the knowledge that Blackthorne Keep lived or died with Dominic was like an acid eating into her soul.

War again. Yet God promised man that there was a time for all things under the sun. We have seen the time of hatred, of plucking up that which was sown, of battle and disease and death.

Surely there must be a time for harvest, for babes, for love and renewal, for peace.

More medicine trickled into Dominic's mouth . . . and trickled right out again.

With an oath, Simon stripped off his gauntlets, threw them to the floor, and began pacing like a caged wolf.

"Think," he said urgently. "There must be a way to get it down him. A spoon?"

"Send for one," Meg said.

But there was no real hope in her voice. Dominic needed more medicine, and more quickly, than dripping in with a spoon would allow. Then she remembered another way to take—and give—liquid.

Small falcon. Drink from my lips.

A shudder went over Meg. The amber medicine was very potent. Even holding it in her mouth was a terrible risk. If she swallowed, she would likely die.

And Dominic would surely die if something weren't done. Quickly.

"Stay with me, Simon," she commanded.

Startled, he spun toward Meg.

"Help me lift Dominic just a bit," she said.

With Simon's help, Meg eased one arm beneath Dominic's head and shoulders. The coolness of his hair slid against her wrist and his head settled heavily in the crook of her arm.

"Hold his head tilted back," Meg said. "No, not that much. As though he were looking up at the horizon. Aye! Hold there."

Any lingering uneasiness Simon might have had about the nature of the medicine Meg wanted to administer vanished when she took a mouthful of the liquid herself. She didn't swallow. She simply opened Dominic's mouth again and gave him a small bit of the medicine from between her own lips, sending a few drops of liquid over his tongue so that he must swallow or choke.

Dominic swallowed.

"Aye!" Simon said excitedly. "Well done!"

Quickly Meg gave Dominic another few drops to drink from her lips. Again the drops slid over his tongue, triggering a need to swallow, which he did without hesitation.

The third time, Meg was more bold. She put her mouth against Dominic's partly opened one, pursed her lips, and fed him a gentle stream of medicine. He swallowed again and yet again. When her mouth was empty, she quickly took more medicine and returned to feeding her husband until there was nothing left in the cup.

As Simon watched the gentleness with which Meg gave Dominic the medicine, he silently admitted that he had been too harsh in his opinion of her. Like the tears that had not ceased their slow welling, her actions told Simon that despite the gossip, Meg felt no hatred toward her husband.

In fact, had Simon not been certain that the marriage was unconsummated, he would have sworn that real affection existed between his brother and the Glendruid witch. She was as tender toward Dominic as a mother to her babe.

"His breathing," Meg said urgently. "Does it seem slower than it was?"

The hope that had been uncurling in Simon froze as he realized Meg was correct. Dominic's breath was definitely slowing.

"I wasn't in time!" she cried. "Dear God, I wasn't in time!"

Meg flung the bowl into the floor and reached out to shake her husband's shoulders.

"You must breathe!" she said urgently. "You simply must!"

As though she would give him air as surely as she had given him medicine, Meg bent to her husband once more.

"Take back the breath of life," she whispered. *"Take it."*

She sealed her mouth over Dominic's and forced her own breath into his body again and again when he breathed too shallowly and too slowly for himself.

Astonished, Simon held his brother and watched for long minutes as Meg fought for every breath Dominic took. Her determination that he live was so great that it was almost tangible.

A tingling sensation went down Simon's spine, a primal recognition of a will as deeply trained and disciplined as that of Dominic himself. Except for his brother, Simon had never encountered such strength of purpose. He hadn't even believed it existed.

Simon sensed Dominic stirring almost as soon as Meg did. She gave him a final breath and collapsed onto her knees with her cheek against his chest, trembling from an effort that was as much mental as physical.

"Does he—breathe?" she panted.

"Aye. Slowly, but not fearfully so. And he draws air more deeply."

The breath Meg took was almost a sob. She lifted her head. Dominic was less pale now. She touched his cheek. His skin was warming where it once had been cool. Yet still his breaths came with painful slowness.

Meg watched anxiously, knowing the antidote should have had more effect. Made from new leaves, it had twice the potency of medicine made in summer.

"Sir," called Dominic's squire from the hall door. "A few of the knights are a bit slow, but none complain of it. They simply say the ale was unusually strong."

Simon looked at Meg.

"If they were going to succumb, they would have done so by now," she said without looking away from Dominic.

"Go back to your post," Simon said. "We'll call you if we need anything else."

The squire hesitated. "Sir?"

"Dominic is getting better with every breath," Simon said through a false smile. "Tell the people of the keep that their lord will be well on the morrow."

Jameson's relief was clear. "Thank you, sir."

The squire turned to go, then turned back. "I almost forgot. Thomas the Strong wants to know if he should let the drawbridge back down in the morning."

"Nay," Simon said flatly. "I want no coming or going."

"Yes, sir!"

Beneath Simon's baleful eyes, the squire retreated with more speed than ceremony. When Simon turned back to the bed, he saw Meg's fear written in her pale face. Her hand was resting on Dominic's heart, but it was his breathing that frightened her.

"It isn't enough," she whispered. "He'll die before he wakes. I must risk it."

"What? You aren't making sense."

Ignoring Simon's question, Meg pushed to her feet. As she reached for the small, stoppered bottle, her foot kicked the bowl she had thrown aside in her fear. She picked up the cool metal, filled it half full of water, and upended the bottle until nothing of the brilliant amber liquid remained.

When Meg turned back to the bed, Simon moved aside to give her more room. Her fingertip slid along

Dominic's mouth, which opened more readily this time. She drank from the bowl of potent medicine, bent to him, and fed the precious liquid onto his tongue.

After the first searing mouthful, it went quickly, for Dominic was less in the thrall of the poison with every heartbeat that speeded the medicine through his body. When Meg bent to him for the last mouthful, he drew the medicine from her lips as naturally as a babe taking nourishment from his mother's breast.

Even when the bowl was empty, Meg lingered over the final drops, for Dominic had taught her to enjoy the intimacy and warmth of his mouth.

After a final gliding pressure of her tongue over his gave Dominic both a caress and the last drop of medicine, Meg straightened. When she realized that Simon was watching her with a combination of compassion and surprise, she flushed. Without a word she went to the water pitcher, rinsed the bowl, and then rinsed her own mouth thoroughly.

Despite Meg's care, enough of the potent medicine had seeped into her body that she found it impossible to be still. She paced the room with quick strides that set golden bells to singing. When that was not enough to ease her, she grabbed the stone bottle and rolled it between her palms as though it was a cool, soothing river pebble.

Simon watched Meg, then his brother, then Meg once more.

"What next?" Simon said.

"We wait."

"Until . . . ?"

"Until one or the other medicine wins," Meg said simply.

Simon looked at the bottle in Meg's hands. The careless way she held it told him that nothing of value remained. There was no more medicine to give.

"When will we know?"

"I can't say," Meg whispered. "Any man less strong would have died twice by now."

"Twice?"

"Aye," she said curtly. "Once from the poison. Once from the medicine to counter it. 'Tis a stimulant strong enough to make a swine jump over the keep's highest wall."

"Is that why you're pacing like a squire before his first battle?"

Meg nodded her head.

"Are you at risk?" Simon demanded.

"I don't know. If Dominic awakens and I'm not—" Meg's words stopped abruptly. "Give him water and more water until he can take not one more drop. It will help to purge his flesh of any remaining poison."

Simon released his brother and went quickly to Meg. "Is there nothing you can take for yourself?"

"No. I haven't Dominic's great strength. I would lose the tug-of-war between the two most potent medicines Glendruid knows."

When she saw the concern in Simon, Meg smiled despite the too-rapid breaths that the medicine was forcing upon her. Her heart speeded wildly.

"Don't worry. The stimulant—spends itself—quickly."

Meg's jerky words and breathing did nothing to reassure Simon.

"You should have told me to give the medicine to Dominic," he said. "Or is the method a Glendruid secret?"

She laughed oddly and paced even more quickly, setting bells to jangling wildly.

"Glendruid?" she said. "No. Dominic taught me."

Simon looked startled.

"You see, my husband wants a son more than he wants anything on earth or in Heaven. He plans my seduction with the care he planned his most grueling battles."

Bells cried urgently as Meg spun to pace the room again. Like her walk, her words were quick and nearly wild.

"But a son is not mine to give or withhold. When Dominic understands that, he will hate me as savagely as ever a man hated a woman."

Bells jerked and screamed in tiny golden voices that made the hair on Simon's neck rise.

"Glendruid," Meg said raggedly. "Curse and hope in one. Every Glendruid girl has borne the curse. None has borne the hope."

Before Simon could answer, Meg began to breathe like a charger after a long race to battle. Her steps became shorter and shorter until she was all but running in place while bells trembled and cried with a ghastly music. Gasping, shaking, Meg tried to stay upright while the stimulant raged through her body like lightning.

Simon caught Meg and held her when she would have fallen. She gasped convulsively yet seemed to get no air. As he watched her struggles, he realized how badly he had misunderstood his brother's wife.

"God forgive me," Simon said, shaken. "I thought you wanted Dominic dead. Yet you risked yourself to give him a chance at life."

Meg didn't hear. There was a savage cacophony in her brain. She lifted her hands to tear at her hair, but Simon prevented her. She fought with incredible strength before she realized what she was doing. Clenching her teeth, she stopped fighting and let the stimulant rage through her body.

The seizure passed as quickly as it came. With a shuddering sigh, Meg slumped against Simon.

"Meg?" he asked, forgetting formality in his need to know that she was all right.

"The worst is spent," she said.

A low voice called from the bed. Meg pushed away from Simon's support and stumbled to her husband's side.

"Dominic?" she said urgently.

His eyes opened, but he did not see her. Sounds poured from his mouth, but they were only that—sounds without meaning.

Meg gave an anguished cry.

"God forgive me. I have saved his body but his mind is gone!"

18

FOR A MOMENT SIMON DIDN'T understand why Meg was so upset. When he did, he bit back a laugh of relief and triumph and tried to soothe her.

"Nay, Meg. You saved all of him."

"Are you mad? Can't you hear that babble?"

"Yes. I never thought to savor the speech of my enemy, but God, it is sweet!"

Meg looked at Simon as though she feared he, too, had lost his wits.

"He is speaking Turkish," Simon said.

And then he laughed until the walls rang.

Meg smiled rather uncertainly as she watched the blond warrior who at times reminded her almost painfully of her own husband.

"Turkish?" she asked when Simon stopped laughing. "Then his words have meaning?"

"Yes."

"What is he saying?"

Simon listened, hesitated, and gave Meg a rueful look.

"Er, he's talking about a certain sultan's ancestors."

"Ancestors?"

"Somewhat, yes. Donkeys, baboons, slime, and, er, excrement."

"I fear the poison went to your head after all," Meg said unhappily. "You make no more sense than your brother."

A smile flashed across Simon's face, increasing his resemblance to Dominic until Meg felt as though her breath would stop. Only at that moment did she admit to herself how much she feared she would never see her own husband's smile again. She would willingly wear bells and be fed from his hand for the next year if it meant that Dominic would be sane and healthy again.

"The sultan was an unpleasant man," Simon said.

"Much the same is said of all Turks."

A torrent of words from the bed made both people turn to Dominic. The only word Meg recognized was Simon's name. The distress in Dominic, however, needed no words to be understood. She sat on the bed and pressed Dominic's hand between hers.

"Rest, Dominic," Meg said clearly and calmly. "You are safe."

"Simon. Simon! He is taken."

Though spoken in a low voice, Dominic's cry was as urgent as a shout. Simon took his brother's left hand and squeezed as though to imprint his presence on Dominic's flesh.

"I am here," Simon said. "You ransomed me from that pit of Hell. I'm safe, brother, and so are you."

Dominic cried out again, but with less urgency. Then he was still but for the restless movements of his body.

"What happened in Jerusalem?" Meg asked in a low voice.

"Twelve knights were captured. I was one of them. We were given as a gift to a sultan whose name none of us could pronounce, so we called him Beelzebub. Dominic ransomed us."

"It must have cost dearly."

"More than any of us know."

Meg gave Simon a quick look, caught by something grim lying beneath his simple words.

"What do you mean?" she asked.

"The sultan didn't care about twelve infidel knights. There was only one infidel whose mettle he wanted to test."

"Dominic?" Meg whispered.

Simon nodded. "Aye. Dominic le Sabre."

"What happened?"

"Dominic gave himself to the sultan in our place."

Meg's eyes widened. "Dear God."

"God had little to do with the sultan. A more cruel man never drew breath. Some men like women. Some like boys. Some like giving pain. Beelzebub lived to break men stronger and more decent than he was. He had developed a rather astonishing variety of tools for that purpose."

A shudder went through Meg.

"The hand you hold bears the mark of the sultan," Simon said. "If your marriage were normal, you would have seen still more scars on your husband's body."

Meg turned back toward Dominic. His hand was much larger than hers, stronger, hard with the uses of war; yet he had touched her with great gentleness.

Delicately, Meg's fingertips traced scars long ago healed. When she came to Dominic's fingers, her breath stopped. She had seen enough accidents with axes or stones to recognize the marks of a finger that had been smashed and had healed, but not completely. His smallest finger had only half the nail it should. His next nail held deep dents.

"It's the same on this hand," Simon said. "Pulling

out Dominic's nails was the least of what the sultan did."

A low sound of pain came from Meg. She held her husband's hand and stroked it as though simple touch could somehow take back the cruelties of the past.

"How did Dominic win free?" Meg asked after a moment.

"When word went out of what had happened, knights from all lords and lands gathered. When we were finished, not one stone of the sultan's great castle was left standing."

"And the sultan?"

"He was dead when we found him."

Again, it was Simon's voice rather than his words that told Meg the most. And his smile was like a preview of Hell.

"How?" she asked starkly.

"It was difficult to tell. You see, Beelzebub amused himself with his harem when there were no fresh infidels to torture."

Meg waited, afraid to breathe.

"While the sultan's guards were otherwise occupied, Dominic grabbed the sultan, threw him into the women's quarters, and locked the door."

Simon saw the shock on Meg's face and smiled again.

"My brother," Simon said softly, "always understands a man's weak points. There was nothing he could do to the sultan that would have been half so cruel or inventive as the punishment meted out by concubines who had waited a lifetime for the opportunity."

Dominic moved restlessly, groaned, and grabbed his shoulder. He cursed in English and Turkish, raging at a knight called Robert the Cuckold.

"What is it?" Meg asked, looking at Simon.

"Robert married a Norman wench raised in Sicily. She had a taste for men. Many of them. Robert thought Dominic was one of them, and led us into ambush."

"Dominic was wounded?"

Simon nodded. "He killed Robert and offered Marie his protection. It was the only way to keep peace among his knights."

Meg's mouth flattened as she realized how the leman had come to be among Dominic's retainers.

"How clever of Dominic to sacrifice himself for the honor of his knights," she said sardonically.

"Dominic could hardly sell Marie as a slave to a sultan, could he?"

"Why not?" Meg muttered. "From what I've seen, the wench was born for the harem."

"You should be grateful to her."

The sidelong look Meg gave Simon made him struggle not to smile.

"Without Marie—and the eager Eadith, of course—Dominic's knights would be causing havoc among the keep's unwilling maids. Normans are not well liked here."

"Give us time," Meg said dryly. "That's a fine, strapping lot of knights Dominic has, stout of arm and thick of head. I'm sure the maids will weaken soon."

"Do you think so?" Simon asked wistfully.

"Why not? In the dark, 'tis impossible to tell Norman from Scots or Saxon."

Simon laughed outright. "You will run Dominic a merry race, Meg. It will do him good. He is too cold since Jerusalem."

Smiling slightly, Meg turned aside and poured water into the metal bowl. When the cool metal rim touched Dominic's lips, he turned away with an impatient jerk of his head.

"My brother may be delirious," Simon said in a dry tone, "but he isn't stupid. He would rather take liquid from warm lips than cold metal."

Color stained Meg's cheeks as she took a mouthful of water, bent over Dominic, and offered him drink from her lips. It took no coaxing to gain his attention. As soon as her mouth brushed his, he turned hungrily toward her. Not until two bowls had been drunk did he get restless and begin his verbal rambling again.

This time the words were in English. Meg found herself wishing they were not.

" . . . endless bloody slaughter. James, dead. John the Small, dead. Ivar the Heathen, dead. Stewart the Red . . ."

Dominic's voice was that of a monk chanting an alien mass. While name after name fell from her husband's lips, Meg leaned over and stroked his head as though to soothe a fevered child.

But it wasn't fever that drove Dominic, nor was he a child. He was a man who had known the gore of swords slashing and hacking, the havoc of lance and charger churning through men afoot, the slow wasting of siege and disease until children starved and women fought with cats over rats as thin as shadows.

Dominic recited the roll call of the starving, maimed, and dead repeatedly until Meg thought she would scream if she heard one more name.

"There must be peace!"

Meg thought it was her own cry until the echo came back and she knew it was her husband's voice.

"Do you hear me, Simon? There must be peace!"

"Aye," Simon said clearly. "You will bring peace to your land, Dominic. I know it as surely as I know the sun will rise on the morrow."

When Dominic cried out again, Simon answered

in the same way, trying to reach past the delirium of poison so that his brother could rest.

Dominic's pain, so well shielded when he was in control of himself, made Meg ache with compassion and something more, the enduring Glendruid hope that was her birthright and curse.

No matter his motive, he touched me with great kindness. He was driven by a need as great as mine, yet he wooed rather than demanded.

He could have slain every Saxon in the keep, yet he stayed his hand.

Peace, not war.

Dear God, would that I had the power to grant Dominic's greatest desire.

Yet Meg could not, and she knew it: the fabled Glendruid son would be born of love and love alone. She might feel a woman's normal passion for a man, she might feel compassion for her husband's past suffering, she might respect his intelligence, discipline, and ambition, she might grieve for all that could have been between them had she seen him less clearly and had he seen her more so; *but she could not make herself love a man who could not love her in return.*

It was too much to ask of any woman. It was simply beyond her ability . . . as love was beyond his ability.

Meg brought Dominic's hand to her lips and held it there while the tears she couldn't stem fell from her cheeks to his fingers. All of Dominic's hopes were for naught, as were Glendruid's. She was like every Glendruid woman before her.

Cursed.

"Dominic changed after being the sultan's captive," Simon said in a low voice. "He had always been a wise soldier, but he became both brilliant and utterly ruthless. He planned each battle with great care. Not simply to win, but to destroy as little as possible in the process. Yet what he did destroy . . ."

Simon's voice faded, then strengthened. "What he did ruin was laid waste in such a way as never to be made whole again."

Meg brushed her lips over Dominic's palm.

"There is an unnerving coldness in him now," Simon continued. "No matter how greatly provoked, he will show mercy to the wise because it is intelligent to do so. To fools he shows only the sharp edge of his sword, no matter how minor the offense."

Silently Meg kissed Dominic's palm again and wondered whether he would call her wise or foolish after she had broken her word to him to stay in her rooms.

"When Dominic walked away from the wasteland that had once been the sultan's domain," Simon said, "my brother vowed that he would get land of his own at the farthest edge of the civilized world, away from the ambitions of kings and popes and sultans. He would husband that land so carefully there would be neither famine nor want. And then Dominic vowed to take a noble wife and breed strong sons who would also breed strong sons."

"So that something of his accomplishments would live forever?" Meg asked.

Simon shook his head. "Dominic learned that peace is possible only for the strong. For the weak, peace is naught but a cruel dream, and he would have no more of cruel dreams."

Land, a noble wife, sons . . . and peace. Above all, peace.

The litany of Dominic's desire rang through Meg's mind as she looked at the lines pain had drawn on her husband's face. In silence she raged against the malice of circumstance and men, the irony of Dominic's marriage to a Glendruid wife like a knife turning in her heart.

You have earned peace, land, a noble wife. . . . Of all women on earth why did God send you to me?

"Will he have sons of you?" Simon asked.

Meg's only answer was the soundless flow of her tears. She held Dominic's palm pressed to her cheek when he began talking again, returning to the sultan's carefully wrought hell.

For a long time she listened to Dominic's delirious nightmare and his equally delirious dream of peace. The pained cries that would never have escaped his lips if he were awake tore at her heart.

Watching Dominic and hearing the echoes of his old agony taught Meg that the Norman warrior who had condensed out of the mist beyond Blackthorne Keep wasn't the cold, invincible force she had believed. He was a man who had been brutally used by life. She wept for him and for the fate that had mated him to a woman who couldn't give him the dream he had earned at such great cost.

Finally Dominic fell silent. Slowly his breathing deepened and his body relaxed.

"Is he all right?" Simon asked.

"Yes. He is sleeping now, a true sleep."

Simon watched the lines of strain fade from Meg's face as surely as they had from Dominic's when he slept. With a soft prayer of thanks, Simon stroked back the thick black hair from Dominic's forehead. The gesture said much about the affection between the two brothers, a bond that went deeper than the accident of a shared father.

"It is so strange," Meg whispered.

"What is?"

"Duncan touched John that way," she said without thinking.

The gentleness Simon had displayed vanished.

"Duncan," Simon said in a low, savage voice. "I'll have his heart for this."

Meg drew in a swift breath. "For what?"

"Poisoning my brother."

"Duncan was nowhere near here!"

"His minions were."

"The Reevers are gone."

"God rot them," Simon said coldly. "I'm talking about Duncan's spies within the keep. One of them poisoned Dominic. When I find out who, I will hang him."

Meg looked stricken. "No one in the keep would poison . . ."

Her voice died as she realized that someone *had*. She closed her eyes. Unwittingly she ran her hands up and down her arms as though warding off a cold wind. The thought of someone within her home so hating Dominic as to kill him in this cowardly way literally chilled her.

"Before I watched your struggle to save Dominic's life," Simon said, "I was certain you were the poisoner."

Meg's eyes opened as green and hard as the emerald Dominic had given her.

"I am a healer," she said.

"Aye." Simon smiled almost gently. "Were it not for you, Dominic would be dead. So it is reasonable to assume you didn't poison him in the first place."

"Perhaps no one meant to poison him. Perhaps whoever drugged the ale tipped too much in one of the mugs and Dominic was unlucky enough to get that mug."

Simon tilted his head aside as though considering the matter.

"Perhaps," he said after a time, but there was no enthusiasm in his voice. "It's not very likely."

"What do you think happened?" Meg asked.

"I think someone poisoned the barrel of ale, and

then added more to Dominic's mug to be certain."

"Who? When?"

"The barrel could have been poisoned at any time."

"No. Only since the day before the wedding."

"Why do you say that?"

"That was when I discovered the potion was missing," Meg said.

"Did you tell Dominic?" Simon demanded.

"No."

"God's blood, why not?"

"I wasn't certain what kind of man he was," Meg said bluntly. "In any case, it could have been one of your people who stole the medicine."

Simon made a dismissive gesture with his hand. "Nay. The knights are loyal. Dominic sold his soul to ransom them."

"What of the rest of your people? How many do you know well enough to vouch for their honesty?"

"Give way, sister," Simon said impatiently. "Who of my people could have known about the herbal and the medicines you keep there?"

"None of Blackthorne's people use my herbal but Old Gwyn."

Simon's eyes narrowed. "Where is she?"

"Exchanging knowledge with a wise woman from a settlement a day's walk to the south."

"She could have poisoned the ale."

"If she had, every knight would be dead."

He gave Meg a swift, black look. "How so?"

"Old Gwyn knows the dosage," Meg said succinctly. "There wasn't enough in the missing bottle to kill when mixed in a barrel of ale, unless three or four men divided it among themselves."

Simon smiled slightly. "The ale would have killed them first. So . . . Old Gwyn."

"Nay. Gwyn no more could kill in that way than I could. She is Glendruid, a healer."

"Does Eadith know the doses?" Simon asked.

"No. Why?"

"She served much of the ale. And she hates Normans."

"Truly?" Meg asked in a dry tone. "Is that why she spends more time in the bed of Thomas the Strong than in her own?"

"She served the ale," Simon insisted.

"The leman served it too," Meg retorted. "Do you suspect her?"

"Marie? Of course not. She owes her living to Dominic."

"And Eadith owes hers to me. She can be a tiresome gossip, but that is no reason to suspect her of such a heinous act."

"She is ambitious," Simon countered.

"Yes. She wants a husband and a home of her own. So does the red-lipped leman."

Simon made a sound of exasperation and raked his hand through his hair.

"It must be one of John's knights," Simon said finally.

Instantly Meg started to object, only to be cut off by an impatient gesture from Simon.

"Someone poisoned that ale and nearly killed Dominic," Simon said in a cold voice. "There will be no safety for anyone in this keep until we find out who is the viper at our breast."

Meg looked over to the bed where Dominic slept. As much as she hated Simon's conclusion, she knew he was correct. Blackthorne Keep lived or died with Dominic le Sabre.

And Dominic had nearly died.

19

DOMINIC AWOKE IN THE MIDDLE of the night with Meg's soft warmth lying alongside him and a headache that threatened to tear his skull apart. When he opened his eyes, even the vague shimmer of firelight through the bed draperies was like a knife in his eyes. Stifling a groan, he pressed his hands against his temples and wondered what had happened to him.

Instantly Meg awakened and reached for the basket of medicines that she had kept near her throughout the long hours of Dominic's sleep. With quick motions she mixed a packet of powdered bark into a mug of water Simon had drawn from the well and personally delivered to Dominic's room.

"Here," she said, handing the mug to Dominic. "Drink this. It will ease your head."

Without hesitation, he put the mug to his lips. Though the potion was bitter, he didn't lower the mug until the last drop was drunk.

Meg let out a relieved breath.

"Did you think I'd fight you over the medicine?" Dominic asked dryly.

"I was afraid you might think as Simon did at first."

A black eyebrow lifted in silent query.

"Your brother thought that I was the one who poisoned you," Meg explained.

"*Poisoned.*"

Dominic sat bolt upright, winced, and muttered something in Turkish. Meg sat up and pressed her hands against Dominic's chest, urging him to lie back once more.

"Don't get up yet," Meg said. "Your head must feel as though an ax were buried in it."

"Aye," he groaned. "God's blood, it feels just like that."

"Shhh," she murmured. "Close your eyes. It will help. Even the gentle light of the hearth must seem harsh to you right now."

As Meg leaned down to massage Dominic's temples, the golden bells twined within her loose braids sang tiny songs.

"So you still wear your jesses," he said, remembering more of what had happened with every breath.

"Until you remove them," Meg agreed.

"Yet you break your word to me in other ways."

Her hands paused. She was glad Dominic's eyes were closed; even half-dead from the lingering results of the poison, he would have seen the fear in her.

A wise man shows mercy only once to the same person. Never fight me again, small falcon.

But she had.

"Harry's wife—" Meg began, rubbing Dominic's temples again.

"I remember," he interrupted. "A long, difficult birthing. How does she fare?"

"I don't know. Simon has allowed no one but himself in or out of this room. Even now, he sleeps outside your door."

"Does the woman need you?" Dominic asked.

Meg wondered what Dominic was thinking. His voice gave no clue. Nor did his body. He was fully in control of himself again.

"I think not," she said. "Gwyn returned just before sunset yesterday. If something were wrong with Adela, Gwyn would have come to me."

"And to the devil with Simon's edicts?" Dominic asked neutrally. "Or mine?"

Meg wondered how to explain to her husband that she was responsible for the people of the keep in a way that transcended the normal duties of a lord's wife.

"Knowing people hurt when I could bring ease," Meg said haltingly, "that they sicken when I could bring health, that they die when I might have helped them live . . ."

Meg fought the ache constricting her throat as she searched Dominic's face for a hint of his thoughts. There was none. His expression was like his voice: ruthlessly disciplined, almost inhuman in its lack of emotion.

"Whatever punishment you mete out to me for breaking my vow," Meg whispered, "could be no worse than knowing one of my people died when I could have saved her."

Dominic's hands closed over Meg's, stilling her soothing motions against his temples.

"You broke your vow to me," he said.

"Yes," Meg said, closing her eyes.

"You will do it again if your people need you."

"Yes," she whispered. "I'm sorry, husband. I can obey you in many things, but not in that."

"And you are prepared to take whatever punishment I find suitable."

She took a deep breath and said, "Yes. Just don't truly lock me away. I couldn't bear that."

"Nor would the people," Dominic said. "Is that it?"

Hesitantly Meg said, "Aye."

"You are truly a double-edged sword, wife."

"I don't mean to be. I am simply . . . what I am."

"Glendruid."

"Yes."

After a moment Dominic asked, "How did you get out of the keep?"

Meg did not answer. Nor did she open her eyes. She didn't want to confront the cold anger of her husband.

There was silence for such a long time that Meg finally risked a glance at Dominic. He was watching her with a clear calculation that once would have chilled her. Now, knowing what drove him, she felt only the same compassion that she did for the people of Blackthorne Keep, caught in lives that were rarely of their own making.

"You are a very brave woman," Dominic said coolly. "But then, you are well protected. If the least thing displeases you, you simply hold your 'people' over my head like the sword of Damocles."

"That's not true!" Meg said passionately. "I hated being shut away from the sun like a falcon newly come to the mews, but I didn't cry my unhappiness from the windows. I detested being a steppingstone on the way to men's ambitions, but I said nothing to the people of Blackthorne Keep when the king decreed my marriage. Even when John beat me, I said nothing!"

"But the people knew just the same."

She hesitated, then nodded, for it was the truth.

"Just as I know about their pain," Meg said simply. "We are . . . joined."

Dominic let the silence stretch while he considered the Glendruid wife who kept surprising him with her combination of vulnerability and intransigence.

"Obviously there is a bolthole in this keep," he

said finally. "You will show it to me, and only to me."

Meg didn't want to reveal her secret route from the keep, yet it was Dominic's right as the lord to know where the bolthole was.

"Yes," she said softly.

The corner of Dominic's mouth kicked up. "Was it that hard, small falcon?"

"What?"

"Giving me what is my due as your lord."

"You make me sound cold and selfish."

"No. Just untamed."

Meg's bleak smile surprised Dominic.

"Untamed?" she asked. "Is that how you see me?"

"How else could I see you? You obey no one, not even your husband."

"I obey everyone, answering the needs of even the lowliest of Blackthorne's people. Not once—*never*— has anyone asked me what my own desire was."

"What is it?"

"Freedom, lord. Just that."

Slipping her hands from beneath Dominic's, Meg got out of bed to tend the hearth.

"Sleep. Your body has much healing to do."

"I will heal more quickly with you beside me."

Meg hesitated in the act of adding a piece of oak branch to the fire. Tiny flames lifted toward the wood as though sensing that their destiny was to burn, and in burning, to warm lives that would otherwise go cold.

Slowly Meg lowered the branch among the coals. Before she could take a full breath, tongues of fire raced over the oak, cherishing it and setting it ablaze. After a moment she stood and went back to Dominic's bed. She pulled apart the heavy drapes surrounding the bed.

Dominic was waiting for her. He held the covers

aside, silently inviting Meg to come to bed. She slid
quickly beneath the covers, not wanting any warmth
to escape. Behind her, the drapes fell shut once more,
cutting off the drafts from the shutters.

"You'll catch a chill if you don't keep the covers
snugly around you," Meg said.

"You'll warm me."

Dominic's strong arms reached for Meg, tucked
her alongside his body, and pulled her close in an
intimacy that had become familiar in the days since
their marriage. Usually his was the greater warmth,
but not tonight. Tonight, the last of the poison still
touched Dominic's body with cool fingers.

Meg wrapped the covers closer around both of
them and tried to cover as much of his flesh with her
own as she could. The warmth of her body radiated
against him. The feel of it sent a shimmer of simple
pleasure through Dominic.

Smiling, he brushed his lips over Meg's forehead,
smoothed her cheek with his palm, and gave himself
back to healing sleep. Meg quickly followed, her
body relaxing along her husband's until both were
warmed.

Then the dream came and icy fingers clawed Meg's
heart.

"*Nay!*"

She sat upright in a rush, her heart racing like a
runaway horse, shaking her.

Dominic sat up an instant later, a knife in his
hand. A quick glance told him that the draperies
around the bed hadn't been disturbed, for only a
thin glimmer of light shone through the crack where
the hearth lay.

"Dominic?" Simon called harshly from beyond the
door. "Is all well?"

"Yes. It was only a dark dream."

Simon muttered something about witches and

nightmares as he settled against the door once more to get what sleep he could from the remaining night.

Beside Dominic, Meg shivered and murmured sounds which had no meaning except that of fear and denial.

With a swift motion, Dominic slid the knife under his pillow once more, threw back a drapery, and lit a fresh candle from the guttering remains of the one on the table. The room was cold. Only bare embers remained of the fire. Yet he doubted that was why his wife shivered.

"Meg?" Dominic said in a low voice, stroking her cheek. "What is it?"

At first Meg didn't hear him, for she was still in the grip of nightmare.

"Meg?"

Her eyes opened and she glanced around as though disoriented.

"Dominic? Is something wrong? Do you feel ill again?"

"No. 'Tis you, Meg. You cried out."

"Oh."

Rubbing her palms up and down her arms, Meg looked around, truly seeing the room for the first time since waking. A fresh candle burned brightly a few feet from the bed. Embers glowed in the hearth. No hint of light came through the narrow gap in the shutters.

"The fire," she said absently.

"I'll tend it."

"No. You'll take a chill."

Dominic turned Meg's face until she looked at him.

"What is wrong?" he asked.

She opened her lips but no words came out. Shivering, she rubbed her arms again as though to put warmth back in skin that had gone cold.

"Lie down," Dominic said, pushing Meg back onto the bed as he spoke. "You'll take a chill."

He got up and fed the fire with a few quick motions that spoke eloquently of returning health. When he came back to bed, he pulled Meg close but made no move to pull the draperies around the bed once more. He suspected that light was more important to his wife right now than warmth.

Slowly Meg's arms stole around Dominic. Her breath came out in a long, soundless sigh against his chest.

"Can you tell me now?" Dominic asked.

At first he thought she would refuse to speak. Then her breath came out in another noiseless rush of warmth.

"Just a dream," Meg said.

"Do you dream like that often?"

"No."

Dominic waited.

Meg said no more.

"Are you afraid of me?" he asked after a moment. "Of how I might punish you?"

"No," she whispered. "Though I should be."

"Why?"

"You are so much stronger than I am."

He made a sound halfway between harsh laughter and disbelief. "Am I? Is that why I find myself unable to get the most simple form of obedience from you?"

"But—" Meg began.

The pressure of Dominic's fingers on her lips cut off her protest.

"Tell me," Dominic said in a low voice. "Why are you afraid?"

"Sometimes—sometimes I dream," Meg said in a rush.

"Most people do."

"Not—like this. There is danger. I know it."

"Night fears are common," he said calmly.

"Do you have them?"

"Yes."

Meg shifted her head until she could see Dominic's profile outlined in firelight.

"Of what do you dream?" she whispered.

"I don't know. I know only that I awake cold and sweating."

"You don't remember your dreams?"

"Some of them," he said.

"But not those that wake you?" she persisted.

"No. Not those."

Meg's long sigh sent warmth rushing over Dominic's skin.

"I wish I didn't remember," she whispered.

"Can you tell me what you remember? Or is it a Glendruid matter?"

"I—don't know," she said. "Old Gwyn and I don't talk about it and Mother never said anything at all."

"But you think it is Glendruid."

There was no question in Dominic's tone. Though his voice wasn't harsh, it was clear he meant to pursue answers until he was satisfied.

"Yes," Meg whispered.

"Tell me, small falcon."

Dominic's voice was gentle, but his eyes burned with reflected fire.

"There has been little of peace in my life," Meg said in a low voice. "My fath—that is, Lord John was ever trying to wed me to a powerful Scots thane or Saxon lord."

Dominic made a sound of encouragement.

"And all the while," Meg said, "Saxons whose land had been taken by the Normans roved in bands, fighting and stealing and trying to get back their former family holdings."

"Like the Reevers?"

Meg nodded.

"John," she continued, "was the son of a Norman knight and a lady who was both Scots and Saxon. Father and son both had to fight to hold his land. While they fought, crops were ignored and flocks were raided. That was why John took a Glendruid to wife. He wanted a time of prosperity for his lands so that he could afford more knights."

Dominic smoothed back a wisp of fire-bright hair that had fallen across Meg's cheek.

"But it didn't happen that way," she said sadly. "Both lost."

"Both?"

"Glendruid and John."

"What did the Glendruids lose?" Dominic asked.

"The Glendruid Wolf. Old Gwyn believed that my mother would bear a son."

"Instead, she bore a daughter."

"A disappointment," agreed Meg.

"Not to me. Without you I would have died," Dominic said simply. "To me you are a delight."

"You didn't sound delighted earlier, when you discovered I had left my room."

Wisely, Dominic said nothing.

For a time there was no sound but the soft whisper of fire and the even softer whisper of Dominic's hand smoothing over Meg's hair as he remembered her passionate words.

I obey everyone, answering the needs of even the lowliest of Blackthorne's people. Not once—never—has anyone asked me what my own desire was.

"What did you want, Meg?" Dominic asked finally. "Why did you agree to marry me? Why didn't you cast your lot with Duncan of Maxwell, for whom you feel 'affection'?"

Dominic sensed the change in Meg's body, a stillness that went all the way to the marrow of her bones.

"I wanted no more war," she said flatly. "I hate the endless cruelty, the violence, the lives cut off before they are ripe. I knew if a strong man with many knights held Blackthorne Keep, the landless thanes would look elsewhere to feed their ambitions. And I heard that no stronger knight than Dominic le Sabre lived between here and Jerusalem."

She took a swift, deep breath and continued before Dominic could speak.

"And now I find myself caught in whispers of adultery when I have touched no man save my husband. I find my husband poisoned and myself suspected of the vile act. I find knights in chain mail prowling the keep, seeing enemies in every familiar face."

"I don't suspect you," Dominic said.

Meg kept speaking as though she hadn't heard.

"I am a healer. I want to heal this land's hatred, for it is a greater sickness than any I've ever known. Hatred is the bitter soul of war. I want to bring peace to the land!"

Dominic's breath caught. He had never thought to hear his own dreams so clearly stated. Slowly he turned Meg's face up to his.

"I share your desire," he said in a low voice. "Work with me, wife. Help me to bring peace to the land."

"How?"

"Blend Norman and Glendruid blood. Give me sons."

Sudden tears fell from Meg's eyelashes. The heat of the drops was scalding.

"That is beyond my control," she whispered. "You are a warrior who can be wise, who can be restrained, who can look after the welfare of your vassals, who can do much for your people . . . *but you cannot love.*"

Dominic didn't deny it. The sultan's hell had burned out much of Dominic's soul, and he knew it. As much as he wanted sons, he could no more magically transform himself into a man who was capable of love than he could fly as a falcon flew.

He could only do what a falcon master did—get a small falcon to fly for him.

"Aye," Dominic agreed. "I am a warrior who cannot love. You are a healer who cannot hate. Don't you see the way out of the trap?"

Meg shook her head slowly.

"Old Gwyn told me that Glendruid women are cursed by seeing into the souls of men," Dominic said, "and only God could love a man so clearly seen."

"Yes," Meg whispered.

Tears welled as she looked into the eyes of the warrior who could not love.

"I don't believe that all Glendruid women are so cold," Dominic said. "I believe that a Glendruid *healer* would look differently at a man who could bring peace to a land torn by war. I believe she would see past the imperfections of his soul. I believe she could love him.

"Look at me and see peace for Blackthorne Keep," Dominic said. "Love me, Meg. Then heal the land with my sons."

"You ask too much," she whispered, appalled by his logic. "*I see you too clearly.*"

"I ask what I must. It is the only way out of the trap. For both of us."

20

FROWNING AND TUGGING AT cloth, Marie worked over the last adjustments on Meg's new dress while church bells rang out, telling the people in the fields that it was time for their mid-morning food. Voices fell silent in the bailey as servants halted their tasks long enough to enjoy the melodious song of the bells.

The bells rang again, reminding Meg of a time five days past, when she and Dominic had walked from the keep to the church and stood in a chill mist while John of Cumbriland was buried. The ceremony was brief.

There will be no time of mourning, Dominic had decreed calmly. *John of Cumbriland was not your father.*

With that Dominic had turned from the freshly filled grave while the bells were still tolling the end of John's life. He led Meg away with him through the thick mist of a day that would neither rain nor allow the sun to shine.

Meg hadn't objected to the lack of ceremony. She felt only relief at John's burial. Part of her hoped it would mark the end of the old time of savage strife and the beginning of a newer, more peaceful day.

She hoped, but she also feared. It was now a week since Dominic had thrown off the effects of the poison, and still she dreamed. Then she awoke crying and cold with dread.

There was no one to hold her now. Since Dominic had fully recovered from the poison, he did not sleep in her bed. Nor would he, for she had not yet bled. He had freed her from the intimate mews, with the result that she rarely saw him.

Dominic hadn't raised the subject of love, peace, and sons again, except for the time when he had handed Meg a bolt of silk cloth. The fabric was as green as her eyes, richly shining, cool and smooth to her fingertips. It was as beautiful as the cloth of the ritual Glendruid garment she had worn for her wedding, a dress Old Gwyn had removed while Meg slept.

But Gwyn wouldn't come and take the green silk from Meg. The silk was Dominic's gift to her, which made it doubly precious, as though a swath of spring had been spun and woven into cloth just for her.

Dominic had seen her pleasure in the fabric and smiled. Yet his eyes were cool, intent, unsmiling, and his voice was harsh with restraint when he spoke to her.

Think of what we talked about. Think of loving me, Meg. With your love, anything is possible.

Even peace.

He had said nothing of his hope for sons, but it was there in his searching eyes, in the hunger of his voice, in the tension that hummed throughout his powerful body.

Sons.

Love me, Meg.

Yet Dominic didn't love her. Meg knew it as surely as she knew her eyes were green. She doubted that

he would ever love. He who loved, risked. The
ruthless practicality of Dominic's nature would not
allow it. His love of his knights had nearly cost
him his life in Jerusalem; it had certainly cost him
whatever softness lay in his soul. No matter how
gentle his apparent seduction, it was the result of
calculation rather than of any true tenderness in his
feelings for her.

Meg could not blame Dominic for that any more
than she could blame an eagle with a broken wing
for not flying. She could only wish that he had not
come to her with a hurt that was beyond her ability
to heal.

Closing her eyes on a wave of sadness, Meg
smoothed her hand down the marvelous green silk
cloth. The movement made the golden bells at her
wrist shiver with hushed music.

"The cloth is so fine," Meg said after a time.

"Your skin is finer," Marie said without glancing
up from her tiny stitches.

Meg looked down at the small, quick woman
who was sitting cross-legged on the floor while she
worked over the hem of the dress she had sewn.
The Norman woman was an enigma to Meg. Marie's
combination of blunt sexuality and quick, rather
cynical intelligence intrigued Meg—so long as Dominic was nowhere in the vicinity. Marie's lush body
and exotic perfumes had the knights of the keep sitting up and howling like dogs after a bitch in heat.

Only Dominic and Simon seemed immune. But
then, if they wanted Marie, all they had to do was
crook a finger and she would be at their side. She
knew who was the master of the keep and who was
the master's right hand.

"You need not flatter me," Meg said.

"I don't," Marie said casually. "Your skin is as
fine as a sultan's most prized pearl. No flattery,

lady. Simple truth. Turn to your left, please."

Meg obeyed. Bells shifted and murmured musically.

" 'Tis a pity your lord is so possessive of your beauty," Marie continued.

"Pardon?"

Marie looked up from her fussing over the straightness of the hem long enough to catch the surprise on Meg's face. The Norman woman smiled rather wryly at this further proof of the Glendruid witch's innocence of carnal matters.

"Dominic directed me most carefully to be certain that your shoulders, wrists, breasts, and ankles were covered by the silk," Marie explained.

"But of course."

Marie shook her head. "Nay, lady. Not 'of course.' The sultan's women knew how to dress to catch a man's eye."

"How was that?"

"They wore cloth many times lighter than this, as frail as a breath, and nearly as transparent, too. Layer upon layer, so that when a woman walked, her breasts and thatch and the curve of her buttocks were revealed and then concealed before a man could be certain of what he had seen."

"Do you jest?" Meg asked, startled.

"No, lady. Look straight ahead, please, else the hem will be crooked."

"You could see through the cloth? Truly?"

Marie's smile flashed. "Truly."

"Astonishing."

"To the English, perhaps. To the Turks, it was accepted. And," Marie added slyly, "much appreciated by the men."

"Have you worn such clothes?"

"But of course. Your husband found them particularly attractive."

Meg jerked.

With a muttered phrase in Turkish, Marie went back to fussing over the hem.

"You Saxons," Marie said after a moment, shaking her head. "A man's desire to possess a wife, that I can understand. He wants to be certain he will raise only his own children. But a possessive wife . . ."

Marie shrugged, checked the length of thread on the needle, and resumed stitching.

"Once married, there is no divorce for a Christian," Marie continued, "therefore no need for jealousy. You have Dominic's protection, title, and wealth for the rest of your life. What else of worth remains of him to possess?"

"His affection. His respect. His . . . love."

"Gold and jewels last longer," Marie said. "They can be sold for food and clothing when war or famine comes. Affection is amusing for a time, but it is as fickle as the wind. As for love, it is a fancy of the mind, nothing more."

Marie knotted the thread and severed it with a quick flash of her teeth.

"There," she said, satisfied. "It hangs as it should now."

She stood with the grace of a woman accustomed to sitting on pillows scattered across the floor rather than on chairs. Deft fingers flew as she began unlacing the closely fitted dress.

"Marie."

"Yes, lady?"

"Save your sexual wiles for the garrison," Meg said bluntly. "Don't use them on my husband. Whether you succeed or fail, you shall rue the attempt."

There was a moment of surprised silence before Marie laughed out loud.

"I can see why he calls you his small falcon," she said. "Step out of the dress, lady."

Meg did so and then waited, watching with eyes that were frankly predatory while Marie carefully put the dress into a wardrobe.

"Marie?"

"As you wish," she said calmly, turning back to Meg. "But you must know that what you wish holds true only so long as your master wishes it, too."

"What do you mean?"

For the space of a breath, Marie looked at Meg with something close to compassion.

"How you could have reached nineteen and be so innocent . . ." Marie sighed heavily and explained. "Dominic is wooing you most carefully. While he does, he looks not at me. When that changes—and it will, for he is but a man—then I will go to his bed for as long as he wants me. He is master in this keep, not I. Nor are you, my lady. No woman is."

Marie picked up the small sewing basket. "Is there anything else you wish?"

"No."

After a slight nod of her head, Marie walked from the room. With each step her hips swayed like a candle flame in a draft.

Meg let out a pent-up breath and a few words that would have drawn a horrified look from the good father. The worst part of it was that Marie was correct. If Dominic chose to favor his leman over his wife, there was little Meg could do about it.

She can't give him legitimate heirs. Only I can do that.

Yet Meg wasn't certain she could. When all was said and done, it seemed that few Glendruid women were fertile.

Frowning, Meg threw a mantle about her shoulders and headed for the bathing room. The oddly pointed cloth slippers Dominic had given her whispered over the floor and gleamed metallically in the illumination from lamps. The fragrant oil in the lamps offset the damp, cold smell of the keep's stone walls. Since Dominic's arrival, the keep had begun to shine like a butterfly recently released from its chrysalis.

"There you are," Eadith said. "I thought you had displeased your lord and been confined to your rooms again."

Meg smiled rather grimly. "I've been confined to green silk while Marie fusses over the hem."

"Ah, the leman. Dominic promised her silk of her own if she made you a dress that pleases him."

The enjoyment Meg had taken in the green silk faded. Turning away from her handmaiden, Meg removed the mantle, set it aside, and began untying the ribbons on the silk undergarments Dominic had given to her along with the slippers embroidered in gold thread.

Eadith tested the heat of the water in the tub, found it satisfactory, and turned to help Meg.

"Such delicate cloth," Eadith said as she removed the top. "And such pretty designs, like the priest's Bible."

Meg said nothing. The thought of Dominic giving gifts to Marie made Meg both uneasy and angry.

. . . I will go to his bed for as long as he wants me. He is master in this keep, not I. Nor are you, my lady. No woman is.

With a sideways glance at her unhappy mistress, Eadith went about laying out the soap and perfume, unguents and creams that were part of Meg's Glendruid ritual. Privately Eadith thought it all a great waste of time. On the other hand, Dominic's knights had shown a pronounced preference for the Saracen-raised woman, and she bathed almost as often as Meg. Perhaps there was more to the matter than Glendruid fetish and heathen Saracen ways.

Golden bells sang sweetly as Eadith twisted Meg's braids into a crown on top of her head and secured the hair with combs of emerald and gold—more of Dominic's presents.

"Such lovely combs," Eadith said.

"Yes," Meg said, but there was little pleasure in her voice.

"They look pretty against your hair."

"Thank you."

"Thomas gave me some silver combs. He said they suited my hair."

"Do you care for Thomas?" Meg asked. "You talk of him often the past week."

Eadith shrugged. "He is kind enough for all his size."

"Should I ask Dominic to offer a marriage?"

"Nay," Eadith said. "Thomas hasn't enough wealth to keep two squires, much less a wife. Unless Dominic is going to give his knights estates . . . ?"

"I don't know."

"Well, I doubt it," Eadith said, sliding in another glittering comb. "Even when his other knights arrive, he'll have few enough men to defend the keep and manors as it is. If the knights are off defending their own land they won't be able to defend his."

"True enough."

Eadith slid in a final comb. "Do you know when the knights will be coming? The steward is in a knot over the amount the men eat as it is."

Meg grimaced. The steward complained of the quickly vanishing stores to her every time he saw her.

"Gwyn said there was much talk in the south of the sea's wildness," Meg said. "Perhaps the knights are still in Normandy awaiting passage across."

"At least a fortnight, then." Eadith stepped back. "Into the bath with you."

Meg took off the golden slippers, handed them to Eadith, and got into the steaming, herb-scented water. With a sigh of pleasure, she immersed herself up to her chin, stilling the musical cries of the bells except for those remaining in her hair.

" 'Tis a wonder Glendruids don't have scales and fins," Eadith said, watching Meg give herself to the water.

Laughing, Meg moved her hands to make the water swirl.

"Do you need aught else?" Eadith asked.

"No."

"I'll leave you to your chanting, then."

Meg's mouth curved with amusement at Eadith's stolid disapproval of Glendruid ways.

"If I'm not back when you need me," Eadith said, "raise a cry. Your two-legged hound is just down the hall. He'll fetch me."

The reminder that Dominic's squire was always a short distance away made Meg's mouth flatten. The "small falcon" had been released from the mews, but was hardly free. When Dominic wasn't with her, Jameson was always within calling distance.

Does my husband really distrust me so much?

The answer was as immediate as it was inevitable.

Aye. Why else hasn't he made me his wife in truth as well as in name? His body certainly is capable. But until my monthly flux passes, he won't trust that whatever grows in my womb is his.

Only love would have that kind of trust, and he loves me not.

Slowly Meg's unhappy thoughts dissolved in the soothing heat and fragrance of the water. She closed her eyes, inhaled the complex, scented herbal steam rising from the water, and began softly chanting the ancient ritual of purification and rebirth. With graceful, rhythmic strokes she washed the old mistakes and regrets from her body, and then smoothed on the scented soap of possibility and renewal.

When Meg was finished, she opened her eyes languidly, feeling both calm and vibrant with energy. The calm vanished when she realized that Dominic was standing very close, watching her with eyes that shone like hammered silver. His heavy, dark mantle was a thick slice of midnight within the candlelit room.

"I—I didn't know you were here," she stammered. "How long have you waited?"

"A thousand years," he said in a strange, husky voice.

Meg's breath wedged in her throat as her heartbeat went wild. Wary and hopeful at the same time, she looked up at Dominic with luminous emerald eyes. He held out a drying cloth that was as large as a mantle.

And then he smiled and whistled sweetly, the same intricate five-note call she had used to charm the peregrine.

"Fly to me, small falcon."

Meg smiled almost shyly, hesitated, and then rose from her bath in a graceful motion. Water hastened from her body in silver rivulets while golden bells whispered and sang as they were freed from the water's muffling embrace.

Dominic's hands tightened on the cloth as he saw his wife's body glistening with water and candlelight. Silently he questioned his wisdom in coming to her in the scented intimacy of the bathing room. He thought he had been impatient to ask her to ride hawking with him. Now he realized that he had been impatient to see her, period.

Meg looked very beautiful to him wearing only chains of golden bells and glistening water. Beneath the concealing mantle, his body hardened in a rush that left him aching from his forehead to his heels. It also left him feeling powerful, fully male, eager to take what Church and law decreed was his.

God's teeth, I've never wanted a maid like this! Will she never bleed? Perhaps I should do as Simon suggested and slake my body's thirst at Marie's willing well.

Yet even as the thought came, Dominic ruled out taking the leman for his own temporary ease. He needed Meg's love far more than his body needed relief from its relentless sexual hunger. And he sensed quite certainly that Meg would be angry if he showed the leman any attention. An angry girl wasn't likely to be a loving one.

Patience.

In the name of God, patience has never been so difficult. What is wrong with me? I'm not a beardless squire to slaver after a girl.

"You look quite fierce to whistle so sweetly," Meg said uncertainly as she reached for the drying cloth.

Dominic wrapped the cloth around Meg, capturing her arms against her side.

"I feel rather fierce," he said.

His voice was rough rather than seductive, but he could no more help its aroused huskiness than he could soften the masculine sword that had sprung to readiness at the sight of Meg's naked body. He knew he should turn and walk from the room, but that, too, was beyond his ability.

Slowly, taking entirely too much pleasure from such a simple thing, Dominic began rubbing Meg dry, beginning with her neck and shoulders.

"Is something wrong with the keep?" she asked anxiously.

"No." Dominic took a corner of the cloth and dried the hollow in Meg's throat where drops of water had collected. "Just with the keep's lord."

"What is it?"

"I came here in a fever to take you hawking. I fear I will leave in a greater fever."

"Hawking?"

Meg was so excited at the prospect that she danced in place, making golden bells chime.

"Oh, aye, Dominic! Let's go hawking! Send Eadith to dress me and I'll be ready before you know it!"

He smiled at the pleasure animating Meg's face. The smile became somewhat dark as his hands rubbed down the elegant length of her back. Even with cloth separating him from her skin, he could feel the smooth resilience of her flesh.

And he could remember what it had been like to touch her naked skin.

"We don't need Eadith just yet," Dominic said. "I'll tend you."

"But it will be quicker if Eadith dresses me."

"Are you in that much of a fever to go hawking?"

"Aye. John rarely let me go, for all that I helped train many of the falcons."

A distant reverberation of thunder made the air tremble with low sounds. Meg cast a worried look at the long slit of the window. More cloud than blue sky showed.

"Hurry," Meg said. "A storm threatens."

"Indeed. It has already overtaken me."

Dominic's fingers stretched, circled her buttocks, and flexed deeply. Meg gave a startled cry as heat shot through her body, weakening her knees.

"So," he whispered. "It is the same for you."

"W-what?"

"Lying with me at night as we once did, breathing my breath, sharing my warmth . . . You have sunk through my skin to the marrow of my bones. You are a fire in me, Meg."

She started to answer, but his hands flexed again, sending lightning strokes of heat through her body. As she moaned, she saw the blaze in his eyes and knew that he was right; somewhere in the long nights they had lain chastely together heat had begun to burn deeply within her.

"And I have become a fire in you," Dominic said, savoring the moan he had drawn from Meg's throat. "We will burn together. We will burn. . . ."

"Dominic," she whispered.

Before Meg could say another word, his mouth covered hers and his tongue sought hers in an intimate duel that lasted until she was breathless, leaning heavily against him, lost to the kiss. She had never known anything like the pleasure Dominic gave her. She had no defenses against it. Nor had she any defense against the Glendruid hope that burned as fiercely as desire within her.

Surely love is possible. Surely . . .

After a time Meg began to struggle against the embrace. Reluctantly Dominic lifted his head and looked down at Meg's flushed cheeks. Her breath was rapid and her nipples stood like small pebbles against the soft cloth.

"Why do you fight me?" he asked in a deep voice.

"Not you. The cloth. I want to stroke your hair, but I'm trapped like a fish in a net."

The sight of Meg's hard nipples so intrigued Dominic that it took a moment for him to realize that he had indeed wrapped her so tightly in the drying cloth that her arms were imprisoned at her sides.

"Do you want to pet me like Black Tom?" he asked. "Head to heels and back again? Will you run your cheek all over me as well, the way you do with him?"

The thought of it shortened Meg's breath.

"Would you like that?" she whispered.

"Aye," Dominic said in a low voice. "Every morning when I watch you pet that cat from bailey to gardens and back again, I think what it would be like to have your hands on me in the same way."

Thunder rumbled beyond the open shutters. Wind gusted, bringing the scent of rain and new leaves and freshly opened flowers.

Meg barely noticed the building storm. The quicksilver blaze of Dominic's eyes consumed her. The sensual depth of his voice caressed her like sunlight. Whether he loved her or not, there was no doubt that she held his whole attention right now.

Perhaps he could, if only for the moment, forget the cold calculations of dynasty and sons. Perhaps she could help him forget those things. Perhaps she could burn so brightly that he would be the moth and she the flame.

And then he would succumb to her, wanting only her, forgetting everything else.

"Do you purr?" Meg asked with a catch in her voice.

"Never yet. But with you, I think I might."

Dominic's hands shifted from Meg's hips to her back. He hooked his thumbs in the drying cloth and began slowly dragging it down her torso.

"What about you?" he asked in a husky voice as the high curves of her breasts were gradually revealed. "Do you purr at a man's touch?"

Meg couldn't answer. The expression on Dominic's face as he looked at her breasts made it impossible for her to think, much less to answer questions. He was watching her as though he had never seen anything as beautiful. The intensity of his eyes was a caress.

Soft, glittering sensations rippled through Meg as her breasts tightened on a swiftly indrawn breath.

"You are more beautiful than any spring buds," Dominic said in a low voice.

Thunder rumbled and the wind freshened, sending a quick draft through the room, making candle flames bend and tremble. Meg shivered from the opposite sensations of coolness and heat. Her nipples gathered into hard crowns that were as pink as her tongue.

"Are you cold?" Dominic asked.

"Aye. That is, nay." Meg made a breathless sound that was neither laugh nor word. "I don't know. I can't think when you look at me like that."

"Like what?"

"Like I'm a Turkish sweet of unknown flavor."

Dominic's mouth shifted into a sensual smile that sent more heat through Meg.

"Are you?" he asked.

"W-what?"

"Sweet."

Before Meg could answer, Dominic bent his head to taste her. His tongue darted out and licked the peak of one breast as delicately as a cat.

"*Dominic.*"

He made a low sound that was rather like a purr and licked her again.

"Sweet but not cloying," he said. "You taste like spring itself."

The end of his tongue tested Meg's nipple, circled it, and then slowly drew the tip of her breast into his mouth for a thorough tasting.

Heat cascaded through Meg, loosening her body as though she lay in a meadow caressed by the summer sun. The changing texture and pressure of Dominic's unexpected caress made her dizzy with delight. Pleasure gathered and burst softly deep inside her, drawing a low moan from the back of her throat.

The sound acted on Dominic like a whip laid across naked skin. His whole body tightened as he drew Meg more heavily into his mouth. The caress changed from teasing to intense as he shaped her breast to the urgent demands of passion. A ragged cry and the pressure of her nails against his biceps only added more heat to the desire that was rapidly burning through his usually indomitable self-control.

Dominic's hand caressed down Meg's naked back to her waist. With an impatience he could barely reign in, he slid his fingers beneath the drying cloth. A long finger traced her spine to the cleft of her bottom. He knew he should stop there, satisfying himself with the startled cry of discovery and desire he drew from Meg when he cupped the flare of her hip in his hand and squeezed carefully.

Yet even as Dominic told himself to withdraw until he could slow the hammering of his blood, his hand returned to the small of her back. There he delicately teased the sensitive hollow and savored the heat rising from her skin.

When Meg murmured and sighed with pleasure, Dominic traced her spine from nape to base once again, but this time he couldn't resist following the line of her body until his fingertips again found the warm cleft dividing her hips. He followed it slowly on down, dragging a shivering cry of surprise from her.

The cloth fell from Meg's hips to the floor. The cool air of the room made an intense contrast to the heat expanding through her in shimmering waves with each tug of Dominic's mouth on her sensitized breast, each gliding foray of his fingertips down her back to the alluring cleft where passionate embers smoldered on the edge of flame.

Then his long fingers sought more deeply, discovered, parted, penetrated her satin warmth as lightly as fire itself. The sensations that burst through Meg made her cling to Dominic for balance while everything else in the room was drawn into a dizzying spiral of invisible flames.

"My lord," Meg whispered. "What are you doing to me?"

Reluctantly Dominic released her breast, but not the silky, secret heat he had barely touched.

"I'm discovering you," he said in a husky voice.

As Dominic spoke, he probed lightly again, and again was rewarded by Meg's broken breath and a moisture that owed nothing to her recent bathing ritual.

"I can barely stand," she whispered.

"Then hold on to me."

"I am."

Dominic smiled despite the hammer blows of desire that were shaking him, breaking his breath as surely as hers.

"So you are," he said. "I can feel your delicate talons."

Belatedly Meg realized she was indeed clinging to Dominic with fingernails as well as hands.

"I'm sorry. I didn't mean to hurt you."

His low, masculine laugh sent more heat snaking through her body.

"Hurt?" Dominic asked. "Nay. I like the feel of your hunger rising to fly with mine. Go ahead, small falcon. Test your strength against me. And I . . ."

His hand glided from her hip to the hollow of her throat. As he watched Meg with smoky gray eyes, his fingertip traced the center of her body from breastbone to navel to the cloud of red hair that concealed the same cleft he had stalked from the other side.

" . . . I shall test your softness," Dominic whispered.

Unerringly his fingertip parted the lush thicket, discovered the hidden bud and circled it slowly before going on to the sleek petals that had begun to fill with desire. He drew his fingertips slowly over Meg, probing softly, insistently, but her gate was too well defended from front.

"Open for me," he said hoarsely.

"What?"

"Give me the freedom of your warm keep."

Before Meg's mind understood Dominic's request, her body did. Her legs shifted, allowing him a greater intimacy. She was rewarded by a gliding caress that made fire splinter through her.

She knew then that she had wanted this since her wedding night, when she had first felt the hard warmth of Dominic's hand sliding up beneath her dress.

"More," Dominic said hoarsely, watching Meg through narrowed eyes. "You are still closed against me."

She shifted again, then gasped at the slow penetration of his fingertip. When she would have closed her legs once more, she found she couldn't. He had thrust his thigh between hers, holding her legs apart. Her eyes opened, startled.

Dominic was watching her with eyes of silver fire.

"I should not do this," he said hoarsely.

"What?" she whispered.

"This."

He circled Meg's sleek sheath. The shivering cry he drew from her made his head spin with passion.

"So tightly held against me," Dominic breathed, "yet you wear your desire like a perfume."

" 'Tis only—my bath."

" 'Tis your passion, Meg. There is no perfume like it."

She would have said more, but he was between her legs again and she couldn't breathe for the rings of pleasure expanding through her body, crowding out all else but a delicious, pulsing heat.

"Dominic, I fear I cannot stand much longer."

Without a word he lifted Meg and seated her on the trestle table. The cool, smooth wood was another kind of caress, one that served to focus the heat of her own body and that of the man who was standing in front of her, his face drawn with passion. Beneath his concealing mantle he worked at his clothing. Then he swirled his mantle over both of them.

"Wrap your legs around my waist," Dominic said.

His voice was hoarse, urgent, and even while he spoke he was drawing Meg's legs around his body.

"Yes, like that," he said. "Now come closer. Closer, Meg. Closer . . . yes, a bit more . . ."

Meg's breath came in swift and hard as she realized that it wasn't Dominic's hand caressing between her legs. Her fingers dug into his arms as she felt something broad and smooth and solid probe the edges of her softness.

"Dominic?"

He shuddered heavily as he nudged the sultry sheath, felt the liquid heat of her response, and knew that he must be held hotly, deeply, tightly. *Now.*

"Hold on to me, small falcon. Soon we will fly."

"The devil take you, squire," Eadith said loudly from the hallway. "If I want to speak to my mistress, I will!"

The drapery whipped aside as the handmaiden entered the bathing room. "Cook wants to know if—Oh!"

Though Dominic's mantle covered both himself and Meg, the circumstances left little doubt as to what Eadith had interrupted. The shock on her face would have been amusing to Dominic if he hadn't been ready to throttle her on the spot.

"Beg your pardon, Lord Dominic, lady," Eadith muttered as she withdrew hastily.

Dominic sent a barrage of searing Turkish oaths after the handmaiden while Meg struggled to disentangle from her husband. At first he wouldn't permit it. Then, with a final oath, he released her.

"It's just as well," Dominic said savagely. "I never meant it to go so far before you bled."

A savage crack of thunder shook the keep. The last, rolling reverberations were drowned by the pouring rain.

Fortunately, the rain also drowned out Meg's words to her husband. Though each word was carefully chosen, not one of them was fit to pass a lady's lips.

21

THE COLD WIND AND RAIN WAS followed by a cold drizzle, which was followed by another wild and blustery storm. It was two days before the sun came out again.

Meg was as unsettled as the weather. The body she had thought she knew quite well turned out to be something not very well known at all. The sound of Dominic's voice at a distance set her heart to racing. The sight of him striding into a room shortened her breath. The simplest touch of his hand sent pleasurable chills over her skin. Remembering how he had caressed her in the bathing room made a liquid heat coil deep within her body.

Meg's only satisfaction—and it was a paltry one—was that Dominic himself had not been unaffected. She suspected he did not trust his own formidable self-control any longer where she was concerned.

Have you bled yet?

No.

Tell me when you do, small falcon. Then we shall fly together—and not before.

Dominic's decree angered Meg. It was bad enough that he didn't trust her not to be breeding Duncan's bastard. It was unbearable to be wanted simply for the fruit of her womb rather than for her laughter and her companionship, her warmth and her wit, her silences and her hopes. She had so much more to share with Dominic than a future heir.

Yet even as Meg dreamed of being able to seduce Dominic from his discipline, she feared the cost if she should quicken and not be able to convince Dominic that the babe was his.

He did not love her.

Nor did gossip encourage trust. The countryside was alive with whispers about Duncan and Lady Margaret, lovers destined for one another but separated by a harsh Norman master. No matter how emphatically Meg denied any liaison with Duncan to every person she met, no matter how she praised her Norman husband, the gossip persisted.

Meg prayed that Dominic hadn't heard the whisperings, yet she knew he must have. Little that happened in and around Blackthorne Keep escaped his attention. The servants could attest to his keen eye. The keep glistened with its recent cleaning. From every floor rose the fragrance of rushes and herbs freshly laid. The spices he had brought from the East scented the air around the kitchen, making the end of winter's stores smell like a feast.

But it was the contents of the treasure chests that fascinated most men. Each time Meg appeared with golden bells chiming and gems glittering in her hair, everyone within hearing stopped what they were doing and stared.

With mixed feelings of pleasure and frustration, Meg looked at Dominic's latest present to her. It was an extraordinary pin of gold and emeralds in a fanciful design that somehow evoked a falcon riding the wind. Larger than her hand, set with countless perfect emeralds, the pin secured a mantle of scarlet wool whose floral designs were emblazoned in costly gold thread. Tiny golden bells had been sewn into the design. When she walked or turned or sat, delicate music followed each movement.

Small falcon with emerald eyes and jesses of gold. Wear this and think of me, of healing the land.

Of sons.

"Mistress?" Eadith called. "Where are you?"

Startled, Meg whirled around. Bells trembled and chimed, marking her sudden motion.

"In the chapel," Meg said.

She stood as Eadith came into the small room which occupied the third floor of a corner tower.

"What is it?" Meg said.

"Your lord wonders if you would like to go hunting."

"Aye! When?"

"After dinner."

Meg looked at the angle of the sunlight slanting into the chapel. Almost noon. She had little time to change.

"Quickly, then," Meg said.

In a flurry of golden music, Meg raced up the winding stairs to her quarters, followed by a grumbling Eadith. But complaining or not, the handmaiden's fingers were quick about their work. Before the noon bells rang, Meg was seated in the great hall, surrounded by knights whose falcons waited on perches along the wall behind the knights' chairs. The perch behind Dominic's chair was empty.

"Did my lord decide not to bring his peregrine to table?" Meg asked Simon, who was seated to the left of the empty chair Dominic would occupy.

"No. Something about the jesses had to be changed. He should be here soon."

"Is she calm?" Meg persisted.

"Aye," Simon said with clear satisfaction. "Fatima rides her master's wrist with great assurance. She is a queen among peregrines. By summer's end she will bring many fat ducks to our plates."

A snarl came from beneath the table, followed by a flurry of yips.

"Baron!" Meg said clearly, not bothering to look. "Stop tormenting Leaper."

A greyhound's head appeared next to Meg's thigh. Baron gave her a woeful glance. She rubbed his ears absently.

Simon stared. "If I called him down like that, he'd have my hand."

"Baron? Nay, he's a gentle beast when he's not on the hunt."

Laughter and a shake of his head was Simon's only answer.

A feeling of imminence came over Meg, telling her that her husband was near. She turned from Simon to the entrance to the great hall. An instant later Dominic appeared.

Despite the sunlit promise of the day, Dominic was wearing his heavy black mantle. On his wrist rode the large falcon. When he walked through a shaft of sunlight, the subtle gray and cream coloring of Fatima's feathers shone like steel and pearl.

The peregrine knew her own aristocracy. Certainty of prowess was in every line of her body. Her clear, penetrating black glance summarized and dismissed the cheerful chaos of dinner in the great hall. With the indrawn stillness of a supremely patient predator, the falcon awaited the signal for a hunt to begin.

Murmurs of admiration and excitement rose from the rank of knights as Dominic strode past with the peregrine riding calmly on his wrist. Many of the other birds, some of them with long training, went hooded to their perches in the great hall. Not Dominic's falcon. Her eyes were calm with elemental knowledge of life and death.

And from her legs dangled new jesses studded with emeralds and precious golden bells.

"By God, she is a beauty," Simon said.

Dominic smiled and held his wrist next to Fatima's perch behind his chair. She stepped onto the perch without a fuss. Then she cocked her head from side to side and looked at the banquet hall as though trying to decide if there were anything worthy of her predatory attention.

"I pity any mouse brave enough to venture into the hall," Simon said.

"Nay. Fatima won't be bothered by such tiny prey," Dominic said.

"Try not feeding her for a day or two," Meg retorted. "She'll catch mice fast enough to put Black Tom to shame."

Dominic gave his wife a sideways look. He had been careful not to be alone with her since he had so nearly taken her in the bath. Staying away from her hadn't been easy; just remembering the act of opening her thighs and beginning to press into her as she sat on the table had the ability to make him hard, hot, ready.

With an inner curse, he stifled his lusty thoughts. Before he touched her again, he must be certain she wasn't breeding. He could not trust himself to hold back a second time.

"You look beautiful, as always," Dominic said.

He lifted Meg's hand and brushed a kiss against the underside of her wrist. The sudden, frantic race of her pulse beneath his lips made him want to groan with a mixture of triumph and sexual hunger.

Will she never bleed?

" 'Tis the jewelry and mantle," Meg said. "They are beautiful, not I."

" 'Tis you," Dominic said flatly.

Though Meg said nothing more, Dominic read her disbelief in her expression. His mantle flared almost impatiently as he sat down next to Meg.

"Duncan must have been a miserable lover," Dominic muttered under his breath as he sat between Simon and his wife.

Meg couldn't believe what she had just heard.

"I beg your pardon?" she whispered.

"Duncan must have been a miserable lover," Dominic repeated obligingly.

Simon made a choked sound and carefully looked away from his brother.

"What are you saying?" Meg asked, shocked.

"He never got around to mentioning your beauty," Dominic said in a matter-of-fact tone. "Therefore the bastard must have been a miserable lover."

" 'Tis hardly surprising the matter never came up," she retorted. "I am not beautiful and he was never my lover!"

Dominic's eyes gleamed as he remembered Meg's body gilded with water and passion, each of her breaths echoed by softly crying bells. The familiar rush of blood pooling into rigid flesh made him want to laugh and curse at the same time. By the time Meg bled, he was going to be walking around doubled over from the pain of constant arousal.

"You are wrong," Dominic said in a low voice. "I have never seen another woman as beautiful to me as you."

The sensual blaze of his eyes and the rasp of desire in his voice told Meg that he, too, remembered the intimacy of the bath.

"Duncan has never seen beauty in me," Meg said huskily. "Not as you have."

For a vivid instant Dominic remembered just how much of her beauty he had seen. With a wrench he pushed the image of her open thighs from his mind.

Deliberately he turned away from Meg and signaled for the meal to be served. When he turned back to her, his mind—if not his unruly body—was under control once more.

"That's not what everyone says," Dominic said coolly. "Each day that goes by, more gossip breeds about your lover waiting for you where the forest gives way to the northern fens."

"I can't control wagging tongues," Meg said in a tight voice.

With a shrug, Dominic reached for his mug of ale. "So long as gossip is all that's breeding, it matters little."

"Is it so hard for you to believe in my honor?" Meg demanded.

Dominic's hand paused in the act of lifting the mug.

"Honor is many things to many people," he said after a moment. "In Jerusalem, God's honor demanded that Turks die. For the Turks, God's honor insisted that infidels die. In England, honor demands fealty to king. In the northern marches, honor requires that the king of England be denied. I do not know what Glendruid honor requires beyond that you do not use your healing skills to kill."

"It requires healing," Meg said succinctly. "Betraying your trust in my fidelity is hardly a healing thing."

"For me, no. But for Duncan? Ah, that is a different matter. Nay," Dominic said abruptly when Meg would have spoken. "Don't ply me with soothing words, wife. 'Tis not words that matter, but deeds."

"Truly? Then why does gossip trouble you?" she asked. "It is but words."

"Describing deeds—"

"Which never occurred," she shot back.

"I hope you are right. But hope, too, is merely a word."

The fish course arrived, interrupting the conversation. In silence Dominic applied himself to the boiled eel and its savory broth. The same silence prevailed through the fowl course. The pigeons were lean but decently spiced and quite brown from the spit. Dominic ate two of the birds with the same precision and restraint he did everything else.

Rather grimly Meg wondered if Dominic ever slipped the leash on his self-discipline, or if he was truly as cold as he seemed. No sooner had the thought come than she remembered his expression when he had stood between her thighs in the bath. His face had been drawn with the same passion that had made a shudder run visibly through him when his blunt, aroused flesh had first probed against her sultry gate.

Heat flushed Meg at the memory. She reached for her ale and drank quickly, hoping to cool the uncanny fires Dominic had lighted within her.

Beside her, Dominic lowered his own mug to the table with a thump and turned to his brother.

"What news, Simon?"

"The same. The Reevers are prowling through your estates like the wolves they are. When we come upon them, they vanish. When we turn our backs, they reappear."

Though Simon spoke softly, Meg heard him above the genial clamor of the meal. Her breath tightened in her throat until she ached.

She still dreamed, and she still awoke chilled and sweating at the same instant.

"God's teeth," Dominic muttered. "Duncan will get naught for his trouble but hunted down like a wolf and slain. He seemed a wiser man than that."

"He is a bastard," Simon said matter-of-factly. "He will do what he must to get land. Obviously he has spies here. He knows your knights haven't yet arrived. That's why he is so bold."

"Aye," Dominic said grimly. "What news did Sven have from the south?"

"Ten days or more before the rest of your knights and your riding household arrives. The storms have been severe."

"God's *teeth*. Had I known, I would have waited to marry."

Simon smiled thinly. "I doubt that, brother. It was rumors of Duncan that spurred you north in the first place."

A platter of whole roasted pig appeared in front of Dominic before he could answer. The boar was winter-lean and old, but the kitchen had done its best. The ears were nicely burnt yet still intact, and the skin was a deep brown, promising as succulent a roast as the animal's age and condition permitted.

"I hope the hunt is successful," Dominic said. "If the cooks can do this well with a doddering old boar, imagine what could be done with venison."

"Stop. You will make me drool," Simon said.

The greyhounds set up a snarling, yipping turmoil beneath the table.

"Baron," Dominic said curtly. "Enough!"

After a few yips and a soft growl, the hounds subsided.

Dominic pulled his belt knife and sliced portions of meat for himself and for Meg. Steam rose and savory juices ran onto the platter, pooling like hot rain. A stuffing of figs, onions, and rosemary spilled out. Hot bread was passed along with the meat.

When a bowl of cooked greens appeared, Dominic looked askance at his wife. Smiling, Meg put the greens next to her meat, broke off a crust of bread to catch the juices, and began eating with delicate greed.

Soft whines issued from beneath the table.

Meg ignored them. But she couldn't ignore the sudden pressure of her husband's leg against hers when he reached for the saltcellar. Even through the weight of her clothing, she felt the heat of his body. Her hand shook and a bite of meat fell to the floor.

Hounds seethed suddenly around Meg's legs. Teeth snapped, startling her from her sensual distraction with her husband's warmth. She pushed back from the table so quickly that her heavy chair teetered on the edge of falling.

Dominic moved in a blur of speed. One hand righted Meg's chair and the other hand vanished beneath the table, only to reappear immediately holding Leaper by the scruff. A torrent of Turkish poured over the hapless hound while she was soundly shaken for frightening Meg. As soon as the greyhound was released, she slunk off to sit under someone else's feet.

"Are you bitten?" Dominic asked, concerned.

"No, just startled. I was thinking of something else, and Leaper isn't usually so bold about snatching food from the males."

"She is coming into heat." Dominic smiled faintly. "She knows it, so she starts testing all the males."

"Gets away with it, too," Simon said.

"How nice to know that every bitch has her day," Meg said blandly.

Dominic leaned over to her and said softly, "Don't get any ideas, wench. Men are brighter than dogs."

"Dazzling thought, that. We all know what an intellectual marvel the average long-tongued hound is."

"The bitch is brighter than some women," Dominic said.

"How so?"

"When her time comes, she knows what is her due from the males, and she demands it."

Meg knew better than to ask what the bitch's "due" was. Heat flushed her cheeks.

The smile on Dominic's face told Meg that he guessed her thoughts. He leaned even closer to her.

"Have you bled yet?" he whispered.

The color of her cheeks deepened.

"How long?" Dominic persisted.

Without a word, Meg bent her head and tried the roasted pork. Dominic's smoky glance watched every morsel slide between her lips.

"If we were alone, small falcon," he said in a low voice, "you would be taking food from my hand. And I . . ."

Meg looked up, saw the sensual burning in Dominic's eyes, and knew that if they were alone, he would be doing a good deal more with his hands than feeding her.

Abruptly Dominic stood. "It is time for the hunt."

FOUR knights, five squires, a single lady, a pack of hounds, and the hound master rode to the hunt. Only the presence of Meg betrayed that it was a hunt rather than a battle being sought. Dominic and his men broke custom and hunted in hauberk, sword, and helm, astride destriers and followed by squires carrying lances.

It was an awkward way to hunt, but not as awkward as coming unarmed upon a nest of Reevers would have been.

Ahead of the hunting party, the rugged fells thrust steeply into an unusually clear sky. Neither as large as the mountains Dominic had seen in his travels, nor small enough to be dismissed as hills, the rocky fells were covered with the shimmering green mantle of spring. Hidden by distance and the rugged land was a long, ragged lake from which flowed the headwaters of the Blackthorne River. With the river as their guide, Simon hoped to find a shortcut to the place where he had come across a large stag's spoor when he had backtracked Meg.

In sheltered places on the hillsides, trees found a foothold and lifted their countless branches to the sky. A blush of green hazed the branches, telling of buds coming gently unwrapped beneath the warm sun. Wildflowers bloomed in vivid colors of yellow and blue, purple and gold, greedily absorbing sunlight in the days before the leaves of oak and birch, willow and alder opened to create a dense forest canopy. Once the trees were fully leafed out, little sunlight would reach the ground. Then mosses would swell and thrive, and ferns would unfurl their ancient green bouquets.

Despite the armed knights at every hand, and the aging palfrey that was her mount, Meg was enjoying the ride. The pretty sounds of the bells in her jewelry and mantle seemed to incite the songbirds to greater outpourings, making the day alive with music.

Overhead an eagle quested for prey, its keening cry an untamed song of freedom. Meg shaded her eyes with her hand and looked up, measuring the effortless flight of the bird. As always, she yearned to know what it would be like to soar within the sunlit beauty of the sky.

"Simon?" Dominic asked, reining in his stallion. "Is this the place you spotted the stag's spoor?"

Simon considered the area just ahead, where tributary creeks braided down from the fells into Blackthorne River. Too wet for trees, the ground became a marsh dotted with quiet pools. Rivulets of moving water wound among the brown sedges, joining them with a liquid network that was silver or blue or black, depending on the time of day.

"It looks like it," Simon said finally. "I approached from over there. The heathen place is beyond, to the west."

Simon pointed away from the cart road which led to Carlysle, the northernmost of the six manor houses Dominic had acquired along with John of Cumbriland's only heir and daughter. On the other side of the fen, the fells rose steeply. Many of the ridgelines were brushed with snow from the past storm. The crags themselves wore shimmering white crowns that would not melt until summer was well advanced.

"Meg?" Dominic asked. "Is there a way here through the fen to yonder vale?"

She looked beyond the marsh to the wild glen that cut across the fells. In the summer the vale would be a mosaic of green forest and sunny glades thick with grass. At the moment it was a pale-trunked, dark-branched ghost wood where only the undergrowth had turned green in its yearly race for the sun. A creek stitched brightly through the glades where new grass pushed through the dun mat of last summer's growth.

"A game trail cuts to the left," Meg said, pointing. "It will be slow going through the fen, but after that the way is easy enough."

Dominic gave the countryside a sweeping glance, memorizing the lie of fells and dale, forest and glade and fen. He glanced at the hound master, who nodded eagerly. The hounds, too, were keen for the hunt.

There had been little sport for them since they had left Normandy.

Abruptly Dominic motioned the hound master forward. When the game trail winding through the fen was discovered, the man blew a short note on his horn, rallying the dogs.

"You go first," Dominic said to Simon.

Surprised, Simon reined his stallion past his brother. Equally surprised knights were waved forward. Dominic fell in behind Meg's palfrey. She turned and gave him a curious look.

"I didn't want you trampled by the war stallions in the heat of the chase," Dominic said. "Your mount is willing, but a bit long in the tooth for hunting in country such as this."

"What of you?" Meg asked. "If I fall behind, you'll miss the kill."

"There will be other hunts."

"My palfrey will be the same."

"Aye, but you won't be riding her. When my knights arrive, you will have a Saracen palfrey whose coat is as red as your hair."

"Truly?" Meg asked, excited.

"Truly. She should have fine colts from Crusader."

"Breeding again," Meg muttered under her breath. "Is that the only use you can think of for a female?"

If Dominic heard, he said nothing in response.

Meg had been correct about the first part of the trail being difficult. By the time her mare picked a careful route through the traps and snares of the sedges, the palfrey was breathing deeply and had fallen a hundred yards behind the other knights. Despite carrying much more weight, the stallions were unaffected by the hard going, for Dominic conditioned the war-horses as carefully as he conditioned his knights. A mount that lost wind or strength on the battlefield was worse than useless.

When Meg's palfrey finally cleared the boggy stretch, Dominic came alongside and waved the squires on past. Almost two hundred yards ahead now, the knights followed the creek through grass and scattered trees, and then into forest. Even without leaves, the trees and underbrush were sufficiently thick to swallow up the knights and the pursuing squires without a trace.

Meg and Dominic had covered a thousand yards when the sound of a hunting horn echoed through the day. They pulled up and listened. The horn cried again and then again, marking the twists and turns of the chase.

"They turned up a side creek," Meg said, listening.

The horn sounded again, urgently.

"The stag has been sighted!" Dominic said.

Breath held, they listened to the fading sound of the horn. The stag was leading the hounds a fine chase through hill and dale. Dominic had been right; the pace was breakneck. Her palfrey would have been badly outrun.

Without warning, unease slid like ice down Meg's spine. She looked around quickly in the manner of prey seeking any escape route.

"What is it?" Dominic said.

"I don't know. Suddenly I feel like the stag. Hunted."

"Does this happen often when the quarry is sighted?" he asked curiously.

"Never before. I—" Meg's voice broke off as though slashed with a knife.

A horn sounded from the east, directly between Dominic and Meg and the knights pursuing the stag. The note of the horn was not that of the hound master of Blackthorne Keep.

"Do you recognize the horn?" Dominic asked.

"It can't be," Meg said. "He wouldn't."

"Who?" Dominic demanded.

"Duncan. 'Tis the battle horn of the Reevers."

The horn sounded again, closer now. The Reevers were pursuing not the knights and squires, but the two who had strayed perilously far behind.

"God's eyes," Dominic hissed. "Is there a place nearby that one man can hold against many?"

"There is a place where no man will go."

"Lead on!"

"It's that way," Meg pointed, "but my palfrey can't—"

Before Meg could finish speaking, Dominic snatched her from her mount, settled her astride in a wild flurry of cloth in front of him, and put his spurs to the big stallion.

Behind them rose the shout of men who had just spotted their quarry.

22

MEG CROUCHED PERILOUSLY FAR over the right side of the stallion's neck while the lowest branch of a great oak threatened to sweep her from the saddle. Behind her, Dominic bent to the left. They passed under the branch so closely that his hauberk scraped bark.

What sounded like shouts came from behind them. If it was the Reevers, they had fallen back in the frantic scramble up the hill.

A hound bayed. The sound was deep-throated and supple, the voice of an animal whose wolf ancestors were only a few generations removed.

"They're tracking us with dogs!" Meg cried, trying to see over her shoulder.

"Don't look back," Dominic commanded. "You'll lose balance."

Without answering, Meg buried her face once more against the stallion's muscular neck and hung on with both hands until her muscles ached. Even so, if it hadn't been for Dominic's hard arm around her waist, she would have fallen. She wasn't accustomed to blazing across the countryside on a horse of Crusader's size and strength.

Meg's frantic heartbeat blended in her ears with

the rolling thunder of Crusader's hooves, his deep breaths, and the urgent chiming of golden bells. Black mane whipped against her face. Tears were ripped from her eyes in the wind caused by the stallion's furious pace as he lunged over a rocky hilltop and raced down the far side.

Forest closed around them again, concealing them from their pursuers. Several hundred yards beyond the bottom of the hill stood a grove of massive oaks. They grew so thickly it was impossible to gallop through. In any case, Crusader was showing an abrupt reluctance to go forward at any speed.

"God's teeth!" Dominic swore, spurring the stallion. "What is possessing you, Crusader?"

Crusader flattened his ears and balked, refusing to move another step.

"Off!" Meg said, sliding down in a jangling of golden bells. "Quickly!"

Dominic dismounted as though for battle, leaping off to land on both feet, his hand on his sword, his body poised and ready to fight.

Meg whipped off her head cloth and held it out.

"Blindfold Crusader," she said, "then follow me. If the stallion balks again, leave him. Quickly! They will be upon us!"

Dominic grabbed the head cloth, wrapped it around Crusader's white-rimmed eyes, and tugged on the reins. Snorting, pulling back in alarm, the stallion swung like a pendulum at the end of the reins, trying to go everywhere but forward.

Despite the urgency goading him, Dominic spoke soothingly to the stallion and applied a steady pressure on the reins.

"Hurry!" Meg called from ahead. "I see a dog!"

Crusader snorted, minced, and gave in, following Dominic as he had so many times before, even into the dank, wretched hold of a ship. Walking quickly, then trotting, Dominic led the stallion between trees that grew older and more magnificent the deeper the grove was penetrated.

Standing stones taller and thicker than Dominic loomed without warning between the trees. The stones had been in place so long that they wore thick robes of moss and lichen, as though tiny gardens had been planted in rocky hollows no deeper than a finger's width.

After three hundred feet, more stones loomed. These were half a man's height and set so close together that no trees grew between. After the second ring of stones came a circle of grass seventy feet across. In the center of the circle was a large, overgrown mound of earth and rock.

The hair on Dominic's neck lifted in animal awareness. At some primal level of his mind he sensed what had made Crusader shy off from penetrating the grove. There was a sanctuary within the concentric rings of stones that wasn't meant to be disturbed heedlessly.

Glendruid.

Wary and curious at once, Dominic looked around as he led his blindfolded war stallion into a place of peace and protection. There was sunlight and grass in the widening spaces between oaks. Wildflowers sang their silent, colorful songs everywhere he looked. The trees were more fully leafed out here, as though the sun came sooner and stayed longer in this one spot.

From beyond the first ring of stones came the frantic baying of a hound that had been deprived of its prey. Oddly, no other hound voices joined it. Dominic looked questioningly at Meg.

"Does Duncan hunt with but one hound?"

"Only when he seeks poachers. Besides, we can't be certain it's Duncan."

"Leave off defending the bastard," Dominic said harshly. "Who else would it be?"

Meg said nothing. There was nothing she could say to deny the logic of Dominic's words, but the logic of her emotions was something entirely different.

"I should have let Simon gut the Scots Hammer in the church," Dominic muttered.

He looked around the sunny glade with its ancient mound. There was no place where a lone knight might have his back safe while defending his front.

"Keep going," Dominic said to Meg. "We haven't reached a haven yet."

"There is no better haven except the keep, and no way to get there but the way we took coming here."

Meg didn't add that the Reevers now occupied the ground between the haunted circle and Blackthorne Keep. She didn't have to point out the obvious. Dominic's scalding oaths told her that he realized their predicament as well as she.

"Then we are well and truly caught," Dominic said. "It would take many knights to defend this place."

"Nay. Not one Reever will pass the outer circle of stones."

"Duncan is more than clever enough to blindfold his horse and follow our tracks here."

"I doubt it. I wasn't certain it would work myself."

Dominic stared at Meg. "Then why did you suggest it?"

"I knew you wouldn't leave your stallion until it was too late. The Reevers would have killed you like a stag brought to bay before you made it through the outer ring."

He grunted. "They may do it yet."

"I think not. In a thousand years no man has ever

passed the standing stones. Not even my father."

"Did he try?"

"Once."

"Why?"

Meg shrugged. "He thought the secret to having a son lay inside the stones rather than inside his heart."

"Or inside his wife's heart?" suggested Dominic.

Suddenly Crusader's head came up. He tugged sharply at the reins.

"Gently," Dominic said in a low voice, stroking the stallion's neck. "There is nothing to fear in this place."

"He scents the water," Meg said, pointing toward a tumble of rocks and lush undergrowth that lay at the base of the mound.

"A sacred spring?" Dominic asked neutrally.

"Nothing Glendruid will be offended if a stallion slakes its thirst. Is that what you mean?"

Without a word, Dominic removed the stallion's blindfold. Crusader looked around curiously, but showed no fear. Dominic led the stallion to the spring and waited while Crusader drank the crystal water.

It was easy to follow the progress of the Reevers around the outer ring of stones. Faint shouts and the sad baying of a hound were heard from various points around the circle as the renegades tried to pick up the trail on the other side of the haunted ground.

Between the stones themselves, nothing moved but the wind.

"What lies at the center of the mound?" Dominic asked.

"A chamber with no ceiling."

"Is there room inside for a horse?"

Meg hesitated.

"Never mind," he said, reading her reluctance. "I'll tie Crusader out here."

"Nothing will bother him."

"Go to the mound chamber," Dominic said. "If Duncan is brave or clever enough to get through the rings of stones, the chamber will be easier to defend than this open space."

"What about you?"

"I'll be along as soon as I see to Crusader. Or will I need special spells and incantations to get inside?" Dominic asked sardonically.

"Nothing more exotic than the eyes God gave you," Meg said in a tight voice. "If this were an evil place, my cross would not tolerate it."

Dominic shrugged. "It matters not. I would trade with the Devil himself for shelter from Duncan and his Reevers."

"Nay!" Meg said, horrified. "Never say that!"

He laughed. "What an odd witch you are."

"I am not a witch," Meg said, spacing each word. "I am Glendruid. It is not the same thing."

"The common folk have trouble distinguishing between the two."

"That is why they are common," she retorted.

"Go to the mound, Glendruid wife. I'll join you there."

Meg walked around the mound until she came to an opening where the earth and rocks either had been sliced away or never piled up in the first place. The passageway was narrow, stone-lined, and thick with last season's leaves. After a few yards it opened into a circular chamber. If the area had ever been roofed over, all sign of it was gone.

Grass and wildflowers grew in a thick carpet. To the western side, last year's leaves had piled at the feet of four odd white stones. They could have been supports for a shelter or obelisks surrounding a vanished altar or reference points capturing the slanting light at the change of a certain season. No living person knew.

If the Glendruids had ever known the purpose of the mound, the chamber, or the obelisks, that knowledge had not survived the ages since brother had turned against brother and the Glendruid Wolf had been lost; and with it, the peace of the land itself.

"You look sad," Dominic said from behind Meg. "Is this a melancholy place for you or are you unhappy that Duncan missed his chance to take you?"

"Is that what you believe?"

The temptation to goad Meg nearly overrode Dominic's good sense. With a muttered oath, he reined in his tongue. His temper was always volatile when his blood was up after a battle. His men had learned to walk carefully around him.

"Let me just say I am sick unto death of hearing about you and Duncan of Maxwell," Dominic said bitterly.

"So am I." Meg's tone was as bitter as her husband's.

It was a visible effort, but Dominic held on to his temper.

"Stay here," he said. "I'll stand guard outside."

Without a word Meg watched Dominic stalk out of the chamber. It took only a short time for her to find a comfortable place amid the grass and wildflowers. She removed her mantle, turned it inside out to protect the elaborately brocaded cloth, and made a pillow for herself. Her head cloth had come awry in the frantic ride, as had her braids. She removed the golden jesses, shook out her hair, and set to work on it with the jeweled comb that had been Dominic's gift.

From the top of the mound where Dominic now sat, the shift and ripple of Meg's hair was like fire combed by fingers of gold. The small chiming of the bells she wore at her wrists and around her hips fit the day as perfectly as did the songs of birds.

No matter how sternly Dominic told himself he must watch for Reevers, the music and beauty of his wife kept drawing his eyes. With a muttered curse he closed his eyes and listened for anything more sinister than the tiny bells and the liquid calling of songbirds.

Nothing came to his ears but the languid drone of insects and the secret sighing of the breeze through the tender leaves of spring. Dominic looked toward Crusader, trusting the stallion's instinct for danger.

The horse's head was lowered and he was lipping lazily at some tender shoots. From time to time Crusader lifted his head and scented the breeze with flared nostrils and pricked ears, sifting the wind for any hints of danger. Apparently no odor of strange men, horses, or dogs—or familiar ones, either—came to the stallion, for he resumed nuzzling at foliage in the manner of a horse that is bored rather than hungry.

The sun was a warm blessing on the land. Relaxation began to steal over Dominic, drawing away the tension of flight and battle. He looked back into the chamber and saw Meg stretched out in the grass, her hair fanned in silky glory around her head. The temptation to join her was as great as any he had ever known.

Dominic resisted the siren song of peace and relaxation for some time, but nothing in the calm day rewarded his vigilance. Finally he climbed down off the mound, led Crusader to the passageway, and tied him just outside where no man could get past without alerting the stallion.

Inside the chamber, Dominic wearily eased off his

helm and set it aside. His dark mantle made a fine
bed over the grass and flowers. As soon as it was prepared, he lifted Meg onto the mantle and lay down
beside her. The weight of sunlight unraveled him
as deeply as any ale ever had. He threw off his hauberk and chausses, savoring the freedom from war's
weight. With a long sigh he drew Meg into his arms.

For the first time since he had traded his own
freedom for that of his men in Jerusalem, Dominic
le Sabre slept without dreaming.

WHEN Meg first awoke, she didn't
know where she was. Even so, she felt no fear. The
heat of the sun and the sweet trilling of forest birds
assured her that she was safe before she opened her
eyes. Even more reassuring than birdsong was the
heavy warmth of Dominic's arms around her and
the steady, relaxed beating of his heart beneath her
cheek.

Abruptly Meg remembered the frantic flight
through the forest. She lifted her head just enough
to see through the passageway to the glade and
the trees that surrounded the ancient site. Crusader
stood at the entrance to the mound with his head
down and his weight on three legs, sleeping on his
feet after the manner of horses.

The shadows at the mound entrance had shifted
very little, telling Meg that her sleep hadn't been a
long one. Yet she felt curiously refreshed. She always
did when she came here. It was as though the peace
of a thousand years had pooled here to be drunk by
those wise enough to slip between standing stones
to the sunlit mound.

When Meg turned her face back to Dominic, she
realized that he had taken off his battle gear to lie in
the sun with her. He, too, must have felt the healing
touch of the ancient place.

The realization went through Meg like lightning. Old Gwyn had known of no man for a thousand years who had been able to put aside his unease long enough to enter the inner ring of stones, much less to surrender himself in sleep to the venerable peace of the mound.

Yet Dominic had done just that.

The proof of that incredible fact lay before her now, his powerful body relaxed, his eyes closed, sleeping as deeply as any babe. Dominic le Sabre, a warrior so powerful that he made even the king of England uneasy, had a baffling communion with peace.

Work with me, wife. Help me to bring peace to the land.

The words were so distinct that at first Meg thought Dominic had spoken aloud to her. With the next breath she realized it was the past she was hearing, when Dominic had emerged from poison's snare and looked at her with eyes as clear as the sacred spring at the base of the mound.

Work with me, wife. Help me to bring peace to the land.

How?

Blend Saxon and Norman blood. Give me sons.

In a silence that brimmed with possibilities, Meg looked at the thick, ragged fringes of Dominic's eyelashes and the loosely curling forelock that was often concealed beneath a battle helm. She remembered how soft and cool his hair felt between her fingers, how warm it was at his scalp, and how well he liked to feel her nails lightly drawn over his skin.

Gently Meg ran her palm over the supple leather shirt Dominic wore beneath his hauberk. Under the shirt's laces lay a thatch of dense black hair. Thick, springy, it was unlike the smooth hair on Dominic's head. She wondered if this hair would feel as intriguing between her fingers as it did to her fingertips. No sooner had the thought come than she found herself picking apart the laces so that she could slide her fingers unhindered beneath.

With a small sound of pleasure, Meg discovered that the muscular contours of Dominic's chest were both warm and resilient, and the dark furring of hair teased her palm irresistibly. She caressed him with slow movements of her hand, smiling at the pleasure it gave her to touch him so.

A subtle change in the tension of Dominic's body told Meg that he was awakening. Reluctantly she ceased her petting and began to ease her fingers from his shirt.

A hand hardened by war came down over Meg's, holding her palm against Dominic's chest.

"Don't stop," he said huskily, "or I shall be even more jealous of Black Tom than I already am."

Meg's smile widened. She lifted her head until she could look down into eyes that were the clear, uncanny silver of a sacred Glendruid spring.

"Or do you prefer stroking Black Tom because he has more fur than I?" Dominic asked whimsically.

"I doubt that. You feel quite wonderfully furry to me."

Dominic's breath came in swiftly when Meg's hand slipped inside his leather shirt and she began petting him once more. Pleasure rippled through him, for the expression on her face told him that she was enjoying the stroking as much as he.

"Are you cold?" Meg asked, concerned.

"Nay."

Dominic's voice was very deep and his eyes were smoky with a lazy, teasing sensuality that Meg had never before seen in her husband.

"You shivered," she pointed out.

"Yes."

His hand shifted. The back of his index finger caressed Meg's cheek, her jawline, the nape of her neck, the hollow of her throat. The caress drew a quivering sigh from her.

"Are you cold?" Dominic asked.

His eyes said he knew very well what the answer would be.

"Nay," Meg said. "Is that . . . ?"

He made a questioning, almost purring sound and pressed her hand beneath his once more. He rubbed her palm over his chest, and as he did, he twisted slowly against her touch like a cat.

"Is that why you shivered?" Meg asked curiously. "My touch?"

"Yes. Your touch. And you shivered at mine. Touch me some more, small falcon. Make me tremble."

"Will you like that?"

"I don't know. I have never trembled at a woman's touch before now."

Hesitantly, then with greater confidence, Meg stroked Dominic's chest beneath his shirt. The warmth of him was delicious, as was the deliberate movement of his body against her hand, redoubling the sensual petting.

"You are indeed like Black Tom," Meg said.

"Furry?"

"And warm. And supple." She tested Dominic's muscular chest with her fingernails. "And strong. And sleek. And . . . altogether quite wonderful."

Laughter and sensual response tangled in Dominic's throat. The result was a low, rough sound.

"And you purr, too," Meg teased. "What a wonderful thing is a catlike man. Do you also catch mice in your teeth?"

"I fear not."

"Ah well, perhaps Black Tom can teach you."

Dominic laughed in the moments before his breath caught. Meg's slender fingers had found the smooth skin around one nipple. The contrast between hair and skin must have pleased her, for she returned to circle the nipple again. When it hardened into a tiny point, she lifted her hand, startled.

"Again," he said huskily.

"You like it?"

"The only thing I would like more is your warm tongue."

The memory of how Dominic had caressed her own nipple went through Meg in a liquid wave of heat.

"Aye," she whispered, eyes closed. "I remember."

Dominic pulled off the leather shirt. Beneath it was nothing but the warm skin, muscle, and springy hair she had been enjoying. Eyes still closed, she explored him with her fingers.

"You are . . . beautiful," Meg whispered.

"Nay," Dominic said, running his fingertip around her lips. "You are the beautiful one. I am scarred from head to heels."

Meg blinked and opened her eyes. For the first time she saw the scar running across Dominic's chest and shoulder. Her breath came in with a low sound as she thought of the pain the wound must have caused him.

Silently cursing himself for his stupidity in undressing beneath full sunlight, Dominic reached for the shirt he had so recently cast aside.

Meg's hand darted out, preventing Dominic from pulling the shirt over his head.

"Give way, wife. I'm better seen in darkness than in light," he said flatly.

"Nay," she said. "You are a pleasure to my eyes."

"You can barely bring yourself to look at me. Let me dress."

"It was the pain."

"What?"

"Your pain cries out from the scar," Meg said simply. "I wasn't expecting that. I won't be taken by surprise again. Let me see you, my warrior."

Let me heal you.

Slowly Dominic's fist opened, giving up the shirt. Meg put it aside and looked at her husband. After a taut, silent moment she began tracing the muscular lines of his body with caressing fingertips.

"I have sensed your male power before," Meg said after a time. "I have felt it when you lift me. I felt it differently just a few moments ago, when you were as warm and supple as a cat beneath my hands. But I have never seen your naked strength before now."

Dominic's eyes narrowed against the violence of the passion surging through him at each delicate caress from his wife's hands. Meg was looking at him with an admiration that was more than sensual and less than innocent.

"You are splendid, my warrior. Quite . . . magnificent."

Delicately Meg stroked the length of the scar with her fingertips. The caress dragged a low sound from Dominic, for there was nothing of horror in his wife's voice or touch. He knew as clearly as he knew his own heartbeat that he was beautiful in her eyes.

The realization stunned Dominic, for he also knew that only great emotion could overlook the ugly scarring that war had left upon his body.

"This is part of your power," Meg whispered, tracing the scar once more. "I would take the pain from you if I could, but I would not take the mark of honorable battle. Never fear going naked before me, husband. I find you as handsome as you are strong."

A shudder ran the length of Dominic's muscular body, pleasure and something even more powerful, a yearning of the spirit that ravished him as gently as sunlight.

"You are unraveling me," Dominic said huskily.

"Then I will have to knit you up again. But without the pain, my warrior. Without the pain . . ."

As Meg bent to kiss Dominic, her hair fell like cool flames over his skin. He threaded his fingers through the silky mass and pulled her close for a deep, lingering kiss. When he finally released her, she was flushed with pleasure and her fingers were hungry on his chest.

"You are like tasting sunlight and warm rain at once," Dominic said.

"And you are like wine," she whispered. "You make my senses spin."

"Then you should lie down."

With one hand Dominic gathered up the silk and fire of Meg's hair. With the other he pulled her close as he turned over, taking her with him, kissing her until she clung to him as though to life itself. When he dragged his mouth from hers long enough to look at her, she was lying half beneath him, her eyes were languid, and her hair was a smoldering fan spread out over the midnight of his mantle.

"Are you less dizzy now?" Dominic asked, smiling.

Meg started to speak, was caught by a sensual shiver, and stroked her hands down her husband's back instead of trying to tell him how she felt. Beneath her fingertips she felt a network of scars, the kind that could come only from being tied up and whipped until skin broke and flesh became a bloody ruin.

Dominic's body became still, almost distant, as though he had withdrawn from sunlight to a dark, inner place.

"Not exactly scars of 'honorable battle,' are they?" he asked ironically.

"You are wrong," Meg said. "There is no greater honor than trading your own pain for that of your knights."

His breath came out in a rush. "Who told you?"

"Simon." Meg looked up at Dominic's shadowed eyes. "He assured me the sultan's death wasn't easy."

"The sultan died as badly as any man ever has."

"Excellent," Meg said on a long, exhaled breath.

And she meant it.

Surprise widened Dominic's eyes. "You are astonishingly savage for a healer."

"Spring heals winter's wounds, but spring is rarely a gentle time. The wounds of winter are starkly revealed before they are healed by spring, and only the most hardy of living things survive renewal. Healing is not for the faint of heart."

For a long moment Dominic looked at the enigmatic, sensual Glendruid girl who kept surprising him.

"Will I ever know you?" he asked.

Before Meg could answer, Dominic lowered his head and claimed her mouth once more. Closing her eyes, she gave herself to the kiss and to the warrior whose scarred body called to her senses as nothing ever had, not even the first, delicate tremors of spring stirring through the wintry land.

Dominic's embrace was like falling into a magical fire, heat without harm, burning without pain. When his long fingers opened Meg's clothing and pushed it to her waist, she felt sunlight on her naked breasts for the first time in her life. The caressing warmth made her lift instinctively, trying to come closer to the source of her pleasure.

Breath came out of Dominic as though at a blow. He groaned and tasted one breast, teasing the coral peak with sensual forays of his tongue. The rippling cries he drew from Meg made his whole body tighten with violent hunger. He slid his powerful arm beneath her and arched her like a drawn bow. Then he held her there, feeding on her breasts until she moaned and twisted from the searing delight of his caresses.

The taste and scent and feel of Meg sank like sweet talons into Dominic's body, drawing him into an arousal that would have been agonizing if it weren't so great a pleasure. He lifted her higher, holding her with one arm while the other swept clothes from her body.

When he was finished, he stretched her out on his mantle and looked at her with eyes that burned while he stripped away his remaining clothes. He was fully aroused, hot with passion and hard with generations yet unborn.

Meg's eyes widened. She made a ragged sound as Dominic knelt beside her.

"Do I frighten you?" he asked.

"I was just . . . surprised."

Then she looked at Dominic frankly and smiled in a way that made his blood beat visibly in his erect flesh.

"But I should have known," Meg murmured, cupping him in her palm, "that a great knight such as you would have a redoubtable sword."

Passion almost ripped apart Dominic's control. He clung to it by the thinnest margin, ceding only one scalding drop to Meg's unexpected caress. With a low word that was both reverent and profane, he lay beside her, looking at her with fierce hunger.

"You are the riches, not I," he said huskily. "Riches fit for a king. Emerald eyes and skin as fine and smooth as silk."

Dominic kissed Meg's taut nipples until they were flushed and hard from his mouth.

"Rubies," Dominic breathed. "But warm, as warm as the breath of life."

When Meg's eyes closed on a wave of pleasure, Dominic's hands slid down her body, shaping her breasts and waist and thighs, returning to the darker fire that burned at the apex of her legs. Gently he drew her legs apart until he could caress the soft, scented flesh that had haunted him since he first had touched it. Tenderly, relentlessly, he eased his fingers through the tight curls of hair until he found what he sought.

"The jewel beyond price," Dominic whispered.

Meg trembled with the onslaught of pleasure both unexpected and consuming. She tried to speak but her breath broke on a sound of surprise as she convulsed in secret, spilling warmth from her body to Dominic's hand. The scent of passion swirled around him like a wild caress.

"Sandalwood and spice," he whispered, savoring her again. "Most precious of all perfumes."

Pleasure swept through Meg. The ragged sound she made was both Dominic's name and a question. His answer was another circling, tugging caress that made her body weep passionately once more.

"You are perfect," Dominic said huskily. "You are fire that burns me without hurt, and your flames are tipped with diamond tears. What is the heart of your fire like, sweet witch? Will it give me pleasure or pain?"

Dominic watched Meg, enjoying her passionate shivering while he traced the humid, sleek sheath that cried out to hold his sword. When he probed lightly, her helpless response welled up, caressing him in return, luring him unbearably.

"Coral gates guarding a sacred spring," Dominic said, sliding deeper into her thrall. "You are truly magic, my Glendruid bride."

Meg's eyes opened slowly. She saw Dominic's face drawn as though in agony while he watched her with burning silver eyes. Her hands went from his cheeks to the clenched muscles of his torso and from there to his rigid flesh. He shook beneath her tender caresses as though she were flaying him alive.

"You are in pain," she said raggedly. "Let me heal you."

"Only one thing can heal me."

"Then I give it to you."

With fiercely controlled power, Dominic settled between Meg's slender legs. He separated her soft gate with his own blunt flesh, forcing himself to press slowly forward despite the waves of passion that pounded through him, demanding a faster release. She was sultry, welcoming, yet so tight he feared hurting her.

Then he felt the taut veil of virginity and froze. He hadn't dared believe in her innocence, yet the proof of it was pressing against him right now.

Dominic's passion doubled and redoubled in two heartbeats. Sweat glistened on his body as he fought for the self-control he had worked a lifetime to develop.

Instinctively Meg tried to pull him closer, but he resisted with an easy strength that reminded her just how powerful he was.

"Lie still," Dominic whispered hoarsely against Meg's neck. "No good will come for either of us if I hurt you."

"Will it be a greater hurt than John's fist?"

"Nay," Dominic said, giving Meg's cheek tender,

biting kisses. "Never would I hurt you like that. But you are a virgin. If I press deeper, you will bleed."

" 'Tis the nature of swords to draw blood."

"Only once in sensual battle. I promise you, small falcon. Only once."

With a sinuous shift of her body, Meg lured Dominic more deeply into her. This time he didn't pull away. Instead he slipped one hand between their bodies until he could cherish the jewel of her passion with sultry fingertips.

Meg's eyes widened as fire shimmered up from Dominic's touch. Instinctively she raised her hips, rocking against him. He rocked back gently in turn and smiled to see and feel the waves of passion melting her until she moaned and lifted herself again.

"Do you want more?" he asked as he plucked delicately at the living jewel that was set within her softness.

"*Aye*. Dominic, I—" Meg's voice broke.

"How much more? This much?"

His fingers stroked, circled, pressed, tugged, until sensual fire licked over Meg with hot golden tongues. She began to writhe beneath him, calling his name, twisting, desperately needing something she sensed waiting just beyond her reach.

And then it flared all around her, convulsing her subtly, relentlessly, consuming her to her core.

With a low sound of need held in check too long, Dominic drove into the center of Meg's golden fire. If she felt any pain it was overwhelmed by the far greater pleasure that came of being joined completely with her warrior, holding him so closely inside her body that she could feel the pulses of his consummation as distinctly as she had felt her own; and his words echoed in the shivering silence that was also ecstasy.

Love me, Meg. Heal the land with my sons.

23

As had become Dominic's habit in the three days since the Reevers had attacked during the hunt, he stood on Blackthorne Keep's battlement in the condensing stillness after sunset.

From his vantage point Dominic could see mist like silver fire shimmering over fish ponds, river, and the distant lake. He could see the lacy black silhouettes of just-leafed oaks on a nearby ridge and the dense black outline of the fells, where the last rosy bit of light lingered on the crags. He could see the last, laggard sheep being nipped and scolded into their folds for the night by quick-footed dogs. He could see the last skein of waterfowl spiraling down for a night on the lake.

What he could not see was Duncan of Maxwell and his Reevers. Yet Dominic knew they were out there in the twilight and mist, waiting for another chance to strike at the heart of Blackthorne Keep.

Footsteps sounded from the direction of the closest tower. Dominic didn't have to turn his head to discover who was approaching him. The footsteps were almost as familiar as his own.

"A fine evening," Simon said.

Dominic grunted.

"A foul evening, then."

Dominic grunted again.

"A vile mood, perhaps?" suggested Simon.

A hard sideways glance was Dominic's only answer.

"I have news of your knights," Simon said.

That got Dominic's attention. "Where are they?"

"Nine days from here, unless more storms come. The muddy roads mired the carts so badly it was impossible to move for several days."

"God's teeth," Dominic muttered.

"You could order the knights to come ahead of the household goods."

"Fourscore and nine animals laden with expensive goods," Dominic said savagely. "Without knights to defend it from bandits, my traveling household is as helpless as a bird with a broken wing."

Simon's fist smacked into his palm. "Would that I and my knights had come upon the Reevers instead of you and Meg."

"Aye. But even if you had, the Reevers wouldn't have held and fought. Duncan is too clever for that. He knows he would lose a pitched battle. Most of his men are ill trained."

"Sven agrees."

Dominic turned to face his brother. "Is he back?"

Simon nodded.

"Send for him."

Even as Dominic spoke, a man walked from the corner tower. His soft leather shoes made no noise on the stone battlements. It was part of Sven's odd skill in blending into whatever surroundings he found himself among. Dominic had never known a man more quiet, or more deadly.

"Have you supped?" Dominic asked.

"Yes." Sven's voice was soft. "Lord, I haven't

much time. I must be back at the Carlysle Manor before long to tend my flocks."

Dominic's smile flashed whitely in the twilight. The thought of a man as fierce as Sven tending sheep was preposterous.

"What have you learned?" Dominic asked.

"The Reevers are growing in number."

"How many?"

"Eight knights, twelve squires, thirty attendants."

"Mounted?"

"That is their problem. Only two of the knights are riding chargers. The rest are mounted on ill-trained animals. Better horses are expected from Scotland within a few days."

"Arms?" Dominic snapped.

"The knights are as well armed as we are. Not as skilled, but the men are as hard and unforgiving as stone. The Solway Scots have much Viking blood in their veins."

Dominic's mouth curved in a faint smile. Sven's fierce pride in his Norse bloodlines was a source of much amusement among the knights. But no wise man baited Sven on the subject.

"The squires are old enough to be blooded," Sven continued. "Indeed, some of them have been robbing their betters since they were old enough to draw a bow."

A shout from the bailey caused Sven to turn so quickly that his dark gray pilgrim's garb flared. Light gleamed in his pale eyes as they searched for movement below.

" 'Tis naught but Leaper caught stealing bread," Dominic said. "It happens as regularly as the sun sets."

"When will the rest of your knights arrive?" Sven asked bluntly.

"Nine days. Perhaps more."

"Not soon enough. The Reevers will be ready to attack in half that time."

"We can hold out," Simon said. "The keep is secure for a siege."

"Then they will simply attack the traveling household first and come at us later," Dominic said.

"Aye," Sven said. "That is Duncan's plan. He is a shrewd one, lord."

"What of the Reevers themselves? Are they content to follow Duncan?" Dominic asked.

"The best are. The worst would follow anyone who promised bloodletting, including Rufus."

"Duncan's cousin," Dominic said musingly. "Is he half the leader Duncan is?"

"Nay. Duncan is like you, lord. Men would follow him into Hell itself. Only dogs would follow Rufus across a room, and then only if he carried bloody meat in both hands."

Dominic looked thoughtfully out over the fields, letting the tranquility of the evening wash over him.

He needed it.

Since Meg had become his wife in truth as well as in law, she had awakened each night with her dreams a chill sweat on her skin. When he questioned her, the answers were always the same, because the dream was always the same.

Danger comes.

What kind of danger? Plague? Siege? Poison? Ambush?

I don't know. I don't know! I know only that danger stalks Blackthorne Keep. Each night it comes closer, closer, closer! Hold me, Dominic. Hold me. I fear for you, my lord. I fear . . .

He held her, stroked her hair, warmed her with his own warmth. And in time, dawn came.

But night always followed day.

"Well," Dominic said finally, "at least I know what the danger is now. You may go, Sven. Thank you. As always, your information is invaluable."

Simon waited until Sven's retreating footsteps faded into silence.

"What do you mean that now you know what the danger is?" Simon asked.

"My Glendruid wife dreams, but not clearly."

"Yet she is your true *wife*," Simon said, emphasizing the final word. "Whatever her feelings might be for Duncan, she has given herself to you."

"Aye," said Dominic in a low voice. "She is my true wife."

But she speaks not of love to me. She speaks of pleasure, of danger, of laughter, of the keep, of the garden, of spring's green embrace . . . but not of love.

Heal me, Meg.

Love me.

Give me sons.

Simon clapped Dominic on the back with silent affection.

"The people of the keep knew it," Simon said with satisfaction. "The moment you returned from the hunt with Meg shining like the sun in your arms, they knew."

There was no answer.

Motionless, silent, Dominic looked out over the serene land until nothing was left of light in the sky but the moon's scimitar smile.

Simon waited for his brother's attention without impatience. He had waited in just this way many times after Sven had given a report and Dominic stood on a vantage point to study the place he must take by force or guile.

"I think," Dominic said finally, "it is time to give the Devil his due."

"Pardon?"

"John of Cumbriland, Lord of Blackthorne, shall have a funeral feast."

Simon was too shocked to speak.

"There will be music and mummers and games," Dominic continued.

"Games," Simon said neutrally.

"Aye. It is time that Duncan and his Reevers test the mettle of Blackthorne Keep's knights."

There was a startled silence followed by a short bark of laughter.

"Battle without bloodshed," Simon said in admiration. "Very clever. But very dangerous. What if the Reevers decide to hell with games and fight in earnest?"

"Then the dogs of war will feast on flesh again."

What Dominic didn't say was that the flesh would likely be his own. The Scots Hammer was as formidable a foe as Dominic had ever faced over drawn swords.

And Dominic would face him in single combat before he would allow the dogs of war to be unleashed.

With a final sweeping glance over the battlement, Dominic turned away from the land he had fought to own all his life, and from the dream of peace that had always eluded him. Such things lay in the unchangeable past or the untouchable future. All that he could reach lay in the present.

And the golden bells she wore called to him.

Dominic left the battlements without a word, walking in long strides to Meg's room. He didn't pause to knock on the door, for he knew it wouldn't be bolted against him. She would be inside, waiting for him, wearing the spicy fragrance that was hers alone.

Eadith made a startled sound as Dominic appeared in the doorway to the inner chamber.

"Leave us," he said.

The handmaiden dropped the jeweled comb she had been wielding over Meg's hair and obeyed with unusual speed. Dominic wore the bleak calculations of the battlement like a dark aura. Only his eyes were alive, and they saw only Meg.

As soon as Eadith left, Dominic shot the iron bolt. When Meg rose from the stool where she had been perched, bells stirred and murmured sweetly. Meg barely noticed the lovely sound. The intangible darkness around her husband made her heart clench.

"What is wrong?" she whispered.

Dominic's silver eyes slowly swept the length of his wife. Her hair tumbled to her hips in a cascade of fire that was held back only by a frail circlet of emeralds and gold. A closely fitted tunic of green silk followed the curves of her body, emphasizing her breasts and narrow waist and the feminine flare of her hips. Several of the delicate gold harem chains served as a girdle. The smallest motion of her body set bells to shivering.

Slowly Dominic walked toward Meg. When he reached out to run a long tendril of her hair through his fingers, his hand trembled from the fierce yearning in his heart.

"You are ... beautiful," Dominic said in a low voice.

Abruptly he closed his eyes and let Meg's hair slide from his fingers.

"Beauty is such a pale word to describe what you are to me," he whispered. " 'Tis like saying winter is cool and sunlight pleasant."

"Dominic," Meg said, catching his hand. "What is wrong?"

He opened his eyes and looked at her as though memorizing the elegant arch of her eyebrows, the faint tilt and clarity of her emerald eyes, the creamy texture of her skin, the sensuous color and curves of her lips. With aching care he brushed the backs of his fingers over her mouth.

"I tried to stay away," Dominic asked huskily. "But I cannot. I need you, Meg. Are you healed?"

"Healed?"

"When we lay together in the ancient place, I hurt you. Are you healed?"

"You never hurt me," Meg said.

"You bled."

"I felt only joy."

Meg kissed the battle-scarred fingers that were caressing her mouth. A subtle tremor went through Dominic.

"Does that mean you will come willingly to me?" Dominic asked. "Will you let my body worship yours?"

It was impossible for Meg to conceal the thrill that went through her at the thought of once more being joined with her husband.

Dominic's breath caught as he saw the sensuous shiver take Meg. His fingers drifted from her lips to the quickened beat of her pulse in her throat.

"I thought you wouldn't want me so soon," Meg admitted.

"Soon?" Dominic asked, startled. "It has been days."

"Eadith said that it takes time for a man to want a woman again."

An odd smile changed the taut lines of Dominic's face.

"If the woman in question is Eadith," he said, "a lifetime wouldn't be enough to raise my, ah, interest. But for you . . ."

"A half day?" Meg hazarded.

Dominic smiled. "For you, my warm Glendruid

wife, a half *hour* would be more than enough time to put steel back in my sword."

"That soon? Even a good ram requires . . ."

Meg's voice died as she heard her own words. She flushed brightly and said no more.

Dominic laughed, feeling the dark chill of the battlement recede.

"If I hadn't been afraid of hurting you more than I already had," he said, "I would have sheathed myself within you at least one more time before we left the ancient place."

Meg's eyes widened. "Truly?"

"Very truly. Did you mean what you said?" he asked in a low voice. "Did I give you pleasure?"

Pink tinted her cheekbones. She glanced away and nodded.

Dominic's hard palm tilted up Meg's chin. "Don't hide from me, small falcon. I must know."

Dark auburn eyelashes shifted, revealing the jeweled depths of Meg's eyes.

"Did I truly please you?" he asked.

The glittering silver of Dominic's gaze held Meg in thrall. Her lips parted on an indrawn breath as a cascade of sensual memories poured through her.

"Aye," she whispered.

Dominic's long fingers slid deeply into Meg's hair as he drew closer for a kiss.

"Did I?" Meg asked against his lips.

"Did you what?"

"Please you."

"Aye." He kissed her. "And aye." He kissed her again. "And aye once more."

"Are you certain? Marie says men get little pleasure of a virgin."

"Hammer Marie," Dominic said, biting Meg's lower lip with exquisite care. "She knows little about virginity and less about men."

Meg looked uncertainly at Dominic, wondering if he were joking.

"I beg to differ, my husband. Marie knows a great deal about men."

"She knows a great deal about spreading her thighs," Dominic said bluntly. "It's not the same thing. But if you don't believe me, give me your hand."

Meg blinked. "Which one?"

"Either will do nicely."

She held up her right hand. Dominic took it, guided it beneath his mantle, and pressed her palm against his rigid arousal. He smiled at the startled sound she made, and then he groaned as he urged her hand even closer. Slowly he guided her hand up the hard ridge of flesh. Even blunted by layers of cloth, the sensation was enough to make his blood pound like thunder through his body.

"Men can lie about many things," Dominic said huskily, "but not this. A man's body can't lie about desire."

The clear skin of Meg's face revealed the blush that claimed her, but she didn't pull her hand from beneath Dominic's.

"You pleased me in the forest," he said deeply. "Just remembering what it was like to press into you is enough to make me harden. You were sleek and tight and untouched, yet you wept your passion for me. You were magic. A virgin spring that welled up at my touch."

With a stifled groan Dominic dragged Meg's fingers from beneath his mantle and kissed them a bit fiercely.

"Will you let me undress you?" he asked.

"Of course," Meg said, turning around so that he could reach the laces of her dress. "It is your right as my hus—"

"Nay." Dominic's voice was sharp. "You are Glendruid. I have no rights but those you give me."

Sadness ached in Meg's throat. "So that is why you are so careful of me. The Glendruid curse."

His fingers paused on the laces of her emerald dress.

"I would woo you with great care in any case," Dominic said.

"Would you? Ah, yes, of course. Men get no heirs of wives who have no pleasure in the marriage bed."

Dominic hesitated, shrugged, and said, "I don't believe that superstition."

Laces slipped from eyelets with a hushed, whispering sound.

"You think a woman who has no pleasure of her partner can conceive?" Meg asked.

"I know she can."

Meg turned and looked over her shoulder at Dominic. "How so? Did you once force a maid and get her with child?"

"Is that what you think of me?" Dominic asked levelly.

With a sigh, Meg turned away. "No, my lord. For all your warrior nature, you take no pleasure in another's pain."

There was silence but for the whisper of laces coming undone. After a few moments Dominic spoke in a low voice.

"Once a knight of mine found a young Saracen girl alone. She was a virgin. He left her so torn and bleeding from his brutal rutting that we barely saved her life. I know for certain she had no pleasure of him, yet she quickened with his seed."

"Dear God. 'Tis little fair in that."

" 'Tis little fair in being born a bastard," Dominic said. "But my brother and I were both born such."

"As was Duncan of Maxwell."

A lace whipped through its eyelet.

"Do you have a penchant for bastards, my lady?" Dominic asked tightly.

Meg made an odd sound. "I? Nay. Rather I would say that bastards have a penchant for Blackthorne Keep!"

Dominic's hands stilled as he fought for control of the anger and despair that claimed him whenever his wife spoke of the terms of their marriage.

"I cannot change how we were married, or why, or what I seek in the way of heirs," Dominic said when he trusted his voice again. "Nor would I if I could. What about you, my reluctant wife? Would you want a marriage that outraged the king of England?"

"No," Meg said after a moment. "That would mean war."

"Would you want a man who cared not for Blackthorne Keep?"

"Nay."

"Would you want a man who couldn't give you children?"

"Nay," she whispered.

"Would you want a man who didn't grow hard with hunger for you?"

Biting her lip, Meg shook her head.

"Then why do you seek a quarrel?" Dominic asked finally. "Do you think I won't defend and protect the land?"

She shook her head.

"Do you think I won't defend and protect my children?"

"Nay."

"Do you think I won't defend and protect my wife?"

Two tears slid from Meg's eyes. Her throat ached so much that it was impossible for her to speak. Slowly she shook her head.

Dominic's long, strong fingers eased the last of the laces free. The green silk dress lay open from the nape of Meg's neck to the shadowed cleft of her hips. He wanted to trace the elegant line of his wife's body so much that his hands trembled with the fierce rushing of his blood.

"Do you think I am unworthy of you in some way?" Dominic asked, his voice tight with strain.

"Nay," Meg whispered. "Never, my lord Dominic."

Her breath came in with a rushing sound as Dominic's mouth caressed the nape of her neck while his fingers undid the frail fastenings of her underclothes.

As his mouth worked slowly down her spine, he eased his fingers into the opening of her clothes and caressed her rounded bottom with slow sweeps of his hands. She was warm and smooth, and he wanted nothing more than to pull off his clothes and bury himself in the sultry heat that he knew awaited within her.

But not yet. First he would hear her crying his name and feel her nails like small talons pricking him into even greater readiness.

With great care, Dominic traced the tight cleft to the hidden softness beneath. The sound of Meg's voice breaking on his name made him smile in fierce triumph.

"Yes?" he murmured. "Is there something you want?"

The feel of Dominic's breath in the naked small of her back made Meg shiver. The exquisitely restrained pressure of his teeth made her heartbeat quicken. The smooth penetration of his finger nearly brought her to her knees.

"You are so sweet to touch," Dominic said.

The feel of his finger testing her depths made Meg moan. Just as Dominic thought he might have hurt her, he felt the pleasure washing through her. Slowly, sensuously, he pressed a second finger into her heat and was rewarded by another searing pulse of response licking over his skin.

"You come undone for me with such delicious ease," Dominic said in a voice roughened by passion, "as though you were a lock made only for my key."

Meg couldn't answer, for Dominic was kissing the small of her back less gently now, his mouth and teeth pricking her into shivering awareness as his hand moved between her legs. Suddenly the pressure of his mouth became fierce and he flexed his hand, stretching her.

Pleasure exploded in Meg, making her sway even as she cried out Dominic's name. One of his arms came hard around her hips, holding her while he repeated the twin, devastating caresses.

She came unraveled in a rippling cry that inflamed him as much as the hot, hidden upwelling of her response. Again he bit her flesh with sensual care as he penetrated her, expanding her supple sheath so that she would be able to receive him without pain.

"*Dominic*," Meg said, sagging against his strength. "I can't stand."

Reluctantly, he began to retreat from Meg's welcoming body, only to discover that he didn't want to release her. Hearing her cries, feeling her softness, smelling her unique perfume . . . he wanted more of these things, not less.

"Once more, sweet witch. Just once."

Before Meg could reply, she felt Dominic's mouth like a passionate brand at the base of her spine. Then he was within her again, pressing sensually, making her bones turn to fire. With a low moan she trembled as liquid heat drenched her.

Dominic made a thick sound of triumph. Slowly he rose to his feet, dragging yet more cries from Meg as he caressed every bit of her even as he retreated. When she swayed against him, he caught her with an arm just beneath her breasts. The creamy, naked line of her spine called out to be traced down and down to the hot feminine core only he had ever touched.

"You tempt me unmercifully," Dominic said in a thick voice.

"How so?" Meg asked.

The husky rasp of her voice was like a cat's tongue. He shuddered once, heavily, fighting for the self-control that was being driven farther away with each hammer blow of his heart.

"You make me want to bury myself in you here and now," he said almost harshly.

"*Yes.*" Meg's nails dug into Dominic's arm as passion shook her. "Yes, my warrior. Take me here and now! I can't bear any more. I feel empty."

Without warning, Dominic lifted Meg in one arm and pulled off her clothes with the other, moving so swiftly that golden bells shivered and rang.

It was many steps to the bed. It was only two to the darning table.

An impatient movement of Dominic's arm cleared the table of colorful yarn and baskets. He sat Meg on top of the table and went to work on his own clothes. The combination of surprise and sensuality he saw in her face made him want to laugh and groan with the fierce prodding of his own passion.

"The table?" she managed huskily.

"It's closer than the bed."

Meg said no more, for the quick motions of Dominic's hands had opened his clothes enough to release his aroused flesh from confinement. The bold thrusting of his body fascinated her.

"May I . . . touch you?" she whispered.

"I shall die if you don't."

Dominic's voice became a low groan at the gentle, fiery brush of Meg's fingertips.

"So hard," she whispered, circling the base of his rigid flesh. Slowly her fingers caressed his length to the blunt tip. "Yet so smooth. Especially here. You shame the finest silk."

"God give me strength," Dominic said through clenched teeth.

A bolt of pleasure lanced through him, shaking him. For the space of a heartbeat, he balanced on the breaking edge of a sensual storm. Sweat gilded his body as he brought his savage need under control with a long, shattered breath.

His hunger barely restrained, Dominic captured Meg's hand and bit her palm.

"Did I touch you the wrong way?" she asked.

"Nay. You touched me all too well. I nearly spilled myself into your hand."

The surprise in Meg's eyes was quickly replaced by curiosity. She looked down at him in sensuous speculation. Then her breath came in with a soft, ripping sound as Dominic wrapped his hands around her knees and slowly drew them apart.

"Shift your legs, sweet witch. Let me stand close."

Meg tried to answer, but couldn't. The controlled strength of the hands opening her had stolen her voice. The silver blaze of Dominic's eyes as he looked at her nakedness made her tremble.

She should have felt frightened, defenseless. Instead she felt oddly powerful, intensely desired. At this moment she was certain that nothing existed in Dominic's thoughts but his hunger for his wife.

Then he was standing between her thighs, testing her with a smooth motion of his hand. The gliding penetration of his finger sent lightning racing through her body. A sensual rain soon followed.

Meg's voice broke over Dominic's name when he redoubled and repeated the caress. Her soft cries charted the progress of his touches. When he plucked the sultry jewel of her passion, she tilted back her head and surrendered herself to the sensations consuming her.

"Yes," Dominic said, watching Meg with eyes that burned. "This is how I want you, hot and sleek and crying for me."

"I can't—bear—any more."

He laughed low in his throat and shuddered as her passionate response licked over the blunt tip of the sword that was even now pressing into her sheath.

"Nor can I," he said thickly. "Wrap your legs around my waist and pull me close. Yes, like that."

Dominic's hands slipped beneath Meg's hips. "Take me now, witch. Take me hard and *deep*."

Meg's answer was a ragged cry as Dominic thrust smoothly into her, sheathing himself to the hilt. For the space of a breath she thought she would be torn apart. He tried to retreat, but could not force himself to give up one bit of the taut, sultry depths that held him more closely than his own skin.

"Is it too much?" he asked through clenched teeth.

"I—"

He began to retreat. The hidden caress of flesh against flesh drew a shudder of pleasure from Meg. The secret rain that followed eased his presence within her. Carefully he pressed forward again. This time the breathless sounds she made came of pleasure rather than surprise.

When Dominic would have retreated once more, her legs tightened around his hips, locking him close. The gesture undid him. With a low cry he began moving deeply within Meg, measuring himself and her with quickening motions.

A strange glittering sensation went from Meg's

breastbone to the pit of her stomach. Shivering, crying softly, she moved with Dominic, reinforcing the shimmering pressure caressing her. She felt her hips lifted in his big hands, felt the raw power of his body, felt the sensual tension spiraling quickly out of control between them.

Meg's nails dug heedlessly into Dominic's muscular shoulders as she called his name on a rising note of urgency. His answer was a thrust that would have hurt her moments before, but not now. Now she was soft and hot, shivering and crying her release as her warrior poured himself deep into her welcoming body.

When Meg finally could breathe again without having each breath break over the echoes of ecstasy still rippling through her, she opened her eyes.

Dominic was watching her as though uncertain of her mood.

"Are you all right?" he asked in a low voice.

Meg started to answer, shivered in remembered pleasure, and whispered, "Aye."

"I didn't hurt you?"

"You are rather, er, formidable," she said. "But you didn't hurt me."

"Are you certain? I meant to take you far more gently," Dominic said. "You have a baffling effect on my self-control."

"You didn't hurt me. Rather the opposite. You gave me great pleasure."

While Meg spoke, she leaned forward to kiss Dominic. The motion shifted him within her. Her eyes opened and her breath broke as bright splinters of ecstasy pierced her.

Dominic felt Meg's response as clearly as she did, for her soft depths caressed him with each flick of ecstasy's silken whip. His eyes narrowed at the sudden, savage rush of his blood. Without separating their bodies, he lifted her and carried her to the bed.

"Don't leave me yet," Meg whispered, holding him.

His breath wedged. "Do you like having me within you?"

"Aye."

She trembled with a backlash of pleasure as Dominic lay full length above her, bracing his weight on his elbows. Even his smallest movement sent hot shards of sensation through her, for he was full and hard once more.

"Did I not please you?" Meg asked.

"You pleased me until I could barely stand."

She moved tentatively. "Did I? But you still feel quite . . . ready."

"Not still. Again."

Her eyes widened. "It has not been half an hour."

Dominic laughed and moved again within Meg, savoring every bit of her warmth, drawing forth a scented rain of pleasure. Slowly he retreated. When he returned, he let her feel his weight and power. The intense, gliding friction set her afire.

"Warrior," Meg breathed.

The heavy pressure within her redoubled, filling her to bursting, seducing her with ecstasy until she could no longer think, only feel. She tried to tell him how good it felt to lie joined with him, moving as he moved, sharing breath and body, but all that came from her lips was a rippling cry of ecstasy.

Dominic laughed with pleasure and the strength coursing through him, a power enhanced and freed by the girl who even now was convulsing sweetly beneath him. He bent and drank her small cries from her lips, gliding and retreating, returning and withdrawing and returning again until her cries became sharp, urgent, almost frightened.

"Dominic?" Meg asked raggedly.

"Hold on to me. This time you will soar very high."

"What of—you?"

"I will be with you. Fly, small falcon. Fly all the way to the sun."

24

SIMON STOOD AT THE GATEHOUSE door, watching the swirls and currents of people around the big meadow where the funeral feast and games had been set up in "honor" of John of Carlysle, deceased lord of Blackthorne Keep. The last of the jousts were being prepared. Thus far, Blackthorne Keep had defeated all but two of the Reevers. Not surprisingly, both of the undefeated knights were warriors returning from the holy crusade.

The Scots Hammer had not yet fought. Nor had Dominic le Sabre.

"You look skeptical," Dominic said in a voice too low to be overheard.

Simon glanced askance at his brother. "You look smug."

"I was afraid Duncan might sense a trap and not come at all."

"He brought every Reever who could ride a horse."

"Aye, but only three of his knights are equal to ours," Dominic said.

"Duncan is equal to two knights."

"Aye."

Simon followed his brother's glance to the rough

arena where four knights stood apart from the general rabble of the Reevers. One of them was Duncan of Maxwell. The others were men who waited and watched the games with the eyes of knights for whom strife and death held no mysteries.

"Interesting that Rufus isn't among the four good knights," Simon said.

Dominic shrugged. "Duncan, damn his eyes, is shrewd. He knows Rufus envies him. The Scots Hammer trusts only those knights standing with him."

"Rufus is a fool," Simon said. "Pity he isn't the Reevers' leader. We could lure him into a pig wallow and leave him floundering."

"Speaking of pig wallows . . . have you seen the priest lately?"

"With a joint of mutton in one hand, a mug of ale in the other, and a sweet bun stuffed between his teeth," Simon said sardonically. "Yes, I've seen him."

"Where?"

"Near Duncan, where else? The Church has made no pretense of its preferences. You should have sent the priest north with John's bastard."

Dominic smiled thinly.

"I thought of it," he admitted. "Then I thought I might have a use for the Church's good offices before Blackthorne Keep was secure in my grasp."

"Have you need of the priest now?" Simon asked curiously.

"Aye. Are the men-at-arms deployed?"

"As you ordered, lord. Now would you kindly tell me what in God's name you have planned?"

"Nothing elaborate. I am going to charge the Scots Hammer with the attempted stealing of my wife."

"Why? I thought it was your death the Reevers wanted."

"Quite probably, but that would raise no cries

across the land. However, to steal a man's lawful wife for purposes of unlawful sexual intercourse . . ."

Simon's eyes narrowed. Then his lips thinned into a smile as feral as Dominic's.

"Even the Reevers couldn't countenance such an act publicly," Dominic continued. "The Church would have to be even more *publicly* horrified. Do you think an excommunicate could lead good knights into battle?"

"You're going to kill the Scots Hammer, aren't you?" Simon said after a moment.

"If I must." Dominic shrugged. "And it seems that I must. The Reevers grow too strong."

The smile on Simon's face faded. "It will mean war."

"Probably. But without Duncan's leadership, the Reevers will be much easier to defeat."

Dominic hesitated, choosing his next words carefully.

Uneasiness blew coolly over Simon's skin. There was a darkness in his brother's eyes that had never been there before, not even after the sultan's infamous torture rooms.

"If I die," Dominic said, "see that Meg—"

"Nay! You'll not die! I'll protect your back myself. Thomas the Strong will—"

"Do nothing," Dominic interrupted. "Nor will you. I will accuse Duncan of wife stealing. He will deny it. The issue will be settled in a manner no one may question—Ordeal by Combat."

"God's blood," Simon said, appalled. " 'Tis too chancy. A pebble could turn under your foot or he could get in a lucky blow or one of his men could—"

Dominic lifted his hand, cutting off his brother's words.

"It is the only way war might be avoided," Dominic said flatly.

For a time there was silence. Then Simon let out a hissing breath.

"Be that as it may," Simon said, "if the Scots Hammer kills you, I will have his skull for a drinking cup and his blood for wine."

A smile showed briefly on Dominic's face. "I believe you would, brother. You are hellish quick with that sword."

"And you are hellish strong."

"So is the Scots Hammer."

Simon didn't disagree.

"Go find the priest before he is too drunk to shrive us," Dominic said.

"He is found," Simon said.

Dominic followed his brother's black glance.

The priest was indeed found. He was standing next to Duncan, talking earnestly while stripping meat from a large joint. Obviously bored, Duncan listened to the priest without taking his eyes from the crowd.

When Simon and Dominic walked up, Duncan sensed instantly that he was at last going to be given the chance to test the mettle of the king's Sword.

"So, you are finally going to join the games," Duncan said with deep satisfaction.

"After a fashion," Dominic said. He turned to the priest. "Are you sober enough to shrive us?"

Duncan became very still. His clear hazel eyes went from Dominic to Simon and back.

"Since when do knights need to be shriven before a simple game?" Duncan asked softly.

"Wife stealing is not a game," Dominic said. His voice was as flat and cold as his eyes.

"Wife stealing?" Duncan repeated, shocked.

Duncan's knights turned and looked at Dominic and Simon as though they had drawn their swords.

"Aye," Dominic said grimly. "Wife stealing."

"When?"

"A few days past, while we rode out to hunt."

Puzzled, Duncan looked at Simon. Where once the possibility of friendship had gleamed in the other man's eyes, there now was only a bleak promise of Hell.

"I don't understand," Duncan said quietly.

For several long moments Dominic studied the Scots Hammer. Reluctantly Dominic concluded that Duncan was probably telling the truth. Whatever had happened the day of the hunt hadn't been Duncan's doing.

Unfortunately, that changed nothing. The Scots Hammer was too strong a leader to go unchecked. His very life threatened the stability of Blackthorne Keep.

"When Meg's palfrey tired of the chase," Dominic said, pitching his voice to carry above the background noise, "I dropped back to ride with her. Soon we heard another hunting horn."

Duncan began talking, only to be cut off by Dominic.

"Meg recognized the horn," Dominic said. "It was yours, Duncan of Maxwell. Further, the dog we heard pursuing us was one of yours, full-throated and savage. It had been put on the trail of human game."

"I did not do this thing," Duncan said distinctly. "I would not run Meggie to ground like a felon to be hanged."

Dominic smiled narrowly. "Indeed? I think you would, Duncan. I think you *did*. You know that Meg is the key to the loyalty of the people of Blackthorne Keep. Whoever holds her, holds the land."

"Aye." Duncan's voice was grim. "On that we agree."

"And because there is 'affection' between you two, you tried to steal the wife God and King Henry had given to me, thinking thereby to steal Blackthorne Keep as well."

"Nay!"

"You may shout nay until the sheep are safely in their folds, but I won't believe you. Nor will any man," Dominic said flatly. "You have a choice, Duncan of Maxwell. You may leave this land, never to return—"

"Nay," Duncan interrupted.

"—or you may face me in single combat here and now."

A hush spread outward from the group of men across the meadow like ripples in a pond.

Meg, who had been talking with the midwife and Old Gwyn about Adela's recovery, looked up. In the wake of the odd silence came excited words as news of the coming battle spread.

The Sword.

The Scots Hammer.

Ordeal by Combat.

Blood left Meg's face. She swayed in the instants before she gathered her self-control.

"They cannot," she whispered.

Yet Meg knew even as she spoke that Duncan and Dominic would fight.

And one would die.

She picked up her long emerald skirt and ran to the knot of knights. The people in the meadow made way for her, warned by the sweet golden cries of the bells she wore.

The knights were also warned. As one, men turned and looked at the Glendruid girl who was running toward them, her long hair lifting like flames on the wind.

Meg had eyes for only one of the men. She needed

his closeness as she had never needed anything, even breath itself. Heedless of hauberk and sword and the cold scrape of steel over her skin, she flew to him.

"Small falcon," Dominic whispered, catching her close.

It was all he could say.

The feeling in Meg's eyes stunned Dominic. Uncaring of the watching people, he closed his arms around his wife and held her, sensing the wild emotions that shook her. When her body was finally still, he slowly released her.

"It will be all right," Dominic said softly. "No matter who wins, you will be cared for. You are the key to Blackthorne Keep."

Meg simply looked at her husband with tears of fear and anger shivering on the brink of overflowing.

"One will kill," she whispered tightly. "One will die. How can that be all right?"

"Blackthorne Keep will survive."

Meg closed her eyes. Two tears slid like liquid moonlight down her cheeks. She tried to speak but could not. Her eyes opened. With fingers that trembled slightly, she traced the hard lines of Dominic's face as though memorizing him.

"The land always survives," Meg said in a low voice. "It is only people who live and die. And love."

Her hands went to her neck. With a quick movement she removed the golden chain holding her mother's ancient cross. Meg kissed the cross and pressed it into Dominic's gauntleted palm.

"God keep you," she whispered.

Dominic took off his gauntlet and held the cross in his naked hand. The warmth of the metal was that of life itself, for the cross had lain between Meg's breasts. He kissed the cross and slipped the chain around his own neck.

Unhappily Duncan watched the girl who had once been his betrothed and the man fate had made his enemy.

"Meggie, I would not have stolen you and forced adultery upon you," Duncan said into the silence. "You believe that, don't you?"

"Aye," she said.

"Well, that is something."

"Here is something else," Meg said.

The tone of her voice made the knights turn and look narrowly at her. She looked back at them, taking particular measure of the men who stood close to Duncan. Her face was pale but for the untamed green fire of her eyes.

"If any of you draw sword before the combat is declared finished," Meg said distinctly, "you will know what it is to face the wrath of a Glendruid healer."

Duncan smiled sadly. "Ah, Meggie, you cannot kill and well you know it."

"Aye." Then she smiled slowly, savagely. "There are things worse than death, Duncan of Maxwell. See that your men don't discover them in their dreams and live them upon waking."

When Meg turned away from Duncan, the priest dropped his well-gnawed bone and crossed himself hastily. All of the men looked uneasy except Dominic. He had attention only for the girl who burned like spring unleashed, forcing life to grow from dead ground. In his mind her words echoed, words that he was only now beginning to understand.

The wounds of winter are starkly revealed before they are healed by spring, and only the most hardy of living things survive renewal.

Healing is not for the faint of heart.

In a silence that was emphasized rather than broken by the priest's stumbling words, Duncan and

Dominic were shriven and final rites administered. When each warrior was prepared to meet his God, the priest's words stopped.

Simon took Dominic's helm from Jameson, fitted it over his brother's head, and removed his mantle. Though not a word was said by either man, Meg's heart ached for the emotion that shimmered unspoken between the brothers.

When she looked at Duncan, she saw not an enemy but the hazel eyes and reckless smile that had lifted her spirits so often in her childhood. Tears overflowed, blurring the features of the man who was in her heart the brother she had never known.

When Meg could see again, Dominic was watching her and Duncan with eyes like hammered silver. She ached to go to her husband, to hold him once more and be held in turn, but it was too late.

The war horn blew, transfixing the people in the meadow. The sliding notes were like a hellhound baying at a bloody moon. In the silence that followed the last echoing note, two war-horses were led to opposite sides of the meadow. Crusader's black bulk was matched by the powerful brown body of Duncan's stallion.

Without a word, the Sword and the Scots Hammer turned and went to their chargers. Both men mounted in the same way, a single tigerish leap, as though chain mail and helm, gauntlets and chausses, sword and shield were made of airy moonlight rather than stout metal. Squires handed over long lances. Each knight couched his weapon, holding it level for the charge to come.

Behind Meg a child cried and a dog growled and a knight's falcon screamed its ire; and throttled within Meg's throat was her own despairing scream.

The two stallions reared and trumpeted a challenge that raised a cheer from the assembled knights.

Instants later the stallions charged across the meadow, sending chunks of dirt and grass flying. Thunder
rolled from the big hooves as the knights raced
toward each other, shields raised and lances braced.

A rending clash and slamming of lances, shields,
and horses burst over the meadow. Both stallions
staggered, recovered, and galloped to the far end
of the meadow for another charge. Again thunder
rolled. Again came the clash of metal and the
thudding of flesh. Again the stallions staggered
and regrouped for another pass.

And then again.

And again.

"They are too well matched," Simon said grimly.
"The stallions are within a stone's weight of one
another and well-trained. Unless Duncan makes a
mistake or a lance breaks—"

The *crack* of a shattering lance punctuated Simon's
words. But it wasn't Duncan's lance that broke.

It was Dominic's.

Though he deflected the force of Duncan's blow
with his shield, the sudden destruction of his lance
unhorsed Dominic. He gained his feet quickly and
ran toward his stallion, but Duncan's charger pivoted to cut off Dominic from Crusader.

Duncan's stallion pivoted again, striking Dominic with his shoulder, sending him rolling. Even as
Dominic pulled himself to his feet, Duncan charged
again. Cheers from the Reevers mixed with groans
and curses from Blackthorne's knights.

Watching in horror, Meg laced her fingers together
and bit back the scream that was tearing her throat as
the massive brown stallion bore down on Dominic.
Duncan's lance was leveled. If Dominic turned and
fled he would be run down by the stallion. If he drew
his sword and tried to fight, he would be killed by
Duncan's lance or run down where he stood.

"Nay!"

No one heard Meg's terrible cry, for every voice was raised in cheers or exhortations. Simon held Meg at his side with fingers like bands of steel, preventing her from running onto the field of battle. She struggled wildly, then stood still, knowing there was nothing she could do.

Dominic stood unmoving, as though he had decided to take his death head-on. Every knight in the meadow expected him to leap aside at the last instant, evading both lance and stallion. It was a common tactic on the battlefield, giving the unmounted knight enough time for a friend to charge over and help the downed knight.

But no one would help Dominic. It was forbidden by custom and by law. God's judgment, not the speed or number of a man's friends, decreed the survivor of ritual combat.

Without help Dominic would be able to evade Duncan for a time, but soon a man afoot would tire or stumble. Then Duncan would be on him and Dominic would die.

The brown stallion charged toward Dominic, picking up speed with every stride. Dominic waited, half crouched, his weight on the balls of his feet, obviously ready to spring to either side. Poised to follow his quarry, Duncan lifted slightly out of his saddle, a savage grimace on his face as he bore down on the Norman lord.

In order to evade the lance, Dominic had to stand until the last possible instant before crossing or turning aside from the charger's path. By the time Dominic moved, the horse was so close that Dominic was pelted with the dirt spurting from beneath the stallion's feet. Just before he would have been crushed beneath the charger's hooves, he sprang away.

An odd sound rose above the crowd, a groan that

could have been for or against the lord of Blackthorne Keep. Again he was charged by Duncan. Again Dominic leaped away at the last instant. The game of cat and mouse continued for several more passes. Each time Duncan charged he leaned a little more forward in the stirrups, eager to end the lopsided battle.

On the sixth charge, Dominic leaped once more, but it was toward Duncan, not away. Grabbing Duncan's right foot, Dominic heaved upward with all his considerable strength. The tactic worked. Duncan lost his seat in the saddle.

Even as he came unhorsed, Duncan dropped the useless lance and grabbed for his sword. Although he landed hard on his shoulder, he rolled as Dominic had, coming to his feet like a cat.

Before Duncan could get set, Dominic hit him behind the knees with the flat of his sword. Duncan tumbled backward. There was no chance to regain his balance or to use his sword; Dominic slid the point of his broadsword between Duncan's chin and the gap in his chain mail hood.

Duncan froze, expecting to die in the next instant. Dominic stood above him, breathing hard from his exertions. Beneath the tip of the sword, blood trickled in a warm stream over Duncan's neck.

"You once told me you bent the knee to no one but your Scottish king," Dominic said in a harsh voice that carried easily over the battle ground.

Duncan waited, his eyes narrowed in expectation of immediate death.

"I give you a choice, Duncan of Maxwell. Die now or accept me as your liege."

For a long breath there was only silence in the meadow. Then the Scots Hammer swore, let go of the hilt of his sword, and smiled crookedly.

"Better your vassal than food for worms," Duncan said.

Dominic threw back his head and laughed.

"Aye, Duncan. Much better."

With an easy motion, Dominic sheathed his sword and held out a hand to help Duncan to his feet. But instead of standing, Duncan went down on one knee and bent his head, making it clear to everyone in the meadow that he would yield to Dominic le Sabre even when there wasn't a sword pricking his throat.

"Stand," Dominic said.

When Duncan did, Dominic picked up Duncan's sword and handed it to him hilt first.

"You have given me your word," Dominic said. "I need no other sign of your loyalty. And an unarmed knight is good to no one, least of all his liege."

Duncan looked from his sword to Dominic's sheathed weapon, smiled oddly, and sheathed his own heavy sword with a quick stroke. As he did, a long sigh rose from people in the meadow.

Dominic turned to the waiting knights, but it was the Reevers who received the brunt of his measuring glance.

"I am giving Duncan of Maxwell a large estate on land disputed by the Scots and English kings."

Duncan turned and stared at Dominic.

"Those of you who follow Duncan have a choice," Dominic continued. "You may ride out unharmed and never again return to my domains.

"Or you may accept Duncan as your liege, *and through him, me.*"

25

WHILE DOMINIC AND SIMON oversaw the departure of the Reevers who had chosen to follow Rufus rather than remain with the Scots Hammer, Old Gwyn and Meg worked in the lord's solar, tending to knights from both sides who had been injured during the long day of games. The solar had been transformed into a makeshift infirmary, for the great hall was being readied for feasting.

"Ouch!" the Scots Hammer yelped, jerking back from Meg's hands. "That hurts!"

Duncan had insisted on being last to be treated, as his wounds were insignificant.

"Do be still," Meg retorted. "You didn't complain nearly as much when Dominic's sword lay at your throat."

"I expected to die. What use were complaints?"

Meg gave Duncan a cool look. As much as she liked the Scots Hammer, she would be a long time forgetting the sight of him bearing down on Dominic, ready to end the combat with a killing blow.

"Tip your head back," she said. "I can't see your throat."

"I don't like the look in your eyes, Meggie. It

would be like baring my throat to a she-wolf."

She glanced at his hazel eyes, saw both the understanding and the rueful amusement, and felt some of her own tension fade.

"If Dominic can spare the life of an enemy," she said wryly, "I can spare the life of a friend."

Ignoring the barely concealed smiles of his knights, Duncan grimaced and tilted his head back to give Meg better access to his neck.

" 'Tis just a scratch," he muttered.

"Is that so?" Meg asked. "What with all your twitching and complaining, I thought your throat was fair slit from apple to ear."

The knights remaining in the room laughed at the sight of a girl scolding one of the most feared warriors in all of England. Meg looked up and smiled at them.

"Go to supper, good knights," she said. "Sir Duncan will be with you soon."

As the men filed past Meg to the great hall, she bent once more and began prodding Duncan's throat with careful fingertips. Duncan had cast aside his battle clothing and was wearing little more than short leather breeches. Meg's hair, as usual, had come undone. When a thick lock slithered forward and threatened to get in her way, Duncan caught it, tugged it lightly, and tucked it behind Meg's ear. The casual gesture spoke of long familiarity between the Scots Hammer and the lady of Blackthorne Keep.

With hooded eyes, Dominic watched Duncan and Meg from the doorway. Each time Dominic drew a breath, he told himself there was no cause for the jealousy that was lying like molten lead in his gut. Yet seeing his wife's hands smoothing over the muscular width of Duncan's neck in search of injuries made vivid every bit of gossip he had heard both before and after coming to Blackthorne Keep.

Duncan's betrothed.

Duncan's leman.

The witch waits, smiling and biding her time.

"You came very close to seeing God," Meg muttered.

"Aye." Duncan tugged on another stray lock of her hair and smiled whimsically. "Would you have missed me, Meggie?"

"The way a cat misses a dog."

Duncan laughed and tucked the fiery lock away beneath Meg's head cloth. Bells chimed when he accidently pulled the cloth askew. He removed and refitted the circlet on her, setting bells to singing with every motion. If she objected to the intimacy, she didn't show it with word or action.

Affection between them.

Pretending to be satisfied with her cold Norman lord.

Smiling and biding her time.

"Ouch! God blind me, are you trying to finish what your husband started?"

"Are you sure you have no trouble swallowing?" Meg asked.

"I'm certain."

"Well, 'tis a lucky scoundrel you are, Duncan of Maxwell."

"Aye," he agreed. "But I'll never have a wife like you, Meggie."

"For that you should thank the lord," she retorted. "Ask Dominic. I'm such a trial to him that he makes me go belled like a cat or a falcon."

"Is Dominic unkind to you?" Duncan asked, his voice no longer teasing.

"To his Glendruid wife? To his sole hope of legal heirs? Does my husband strike you as a stupid man?" Meg asked curtly.

"God's blood, no. The man is as cunning as a wolf."

"He's as cunning as a pack of wolves. And he isn't unkind to me. My jesses, after all, are almost the equal of his fine peregrine's."

Duncan shouted with laughter.

Smiling even as she scolded Duncan to sit still, Meg rubbed a salve into the various bruises that showed on Duncan's broad chest.

Biding her time.

For the Scots Reever she has always loved.

She waits.

"If you should have any trouble swallowing, come directly to me," Meg said as she rubbed salve into a bruise on Duncan's shoulder.

"I always do, Meggie. Your touch alone would heal a man, much less your magic Glendruid potions."

Dominic pulled off his helm and dumped it onto a nearby table with enough force to make ale leap in the bowl Simon had left for the knights to drink.

Meg looked up swiftly. Her green eyes went over Dominic like intangible hands, searching for hidden wounds. What she saw was an icy anger that made her realize she was standing between Duncan's muscular thighs. A flush tinted her cheeks. Hastily she stepped back.

Duncan turned and looked at Dominic. The expression on the liege's face made it clear that he wasn't happy to find his wife alone with a half-naked Duncan of Maxwell. Duncan smiled rather sardonically.

"Now I know why you gave me an estate three days' ride from here," he said.

"See that you get to it quickly," Dominic said in a cold voice.

"Aye, lord. I'll do that. I like my head just where it is."

Duncan stood and strode quickly from the solar, snagging his mantle on the way out. Dominic's cold gray eyes bored into him every step of the way.

"I had Eadith prepare a bath," Meg said. "It should be ready by now. Shall I call Simon to tend you?"

"Nay. I think I will sample the joys of your 'healing touch' for myself."

The words were like a whip. Meg stiffened.

"You have no reason to hint at anything improper," she said angrily.

Dominic lifted a skeptical black eyebrow.

"There is naught between Duncan and me," Meg said. "For the love of God, husband, I came to your bed a virgin!"

"But you can't do that every time, can you? A man can be certain only once of a woman's fidelity."

Meg's eyes widened. "You can't mean that!"

"I can. I do. Once again, I regret not killing that Scots bastard."

Stillness came over Meg like night flowing over the face of day.

"What have I done to earn your distrust?" she asked in a remote voice.

Meg's tone was like adding straw to the fire of Dominic's temper, which was already ablaze with the last, dying echoes of a battle he had come very close to losing.

"You were alone with a half-naked knight who is reputed to be the owner of your heart, if not your body," Dominic retorted. "Were it Marie standing between Duncan's thighs, I would applaud. But it wasn't Marie who was simpering over Duncan's wounds. It was my wife!"

"I have never simpered over any man's wounds. I am a healer, not a prostitute."

Dominic grunted. "At times, 'tis hard to know the difference."

"Duncan has no such difficulty. He knows me for what I am, healer not whore. Would that mine own husband knew me half as well!"

"I'm trying, wife. I'm trying. But I keep tripping over that Scots bastard at every turn. Tell me—for whom did you cheer while we fought?"

"How can you even ask that question?" she whispered.

Turning away, Meg began gathering her medicines with hands that shook from anger and something more, the chill fear that increased each time she understood how little of her husband's respect she had.

And of his trust, she had none.

"I'll send Simon to your bath," Meg said.

"Nay."

The command was as flat and cold as a sword.

"As you wish, lord," Meg said, stalking past her fierce husband. "Though I would think a man who trusted me so little would be fearful of a dagger in his back."

With a hissed phrase in Turkish, Dominic followed. He knew his temper was abrupt and his tongue was as slashing as the edge of his sword, but there was little he could do about the matter at the moment. His usual irritability after battle had turned to fury at the sight of Meg and the half-naked Scotsman.

Dominic stepped into the bathing room and yanked the drape across the doorway into place.

"Do you love that Scots bastard?" Dominic asked abruptly.

"As a cousin, a friend, the brother I never had, aye."

With quick, curt motions, Dominic began undoing his battle gear.

"Did you once love Duncan as a woman loves a man?" he demanded.

"No."

"But he loved you."

Meg made a sound that was too sad and angry to be called laughter.

"Nay, lord. For me, Duncan felt some affection. For Blackthorne Keep, he had great love. Like you, Duncan saw me as a means of becoming a great lord. Unlike you, he was not the man the king commanded me to marry."

"It is a noble woman's duty to increase her family's security through marriage."

"Yes. I have done my duty."

Dominic couldn't argue with Meg's quiet statement, yet he wanted to. He wanted her to say that it was more than noble duty that brought her to his bed, more than duty that made her soften at his touch, more than duty that called forth her sultry, passionate rain.

In a stiff silence Meg assisted Dominic out of his battle gear. When he peeled off the last of his clothing, his heavy arousal made her breath catch in her throat. Abruptly she began to understand why he might have been so angry at finding her with Duncan. The passion of battle had been transformed into another kind of passion altogether.

Meg could understand that, for she had felt the same. The terrible fear she had known while Duncan's charger bore down on her husband had been transformed in the space of a breath to intense desire.

Dominic was alive. She wanted to celebrate his survival in the most elemental of all ways.

"What? No sweet smiles and tender touches for your husband?" Dominic asked harshly as he stepped into the bath. "Aren't you going to stroke me and heal my battle wounds?"

"You look quite wonderfully healthy," Meg said. "But I will stroke you anywhere you please."

The change in his wife's voice from tight to husky both surprised and disarmed Dominic. He looked at Meg in time to see the sensual appraisal in her smile as his loins vanished into the bath. With hungry eyes he watched her remove her mantle and outer tunic, scoop up a handful of her own soap, and walk to the bath.

The water was hot and smelled like Meg's herbal. The soap was soft and smelled like Meg herself. The aches and bruises Dominic had gathered from battle dissolved, but not the hunger that held his body in a sensuous vise, nor the stark arousal that pulsed more heavily with each motion of Meg's hands as she bent over him.

In a low voice Meg sang the Glendruid chant of renewal while she bathed Dominic, washing away the mistakes and pains of the day, coaxing hope to come and live within her warrior's powerful body. When Dominic could bear no more of the tender torment, he took one of Meg's hands and dragged it down his chest to the part of him that ached more than any bruise could.

At the first touch of Meg's fingers on his aroused flesh, Dominic groaned. When her hand curled eagerly around and stroked from base to tip, he thought he would burst like a wineskin overfilled.

"*Meg . . .*"

The word sounded as though it had been torn from Dominic unwillingly.

"Yes, husband?" she murmured.

"Simon tells me I'm beastly after a battle."

"Simon is correct."

Meg pulled her nails delicately over Dominic's eager flesh, drawing another groan from him.

"But now that I know how to pull the thorn from my beast's paw," she added, "I will be more understanding."

"That is not a thorn."

Soft, feminine laughter agreed with Dominic.

"Aye," she whispered, stroking him. " 'Tis a very fine, very magical sword."

"Magic?" Dominic's breath hissed in as pleasure lanced through his whole body. "How so?"

"Though your sword is hard indeed, it is hot rather than cold, it brings pleasure rather than pain, joy rather than sorrow . . . life rather than death. That is a very great magic."

With a throttled groan, Dominic tilted his head back against the rim of the bath and fought for control.

"I have never before been a jealous man," he said, "but the thought of you touching Duncan like this makes me want to kill him out of hand."

As Dominic spoke, his fingers went beneath the hem of Meg's inner tunic. He heard the sudden intake of her breath when he caressed her ankle. Smiling, he stroked his long fingers up the curves of one leg and down again.

"For a knight who is renowned for his logic and tactics," Meg.said breathlessly, "your jealousy makes little sense."

Dominic's eyes narrowed into glittering gray slits as his palm stroked up the length of Meg's leg again. But this time he didn't stop at her thigh. His fingers sought the frail layer of cloth that lay between him and her sensual heat. He pulled once, sharply, and the barrier tore. An instant later his fingers were tangled in the warm thatch between her thighs. The shivering sound she made pleased him as much as the liquid fire his touch drew from her softness.

"Why shouldn't I be jealous of this?" Dominic asked. "A man would kill for such sweet fire."

Meg gently squeezed Dominic's masculine flesh as she asked huskily, "Do you think me too slack-witted to know the difference between paradise and a childhood friend?"

"When you hold me thus, I can't think at all."

Smiling, Meg stroked from blunt tip to base and beyond, cradling the twin spheres wherein his seed strained to be released.

"In your arms I taste paradise," she whispered. "Duncan is my friend, Dominic. I have never touched him thus. I never would. It is only your sword that pleasures me."

"God," Dominic groaned. "You are killing me."

Meg gave him a startled look, then understood he was speaking of sweet torment rather than true agony.

"You'll have me full to bursting all over again," he said thickly.

"Is that so terrible a thing?"

"Nay."

Dominic's burning gaze went from Meg's mouth to her breasts, to the red-gold nest that so tempted him. A primitive hunger lanced through his body. His hands slid up her thighs until he could touch the soft, sultry flesh that gave him so much pleasure.

"But we should have the privacy of a bolted door," he said. "There are things I want . . ."

"What things?"

His only answer was another look at her and a silence that was hotter than fire.

Meg listened. No sounds came but those from the great hall below, where knights drank and boasted of their prowess in battle.

"No one comes," she said.

"If we stay, it will be at your peril," Dominic said.

" 'Tis great danger for me here," Meg agreed with a smile. "I can feel it like a mighty sword against my body."

Dominic gave a crack of laughter. Even though he knew he should make himself go the short distance to Meg's rooms, he wasn't sure he could. He was on fire for his passionate Glendruid witch.

"There are things I heard of among the Saracens that intrigued me," Dominic murmured, looking hungrily from Meg's eyes to the place where their bodies would soon be joined, "but I was never tempted to try them until now."

"What things?" Meg asked again.

"Ways for lovers to tease and pleasure and finally ease, but only after they scream with the sweet torture."

Meg's eyelids half lowered. " 'Tis shameless of me, but I must confess to curiosity."

"Aye, witch. I can see your curiosity." Dominic's smile was dark and fully male. "I shall take great pleasure in satisfying it . . . and you."

The ball of his thumb probed the lush nest between Meg's thighs. When he brushed against the nub hidden within, she flinched with unexpected pleasure.

"You are very sensitive," he said.

Meg shivered.

"My thumb is too hard," Dominic said in a low voice. "I believe my tongue would be better suited to polish the living jewel of your passion."

The startled look on Meg's face made Dominic laugh softly despite the heavy, relentless beat of desire in his body.

"Aye, witch. You begin to understand."

The sight of her nipples taut with arousal and the passionate flush of her body made him want to shout with triumph and hunger. He cupped her breasts in his hands and prodded the nipples sensuously, dragging a cry from her. The cry became a shattered sound of desire when his long index finger caressed down her belly and slid deeply within.

"I want you," he said simply.

"I am yours to take."

"Yes," he whispered. "I can feel the truth of your generosity. I have never known anything like you."

"It is you, not I."

"It is both." A shudder ran the length of Dominic's powerful body. "This time you shall scream with pleasure, my sensuous witch. I swear it."

"What of you? Will you teach me how to give you that much pleasure?"

Dominic groaned. "I shouldn't."

But he finally did.

26

"**A**RE YOU READY TO GO HAWK-
ing this morning?" Dominic asked in a low voice.
"Or is my beautiful falcon still tender?"

The shuttered sensuality of Dominic's eyes made
Meg blush. It had been two days since she had
bathed her warrior husband and discovered just
how potent and demanding a lover he could be.

Before that afternoon, Dominic had held back
much of himself. Meg hoped he would never do
so again. She had discovered she was every bit as
demanding a lover as he was.

"I was tender only for a morning," Meg whispered. "A bath set me right again."

The lazy gleam of his eyes deepened into a hungry
blaze. He touched her smile with the tip of his finger,
then brushed his mouth over hers.

"There is indeed magic in your baths, sweet
witch," he whispered against her lips. "We shall
try one again after hawking."

Meg's breathless agreement did little to cool Dominic's blood. The temptation to deepen the kiss was
very great, but he suspected if he did, the only
hawk that would get flown that day would be a

very special Glendruid falcon.

Reluctantly Dominic lifted his head and looked intently into his wife's unusual green eyes. They appeared as clear and untroubled as sacred springs. Yet each night he spent with her, she awoke at least once chilled and shaking.

Last night had been no different.

Why are you afraid?

I dream Glendruid dreams.

Of what?

Danger.

What danger? Duncan left for the north this morning. The Reevers are divided. Under Rufus, they will soon come to naught. The rest of my knights will soon be here. What danger is left?

I don't know. I know only that I dream.

A peregrine's distinctive, keening cry sliced through the normal noise of the keep.

"Fatima is impatient," Meg said, amused. "She senses that soon she will trail her jeweled jesses across Blackthorne's sky."

" 'Tis a fine day for it."

Meg looked out through the high, narrow window of the upper keep. Sunlight poured into the keep in a soundless yellow torrent.

"Yes," she said. " 'Tis a fine day. Perhaps spring has finally thawed winter's icy breast."

Yet something in Meg's voice told Dominic that she didn't believe winter's grip had been defeated.

The rhythmic beating of hooves in the bailey announced the arrival of horses and knights eager to go hawking. Dominic and Meg hurried to join them. But no sooner had the lord and lady arrived in the great hall than Eadith rushed up from the well room.

"Lady Margaret, wait!" Eadith called.

"What is it?" Dominic said impatiently. "We're off to go hawking."

" 'Tis Marie," Eadith said. "She's spewing her breakfast and groaning like a woman in childbirth."

"God's teeth," he muttered.

Meg sighed. "I must see to her, lord. You go hawking."

"Not without my small falcon."

When Meg turned to go to Marie, Dominic was at her heels. Silently he watched while Meg questioned the sick woman. There was no doubt that Marie was in unhappy straits. Her skin was pale and dull and her normally red lips had no color in them at all.

When Meg finished asking about Marie's condition, Dominic raised one eyebrow in silent question.

" 'Tis likely a piece of spoiled fish," Meg said.

"Excellent. Leave Eadith with her."

Meg dismissed the idea with a motion of her hand. "Eadith is useless at sickbed. When the patient vomits, so does she. Go hawking. I'll join you next time."

Dominic hesitated.

Standing on tiptoe, Meg spoke softly into Dominic's ear. "Go on without me, my warrior. It distresses Marie for you to see her like this."

With a muttered oath, Dominic turned and stalked from the room. Minutes later the clatter and shout of a hawking party leaving the bailey rang through the keep.

Meg barely noticed. She was busy dripping medicine from a spoon between Marie's pale lips. The task required patience, for half the time the drops got no farther than the leman's tongue before she became sick all over again. Eventually enough of the medicine stayed with Marie that she vomited less frequently. Finally she gave a shuddering sigh and slept.

A glance at the angle of the sun told Meg the hawking party would be too far away for her to catch up with them on her aged palfrey. By the time she reached Dominic, the hawking would be done and they would be on the way back to the keep. Sighing, Meg returned her thoughts to Marie.

"Lady!" Eadith cried from the hall.

The urgency in the handmaiden's voice brought Meg to her feet.

"What is it?" Meg asked as Eadith rushed into the room.

"Lord Dominic's horse fell and he was badly hurt. They fear for his life unless you come quickly!"

For an instant the world went black around Meg. Then she forced breath into her lungs and thought into a mind gone blank with terror.

Is this the danger I feared?

"What are his injuries?" Meg asked tightly.

"The squire didn't say."

"Send for my palfrey to be—"

" 'Tis done," Eadith interrupted.

"Old Gwyn?" Meg asked as she rushed from the room.

"I sent one of the kitchen girls to fetch her."

"Stay with Marie. If she vomits again, give her twelve drops from this," Meg said, handing over a tightly stoppered bottle.

Then there was a wild jangle of bells as she raced down the twisting stairway to the herbal. She grabbed medicines, wrapped them in rags against the hard ride to come, and ran from the room. When she reached the bailey, Harry was there. He tossed her up on the palfrey with a strength that belied his old injury.

"The stupid squire bolted back to the hawking party as soon as he told me," Harry said roughly. "Wouldn't even stay to guide you."

"I know the land better than any of the newly come squires," Meg said. "Where is my husband?"

"The boy said the accident happened in the northern fen, just south of the cart road where the Holy Cross Creek comes out of the fen."

"So far," Meg said fearfully.

"Senseless place to go hawking for waterfowl. Any fool knows they have too much cover there for a peregrine to hunt well."

But Harry was talking to himself. Meg had startled the old palfrey into a canter and was clattering out across the drawbridge. She went up the lane with a speed that scattered chickens and people alike. When vassals called out after her, she ignored them.

Only one thing mattered to Meg. Her husband was lying badly injured somewhere ahead. He needed her, and she was not there.

Grimly, Meg kept the old horse at the best pace it could manage while fields and dry-stone fences flew by on either side. By the time the last of the cultivated lands had fallen behind and no more distant cottages remained, the palfrey was sweating. When the way turned more steep and forest closed in, the horse's breathing became deep and hard. Lather gathered on its flanks and shoulders.

Reluctantly Meg allowed the beast to slow for the worst hills. As soon as possible, she demanded more speed. At a normal pace it would have been at least an hour's ride to the place where the accident had occurred. She had no intention of taking that long. Eadith's words were like a knife turning in Meg's soul.

Your husband's horse fell and he was badly hurt. They fear for his life unless you come quickly!

The most steep incline lay just ahead. The way was rough and the forest crowded in on either side of the cart road. Unhappily Meg slowed her horse again.

Reevers galloped out from hiding in the forest, surrounding her before she could flee. She yanked the reins to the right, launching the palfrey at an opening between two knights.

The old horse was too slow. The Reevers spun their agile war-horses on their hocks, closing the opening before the palfrey reached it. Though Meg spurred her mount forward anyway, the Reevers' battle stallions simply braced themselves as they had been trained to do, ready to take the shock of the palfrey's charge.

From the corner of her eyes, Meg saw other men closing in behind her. In a last, desperate attempt to break free, she yanked the reins hard to the left. Before the winded palfrey could respond, a charger leaped forward and knocked the old horse aside.

Even as the palfrey went to its knees, a Reever snatched Meg from her horse's back and set her astride in front of his saddle.

"Nay!" Meg screamed, turning to claw at her captor's unprotected eyes. "My husband is hurt! I must go to him!"

A casual backhand from a chain mail gauntlet sent Meg's senses spinning. By the time she recovered, she was pinned facedown over a Reever's thighs while the charger thundered at a dead run through the forest.

Dominic! My husband, my warrior, what have they done to you?

There was no answer save the drumroll of hooves and the terrible realization of a Glendruid dream come true, danger all around, chilling Meg to the marrow of her bones.

In the silence of her soul, Meg called again and again to the man who had become a part of her.

* * *

"GOD'S teeth," Simon snarled to Dominic. "You're like a cat walking on wet grass. What is wrong with you? Fatima has flown splendidly."

Dominic gave his brother a narrow sideways glance, then resumed watching the eastern fen with cold eyes. Fatima rode calmly on a perch secured to Dominic's saddle. Sunlight caught the soft, gold-embossed hood over her head, bringing the Turkish designs on the leather into fiery life.

"I can't shake the feeling that we should have ridden war stallions and dressed in hauberks," Dominic said after a moment.

"Why? Do you think Duncan will go back on his vow?"

"If I thought that, I would have killed him two days ago."

Simon grunted. "When Duncan left yesterday for his estates in the north, he took the best of his knights. The Reevers are little better than bandits now."

"Aye."

"Rufus is no leader," Simon continued. "In a fortnight, the Reevers will be dispersed like chaff on the wind."

"I told Meg the same this morning, in the dark hours before dawn."

"And?"

"She wasn't consoled."

Simon muttered something about Glendruid witches and the difficulties they gave to the men who married them.

"There are rewards," Dominic said, smiling to himself.

One of them was that Meg's hair looked quite beautiful by candlelight, fanned across her husband's body as her soft mouth taught him that the falcon also flies its master. The sensuous experience had been extraordinary, for both of them.

Abruptly the sense of wrongness that had been plaguing Dominic crystalized into a need to see his wife once more. Without thought, Dominic turned his horse back the way they had come. The gray stallion responded instantly. Though not the size of Crusader, this horse was faster and easier of gait, an ideal mount for hunting or hawking.

"Dominic?" Simon called, surprised.

"I've had enough of hawking for the day," Dominic said flatly. " 'Tis time to check on my own small falcon."

"God's blood. Can't you trust the wench out of your sight?" Simon muttered.

Without answering, Dominic urged Fatima onto his wrist and spurred his mount into a canter. Cursing, Simon put his own hawk on his wrist and turned to follow. The three other knights and six squires rapidly followed suit.

When the hawking party finally came cantering past fields and between dry-stone fences, peasants dropped their tools and stared at the lord of Blackthorne Keep as though he were a ghost.

The first time it happened Dominic thought little of it. But when more and more people stopped work at the sight of their lord riding by, Dominic and Simon exchanged uneasy glances.

"What is it, man?" Simon called to a shepherd. "Why do you stare so?"

The man crossed himself, turned, and fled. Nor would any other vassal come close to the riders. In fact, they seemed terrified of Dominic.

"I like this not," muttered Simon.

Dominic simply urged his horse to a faster pace. Not until he was at the drawbridge did he rein in.

Suddenly Harry limped out of the gatehouse,

stared in shock at Dominic, and grabbed at his hand as he rode by.

"Thanks be to God," Harry said fervently. "I knew the lass would save you!"

"Save me? From what?"

Harry started to speak but no words came. He simply stared, slack-jawed, at the man who bore no marks of injury of any kind.

"The mistress . . ." Harry struggled to swallow.

"Lady Margaret?" Dominic asked sharply.

Harry nodded.

"Speak, man," Dominic commanded. "Where is Meg?"

"A squire came. He said you were sore injured near the northern fen."

Simon started to speak. A curt gesture from Dominic cut off the words.

"As you can see, I'm not injured. Where is my wife?"

"She went to you, lord. To care for you."

"To the northern fen?" Dominic demanded. "That's halfway to Carlysle Manor, isn't it?"

"Aye."

"Who went with her?"

The look on Harry's face told Dominic more than he wanted to know.

"God's *blood*," he snarled. "You let her ride out alone?"

A woman screamed from the bailey. The high, despairing cry made the hair on Dominic's neck rise. He turned and saw Eadith running toward him across the cobbles of the bailey as though pursued by the fiends of Hell.

"Lord," Eadith sobbed, throwing herself at the feet of Dominic's mount. "Don't have me whipped, lord! I did my best but I couldn't talk her out of it!"

Dominic started to speak, but Eadith's sobbing words never paused.

"She has loved him since she was a child. She was determined to follow him. She wouldn't listen to me! I tried, lord. God knows how I tried! But she wouldn't listen to me!"

"What are you saying?" Dominic asked in a deadly cold voice.

"She knew she would never be allowed out alone, so she paid a boy to come running up with a tale of injury to you. In all the turmoil, she simply got on her palfrey and ran off!"

"How long ago?"

"Noon, my lord."

Dominic turned to Simon. "We can overtake her before supper. She couldn't have gotten far on that nag of hers."

Simon looked dazed. "I wouldn't have thought it of Meg. She fought for your life as though it were her own. Do you really believe she—"

"I believe she isn't here," Dominic said in a voice that chilled everyone who heard it. "Do you believe otherwise?"

Simon looked at the fear on the faces of the people of Blackthorne Keep. They had no doubt that disaster had come to them once again.

"No," Simon said. "I believe she is gone. May God damn her soul to ever—"

A single look at Dominic's face cut off Simon's curse.

Eadith looked from one man to the other.

"Waste no time, lord," she said urgently. " 'Tis true, Lady Margaret's palfrey is old, but like as not Duncan will have a better horse waiting for her on up the road."

Dominic gave Eadith a glittering glance before he turned to the mounted men behind him and gave crisp, succinct orders. Men obeyed instantly, for none could meet their lord's feral eyes. They had not seen him look so savage even when they had pulled him from the ruins of the sultan's palace with the wounds of torture still fresh and bleeding on his body.

Within moments a long-tongued hound came dancing from the kennels. When shown the tracks of Meg's palfrey, Leaper took off immediately, following the horse's trail. Simon and Dominic pursued at a gallop. The other knights remained at the keep, carrying out their liege's orders.

When Leaper finally came to the steep incline in the forest, she didn't slacken her stride until she discovered the place where the palfrey's tracks were churned and overlaid by the prints of other horses. In a tense silence, Dominic and Simon reined in their hard-breathing horses until Leaper picked up the trail in the forest. The men spurred forward between trees at a reckless pace.

"I see it!" Simon called, urging greater speed from his horse.

Dominic didn't bother. He, too, had seen the palfrey. He had also seen that her rider was nowhere in sight. Eadith had been correct.

Someone had waited in the forest with a fresh mount for Meg.

Barely able to leash his savage temper, Dominic looked back to the road where the tracks of many horses had churned the earth. There was no way to tell which horse Meg rode now. Nor was there need. Only one thing lay ahead on the cart road. Duncan of Maxwell's new estates.

The palfrey trotted toward Dominic. The golden chiming of bells followed every step the old horse made. Dominic spurred his mount forward and grabbed the palfrey's reins. Tied to the saddle was a rolled piece of parchment and a note written in a priest's fine hand.

Dominic read it with a single, consuming glance. When he looked up, Simon sucked in his breath. It took no great wit to realize that Dominic would sooner kill than speak at the moment.

"Back to the keep," Dominic said flatly.

Simon asked no questions. He simply followed his brother to Blackthorne Keep. No sooner had the horses clattered over the drawbridge than Dominic began looking into the faces of everyone who ran out into the bailey.

The face he was searching for was not there.

"Send for Eadith," Dominic demanded.

A stirring went through the gathered servants, but no one spoke until Old Gwyn stepped forward.

"Eadith is gone to the Reevers."

Though Dominic had expected as much, he couldn't prevent the icy rage from vibrating in his voice.

"Did she leave a message?" he demanded.

"Aye. If you don't wish your wife to become whore to the Reevers, you will deliver the ransom by moonrise tomorrow."

When Dominic neither moved nor spoke, an uneasy murmur rose from the people gathered in the keep.

"Do they have her, lord?" Gwyn asked.

Dominic's clenched fist opened, revealing fragments of the golden jesses his own small falcon had once worn around her ankles.

"Aye, old woman. She is taken."

"What price?"

For an instant Dominic's eyes closed. When they opened, the people closest to him stepped back, instinctively seeking to widen the distance between themselves and the man whose eyes promised all Hell let out for holiday.

"Thrice her weight in gold and jewels," Dominic said distinctly.

"God's blood," Simon said, stunned. "He can't mean that. It would beggar Blackthorne Keep!"

"That is the point," Dominic said. "I am to be stripped of my ability to support my knights. Without them, the keep will soon fall. Not that I will know it."

"What do you mean?"

"I have been instructed to deliver the ransom with no more than one knight to attend me. It is reasonable to conclude that I will be slain despite the good priest's protestations to the contrary."

"You can't do this. 'Tis madness!"

"Aye," Dominic said savagely. " 'Tis madness indeed."

27

When Meg finally was permitted to dismount, she was sore and stiff from the brutal ride. Surreptitiously she glanced around at the Reevers' illegal keep. Nothing she saw reassured her.

There were more than twenty men lounging around the rude forest bailey. Only one man wore the expensive trappings of a knight, and it was obvious that the battle gear had seen better days. The remainder of the men were little more than bandits, poachers, and felons.

Guards sat idly along the edge of the ragged palisade that ringed the bailey. None but the knight had ever been numbered among Duncan's companions. Rough of manner, raggedly clothed, only the Reevers' weapons seemed to have received any care. Swords and knives gleamed in the light from a bonfire that served the needs of both warmth and cooking.

The men watched Meg with blunt lust or animal indifference as she limped over to a big oak and collapsed at its base. Neither the coarse men nor her own bruised body bothered her nearly as much as the waking dream that had come to her during the grueling ride . . . a newborn babe laughing up at her with eyes of Glendruid green.

Have you bled yet, small falcon?

No.

Nor would Meg for nine months more, if she had dreamed truly.

Dominic, will you ever know your child? And if you do, will you believe it is yours?

A hand shook Meg roughly.

"Get up, witch, and serve your betters their supper," Eadith said.

"Eadith! What are you doing here? Did they steal you, too?"

The other woman smiled bitterly. "I haven't a silver coin to my name. Why would any man steal me? Nay, I came to the Reevers willingly."

"Water does find its own level, doesn't it?"

"Mind your tongue, witch," Eadith said, slapping Meg smartly. "I have waited long for this. Move your donkey's arse and serve us supper or I'll give you to Edmond the Cruel for instruction in your new profession."

When she would have struck Meg again, a knight who was somewhat less ragged than the others stepped forward and jostled Eadith aside.

"Rufus wouldn't like that," the knight said calmly to Eadith. "He plans on using the witch first. Any marks on her, he wants to be the one to put them there. He was quite clear about that this morning. Remember?"

Eadith's mouth flattened into a sour line, but she made no move to strike Meg again. Eadith knew very well that Rufus had plans for the Glendruid witch. It had been Eadith who had put many of the plans into the Reever's thick head.

"Is this how you repay Blackthorne's kindness?" Meg asked, rising and adjusting her mantle around her shoulders against the damp mist and covetous eyes of the Reevers. "Treachery?"

"What kindness?" Eadith asked scornfully. "I was the daughter of a keep as great as Blackthorne and I was turned into a common servant."

"Your keep fell to the Normans."

Anger tightened Eadith's already drawn features. Her pale eyes flashed like an animal's with reflected firelight.

"It was not a fair battle," she said curtly. "They came upon the keep through treachery."

"Fair or foul, the result was the same," Meg said. "Your family and husband were slain and you were thrown on the mercy of neighbors who fared no better than you. You were a homeless, childless widow when Lord John rescued you, gave you a respectable position, and promised to find you a husband."

Eadith smiled thinly. "But first, John tried to make me pregnant."

Meg's breath came in sharply.

"Didn't you know?" Eadith said coldly. "The lord of the keep tried to rut on every female before he gave permission for her marriage."

Though Meg began to speak, Eadith gave no opening.

"John promised every girl the same—breed his child and become mistress of the keep. But it never happened, because after his cursed witch wife left him, his staff became so limp no seed ever came from it no matter what whore's tricks were tried."

A shout from the boundary of the rude forest camp distracted Eadith. Rufus was returning to the bonfire with more supplies from Carlysle Manor. As Meg watched, all but one knight and a ragged poacher with downcast face crowded around to see what bounty the manor had supplied this day.

"Ale?" shouted one Reever questioningly.

"Aye," Rufus said as he dismounted, grinning.

He walked to the fire and dragged off his helm, revealing the coarse mane of red hair that was the source of his name.

"Is there food?" Eadith asked rather sharply.

"Meat, bread, and cheese."

"What about a wench?" called another Reever.

"We're promised one of the kitchen wenches as soon as she quits bleeding."

"Why wait?" muttered one of the Reevers. "She'll be bleeding when we finish, like as not. One wench isn't enough to service us."

Meg acted as though she hadn't heard. Beneath the mantle her hands went instinctively to her womb. A chill that had nothing to do with the damp morning condensed beneath her skin.

"Any word from the Norman bastard?" Eadith asked.

A shrug was the only answer Rufus gave. His eyes lit when he saw Meg standing on the opposite side of the fire.

"Stand by me," he commanded.

Outwardly calm, Meg walked around the fire toward Rufus, stopping well short of him. The look in his eyes as he watched her made her stomach clench and bile rise in her throat.

The expression on Eadith's face was both irritated and resigned. The Reever's well-known lust for the mistress of Blackthorne Keep had been one of the levers Eadith had used to pry Rufus from Duncan's side. She was in no position to complain when Rufus displayed that lust for all to see.

"Do at least wait until moonrise tomorrow," Eadith said impatiently. "Rutting on her will be much more satisfying when the Norman bastard is here to watch."

Nausea rolled through Meg. The chill beneath her skin went deeper, despite the bonfire's heat.

"What madness is this?" she asked with aching calm.

"No madness," Eadith retorted. " 'Tis but revenge against the Norman bastard and the Glendruid witch who is his whore."

"What revenge."

There was neither question nor emotion in Meg's voice, simply an unnatural calm that came as ice possessed her soul.

"You should have let the Norman bastard die of the poison I gave him," Eadith said savagely. "Then I could have persuaded Duncan to take the keep and all would have been well. But the bastard lived and I shall have my revenge despite your interfering."

"Duncan. Where is he."

Again Meg's voice was flat, toneless, almost inhuman.

Eadith shrugged. "Gone north with his knights and good riddance. The border clans will cut short that traitor's life before he can enjoy the fruits of his treachery."

"He is not one of you."

"Aye," Eadith snarled. "We have no traitors left among us. Except you, witch, and we won't have you long."

Meg's unblinking stare made the Reevers look from one to the other with growing uncertainty. Muttering ran through them as they measured the uncanny stillness of their Glendruid captive.

Only Eadith was undeterred by Meg's unflinching green eyes. The vengeance Eadith had sought since her family's defeat by Normans was finally within her grasp.

"Let me tell you what is waiting for you, traitor," Eadith said with relish. "At moonrise tomorrow your bastard lord will arrive with thrice your weight in gold and gems."

A hidden motion of Meg's body made her remaining jewelry shiver musically. The small cries were stilled almost as soon as they began.

"We will take the ransom," Eadith continued. "Then you will be given to the Reevers while your husband watches. When there is no more sport to be had from either of you, we will kill him."

Meg said nothing.

"Are you too slack-witted to understand what your siding with the Normans will cost you?" Eadith demanded angrily. "Soon you will know what I endured. You will be orphaned, widowed, childless, and defiled!"

The tilt of Meg's head made golden bells chime. It was the only sound she made for several breaths.

"Dominic le Sabre will not come for me," Meg said.

"He will come. He must. Else you die."

"Then I die. Send for a priest to shrive me."

The certainty in Meg's voice finally penetrated Eadith's triumph. She stared in shock.

"What are you saying?" Rufus demanded, stepping so close that Meg had to tilt back her head to see his face. "Of course Dominic will come to your rescue. Without you, he will lose Blackthorne Keep."

"To whom?" Meg asked flatly. "Duncan will not take it. You cannot."

"We can," retorted Rufus. "We will."

" 'Tis a pity I will already be dead," Meg said, stepping back to look around the camp. "I would enjoy seeing this scabrous band attack Blackthorne Keep. Once the Sword stopped laughing, he would gut you and leave you for the crows."

"There will be no one but Thomas the Strong left to marshal the keep's defenses," Eadith cut in. "He is able enough, but stupid."

"Simon will fight as fiercely and cleverly as Dominic."

"Simon won't be there," Rufus said. "We told Dominic that he could have one knight accompany him with the ransom."

Meg nodded. "I see. That knight will be Simon the Loyal, of course."

"Yes," Rufus said, smiling with satisfaction.

" 'Tis your plan to murder them both."

"There was no other choice after the Norman bastard survived and began doting on you—and you on him," Rufus said. "It was clear there would soon be an heir. If an heir was born, Blackthorne Keep would be lost to us."

"So you tried to murder my husband during the hunt," Meg said. "But we escaped."

"You escaped Rufus," Eadith said. "But you didn't escape *my* snare."

"Ah . . . It was you who made Marie ill so that I would stay behind."

"It was a pleasure to watch the whore vomit. It was an even greater pleasure to watch the Norman bastard's face when he finally returned and I told him you had run off to join Duncan of Maxwell."

"That was stupid of you," Meg said neutrally.

Eadith smiled.

"You are too greedy for revenge," Meg continued.

"How so?"

"You want Dominic to ransom me, yet you couldn't resist twisting the knife by telling him I ran off to another man."

Eadith shrugged. "No matter. It will just make the bastard's desire to pursue and punish you all the greater."

"Then you were the one who kept spreading gossip that Duncan and I were lovers."

Though there was no question in Meg's voice, Eadith answered, relishing every word.

"Aye. Seeing the bastard's jealousy was very sweet. You cast your spell most thoroughly, witch. And now you will pay."

Meg's soft laughter was more shocking than curses could have been. Uneasily the Reevers shifted and looked at the descending darkness as though expecting ghosts to rise from the damp ground.

"Ah, handmaiden," Meg said. "You have outsmarted yourself. 'Tis no great task, granted, but 'tis very amusing to watch."

The cool scorn in Meg's voice was like a whip laid across Eadith's body.

"What are you ranting about?" she demanded.

"Enthralled? The Sword?" Meg laughed once, a sound that made the Reevers flinch. "Eadith, you are a fool to the soles of your feet."

Meg turned to the Reevers. When she spoke, her voice carried clearly despite its eerie calm.

"Hear me, Reevers. Dominic le Sabre wants Blackthorne Keep, not me. If he gave me jeweled jesses and seemed to hang on my every smile, it was in hope of seducing a child from my body, not because I *enthralled* him."

Eadith began to speak, only to be silenced by an abrupt gesture from Rufus.

"Why should my husband give a king's ransom for a faithless Glendruid witch who, even if she is fertile, will not give him a male heir?" Meg asked reasonably. "Dominic kept me only because the vassals would have risen up if he set me aside."

"All the more reason for him to ransom you," Eadith retorted.

Once again Meg laughed, and once again Reevers

looked aside, wishing themselves well away from
the lady who faced them with such amused certainty
of their defeat— and her own death.

"You are so greedy yourself," Meg said to Eadith,
"yet you don't allow for greed in others."

"Speak plainly," Eadith snapped.

"Thrice my weight in jewels and gold will beggar
Blackthorne Keep."

"Aye!"

"Who pays for the knights that protect vassals
from the likes of you?" Meg asked gently. "Who
pays the taxes that will refill the keep's coffers to
buy knights? Whose lives will be made living hell
if their lord is impoverished?"

A muttering ran through the Reevers as they
understood what Meg was saying.

"Aye," she agreed. "The vassals pay. They like
me well enough, but they like feeding their children
better."

"Don't listen to her," Eadith said quickly. "She'll
enthrall you just as she—"

Rufus cuffed Eadith into silence with casual brutality. Meg kept talking, knowing she might well
receive the same treatment herself at any moment.

"While you stand here and count the ransom you
will never receive," Meg said, "I'll warrant that the
lord of Blackthorne is appealing to the archbishop
to have our marriage annulled."

Frowning, Rufus yanked absently at a lock of his
long mustache.

"An abbey should be inducement enough for the
annulment," Meg continued gently, relentlessly.
"But since Dominic is such a clever tactician, he
will probably offer a fine stone church as well."

"What of—"

Meg kept on talking, not allowing Rufus a chance
to voice his question.

"Before my flesh is cold in its grave, Dominic will be wed to a fine, fertile Norman wife who will give him enough heirs to stand hip to thigh across the land.

"You have outsmarted yourselves, Reevers. Blackthorne Keep is Norman now. Thanks to your foolish greed, it will remain so until the Kingdom of God comes again to earth."

" 'TIS shrewd of my wife to demoralize them," Dominic said when Sven paused in his story. "Did she recognize you?"

"I think not. She made no attempt to speak privately with me."

Sven hesitated and looked around the great hall. No one except Simon and Old Gwyn was close enough to overhear.

"I suspect that at least two of the Reevers men spy for Duncan," Sven added.

"No surprise in that," Dominic said. "The Scots Hammer is shrewd when his passions don't rule him."

"One of the spies slipped away from camp well before I did," Sven said.

"Then we shall likely see Duncan soon," Dominic said. "What else did Meg say?"

Sven looked at Dominic and wished himself anywhere at all but Blackthorne Keep. His lord was dressed for battle from helm to chausses. The hilt of his gleaming, well-used sword was never more than inches from his hand.

With a stifled curse, Sven ran his fingers through his artfully dirty hair and spoke again.

"Your lady asked once more for a priest, saying that if she died unshriven she would surely haunt them as Lady Anna haunts the keep."

"Turning the knife." Dominic smiled savagely.

" 'Tis a foretaste of revenge for what they did to her. My small falcon is quite fierce."

Sven looked toward Old Gwyn.

"Is Lady Margaret a good liar?" Sven asked bluntly.

"Nay." The flat denial lay like a stone in the silence. "Meg is like a sacred spring, too clear to hide even the deepest parts of her soul."

"I thought so," Sven muttered.

As Dominic looked from one to the other, the smile on his face faded, leaving the savagery behind.

"What are you saying?" he demanded.

"Lady Margaret believed every word she spoke," Sven said simply. "That's why the Reevers believed her."

"What sane person wouldn't believe her?" Gwyn asked, watching Dominic intently. "It would be madness to ruin your estates in order to ransom a wife who can't give you a son."

"Enough!" Dominic commanded.

Gwyn kept talking as though she hadn't heard. Her words were as calm and relentless as a cold rain.

"After moonrise tomorrow, the Reevers will defile Meg," the old woman said. "Even if she survives what they do to her, it will be impossible for you to keep Meg as your wife. You will set her aside and soon the keep will have a new lady. And you, lord . . . then you will finally have the sons you want more than you want anything else on earth."

"Simon."

Though Dominic said no more, his brother answered the unspoken question.

"You are renowned as a tactician," Simon said, choosing each word with care. "It would be a poor tactician who lost a war trying to win a battle that would gain him nothing."

"Explain."

Simon hesitated. He had never heard quite that tone of voice from his brother. Simon would be well pleased if he never heard it again.

"You came here for land and sons," Simon said after a moment. "That is your war. Half of it is won. The land is yours."

Dominic said nothing.

"If you fight this battle on the Reevers' terms," Simon resumed, "you have nothing to gain and much to lose. Nor will the vassals of Blackthorne Keep require that you sacrifice everything—including them—in a futile battle.

"Meg knows that as well as you do. So, now, do the Reevers."

Simon looked away from his brother. Like Dominic's voice, his expression was a terrible combination of rage and anguish.

"Finish it," Dominic said bleakly.

"God's blood," muttered Simon. " 'Tis clear enough. Meg does not expect you to ransom her."

With a speed that made his heavy war cloak flare, Dominic turned his back on the people in the great hall. He didn't want them to see what must lie naked in his eyes, memories and Meg's words turning like knives in his soul.

I could be a liar, a cheat, a robber, a felon . . . none of it matters to you. One womb serves as well as another, so long as it comes with Blackthorne Keep.

Gauntleted hands became fists.

Is Dominic unkind to you?

To his Glendruid wife? To his sole hope of legal heirs? Does my husband strike you as a stupid man? My jesses, after all, are almost the equal of his fine peregrine's.

Dominic stood rigidly, his fists clenched at his side.

You are in pain. Let me heal you.

Only one thing can heal me.

Then I give it to you.

A tremor ripped past Dominic's control.

Send for the priest, for I will surely die.

For a long time Dominic struggled for the self-control he had learned at such cost in the past. He had been very certain he had nothing new to learn about pain.

He had been wrong.

Meg, I never meant to wound you so. You saw into me so clearly, yet you gave to me so generously.

Would that you could see into me now. . . .

A low sound came from the bailey, hundreds of voices held in unnatural restraint while whisperings gusted through the crowd like fickle winds.

"They still gather, lord," Gwyn said calmly.

"For what?" Dominic asked.

Even the old Glendruid witch flinched at the sound of Dominic's voice. After a moment she answered.

"For you. They are in need and you are their lord."

Without a word or a backward look, Dominic strode through the great hall to the forebuilding. When the vassals saw him appear in the wide doorway with chain mail glittering beneath his heavy cloak, silence spread through the bailey.

Before Dominic could speak, Harry climbed the steps. In his hand was a small leather bag. Coins jingled within.

"Adela and I heard what happened," Harry said. " 'Tis a terrible ransom they demand."

When Harry extended the bag, Dominic was too surprised to move.

"Take it," Harry urged. " 'Tis not much, I know, but 'tis all we have. Please, lord. When Adela was in pain, Meg came to her."

Before Harry turned away, the falcon master was climbing the forebuilding's stairs. In his hands was a wooden bowl holding a few precious coins.

"My second son was trampled by a war stallion when he was four. The lady knelt in the mire and eased his dying pain. She was not yet nine herself."

No sooner had the falcon master set the bowl at Dominic's feet than other vassals stepped forward one by one, holding in their hands whatever small treasure had been gleaned from a lifetime of hard labor. With each gift came a sentence or two.

"She stayed at my father's sickbed."

"When my brother was ill and there was no straw to burn, she gave him her cloak."

"She healed my son."

"My babe would have died but for her."

"She comforted me."

The money Dominic had given to the vassals at his wedding feast fell like a silver rain into the bowl, coin after coin returning, mute witness to the vassals' regard for their Glendruid lady. With the coins came whispered words that told of love beyond price.

"She healed my hand."

"When my wife needed her, she came."

"When everyone called me cursed, she cured me."

"I am blind. Her voice is my light."

Finally no one remained on the steps of the forebuilding but a boy who couldn't have been more than nine years old. At his heels limped a large, tattered dog. Dominic looked at the boy's carefully clenched hand and wondered what a child so young would have to offer, and why.

As though to give himself courage to speak, the boy buried one hand in the hound's thick ruff as he thrust out his other hand. On his palm was his greatest treasure—one of the Turkish sweets Dominic had given to his vassals along with the silver coins. The sweet had been nibbled at one edge only, as though each day the boy took just a bit of the rare treat, savoring it.

"She saved my dog when a snare caught him."

The boy dropped the sweet onto the pile of coins and fled. The hound followed like a ragged brown shadow.

Dominic tried to speak, but could not. Like drops gathering into rills and creeks until a mighty river was born, the gifts and words told the meaning of Meg's life to the vassals of the keep. She was peace and hope in a world of war and famine. She was sunlight and laughter and healing when everything else was pain.

She was all that and more to the warrior who had married for land and sons, and had received life and love.

Finally Dominic was able to speak.

"Our heart has been stolen."

A low sound rose from the people.

"If she isn't returned to us alive and laughing," Dominic said, "there will be a harrowing of the north such as will never be forgotten."

The noise became a growl as though of a beast aroused.

"I will hunt down the Reevers and their families one by one, and I will kill them where I find them, man and woman and child."

Sound rippled darkly, a beast prowling, unleashed.

"I will burn their homes, slaughter their stock, and poison their wells.

"I will tear down their stone fences, slay their game, and salt their fields until nothing can live therein.

"Then I will leave the cursed land to the unshriven ghosts I've made!"

A savage cry of assent echoed through the bailey.

Slowly Old Gwyn climbed the last step and stood before the lord of Blackthorne Keep, seeing for the first time what the vassals already had seen.

From eyes shaded by a battle helm came as many tears as there were silver coins heaped in the bowl.

"I have waited a thousand years for this day," Gwyn said.

With quick, sure motions, Gwyn fastened a heavy silver pin to Dominic's black battle cloak. When she stepped back, sunlight struck the ancient pin, making the silver wolf's head burn. Clear crystal eyes flashed and glittered as though alive.

A great shout went up from the vassals as they greeted the Glendruid Wolf.

AT dawn, knights mounted on chargers galloped forth from Blackthorne Keep, heading north. Steel weapons gleamed and clashed with every motion the war-horses made. Behind them the drawbridge was lifted and the gates were bolted shut.

The Glendruid Wolf had gone to war.

28

"**N**o," DOMINIC SAID FLATLY to Duncan. "You would be recognized and slain out of hand. Don't speak of it again. If you weren't valuable to me alive, I would have killed you twice over by now."

Duncan and his knights had found Dominic in mid-afternoon on the northbound cart road. The Scots Hammer and the Glendruid Wolf had been arguing ever since. Duncan looked up to the oak branches overhead as though expecting to find help in the delicate green flames that burned at the tip of each twig.

"If someone isn't inside the palisade when we attack," Duncan said through his teeth, "Meggie could well be killed before my 'renegade' knight can stop it."

"Do you think I don't know that?" Dominic shot back. "That's why I'm going inside the palisade as soon as it's dark. I'll be able to sneak past the—"

"God's blood!" Duncan and Simon exploded at once.

"You can't do that," Simon continued harshly. "Your size alone would give you away!"

"Not to mention that great shining piece of silver you wear on your cloak," Duncan muttered.

He eyed the wolf's head warily, as though expecting its silent snarl to be transformed into a living wolf at any moment.

"Lord," Sven said quietly. "I will go. 'Tis my favorite kind of work."

"By now they will have missed you," Dominic said, his voice impatient. "What will you say when they ask where you've been?"

"I'll tell them I was worried about my flocks."

Dominic grunted. "It wouldn't convince me."

"Rufus isn't you."

An explosive curse was Dominic's only answer.

"Your lady is chained to a tree," Sven said. "There will be no chance for her to seek cover when you attack. Someone must be there to protect her."

"I can't ask you to do anything that dangerous."

Sven's smile was both savage and amused. "Ah, lord, do you know me so little? Danger is my wife, my mistress, and my child. That's why I like being your knight so well."

A searing oath, a hissing sigh, and Dominic gave in.

"See the priest before you go," Dominic ordered Sven. "This time you may find more danger than even you can survive."

"There are many worse ways to die than defending my liege's lady."

"Aye," cut in Simon firmly. "Let me go with Sven. I can—"

"Nay," Sven objected instantly. "You're as big as Dominic or Duncan. The Reevers would spot you in the blink of an eye. If they didn't, Eadith would."

"You're hardly tiny yourself," Simon retorted.

"They are used to me," Sven said, turning away. "When will you attack?"

"At dusk," Dominic said. "Will that give you enough time?"

Sven glanced at the angle of the sun. "Barely. Send men on foot to attack from the rear. With a bit of luck, the sally port in the palisade will be open."

Before anyone could respond, Sven trotted into the forest and vanished.

"Where did you find that one?" Duncan asked Dominic.

"In a Saracen hell."

"Can he open the sally port?"

"If any man can manage it, Sven can. It won't be the first gate he has opened for me from inside."

"That I believe," Duncan muttered. "He is like a cat in his stealth."

Behind Dominic a horse snorted and stirred restlessly. The other knights and their squires had dismounted while their lord and the two knights argued over who would take the most dangerous position during the attack. Duncan's men were much like Dominic's: hard, competent, and well blooded in previous battles.

Most of the knights had taken off their heavy hauberks and were checking their weaponry. Crossbow and bolts, pike and staff, mace and sword and battle-ax lay in deadly array. The knights talked as they worked over their equipment, laying bets as to which man would be first through the palisades, which would be first to kill, even which would be first to draw blood or have it drawn from his own flesh.

Dominic heard the jests and conversations as though at a great distance. He was focused on one thing and one thing alone: Meg. He would have traded Heaven and taken on Hell single-handed if it would have guaranteed that his small falcon survived moonrise.

"Do you have any instructions for the knights?" Simon asked Dominic when all was ready.

"No quarter. No prisoners."

IGNORING the Reever guards who called back and forth from their perches on the palisades, Meg tugged surreptitiously on the heavy chain that went from her wrist manacles around the trunk of a young oak. Though rusty, the chain was still strong.

She glanced at the sun. It was no longer visible over the raw wood palisade that surrounded the rough bailey. Soon dusk would pool in the shadows and hollows until darkness brimmed over, filling the land. Shortly afterward, the moon would rise in silver glory.

And then the Reevers would come for her.

Eadith paced near the bonfire where the remains of a venison roast congealed on a spit. Impatiently she looked from the fire to the guard who had the best view of the cart road to Carlysle Manor.

"Do you see anything?" she called.

"No," the man said curtly.

Rufus hacked a piece off the roast with a dagger, stuffed the meat into his mouth, and chewed.

"He will come," she insisted. "He is besotted with the witch."

Rufus grunted.

Eadith resumed pacing.

A ragged Reever stepped up to the spit. His knife sliced easily through the tough meat.

"What of you, shepherd?" Eadith demanded. "Did you see riders?"

"No, mistress. My flocks are to the east."

With a muttered curse, Eadith turned back to the guard, who ignored her.

The shepherd wandered toward the back of the

encampment. As he passed by Meg, he dropped the piece of meat. When he bent down to retrieve it, he spoke in a voice that carried no farther than her.

"The Sword comes at dusk."

Meg's eyes widened as she looked at the pale hair and light eyes of the strange shepherd.

"He does *not* come," she said softly.

"Be ready, lady."

Sven smiled thinly, tossed the meat away, and kept walking toward the back gate. As he had hoped, Duncan's "renegade" knight sat nearby, sharpening the edge of a huge battle-ax.

"Dusk," Sven breathed as he walked past.

The rasping of stone on steel paused just long enough to tell Sven that the knight had heard.

"Guard!" Eadith called a few minutes later.

"No one comes as far as I can see," the man answered in a bored tone. The question had been asked and answered many times that afternoon.

Dusk settled over the camp like a cloak. Though the moon had not yet risen, its silver glow shone just above the western horizon. Rufus wiped his knife on his sleeve and looked over at Meg with naked intent.

Casually Duncan's knight stood up, hefting the ax as though to test its balance. He began swinging the weapon one-handed around his head, making the air whistle with the speed of the ax's passage. It was not the first time he had drilled himself with the ax since he had come to the Reevers, but it never failed to intrigue the ill-trained men.

The knight's skilled play with the ax was all the distraction Sven needed and more than he had hoped for. He went to the back gate as though to relieve himself. When he passed the guard, a knife blade gleamed dully and the guard slumped. Sven propped him up against the palisade and pulled the man's mantle around him as though he slept.

A few quick strokes into the earth cleaned the knife blade. Sven returned the weapon to its sheath and waited, knowing the battle would begin soon.

Suddenly the guard at the front of camp shouted and pointed toward the cart road.

"They're coming! Two knights. One is dressed in black. God blind me if it isn't the Norman bastard!"

"Do they have the treasure?" Eadith demanded.

"Aye! Their pack animals are fair staggering beneath their burdens."

A ragged shout went up from the camp. Men jostled one another eagerly to catch the first glimpse of the riches that would soon be theirs.

No one noticed Sven quietly slipping the bolt on the sally port, opening it a crack, and then going quickly to stand near Meg.

"Soon, my lady," he said softly.

Meg was too stunned to answer. As she watched, Dominic slipped through the sally port. In the slowly condensing darkness, he seemed like a part of night itself. Both his drawn sword and the ancient silver pin gleamed as he turned, encompassing the camp with a single glance.

Behind him, Simon and Duncan took shape out of the dusk, their swords drawn, but Meg saw only the Glendruid Wolf gleaming savagely on Dominic's shoulder. Chills coursed over her as she understood that her people's curse had finally been lifted. No longer would each Glendruid girl feel the weight of her people's hope on her shoulders.

A Glendruid Wolf had been born, but not of a Glendruid woman.

Just as Dominic spotted Meg chained to the large oak, a shout came from the men gathered around the front gate.

"To arms! The bastard is among us!"

Reevers snatched up swords and shields and attacked without thought or order. Duncan, Simon, and Dominic took the brunt of the ragged charge, holding the gate open while other knights shouldered through the sally port and into the camp.

Soon steel rang on steel and blood shone blackly beneath the risen moon. Shouting, cursing, clashing, the battle surged back and forth across the churned earth like a mad, bleeding beast.

Meg watched in awe and fear, finally learning how Dominic had earned his name. If any man had questioned the Sword's mettle after he showed mercy in the church and again in the games, no man questioned it now. Dominic hewed through Reevers like a scythe through a summer meadow. There was no mercy in him for the men who had stolen his wife.

Abruptly Meg sensed someone coming up behind her. She spun just in time to see a battle-ax arc down through the dusk. The blade bit through the length of chain that was wrapped around the trunk of the oak. So great was the force of the blow that the blade sank into wood nearly to its haft. A gauntleted hand wrapped around her wrist, pulling her to her feet.

"Quickly, lady. 'Tis not safe for—"

The knight's words ended in a choked cry as a bolt from a crossbow struck his helm and ricocheted off. Without another sound he fell to the earth.

Meg knelt, saw that there was nothing to be done, and stood quickly, dragging six feet of chain with her. With a growing sense of fear she searched for Dominic in the midst of the bloody battle. None of the men lying on the ground had his size, yet the certainty grew in her that the Glendruid Wolf could be lost almost in the same breath that he had been found.

Nay! We have waited too long for him!

Frantically Meg searched the gloom for sight of her husband. Dominic's well-trained knights were making short work of the Reevers. Few of them were still able to fight, but they didn't lack courage for all their wounds. They slashed with swords like madmen, trying to hew through the knights to the Norman bastard who had once again thwarted their ambitions.

Rufus was nowhere in sight. Nor was Dominic. Finally the flash of Glendruid crystal in the wolf's eyes drew Meg's attention. Dominic was at the far edge of the camp, running toward her. Though his sword was still drawn, he ignored the final swirls of battle around him.

Danger.

With uncanny certainty Meg looked to her right. Just a few feet away, Rufus was stepping out from behind the oak that had been her prison. As she watched in horror, he raised his crossbow to murder the Glendruid Wolf.

"Nay!" Meg screamed.

With the strength of desperation, she swung her manacled hands in a fierce arc. Six feet of chain lashed out and tangled with the crossbow, jerking it toward Meg as Rufus fired. The crossbow's deadly arrow hummed harmlessly up into the night.

Rufus dropped the useless snarl of crossbow and chain. As he drew his sword with his right hand, he lashed out with his left hand at the girl who had ruined his aim. A mailed fist thudded into flesh protected only by cloth. Meg spun aside, staggered, and reached out for her husband with chained hands.

"Dominic—!"

Even as Meg crumpled, Dominic leaped forward and caught her with his left arm. His right arm swung in a fierce arc that made his sword flash in the firelight.

Grunting with effort, Rufus began a two-handed swing that was meant to cut Dominic in half, and Meg with him.

The blow was only a hand's span from its target when Dominic's sword sliced up through the darkness, deflecting the blade. Steel rang on steel with a force that sent shock through the men's bones.

Shouting a violent curse, Rufus swung two-handed again. Dominic barely parried the blow in time. He was fighting one-handed, holding on to Meg with the other.

When Rufus swung a third time, Dominic seemed to slip. As he fell, he turned, protecting Meg with his own body. With a cry of triumph, Rufus lifted his sword for a killing blow.

The Glendruid Wolf came up from the ground in a silent, deadly spring. Too late Rufus realized that he couldn't protect himself from the sword that was leveled like a lance at his naked throat.

Before the Reever could plead or flee, he was dead.

Dominic withdrew his sword, knelt, and eased Meg into his arms. She made a low sound and turned toward him. Even in the glow of the bonfire's leaping flames, her face was pale. From across the fire came the last flurry of battle. Dominic glanced up once, then ignored everything but his wife.

"Meg," he said, fear rough in his voice. "Where are you hurt?"

Her eyes opened slowly. Reflected firelight made the silver pin on Dominic's cloak burn. Meg looked deeply into the wolf's savage crystal eyes and sighed. With fingers that shook, she touched first the Glendruid Wolf and then the man who wore it.

"Don't fear, warrior," Meg whispered. "Whether I live or die, Blackthorne Keep and its vassals will be yours."

"Damn the land and damn my ambitions with it!"

Meg's mouth opened but no words came out. Dominic's hands were searching tenderly over her, seeking any wound. What he found was a rent in her clothing where chain mail had ripped through fabric. Her breath broke when he touched her ribs.

"Be still, small falcon. Let me see how badly you are hurt."

" 'Tis but a few drops of blood and a bruise," Meg whispered.

"You fainted."

"The blow took the breath from me."

A few more light touches assured Dominic that Meg was right. She had been pummeled but not badly wounded by the blow. She had also been very lucky. Rufus had meant to maim if not kill her.

The realization of how close Meg had come to death made ice gather in Dominic's stomach.

"You never should have risked yourself that way," he said harshly.

"Rufus would have killed you."

"He nearly killed you! God's teeth, if you had died—" Dominic's throat closed, making speech impossible.

"My death wouldn't have mattered very much."

Meg smiled sadly at Dominic's shocked expression. With a hand that shook, she traced the Glendruid pin on his cloak.

"You are what matters," she said simply. "You will heal the land, not I. The Glendruid Wolf has set you free of John's trap. In a way, I suppose it has set me free, too. I will no longer have to endure the exquisite pain of giving my body, heart, and soul to a man who sees in me only a womb for his sons."

"What are you saying?" Dominic asked, appalled.

"Blackthorne's people are safe without me now. You can have whatever wife you wish, and I can finally be as free as an untamed falcon."

Dominic closed his eyes and struggled to control the combination of relief and fear and rage that battled within him. Meg was alive and safe, but she had never seemed farther from him, slipping away with each word, each sad smile, the trembling of her fingers as she touched cold silver rather than his face.

She had yet to meet his eyes. To *see* him.

"I will never let you go," Dominic said harshly.

"Don't worry, Glendruid Wolf. The people will accept you. Blackthorne Keep is yours for as long as you live. Nothing can change that now."

"Without you, the land and the people are a feast for a dead man. Look at me. *Look into me.*"

"Nay," Meg whispered brokenly. "I can't bear it. I can't bear *seeing* how much I love and how little you do."

For a moment Dominic went completely still. Then he bent and kissed Meg's eyelids tenderly, stealing her tears with the tip of his tongue. He felt the tremors ripping through her, as though he used a whip on her rather than his most gentle caress.

"Look at me and know what I know," he whispered between kisses. "Look at me. *See me.*"

Slowly Meg's eyes opened and she looked at Dominic, *seeing* him, knowing what he knew. With a sound of wonder she touched his lips with her hand.

"Glendruid witch," Dominic said, kissing Meg's fingertips, "you healed my body, my heart, and my soul . . . and then you stole them from me one kiss at a time. With or without heirs, I will have no other wife but you."

As Dominic gathered Meg closely and buried his face against her warmth, he whispered the truth they both finally knew.

"I love you, sweet witch. I will always love you."

Epilogue

WOLFLIKE, WINTER HOWLED, scratching at Blackthorne Keep with claws of ice. Secure in the knowledge of a fine harvest, the people of the keep quietly went about their business. While they worked, they waited for news of their mistress, who had grown big with the Glendruid Wolf's seed.

"I wish Old Gwyn had stayed," Dominic muttered.

"She had paid for her adultery for a thousand years," Meg said. "I couldn't ask any more of her."

Dominic ran a powerful hand through his hair. He still wasn't sure he believed as Meg did. All he could say with certainty was that the silver wedding dress, the crystal-studded silver chain, and the old Glendruid woman were gone as though they had never existed.

An expression of both concentration and unease went over Meg's face. Dominic had noticed just that look more and more often since dawn.

"How do you feel?" he asked anxiously.

"Like I will need both of your strong arms to haul me out of even this shallow bath."

Gently Dominic lifted Meg from the bath and

405

wrapped her in a soft drying cloth.

"Someday we will have to find a suitable hand-maiden," Meg said.

Dominic made a neutral sound as he smoothed his hands over the body that had once been slender but was now swollen with his seed.

" 'Tis unseemly for the lord of a keep to be his wife's servant," Meg pointed out.

" 'Tis a great pleasure for the lord of this keep to feel his babe's life stirring beneath his hands," Dominic countered.

Abruptly Meg's body went rigid with the force of her labor. When she spoke, her voice was strained.

"Call for the midwife. The babe is suddenly quite eager."

While the storm howled around the keep, Dominic carried Meg to the bed she had prepared for the birthing. Fragrant herbs and dried flowers scented the air, and luxurious tapestries cut off drafts from the wind.

The midwife rushed into the room, saw at once that Meg's time was close at hand, and muttered all the way through the Glendruid water ritual Meg insisted she perform.

"There!" the midwife said as she yanked a smock into place. "Are you happy now?"

"Aye."

Meg's voice was a bare thread. Her fingers were clenched on Dominic's hand with enough force that her nails left bright marks on his skin. He smoothed back her hair and kissed her cheek, telling her of his love.

From the corner of her eyes, the midwife looked at Dominic. Such tenderness was rare in any man, much less in one whose ferocity had become famous throughout the northern marches.

No quarter. No prisoners.

And there had been none.

Roving gangs of bandits and knights without lords still harried the northern land, but not one of them troubled the domain of the man who wore the Glendruid Wolf.

The winter storm buffeted the keep, making a loose shutter bang. The long, rising cry of the wind made the midwife look around uneasily.

From Dominic's shoulder, the wolf's eyes gleamed as though alive and watching the Glendruid witch from whose body the future would come.

"You may go about your business, lord," the midwife said. "I will care for her now."

"Nay," Dominic said flatly. "My lady has been by my side through peace and war, sickness and health. I will not abandon her in her pain."

The midwife's shock made her speechless. Before she could regain her tongue, Meg groaned as her body was seized by the urgency of birth.

Wolf's eyes gleamed with every shift of Dominic's body while he shared his wife's labor in the only way he could.

Soon the wind howled with a triumph that was echoed in another strong cry, a baby tasting its first wild draught of freedom.

"Lord Dominic," the midwife said, awed, *"the witch has given you a son!"*

IN the years that followed, Blackthorne Keep rang with the shouts of children at play. As the sons grew older, Dominic taught them the way of the sword and the wolf, giving them the skill to fight when they must and the wisdom to seek peace when they could. Meg's daughters learned the way of water and growing things, of garden and herbal, and that the healing force was both gentle and fierce.

Together, in every word and silence, with laughter and with tears, Glendruid witch and Glendruid Wolf taught their children the most important truth of all: there is no more powerful magic than the generous heart and untamed soul of love.

Hamilton

This book of silly stories
and rhymes belongs to

_____

Silly Stories

This is a Parragon Book
This edition published in 2002

Parragon
Queen Street House
4 Queen Street
Bath BA1 1HE

Produced by
The Templar Company plc

Designed by Caroline Reeves

Printed and bound in Singapore

Hardback ISBN 0 75258 477 4
Paperback ISBN 0 75258 478 2

Silly Stories

Written by
Andy Charman, Heather Henning, Beatrice Phillpotts,
Caroline Repchuk, Louisa Somerville and Christine Tagg

Illustrated by
Diana Catchpole, Robin Edmonds, Chris Forsey
and Claire Mumford

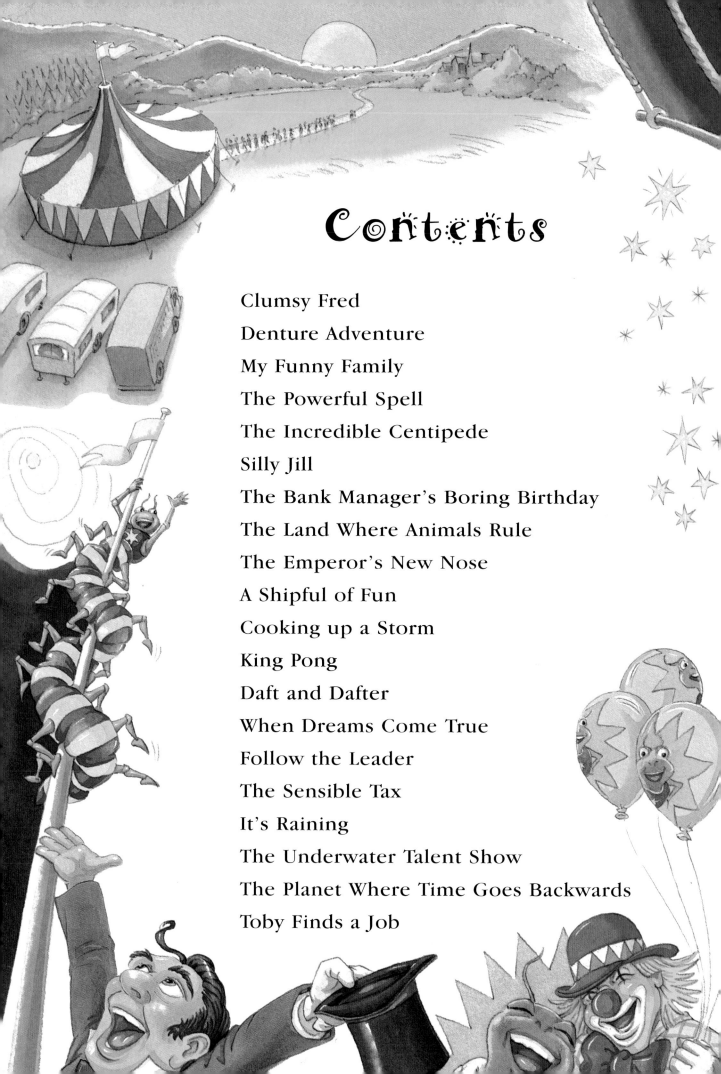

Contents

The Incredible Centipede

Clumsy Fred

Bumping into castles,
Turning homes to rubble,
Clumsy one-eyed monster Fred
Is a load of trouble.

Ooops! There goes a lamp post!
Help! A flying shed!
When careless Fred comes into town
It fills them all with dread.

But why is Fred so clumsy?
Has he gone quite mad?
Or has the friendly monster
Just suddenly turned bad?

We must stop that creature!
But how to save the day?
A monster expert took control –
"We'll do it all my way!"

The expert went to see him.
"I do need help," he cried.
"Why am I so clumsy?
It makes me sad," he sighed.

The expert did a lot of tests,
And then he gave a cry –
"I know what's wrong with you," he said,
"The problem is your eye!"

So Fred put on a monocle,
And suddenly could see.
He wasn't clumsy any more
He was happy as could be!

Denture Adventure

Grandad's teeth grinned broadly as they sat in the glass on the bedside table, next to his spectacles and a dish full of peanuts. Grandad snored while a large African Grey Parrot sat on the brass bedstead directly above Grandad's head. At precisely seven thirty it opened its beak and screeched, "Wakey, wakey," very, very loudly. Grandad stretched out his hand and, without opening his eyes, patted the parrot on the head. The parrot was quiet for exactly nine minutes and then he began again.

"Wakey, wakey," he called in a deafening screech. This continued until seven fifty seven when Grandad sat up in bed, yawned a gummy yawn and handed the parrot a peanut.

Grandad stumbled out of bed, put on his slippers and tripped across the hall to the bathroom. A face not unlike that of a turtle gazed back at him from the mirror, a turtle in Grandad's striped pyjamas. "Oh dear, oh dear," he said, gazing at his curious reflection. "Better put my teeth in."

Back in Grandad's bedroom, Norman the African Grey parrot had similar thoughts and was sitting proudly on the bedstead sporting Grandad's false teeth, which he had helped himself to from the glass whilst Grandad had been in the bathroom.

"Who's a pretty boy then?" he screeched

and the teeth fell out and dropped down behind the bed.

"Oh bother," said Grandad fishing around for them with the end of his best walking stick. But the teeth seemed to have vanished into thin air.

Grandma was in the kitchen making a large apple pie for tea.

"They can't have gone far," she said, as Grandad explained what had happened and, wiping her floury arms on her flowery apron, she climbed up the stairs to help him look.

"Men never look properly," she said getting down on both knees and reaching as far as she could under the big brass bed. She pulled out an old stripy sock with a hole in the toe, a furry mint humbug and a Christmas card from Auntie Beryl.

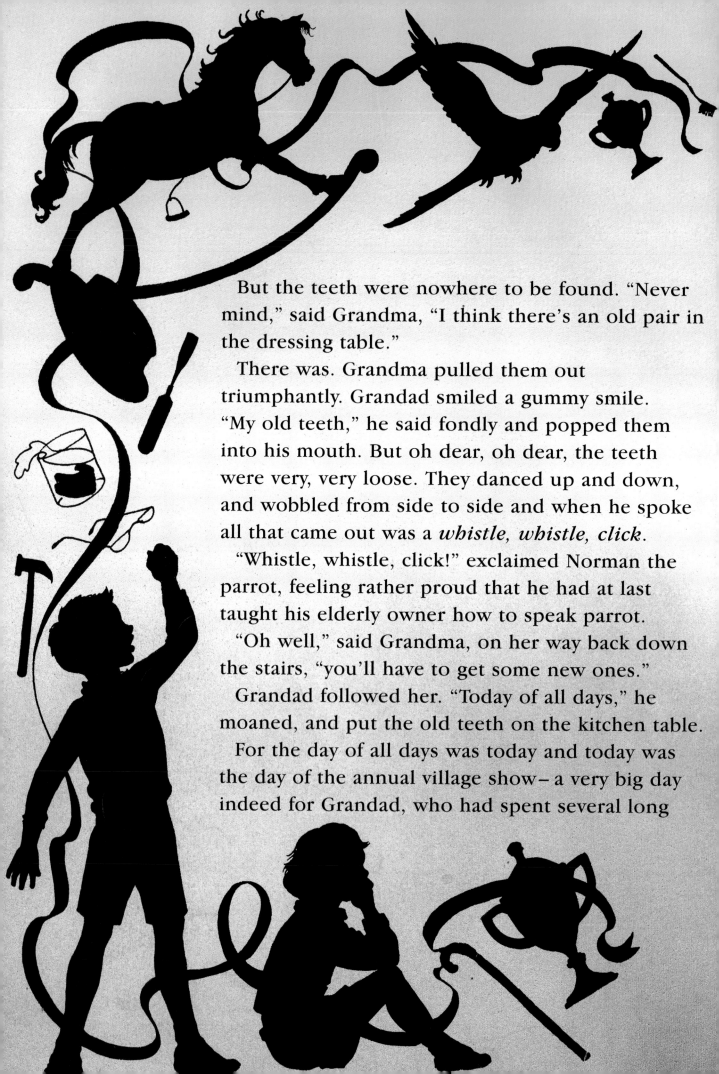

But the teeth were nowhere to be found. "Never mind," said Grandma, "I think there's an old pair in the dressing table."

There was. Grandma pulled them out triumphantly. Grandad smiled a gummy smile. "My old teeth," he said fondly and popped them into his mouth. But oh dear, oh dear, the teeth were very, very loose. They danced up and down, and wobbled from side to side and when he spoke all that came out was a *whistle, whistle, click*.

"Whistle, whistle, click!" exclaimed Norman the parrot, feeling rather proud that he had at last taught his elderly owner how to speak parrot.

"Oh well," said Grandma, on her way back down the stairs, "you'll have to get some new ones."

Grandad followed her. "Today of all days," he moaned, and put the old teeth on the kitchen table.

For the day of all days was today and today was the day of the annual village show – a very big day indeed for Grandad, who had spent several long

months making a magnificent rocking horse which he had entered in one of the craft classes.

"You'll just have to not smile today," suggested Grandma not very helpfully as she lay a large pastry blanket over the fat wedges of juicy apple. "Or talk," she added. Grandad shrugged his narrow shoulders and ambled over to his potting shed, feeling rather sorry for himself.

"Hmm, I wonder," said Grandma as she gazed at the false teeth sitting on the edge of her table. She picked them up thoughtfully and then very carefully and very neatly, she crimped the edge of her apple pie with them. Grandad stood in his shed flicking a duster over the shiny dappled neck of a fine rocking horse. He stood back to admire his work. The horse was perfect in every detail. A real leather saddle and bridle, a silken mane and tail, neat glossy black hooves and two large brown eyes with wonderful long lashes. Grandad rubbed his bristly chin and frowned.

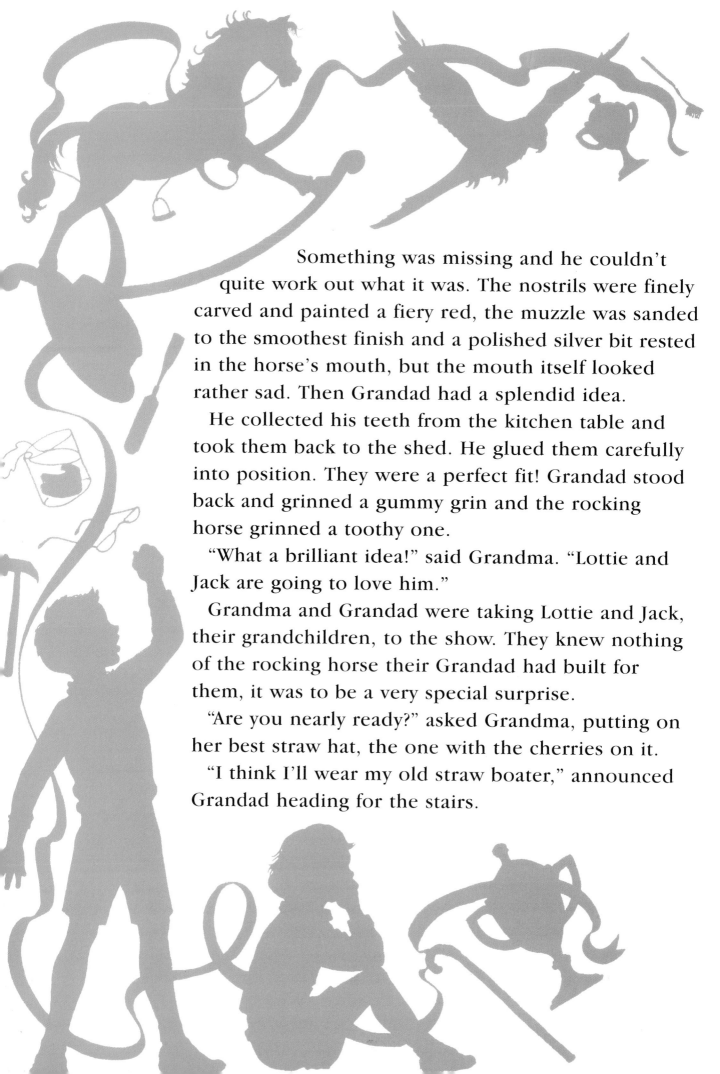

Something was missing and he couldn't quite work out what it was. The nostrils were finely carved and painted a fiery red, the muzzle was sanded to the smoothest finish and a polished silver bit rested in the horse's mouth, but the mouth itself looked rather sad. Then Grandad had a splendid idea.

He collected his teeth from the kitchen table and took them back to the shed. He glued them carefully into position. They were a perfect fit! Grandad stood back and grinned a gummy grin and the rocking horse grinned a toothy one.

"What a brilliant idea!" said Grandma. "Lottie and Jack are going to love him."

Grandma and Grandad were taking Lottie and Jack, their grandchildren, to the show. They knew nothing of the rocking horse their Grandad had built for them, it was to be a very special surprise.

"Are you nearly ready?" asked Grandma, putting on her best straw hat, the one with the cherries on it.

"I think I'll wear my old straw boater," announced Grandad heading for the stairs.

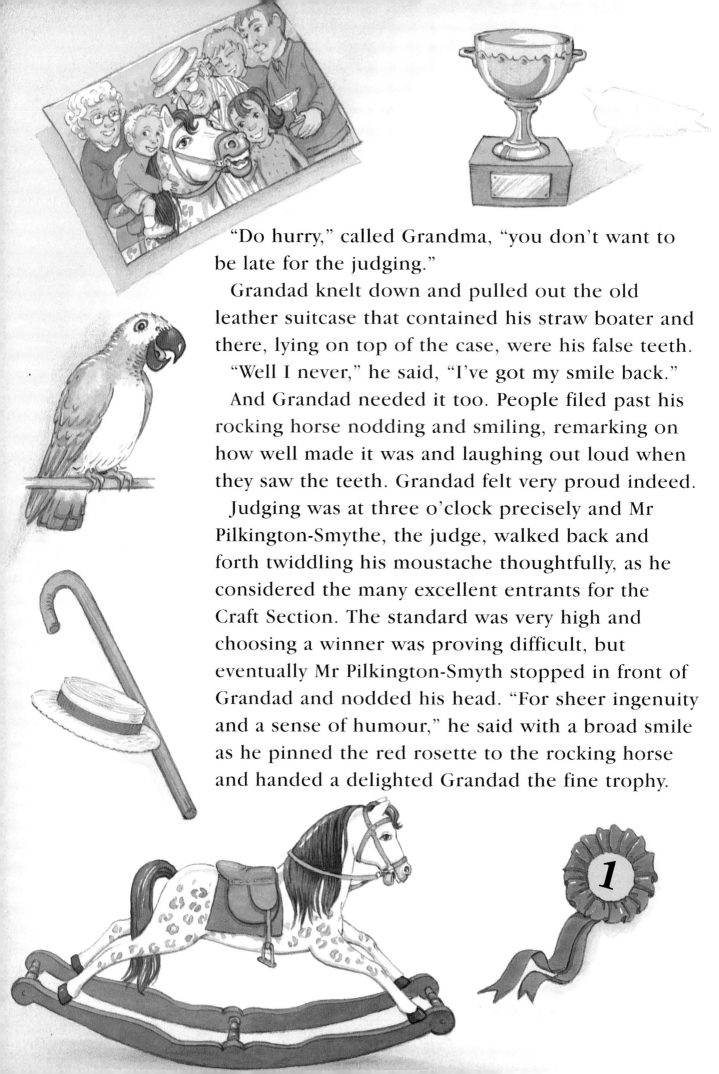

"Do hurry," called Grandma, "you don't want to be late for the judging."

Grandad knelt down and pulled out the old leather suitcase that contained his straw boater and there, lying on top of the case, were his false teeth.

"Well I never," he said, "I've got my smile back."

And Grandad needed it too. People filed past his rocking horse nodding and smiling, remarking on how well made it was and laughing out loud when they saw the teeth. Grandad felt very proud indeed.

Judging was at three o'clock precisely and Mr Pilkington-Smythe, the judge, walked back and forth twiddling his moustache thoughtfully, as he considered the many excellent entrants for the Craft Section. The standard was very high and choosing a winner was proving difficult, but eventually Mr Pilkington-Smyth stopped in front of Grandad and nodded his head. "For sheer ingenuity and a sense of humour," he said with a broad smile as he pinned the red rosette to the rocking horse and handed a delighted Grandad the fine trophy.

The crowd all cheered, everyone had wanted the rocking horse to win and none more so than Lottie and Jack who were very excited, especially as they knew the rocking horse would be coming back home to live with them.

Suddenly a photographer appeared from the local paper and asked Grandad and his family to stand around the horse.

"Smile please," he said and Grandma smiled, Lottie and Jack smiled, the rocking horse smiled, but Grandad smiled the widest smile of them all.

When the photographer had finished Lottie put her arms around the rocking horse's neck to give him a big hug then she gazed inquisitively at his mouth.

"Grandad," she asked in a puzzled voice, "are these your teeth?" Grandma laughed and Grandad bent down and very confidentially told his small granddaughter, "You should never look a gift horse in the mouth."

My Funny Family

My auntie May's got a brain like a sieve –
She forgets where the things in her kitchen all live.
There are plates in the fridge and plum jam in the jug
A chop in the teapot and carrots in the mugs!

My uncle Fred's got ears like cauliflowers –
He listens to the neighbours chat for hours and hours and hours
He can hear an ant whistling from a mile away or more
And butterflies beat their wings and tiny woodlice snore!

My cousin Bob's got eyes like a hawk –
He can see across the ocean from London to New York!
He says he can see unknown planets orbiting in space
And the moon has got a handlebar moustache upon its face.

My sister Sarah's got feet that love to dance –
She's danced from Perth to Benidorm, from Italy to France.
She dances in a dress trimmed with black and yellow lace,
Mum says she looks just like a bee and that it's a disgrace!

My brother Tom's got tricks up his sleeve –
He's got creepy things and spiders, and bugs to make you heave.
He once flicked a baked bean, which fell on Grandad's head
And dear old Grandad didn't know until he went to bed!

My dog Jasper's got a ferocious appetite –
To see him eating up his food is really quite a sight.
He wolfs down fish and chips and when he's really feeling gross,
He'll polish off a cake and several rounds of buttered toast!

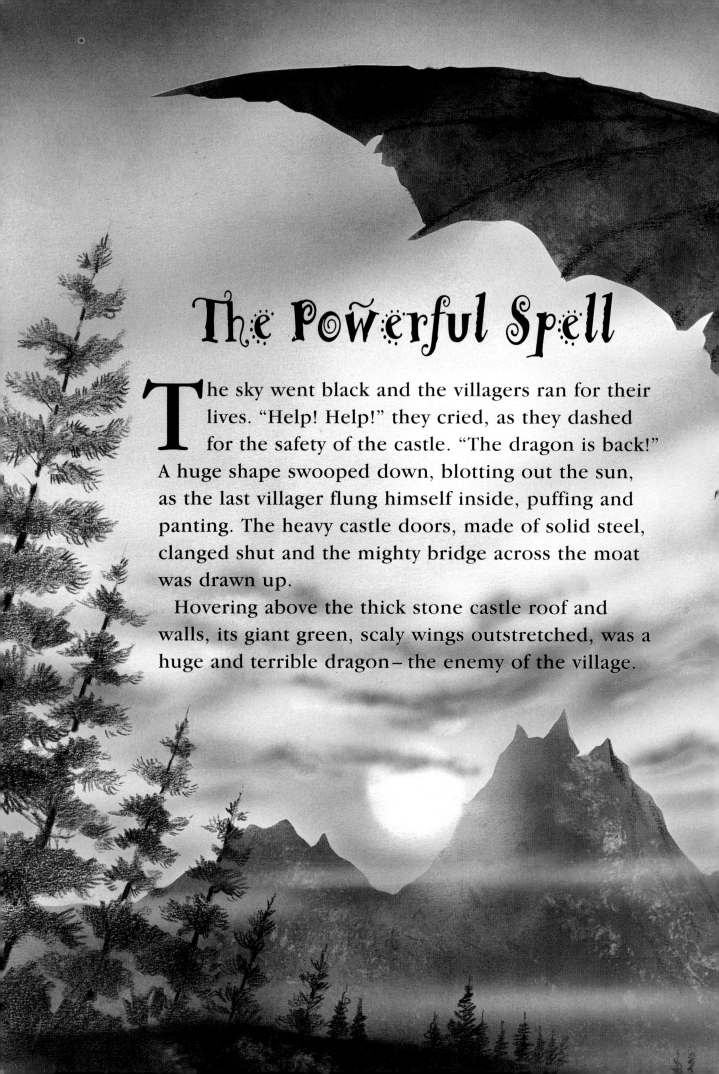

The Powerful Spell

The sky went black and the villagers ran for their lives. "Help! Help!" they cried, as they dashed for the safety of the castle. "The dragon is back!" A huge shape swooped down, blotting out the sun, as the last villager flung himself inside, puffing and panting. The heavy castle doors, made of solid steel, clanged shut and the mighty bridge across the moat was drawn up.

Hovering above the thick stone castle roof and walls, its giant green, scaly wings outstretched, was a huge and terrible dragon – the enemy of the village.

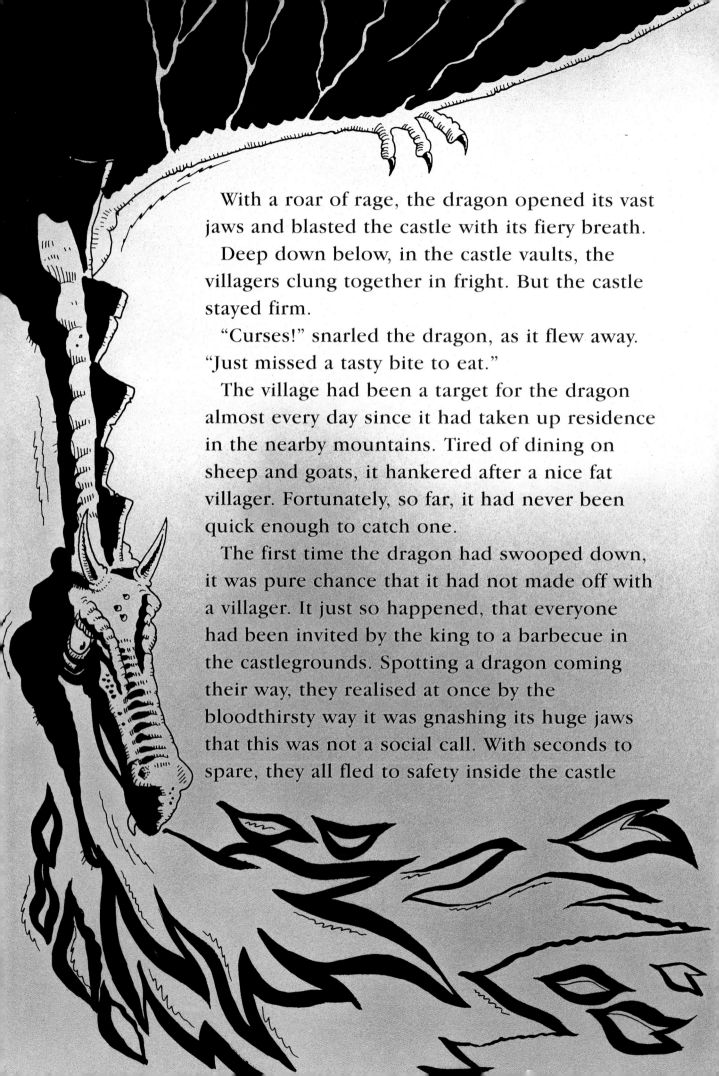

With a roar of rage, the dragon opened its vast jaws and blasted the castle with its fiery breath.

Deep down below, in the castle vaults, the villagers clung together in fright. But the castle stayed firm.

"Curses!" snarled the dragon, as it flew away. "Just missed a tasty bite to eat."

The village had been a target for the dragon almost every day since it had taken up residence in the nearby mountains. Tired of dining on sheep and goats, it hankered after a nice fat villager. Fortunately, so far, it had never been quick enough to catch one.

The first time the dragon had swooped down, it was pure chance that it had not made off with a villager. It just so happened, that everyone had been invited by the king to a barbecue in the castlegrounds. Spotting a dragon coming their way, they realised at once by the bloodthirsty way it was gnashing its huge jaws that this was not a social call. With seconds to spare, they all fled to safety inside the castle

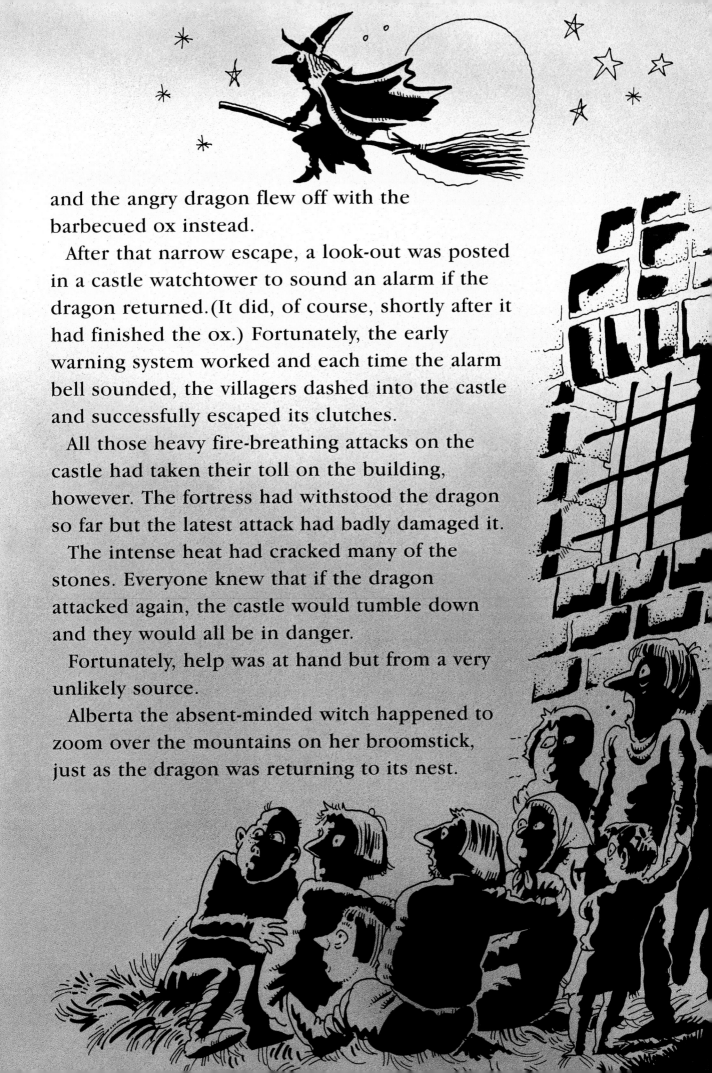

and the angry dragon flew off with the
barbecued ox instead.

After that narrow escape, a look-out was posted
in a castle watchtower to sound an alarm if the
dragon returned.(It did, of course, shortly after it
had finished the ox.) Fortunately, the early
warning system worked and each time the alarm
bell sounded, the villagers dashed into the castle
and successfully escaped its clutches.

All those heavy fire-breathing attacks on the
castle had taken their toll on the building,
however. The fortress had withstood the dragon
so far but the latest attack had badly damaged it.

The intense heat had cracked many of the
stones. Everyone knew that if the dragon
attacked again, the castle would tumble down
and they would all be in danger.

Fortunately, help was at hand but from a very
unlikely source.

Alberta the absent-minded witch happened to
zoom over the mountains on her broomstick,
just as the dragon was returning to its nest.

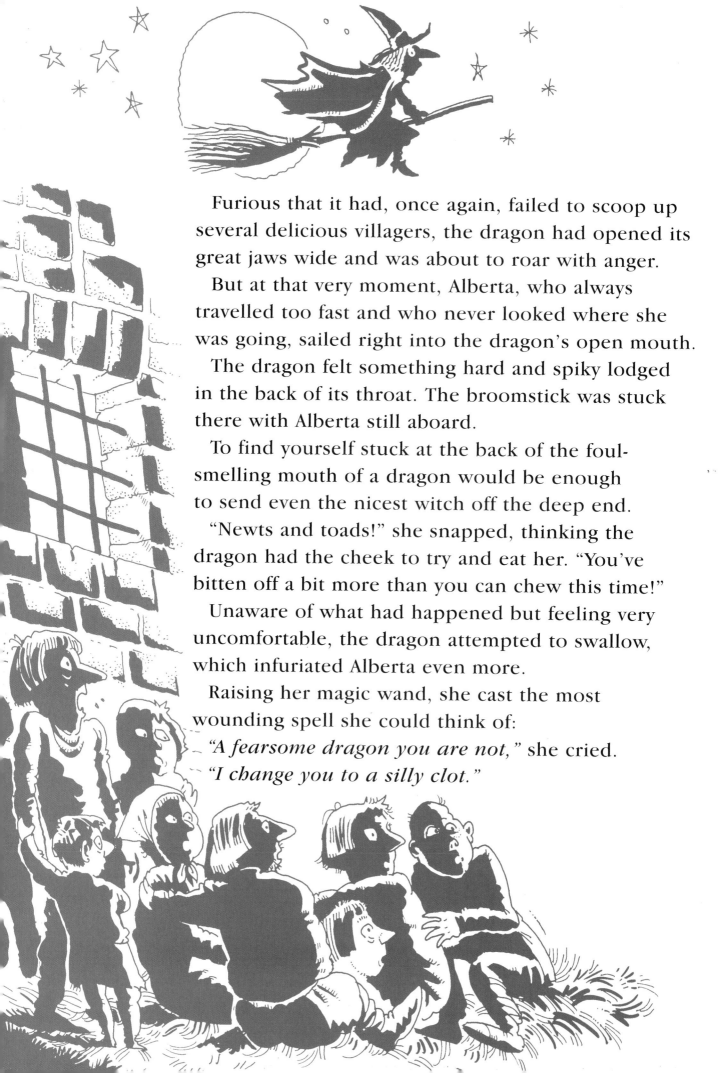

Furious that it had, once again, failed to scoop up several delicious villagers, the dragon had opened its great jaws wide and was about to roar with anger.

But at that very moment, Alberta, who always travelled too fast and who never looked where she was going, sailed right into the dragon's open mouth.

The dragon felt something hard and spiky lodged in the back of its throat. The broomstick was stuck there with Alberta still aboard.

To find yourself stuck at the back of the foul-smelling mouth of a dragon would be enough to send even the nicest witch off the deep end.

"Newts and toads!" she snapped, thinking the dragon had the cheek to try and eat her. "You've bitten off a bit more than you can chew this time!"

Unaware of what had happened but feeling very uncomfortable, the dragon attempted to swallow, which infuriated Alberta even more.

Raising her magic wand, she cast the most wounding spell she could think of:

"A fearsome dragon you are not," she cried.
"I change you to a silly clot."

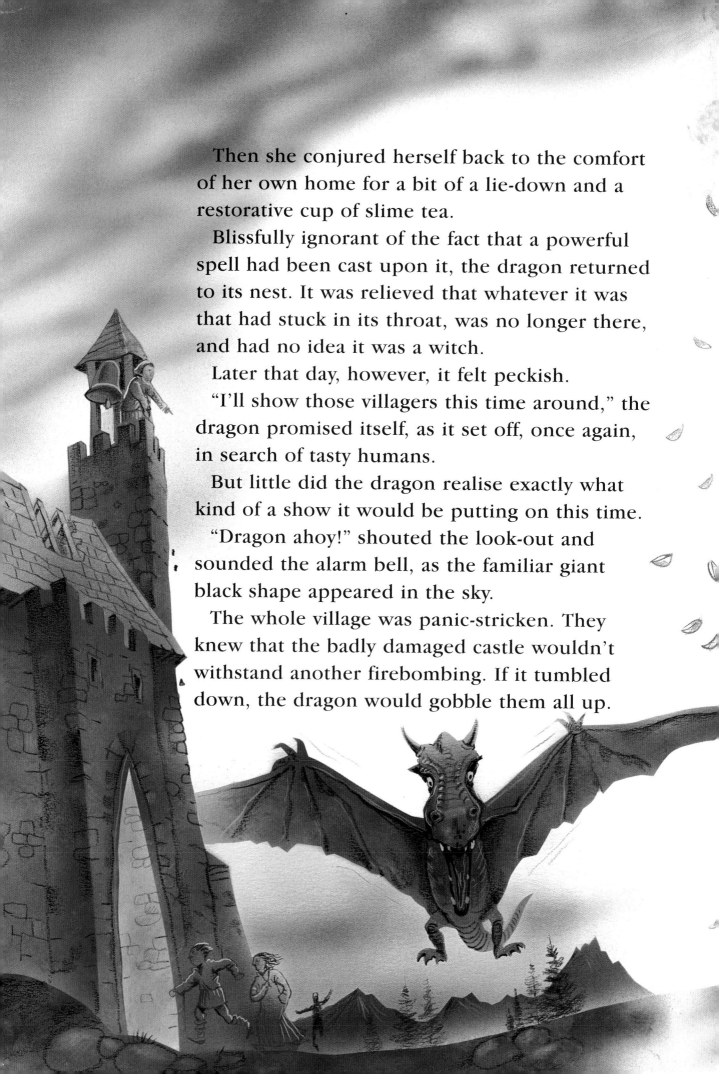

Then she conjured herself back to the comfort of her own home for a bit of a lie-down and a restorative cup of slime tea.

Blissfully ignorant of the fact that a powerful spell had been cast upon it, the dragon returned to its nest. It was relieved that whatever it was that had stuck in its throat, was no longer there, and had no idea it was a witch.

Later that day, however, it felt peckish.

"I'll show those villagers this time around," the dragon promised itself, as it set off, once again, in search of tasty humans.

But little did the dragon realise exactly what kind of a show it would be putting on this time.

"Dragon ahoy!" shouted the look-out and sounded the alarm bell, as the familiar giant black shape appeared in the sky.

The whole village was panic-stricken. They knew that the badly damaged castle wouldn't withstand another firebombing. If it tumbled down, the dragon would gobble them all up.

But there was nowhere else to run to.
So, preparing themselves for the worst,
they shut themselves up inside it, as usual.
Hidden well away from the great holes in the
roof, they clung to each other for comfort and
prayed that somehow they would be saved.

And astonishingly enough, they were.

The dreadful beating noise made by the
dragon's great wings came nearer and nearer.
The blue sky visible through the gaping holes in
the ceiling went black, as the dragon hovered
overhead. But the dreaded fiery jets of dragon
breath never came.

When the enchanted dragon drew a deep
breath and blew out with all its might, no sheets
of flame shot out. Instead, millions of sweet-
smelling flower petals fluttered downwards
from its gaping jaws.

The villagers stared in amazement, as pretty
petals floated through the holes above their
heads and gathered in drifts around their feet.

Scarcely able to believe its eyes, either, the dragon gazed in horror at the beautiful blossom heaped below.

Drawing a second deeper breath, the dragon attempted to obliterate all that beauty with the biggest firebolt it had ever produced. But this time, showers of delicious chocolates rained down on the castle, fell through the cracks in the ceiling and collected in heaps on the floor around the villagers.

The furious dragon gave a great roar of anguish but Alberta's spell ensured that something just as silly as the flowers and chocolates emerged from its fearsome-looking jaws.

Instead of a spine-chilling bellow, the dragon started to yodel in a deep, rich baritone and found to its great embarrassment that it couldn't stop.

"I love you-ee-ou-ee-ou-ee-ou," it sang to the astonished villagers.

Inside the castle, everyone started to laugh. As the dragon continued to yodel a love song to them, they laughed even harder.

The dragon knew it was making a ridiculous spectacle of itself but, thanks to Alberta's spell, it could do nothing about it.

Well, it could do something, the dragon realised. It could fly away and never come back.

And that is exactly what the dragon did.

"Good riddance to you, you silly clot," the king called after the dragon as it flew off over the castle walls as quickly as it could, still singing at the top of its voice.

Then everyone enjoyed a wonderful feast of chocolates, before they rebuilt the castle and lived happily ever after.

The Incredible Centipede

I'm not just an ordinary centipede,
I live in a circus van,
The top performers are known to me
And I have a wonderful plan…

We'll reach a town, and as the sun goes down
The folks will crowd the tent;
With music to thrill, they'll pick up the bill
And read with astonishment:

'Star of the show in the ring tonight
And we hope he does succeed,
Is the enterprising, most surprising
Incredible Centipede!'

The curtains will part and out I'll dart
And shake a leg or six,
Then in spangled tights I'll scale the heights
To perform my amazing tricks.

I'll swing from the wire with a toehold catch
And fold my legs like a clown;
I'll pedal the bike with the balancing pole,
But I'll ride it upside down!

I'll fly though the air without a net–
They'll be standing on their seats.
The crowds will roar, they'll be calling for 'more!'
Of my incredible feats.

It will be so grand, in every land,
Royalty will want to be seen
Meeting the Incredible Centipede–
And I'll shake hands with kings and queens.

The Incredible Centipede

Silly Jill

There was once a girl called Jill Martin and she always thought she knew best. Once, she took pity on a gorilla at her local zoo. She decided he would much rather live with her, than with his wife and babies in the jungle-like park that had been designed especially for them. So, one night, she crept into the zoo and lured him out of his lovely cage with bunches of bananas, while his family was sleeping.

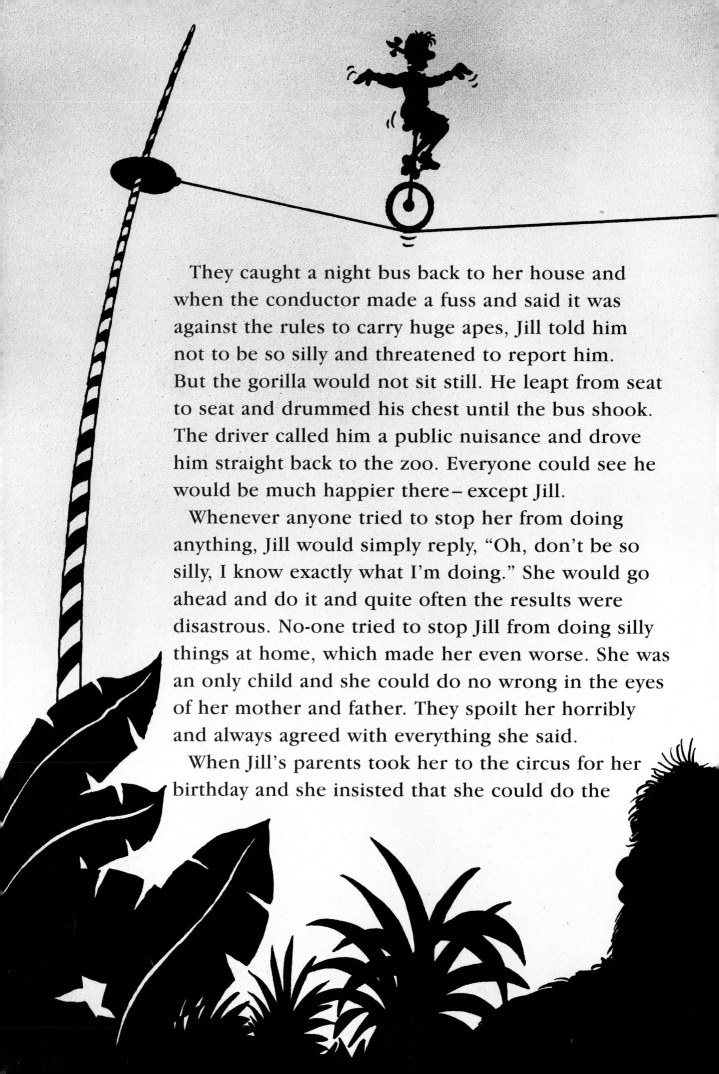

They caught a night bus back to her house and
when the conductor made a fuss and said it was
against the rules to carry huge apes, Jill told him
not to be so silly and threatened to report him.
But the gorilla would not sit still. He leapt from seat
to seat and drummed his chest until the bus shook.
The driver called him a public nuisance and drove
him straight back to the zoo. Everyone could see he
would be much happier there – except Jill.

Whenever anyone tried to stop her from doing
anything, Jill would simply reply, "Oh, don't be so
silly, I know exactly what I'm doing." She would go
ahead and do it and quite often the results were
disastrous. No-one tried to stop Jill from doing silly
things at home, which made her even worse. She was
an only child and she could do no wrong in the eyes
of her mother and father. They spoilt her horribly
and always agreed with everything she said.

When Jill's parents took her to the circus for her
birthday and she insisted that she could do the

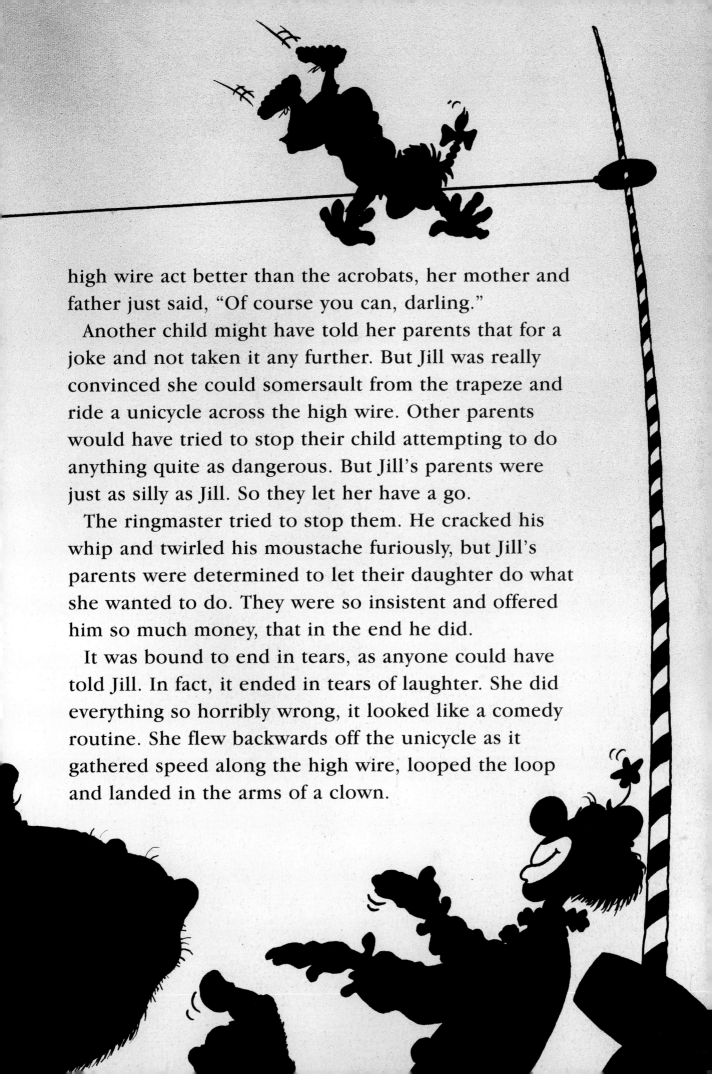

high wire act better than the acrobats, her mother and father just said, "Of course you can, darling."

Another child might have told her parents that for a joke and not taken it any further. But Jill was really convinced she could somersault from the trapeze and ride a unicycle across the high wire. Other parents would have tried to stop their child attempting to do anything quite as dangerous. But Jill's parents were just as silly as Jill. So they let her have a go.

The ringmaster tried to stop them. He cracked his whip and twirled his moustache furiously, but Jill's parents were determined to let their daughter do what she wanted to do. They were so insistent and offered him so much money, that in the end he did.

It was bound to end in tears, as anyone could have told Jill. In fact, it ended in tears of laughter. She did everything so horribly wrong, it looked like a comedy routine. She flew backwards off the unicycle as it gathered speed along the high wire, looped the loop and landed in the arms of a clown.

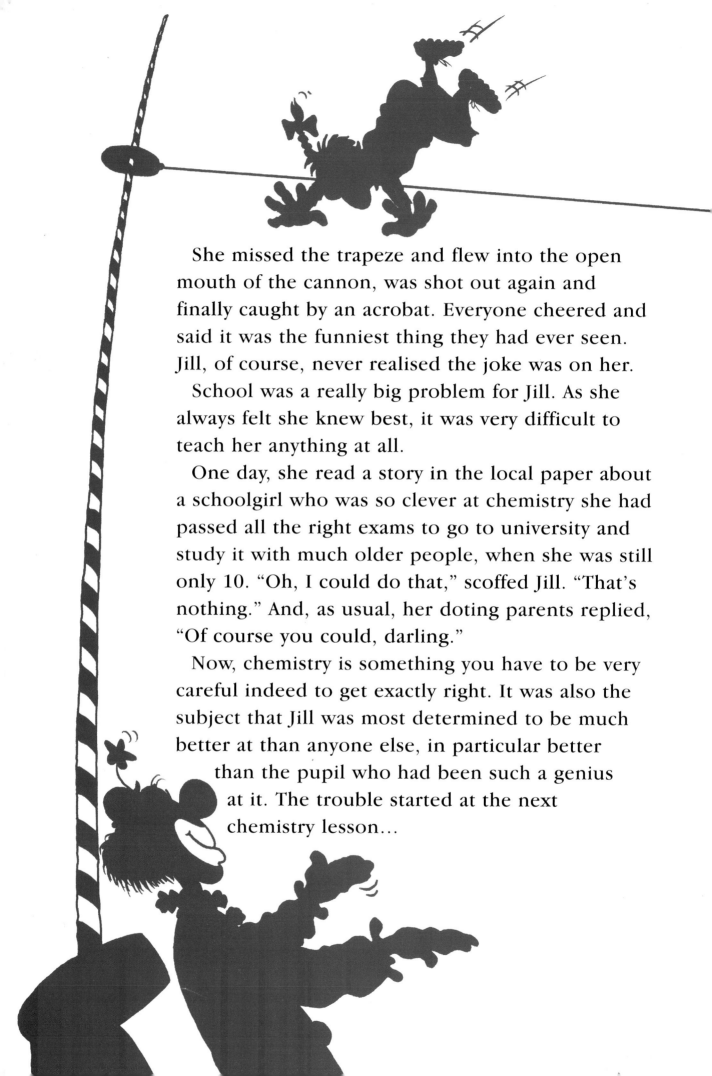

She missed the trapeze and flew into the open mouth of the cannon, was shot out again and finally caught by an acrobat. Everyone cheered and said it was the funniest thing they had ever seen. Jill, of course, never realised the joke was on her.

School was a really big problem for Jill. As she always felt she knew best, it was very difficult to teach her anything at all.

One day, she read a story in the local paper about a schoolgirl who was so clever at chemistry she had passed all the right exams to go to university and study it with much older people, when she was still only 10. "Oh, I could do that," scoffed Jill. "That's nothing." And, as usual, her doting parents replied, "Of course you could, darling."

Now, chemistry is something you have to be very careful indeed to get exactly right. It was also the subject that Jill was most determined to be much better at than anyone else, in particular better than the pupil who had been such a genius at it. The trouble started at the next chemistry lesson…

The rest of the class listened carefully to the chemistry teacher. She explained that in their next experiment it was very important not to mix the wrong liquids. Under no circumstances should blue be mixed with red.

'Huh!' thought Jill. 'I bet it works much better if you mix the blue with the red.' And so, without anyone seeing, she mixed blue and red.

Bang! Jill's flask exploded the moment they were combined and a stream of foul-smelling, smoking purple liquid poured onto the carpet.

"You silly, silly girl!" shouted the chemistry teacher. "What have you done?"

It was difficult to see exactly what Jill had done, the classroom was so full of smoke.

But everyone started to feel what she had done almost immediately.

"Help!" they shouted, as one by one, they felt themselves being lifted off the floor.

A most extraordinary thing had happened. The spilt liquid had made the pile of the carpet grow like grass. Only, instead of growing slowly like grass normally does, the carpet was growing upwards in leaps and bounds, like a meadow that had gone mad.

"Make for the door!" screamed the chemistry teacher, as the long waving pile of the classroom carpet carried them all up towards the ceiling. It was rather like being on a rollercoaster.

So they all did, even Jill. They crawled across the narrow space that was still left as fast as they could, trying not to knock their heads on the lights, while the whole carpet shot upwards in a great mass.

Then, just before they reached the door, the carpet flowered. Fat buds burst out into brightly coloured blooms. Everyone who suffered from hay fever, spluttered and sneezed.

Luckily, the classroom door was open. They squeezed their way through it before the carpet filled the room and then tumbled out into the corridor, chasing the last pupils out of the door.

"Run for it!" commanded the teacher, pressing the fire alarm to alert the rest of the school. And eight hundred pupils, including Jill, thirty members of staff, the caretaker and the cat raced for the safety of the playground, just before the school was completely swallowed up by carpet.

It took every fireman in the town a week to cut the carpet down and for months afterwards it still sprouted the occasional flower.

The school had to be closed, of course, while the giant carpet was scythed, mowed, rolled and finally brought under control. The head teacher was furious with Jill, when she heard how it had all started.

"Your silly, thoughtless behaviour could have destroyed my school and everyone in it," she told her. "I hope this has taught you a lesson and you know now that you do not always know better than anyone else."

Fortunately for Jill – and the school – it had taught her a lesson that she never forgot. From that dreadful day onwards, she stopped insisting she knew best and to everyone's relief, there were no more disasters.

In fact, Jill's terrible mistake turned out to be a fantastic opportunity for the school. An army chief heard about Jill's silly experiment and the amazing result. He decided that a quick-growing carpet would be an excellent weapon. He paid the school a lot of money for the details of Jill's purple mixture. This meant that the school was able to build a swimming pool, ice rink and bowling centre for everyone in the town. And it wasn't long before Jill mended her ways and really did become a star pupil – but everyone still knew her as Silly Jill!

The Bank Manager's Boring Birthday

Mr Smallwood was a very important person. He was a smart, tidy man who believed that there was a place for everything and that everything should be in its place. Every day he put on a crisp, white shirt, tied his tie with a nice tight knot, put on his smart blue suit, shined his shoes until he could see his face in them, and walked briskly across the park to the bank where he worked. He was the manager of the bank and he managed it very well. All in all, Mr Smallwood was a very well-respected figure.

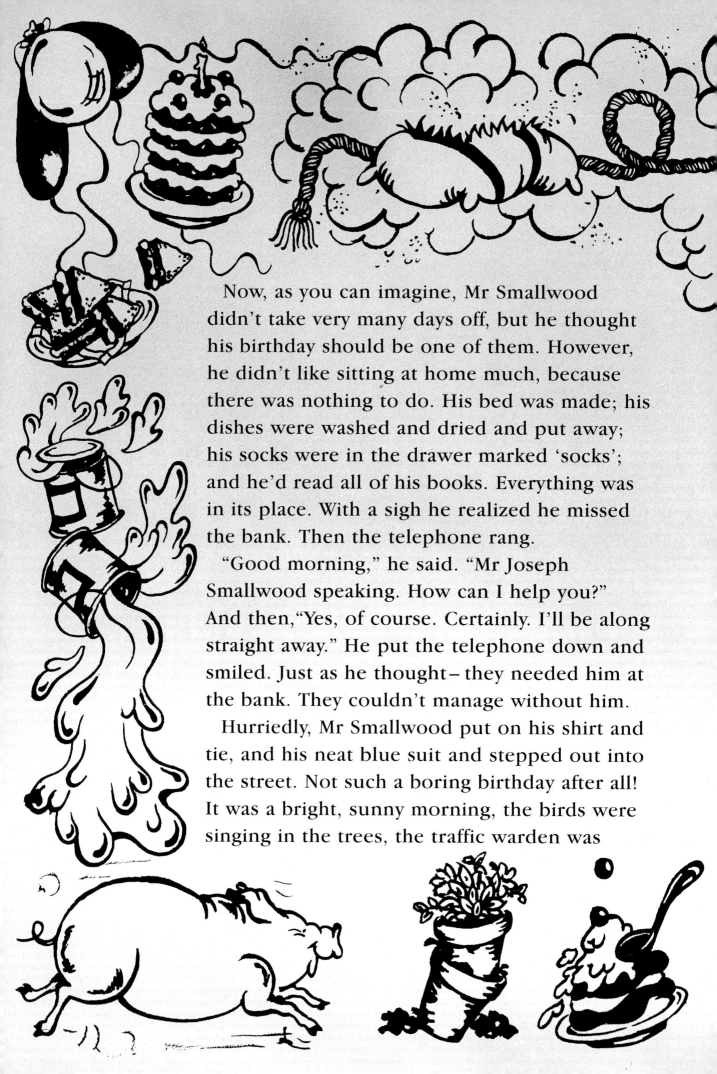

Now, as you can imagine, Mr Smallwood didn't take very many days off, but he thought his birthday should be one of them. However, he didn't like sitting at home much, because there was nothing to do. His bed was made; his dishes were washed and dried and put away; his socks were in the drawer marked 'socks'; and he'd read all of his books. Everything was in its place. With a sigh he realized he missed the bank. Then the telephone rang.

"Good morning," he said. "Mr Joseph Smallwood speaking. How can I help you?" And then, "Yes, of course. Certainly. I'll be along straight away." He put the telephone down and smiled. Just as he thought – they needed him at the bank. They couldn't manage without him.

Hurriedly, Mr Smallwood put on his shirt and tie, and his neat blue suit and stepped out into the street. Not such a boring birthday after all! It was a bright, sunny morning, the birds were singing in the trees, the traffic warden was

writing tickets, the cars were at a standstill. Everything was as it should be. A perfectly ordinary day.

Mr Smallwood hadn't gone far when he came across a pig.

"Now that's not the right place for a pig," said Mr Smallwood. "I should catch that animal and take it to the market." So he chased the pig into the park. But the pig had other ideas. With an excited squeal, it dashed off to hide in the rose bushes. Mr Smallwood made a daring leap. He flew gracefully through the air and stretching out his arms he caught the pig. Then with a loud THWUMP! they landed in a large, smelly heap of horse manure.

"Golly!" said Mr Smallwood, as he stood up. The front of his suit and his glasses were covered with horse manure, but the pig was safely in his arms.

Mr Smallwood set off rather slowly across the park in the direction of the market.

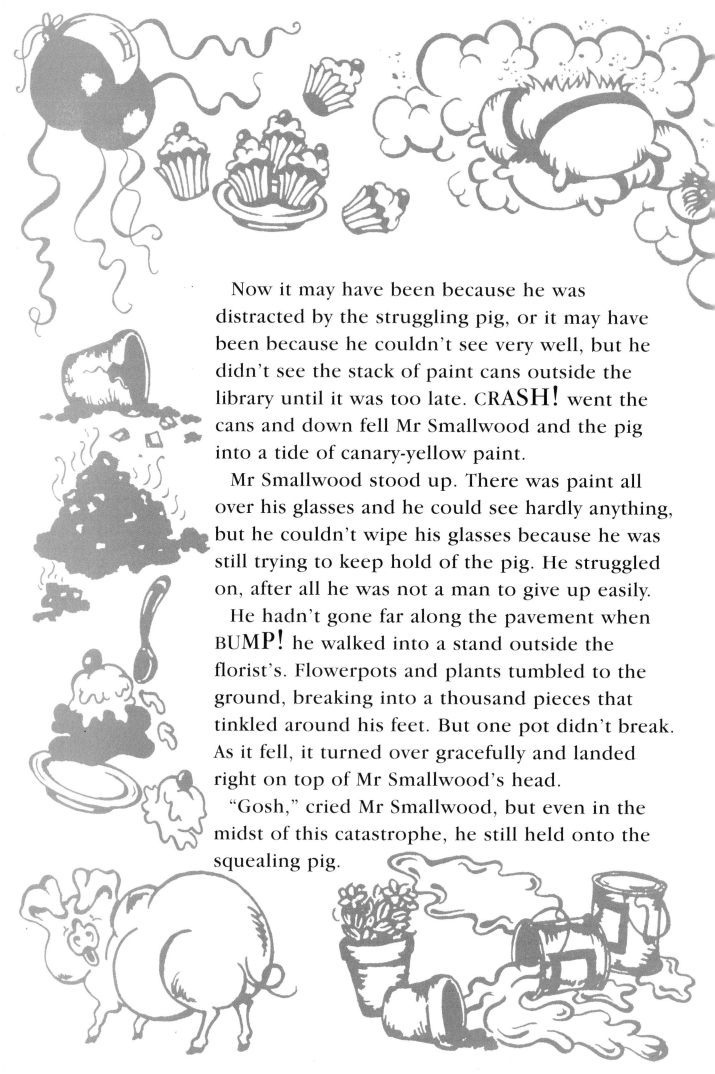

Now it may have been because he was distracted by the struggling pig, or it may have been because he couldn't see very well, but he didn't see the stack of paint cans outside the library until it was too late. CRASH! went the cans and down fell Mr Smallwood and the pig into a tide of canary-yellow paint.

Mr Smallwood stood up. There was paint all over his glasses and he could see hardly anything, but he couldn't wipe his glasses because he was still trying to keep hold of the pig. He struggled on, after all he was not a man to give up easily.

He hadn't gone far along the pavement when BUMP! he walked into a stand outside the florist's. Flowerpots and plants tumbled to the ground, breaking into a thousand pieces that tinkled around his feet. But one pot didn't break. As it fell, it turned over gracefully and landed right on top of Mr Smallwood's head.

"Gosh," cried Mr Smallwood, but even in the midst of this catastrophe, he still held onto the squealing pig.

Staggering somewhat and a little dazed, Mr Smallwood walked on. He hadn't gone very far when a voice cried, "LOOK OUT!" He walked straight into Claude, the waiter at the Crêpe Café. Claude was serving pancakes and ice-cream to some customers, but they didn't get them. Down went Claude, up in the air went his tray, and SLAP! two pancakes landed squarely on Mr Smallwood's shiny shoes.

Always a polite man, Mr Smallwood turned to apologize to Claude and his customers. "Sorry!" he called out. But before he knew what was happening he was falling, stumbling backwards into a hole full of muddy water on a building site.

"Golly," said Mr Smallwood, and, still holding firmly onto the pig, he pulled himself out of the hole. Now, perhaps it was because he was tired by now and not concentrating, or perhaps it was because he had manure and paint and mud on his glasses, but Mr Smallwood didn't realize that he was on a building site. He also didn't realize that he was pulling himself up by a rope attached to a pile of cement bags. The pile swayed, the pile wobbled. The top bag slid off and exploded majestically over Mr Smallwood's head, covering him in a cloud of cement dust.

Mr Smallwood coughed, wheezed and spluttered as the cloud gradually cleared.

The cement began to harden as it soaked into Mr Smallwood's damp suit. He walked away, stiffly.

He hadn't gone far when he heard a familiar voice, and it was calling his name.

"Mr Smallwood! There you are! We were wondering where you'd got to." It was Mrs Tillhead, the assistant bank manager.

Tired and a little shaken, Mr Smallwood allowed himself to be led into the bank. As soon as he entered the building, a cheer went up.

"Hurrah," he heard, and "Happy Birthday!" Someone removed his glasses and cleaned them for him, and he looked around the room. The ceiling was hung with brightly coloured streamers and balloons.

Above the cash desks was a huge banner with the words 'HAPPY BIRTHDAY MR SMALLWOOD' and a table was bending under the weight of crisps, sandwiches and cakes. His staff had thrown a surprise birthday party for him!

Mr Smallwood was very surprised, but not as surprised as everyone else!

Instead of seeing the small, dapper bank manager they expected and respected, they saw in front of them a man walking stiffly in a cement-covered suit, with a flower pot on his head, pancakes draped over his shoes, smelling very strongly of horse manure and carrying a yellow, wriggling pig in his arms.

"Golly!" they cried.

The Land Where Animals Rule

In the land where the animals rule,
The children don't go to school.
They live on farms, and flap their arms,
Just like the chickens used to do.

The post-bears always wear blue,
It's faster on four legs than two.
But it's always better to send it by letter,
Because packets tend to get chewed.

Jaguars and speeding cheetahs,
Are stopped when they go too fast
By policing cats, in pointed hats,
And pandas in people-coloured cars.

Horses take themselves for a ride,
They trot down the road side by side.
In the carriages they own they travel alone,
There's no room for two on the inside.

In restaurants where herbivores go,
They never eat meat so I'm told.
Cows do the cooking while no-one is looking,
It's grass, and it's usually cold.

If you go for a round-the-world sail
You travel on the back of a whale.
Hold on for dear life when he starts to dive,
And look out for that over-sized tail.

It's fun where the animals rule,
No-one tells you what you ought to do.
Their idea of fun is to sleep in the sun,
It's just the place for a person like you.

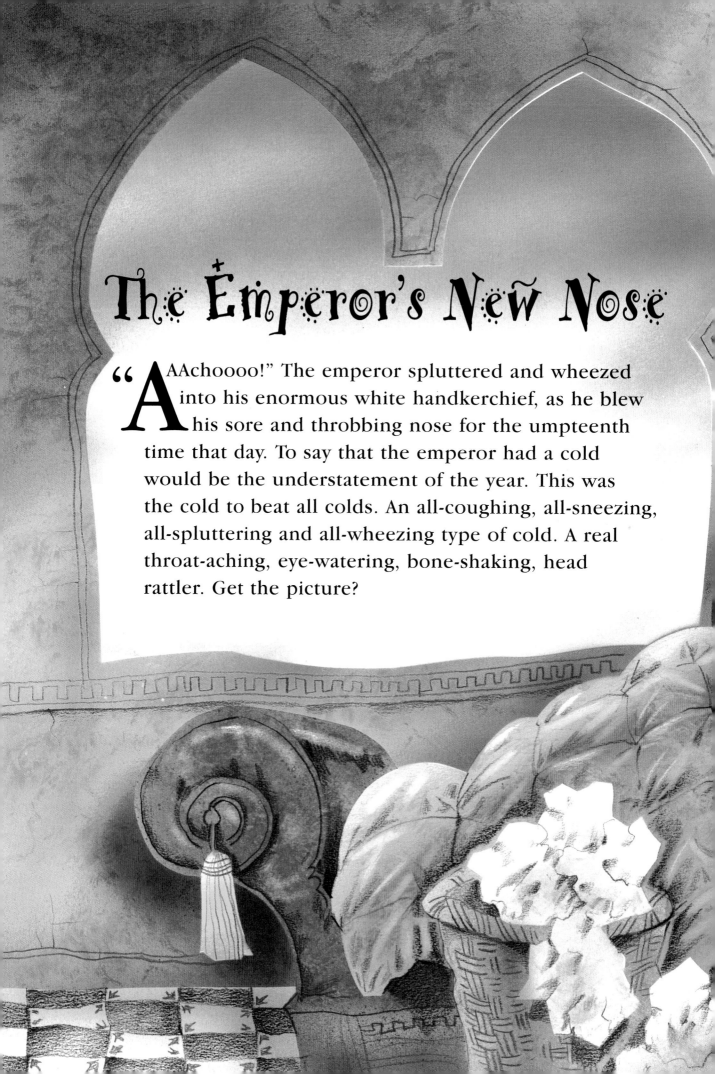

The Emperor's New Nose

"AAchoooo!" The emperor spluttered and wheezed into his enormous white handkerchief, as he blew his sore and throbbing nose for the umpteenth time that day. To say that the emperor had a cold would be the understatement of the year. This was the cold to beat all colds. An all-coughing, all-sneezing, all-spluttering and all-wheezing type of cold. A real throat-aching, eye-watering, bone-shaking, head rattler. Get the picture?

Well, needless to say, the emperor was fed up.
And he wasn't the only one. After all, he was
the emperor – he wasn't going to suffer in
silence. Oh, no! He called all his statesmen and
courtiers to gather in his stateroom, where he
was languishing on a daybed, propped up on
a mountain of pillows, clutching a hot-water
bottle, and sipping a large drink of hot lemon
and honey. To his left was a footman fanning
him with an enormous feather fan, to his right
was another, busy mopping his sweating brow.
The rest of the assembly was required to groan
sympathetically as each cough or sneeze shook
his aching bones. They had been standing there
for three days now, and frankly it was getting
rather tedious. Not to mention the fact that
several of them had started snuffling rather
alarmingly themselves…

As a monstrously loud sneeze shook his large,
overfed frame, the emperor used yet another
giant handkerchief and tossed it into an
overflowing bin. "I'd give anythin' for a new
nodhe," he snuffled. The crowd groaned on

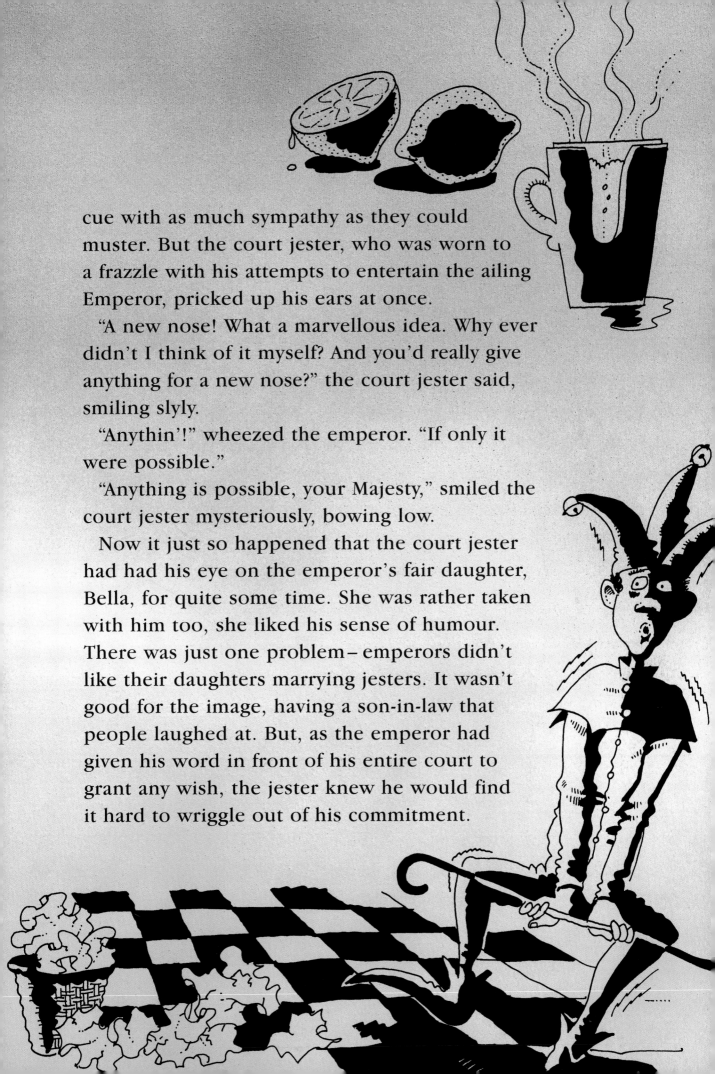

cue with as much sympathy as they could muster. But the court jester, who was worn to a frazzle with his attempts to entertain the ailing Emperor, pricked up his ears at once.

"A new nose! What a marvellous idea. Why ever didn't I think of it myself? And you'd really give anything for a new nose?" the court jester said, smiling slyly.

"Anythin'!" wheezed the emperor. "If only it were possible."

"Anything is possible, your Majesty," smiled the court jester mysteriously, bowing low.

Now it just so happened that the court jester had had his eye on the emperor's fair daughter, Bella, for quite some time. She was rather taken with him too, she liked his sense of humour. There was just one problem – emperors didn't like their daughters marrying jesters. It wasn't good for the image, having a son-in-law that people laughed at. But, as the emperor had given his word in front of his entire court to grant any wish, the jester knew he would find it hard to wriggle out of his commitment.

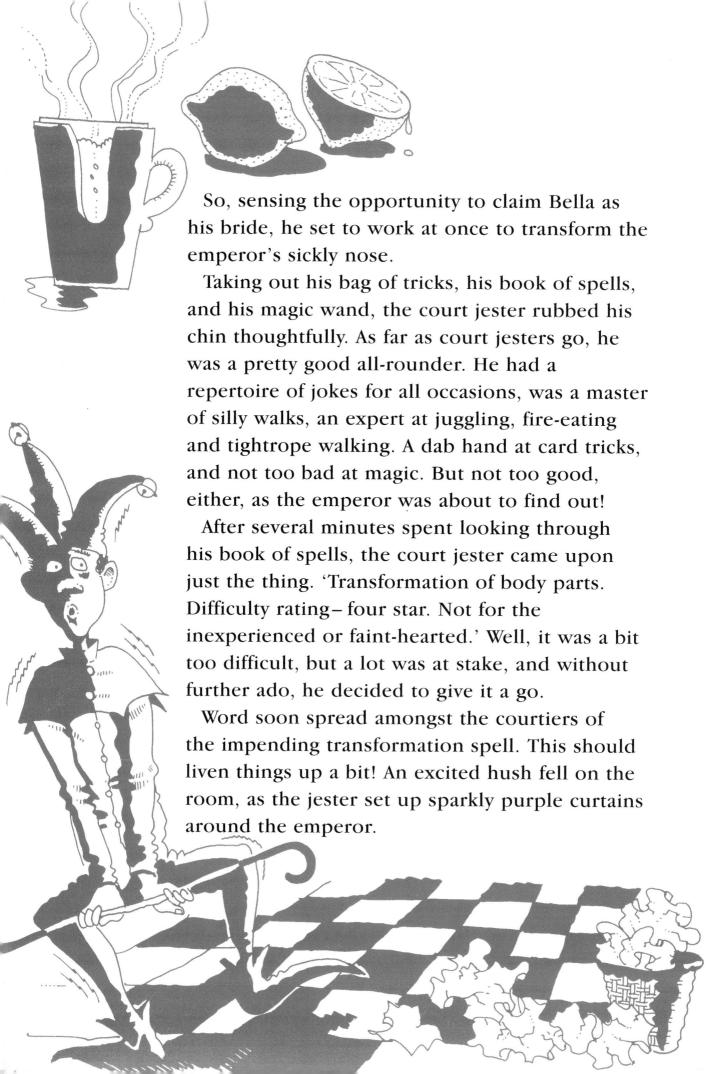

So, sensing the opportunity to claim Bella as his bride, he set to work at once to transform the emperor's sickly nose.

Taking out his bag of tricks, his book of spells, and his magic wand, the court jester rubbed his chin thoughtfully. As far as court jesters go, he was a pretty good all-rounder. He had a repertoire of jokes for all occasions, was a master of silly walks, an expert at juggling, fire-eating and tightrope walking. A dab hand at card tricks, and not too bad at magic. But not too good, either, as the emperor was about to find out!

After several minutes spent looking through his book of spells, the court jester came upon just the thing. 'Transformation of body parts. Difficulty rating– four star. Not for the inexperienced or faint-hearted.' Well, it was a bit too difficult, but a lot was at stake, and without further ado, he decided to give it a go.

Word soon spread amongst the courtiers of the impending transformation spell. This should liven things up a bit! An excited hush fell on the room, as the jester set up sparkly purple curtains around the emperor.

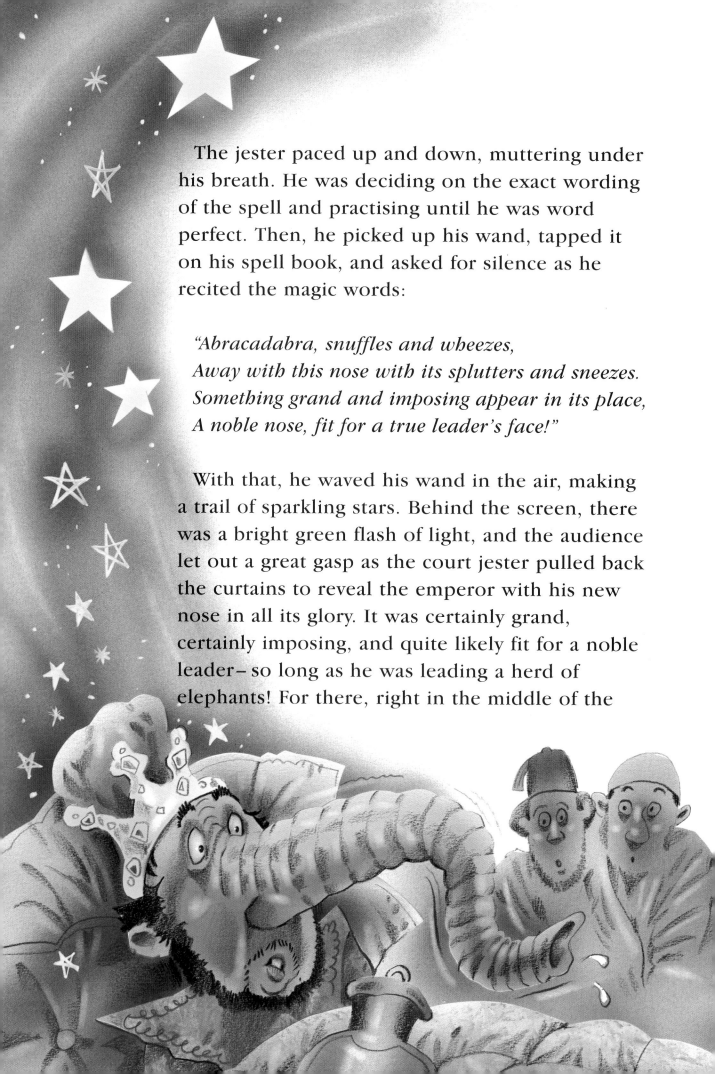

The jester paced up and down, muttering under his breath. He was deciding on the exact wording of the spell and practising until he was word perfect. Then, he picked up his wand, tapped it on his spell book, and asked for silence as he recited the magic words:

"Abracadabra, snuffles and wheezes,
Away with this nose with its splutters and sneezes.
Something grand and imposing appear in its place,
A noble nose, fit for a true leader's face!"

With that, he waved his wand in the air, making a trail of sparkling stars. Behind the screen, there was a bright green flash of light, and the audience let out a great gasp as the court jester pulled back the curtains to reveal the emperor with his new nose in all its glory. It was certainly grand, certainly imposing, and quite likely fit for a noble leader– so long as he was leading a herd of elephants! For there, right in the middle of the emperor's startled and alarmed face, was none other than an elephant's long, twisty trunk!

Well, what a commotion broke out! At first the courtiers were stunned into silence. Then there was a great hullaballoo, since, not knowing whether to laugh or cry, they bombarded the secretly astonished and horrified court jester with questions. I say secretly, because although his magic was not up to much, he was ever the professional, and was not about to let on for one moment that this was anything other than he had intended. He was also well aware that emperors are notoriously easy to fool, and luckily for him, this one was no exception.

"Your Majesty!" he exclaimed bowing low. "I am delighted to report a complete success! What a noble and distinctive nose, what an exceptionally unique profile. Doesn't he look marvellous?" The court jester turned to the courtiers, who, anxious not to offend the emperor, all loudly declared their approval!

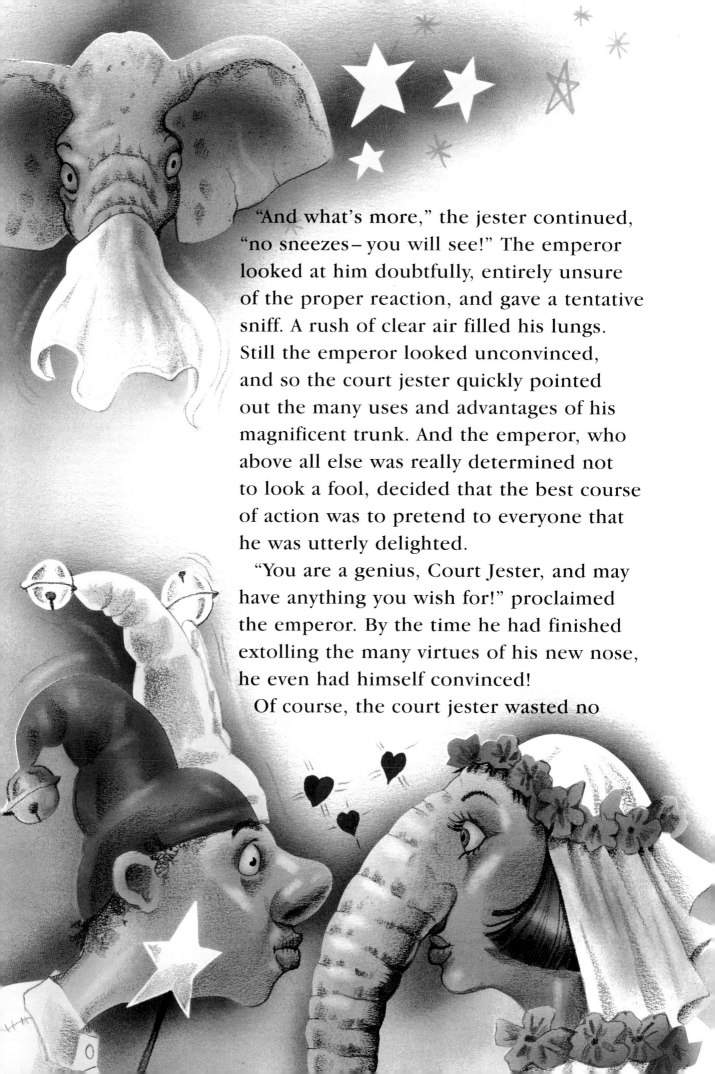

"And what's more," the jester continued, "no sneezes – you will see!" The emperor looked at him doubtfully, entirely unsure of the proper reaction, and gave a tentative sniff. A rush of clear air filled his lungs. Still the emperor looked unconvinced, and so the court jester quickly pointed out the many uses and advantages of his magnificent trunk. And the emperor, who above all else was really determined not to look a fool, decided that the best course of action was to pretend to everyone that he was utterly delighted.

"You are a genius, Court Jester, and may have anything you wish for!" proclaimed the emperor. By the time he had finished extolling the many virtues of his new nose, he even had himself convinced!

Of course, the court jester wasted no

time in claiming the fair Bella's hand, and the wedding was arranged to take place at once. Bella was summoned from her bedchamber, where she had rushed to change into her wedding dress and veil as soon as the court jester had started his spell. The emperor looked on with resignation as his beloved daughter became the jester's blushing bride. And blushing she was...

"You may now kiss the bride!" declared the minister. The court jester eagerly lifted Bella's veil, closed his eyes, puckered up and planted a big, sloppy kiss on her rough, wrinkled and rather hairy... trunk!

Well! Like father, like daughter, I guess! Oh, and as for the elephant, he never did figure out what happened to his trunk, or why he was left with the most terrible c-c-c-c-cold! Aaaachoo!

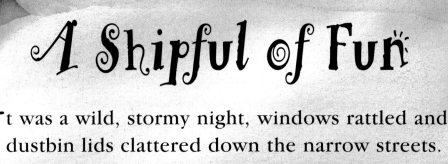

A Shipful of Fun

It was a wild, stormy night, windows rattled and dustbin lids clattered down the narrow streets. Poppy sat wide awake in her bed, listening to the wind howling and the crashing waves. She wondered about the poor seagulls – where would they go on a night like this? Suddenly, her room was filled with bright orange light. A flare! Something was happening at sea! Poppy woke her father and they rushed down to the beach, pulling on their coats. People were appearing from everywhere and there was an air of anticipation as they all gathered on the beach – Poppy had the feeling it would be an eventful night.

Out on the raging sea, Captain Thomas clung to the bow of his lurching ship and shot another flare into the sky. As it lit up the stormy sky, he could see in the orange glow the townspeople gathered on the beach. He was relieved to see the lifeboat being hauled down the slipway and into the crashing waves. He was all alone on his stricken ship and it was heading for the rocks. But the lifeboat was coming, bobbing steadfastly towards him.

Captain Thomas jumped into the foaming water and swam towards the lifeboat. He went under for a second and came up spluttering and coughing, then strong hands grabbed him and stronger arms pulled him into the boat.

"Thank you, thank you," he gasped. The boat turned and took him to the shore. There was a horrible crunching sound as his ship hit the rocks, then it rolled onto its side.

In the morning, Poppy went down to the beach to look at the ship. The sea was calm now, but the ship was wrecked. It was stuck on the rocks and there

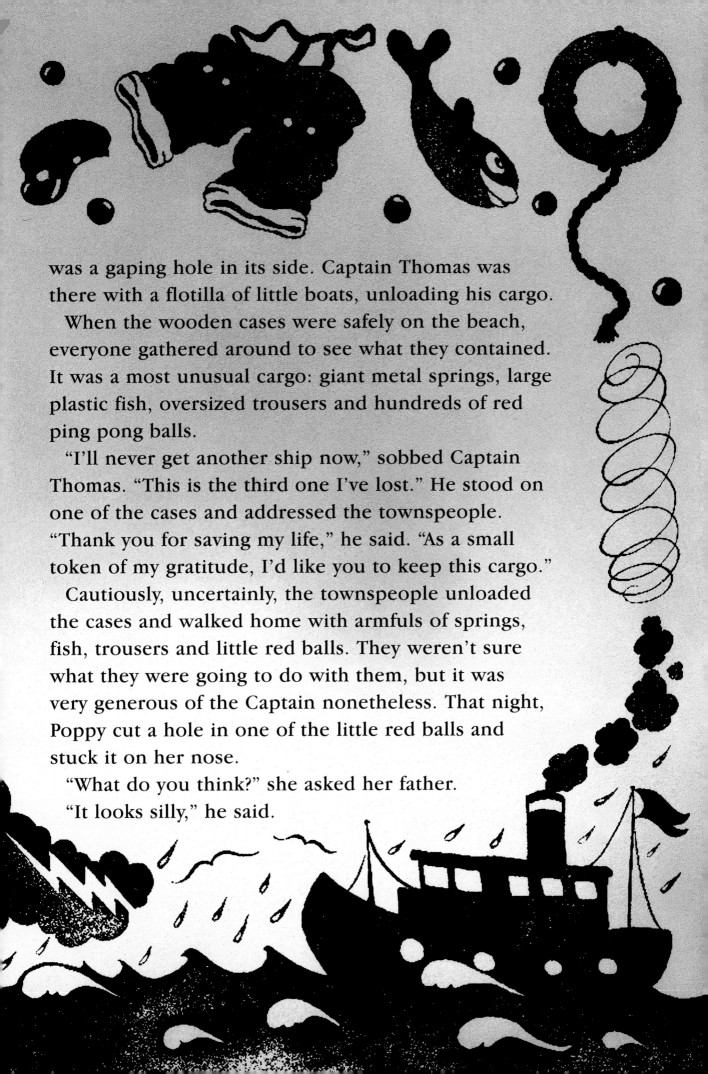

was a gaping hole in its side. Captain Thomas was
there with a flotilla of little boats, unloading his cargo.

When the wooden cases were safely on the beach,
everyone gathered around to see what they contained.
It was a most unusual cargo: giant metal springs, large
plastic fish, oversized trousers and hundreds of red
ping pong balls.

"I'll never get another ship now," sobbed Captain
Thomas. "This is the third one I've lost." He stood on
one of the cases and addressed the townspeople.
"Thank you for saving my life," he said. "As a small
token of my gratitude, I'd like you to keep this cargo."

Cautiously, uncertainly, the townspeople unloaded
the cases and walked home with armfuls of springs,
fish, trousers and little red balls. They weren't sure
what they were going to do with them, but it was
very generous of the Captain nonetheless. That night,
Poppy cut a hole in one of the little red balls and
stuck it on her nose.

"What do you think?" she asked her father.

"It looks silly," he said.

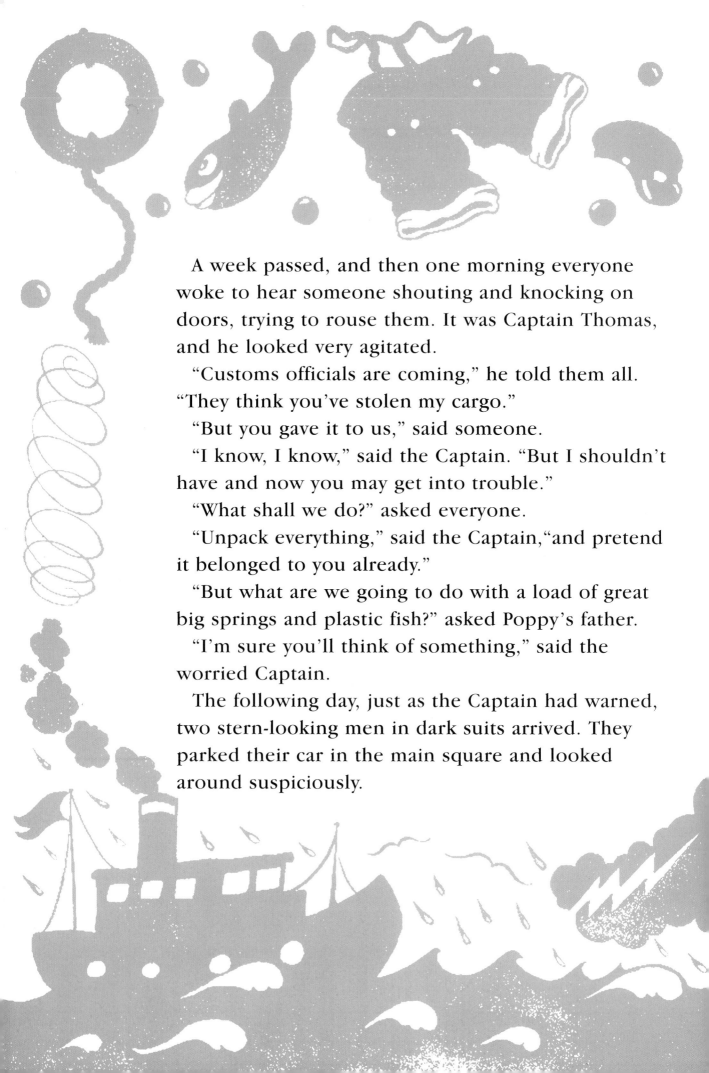

A week passed, and then one morning everyone woke to hear someone shouting and knocking on doors, trying to rouse them. It was Captain Thomas, and he looked very agitated.

"Customs officials are coming," he told them all. "They think you've stolen my cargo."

"But you gave it to us," said someone.

"I know, I know," said the Captain. "But I shouldn't have and now you may get into trouble."

"What shall we do?" asked everyone.

"Unpack everything," said the Captain,"and pretend it belonged to you already."

"But what are we going to do with a load of great big springs and plastic fish?" asked Poppy's father.

"I'm sure you'll think of something," said the worried Captain.

The following day, just as the Captain had warned, two stern-looking men in dark suits arrived. They parked their car in the main square and looked around suspiciously.

"Here we are then," said the taller of the two
men. "Pomberton. A small town which is noted
for its fishing industry and for its long history
of smuggling."

"What are we looking for?" said the smaller man.

"I've absolutely no idea," said the first. "The call
didn't say. But whatever the cargo is, there'll be
lots of it and it's probably stashed away in big
boxes somewhere. Let's have a nose around."

The two men in dark suits walked on down the
street. It was a hot, sunny day. Two small children
with red ping pong balls on their noses ran past.
One of the men laughed, "Kids eh!?"

They went into a shop. The shopkeeper also
had a red ball on his nose and when he walked
his feet made a peculiar slapping sound.

"Goob morning," he said, trying to sound
natural although his red nose made it hard to
breathe. "How can I helb you, gendlemen?"

"Customs officials," said the tall man, waving

his badge in the man's face. "We'd like to have a look around if you don't mind."

"Helb yourself," said the shopkeeper.

Just then an old lady, also wearing a red ball on her nose and a pair of enormous trousers came into the shop. She bought a bag of apples, a bunch of bananas and a packet of washing powder and put them inside her trousers before walking out again. The two men looked at each other and raised their eyebrows. As they walked into the store-room at the back of the shop, one of them glanced down at the shopkeeper's feet. He was wearing two large plastic fish.

"Unusual shoes," said the short man.

"Oh, bery comferdable," said the shopkeeper. "Just righd for this hob webber."

The customs officials found nothing suspicious in the shop and continued down the street.

Everyone they passed wore the same red balls on their noses and slapped along with plastic fish on their feet.

Shoppers came and went with their purchases stuffed into their extraordinarily large trousers. The tall man could hold back his curiosity no longer. He stopped Poppy's father and asked him why everyone was wearing red balls on their noses.

"Is it for charity?" he asked.

"Oh no," said Poppy's father, removing his nose to speak. "It's the smell of the fish. Can't stand it. None of us can."

"I can't smell any fish," said the tall man.

"Can't you?" said Poppy's father. "You had better get your nose checked by the doctor!"

The tall man sniffed and looked worried.

After searching the shops, the customs officials began a house-to-house search.

They started with Poppy's house, where Poppy was outside in the garden, picking apples. She wore a red ball on her nose, of course, and a big baggy pair of trousers. But she also had a giant spring attached to her feet, and she was using this to bounce up to the branches of the apple tree. At every bounce she picked an apple and stuffed it into her trousers. Then she bounced again. The two men in dark suits looked at each other and scratching their heads, walked off.

They continued their search for the stolen cargo. In one house they found a man bouncing up to the ceiling so that he could change a light bulb. Outside, a woman was cleaning the windows in the same way, wiping a patch as she reached the top of her bounce, then dipping her cloth in the bucket on the ground before bouncing up again.

And everywhere they went they heard the 'slap, slap, slap' of people walking along in their fish footwear.

The customs officials searched every house and every shop in town, but there was no sign of the stolen goods. No crates or boxes jammed into cupboards or under beds. Nothing.

When it was time to leave the shorter man stopped to do some shopping. He came out with a red ball and a pair of plastic fish, size 12.

"Very reasonable price, these fish shoes," he said.

The taller man said, as they climbed back into their car, "So, no sign of contraband. They seem like pleasant people here in

Pomberton. Hardworking and honest, I'd say. Completely mad, of course, but hardworking and honest just the same."

"Oh, I donbt bnow about mad," said the shorter man, through his red nose. "These fish shoes are beally quibe comferdable."

Cooking Up a Storm

I'm a wizard in the kitchen,
Or so my friends all say,
Just wait till they discover what
I'm cooking up today!

I've got my biggest cauldron
Heating up on the fire,
And I've gathered the ingredients
This fine spell will require!

First a handful of cat's whiskers,
The tails from three young pups,
A big ladle full of eyeballs,
And froggy slime – two cups!

Add a ton of giant fireworks,
A bunch of old tin cans,
A pair of cymbals, a big bass drum—
All stirred with a frying pan.

Bangs and crashes shake the windows,
It's raining cats and dogs,
Outside the storm is stirring up
A nasty shower of frogs!

For, although it may be August,
So sunny, bright and warm,
You'd better run for cover—
I've cooked up the perfect storm!

King Pong

There once lived a king who was very fond of gardening. The royal garden was the talk of the kingdom, and the king spent most of his time tending the royal blooms. They were the most magnificent flowers you could ever imagine. There were vibrant violets, delicate delphiniums, marvellous marigolds and even lovely ruby red roses. The king could grow just about anything, and everyone said that he had green fingers, but this was largely due to the fact that he never washed his hands.

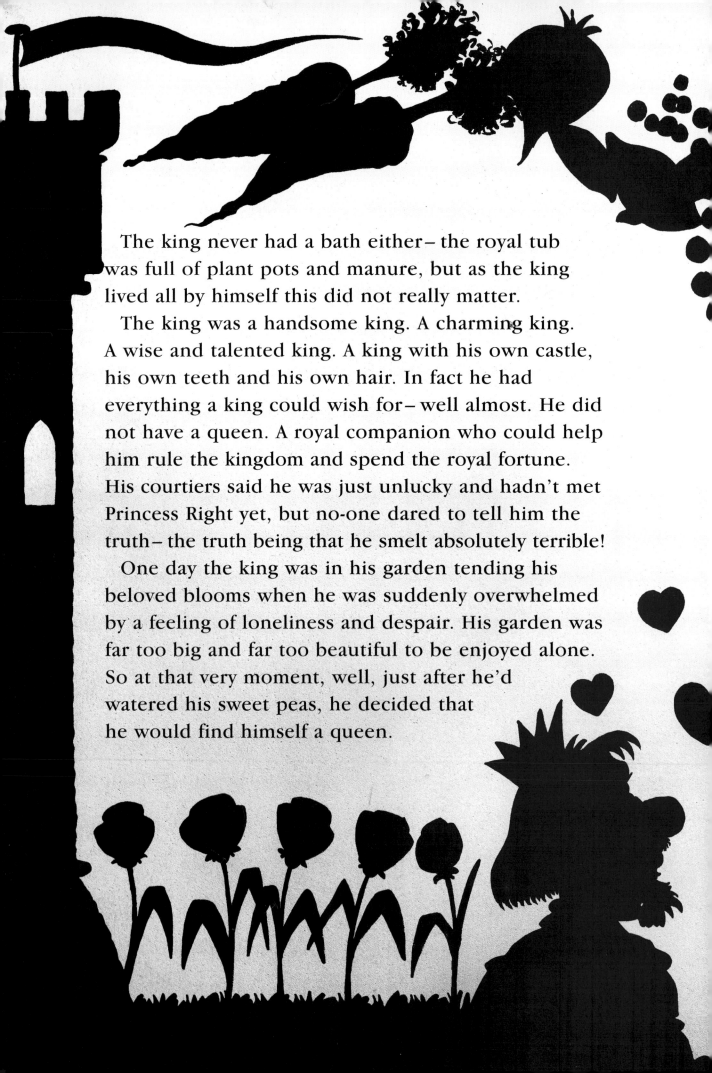

The king never had a bath either – the royal tub
was full of plant pots and manure, but as the king
lived all by himself this did not really matter.

The king was a handsome king. A charming king.
A wise and talented king. A king with his own castle,
his own teeth and his own hair. In fact he had
everything a king could wish for – well almost. He did
not have a queen. A royal companion who could help
him rule the kingdom and spend the royal fortune.
His courtiers said he was just unlucky and hadn't met
Princess Right yet, but no-one dared to tell him the
truth – the truth being that he smelt absolutely terrible!

One day the king was in his garden tending his
beloved blooms when he was suddenly overwhelmed
by a feeling of loneliness and despair. His garden was
far too big and far too beautiful to be enjoyed alone.
So at that very moment, well, just after he'd
watered his sweet peas, he decided that
he would find himself a queen.

That very afternoon the king took the royal rose
pruners and snipped and snipped until he had
a basket filled to the brim with glorious ruby red
roses. He then ordered a single red rose to be
sent to every eligible princess in the kingdom.
Each magnificent rose was to be accompanied
by a gold-edged invitation requesting the pleasure
of the company of the princess in question.
The roses and the invitations were duly despatched
and the king retired to his potting shed to wait.
But alas, although the rich velvety petals and
sweet scent of the roses enticed each princess to
make the journey to the king's castle, none were
able to travel further than the front gate, so
appalling was the smell that wafted towards their
delicate regal nostrils.
The king was about to give up hope of ever finding
a queen when, one day, a small neatly wrapped
parcel arrived with the royal breakfast tray.

Inside was a tiny bottle of vibrant orange liquid and a short hand written note, which read:

Her Royal Highness regrets that she is unable to accept your invitation, but thanks you for the delightful rose, which did incidentally have a touch of greenfly. Her Royal Highness has therefore taken the liberty of enclosing an excellent preparation which should combat this.

The king was intrigued. The very next day he ordered that one dozen royal red roses, minus green fly, of course, be despatched directly to the princess with another invitation asking if she would join him for afternoon tea on Tuesday at four o'clock prompt.

The next morning the king received a large, neatly wrapped parcel containing a splendid Savoy cabbage and a short hand written note which read:

Her Royal Highness thanks you most sincerely for the generous bouquet and trusts that you will accept this cabbage as a token of her appreciation. Sadly she is unable to accept your offer of tea.

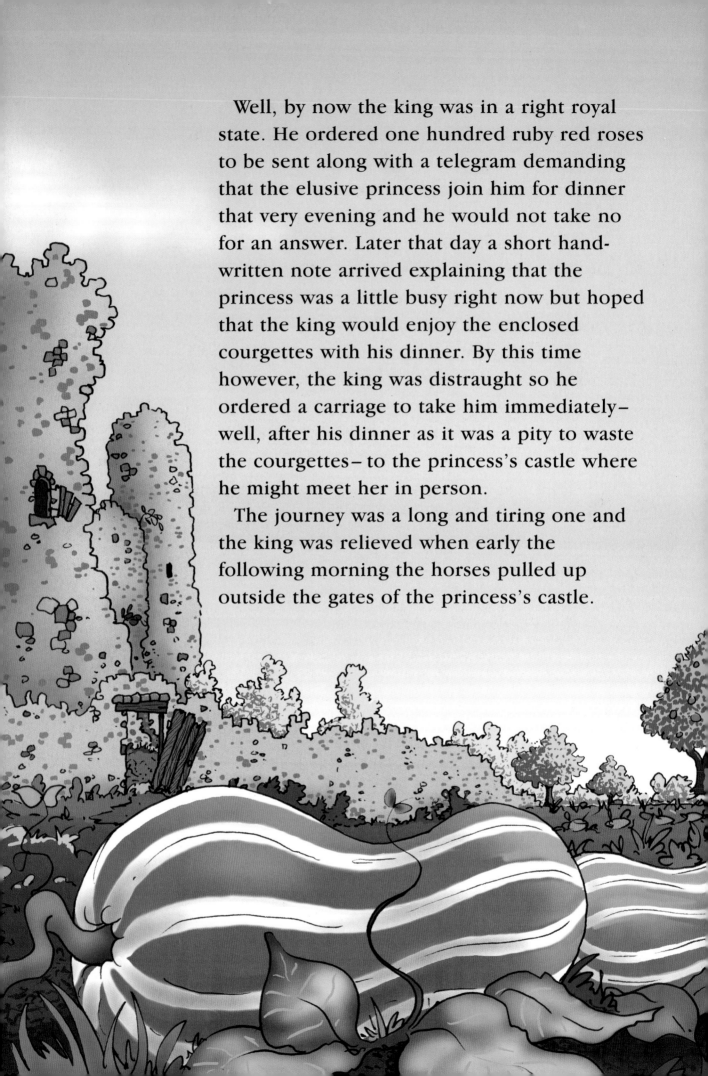

Well, by now the king was in a right royal state. He ordered one hundred ruby red roses to be sent along with a telegram demanding that the elusive princess join him for dinner that very evening and he would not take no for an answer. Later that day a short hand-written note arrived explaining that the princess was a little busy right now but hoped that the king would enjoy the enclosed courgettes with his dinner. By this time however, the king was distraught so he ordered a carriage to take him immediately– well, after his dinner as it was a pity to waste the courgettes– to the princess's castle where he might meet her in person.

The journey was a long and tiring one and the king was relieved when early the following morning the horses pulled up outside the gates of the princess's castle.

The king clambered out and gazed at the crumbling towers that held the crumbling walls of the castle together. It was very very run down. The gates were rusty and one was hanging off its hinges. Unperturbed the king walked up the uneven muddy driveway and knocked at the rotten front door of the castle. There was no reply, so he knocked again and he would have knocked a third time but the knocker came off in his hand so he decided to try round the back instead. He passed through a rickety wooden door set in an ancient moss-covered wall and found himself in the most fantastic vegetable garden he had ever seen.

There were marrows bigger than carriages, great fat pea pods ready to burst, cabbages, cauliflowers and lettuces all growing in perfectly straight lines and in such abundance it took your breath away.

At the far end of the garden he saw a figure effortlessly pulling up bunches of enormous juicy carrots and throwing them into the basket by her side. She was tall and very strong. Her hair was the colour of the carrots and hung in unruly curls about her grubby face. Her patched trousers were held up with string. She paused to wipe her nose on her sleeve and it was love at first sight. The king gave a little cough to attract her attention. The vision of loveliness looked up and the king walked steadily over to her, not noticing that she didn't smell particularly nice. He bowed politely and kissed her grimy hand. The princess blushed the colour of the wonderful beetroots that were sitting in her basket.

"I'm so glad you came," she said, offering him a radish. "It's been lonely since the staff left."

"You're very beautiful," the king told her and he meant it. The princess smiled a shy smile. "Oh you're just being nice," she said. "I'm afraid I've been so wrapped up in the garden I've rather neglected myself."

"Nonsense," said the king. "You are by far the prettiest flower in your garden."

"You are very kind," said the princess – who was far too polite to point out that she only grew vegetables.

The king then knelt in the slimy green mud to propose. Princess Composta, for that was her name, accepted without hesitation.

"We must be married at once," announced the king, and so they were – well, after he'd helped her dig up the spuds.

And they both lived smellily ever after.

Daft and Dafter

"Miaow!"
Tommy looked up at the faint sound of a kitten purring somewhere above his head. Then he blinked in amazement. The kitten was not stuck in a tree – it appeared to be floating down through the sky! Even more incredibly, other kittens were gently falling downwards. It couldn't be true! Were his eyes playing tricks? He looked up again. But it was true! And there were puppies floating down, as well!

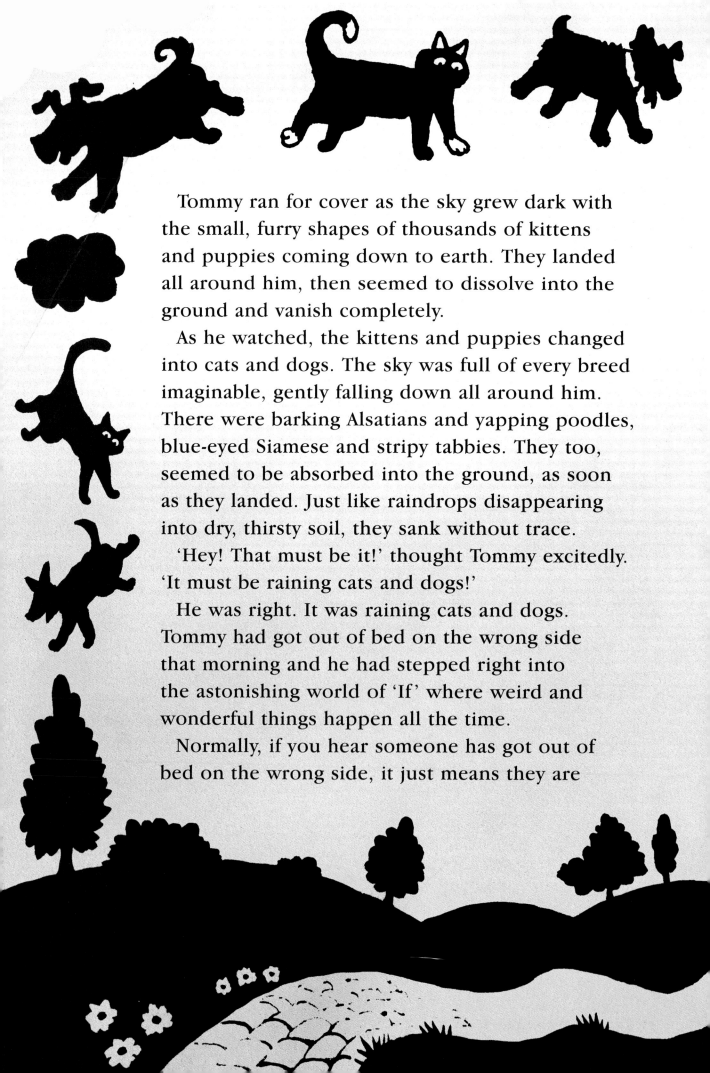

Tommy ran for cover as the sky grew dark with
the small, furry shapes of thousands of kittens
and puppies coming down to earth. They landed
all around him, then seemed to dissolve into the
ground and vanish completely.

As he watched, the kittens and puppies changed
into cats and dogs. The sky was full of every breed
imaginable, gently falling down all around him.
There were barking Alsatians and yapping poodles,
blue-eyed Siamese and stripy tabbies. They too,
seemed to be absorbed into the ground, as soon
as they landed. Just like raindrops disappearing
into dry, thirsty soil, they sank without trace.

'Hey! That must be it!' thought Tommy excitedly.
'It must be raining cats and dogs!'

He was right. It was raining cats and dogs.
Tommy had got out of bed on the wrong side
that morning and he had stepped right into
the astonishing world of 'If' where weird and
wonderful things happen all the time.

Normally, if you hear someone has got out of
bed on the wrong side, it just means they are

very cross. But Tommy was not cross about it at all. On the contrary, he was delighted.

"Wow!" gasped Tommy, as the last dogs and cats vanished into the ground and the sun came out again. "What's going to happen next?"

He was standing in the middle of nowhere but there was a dazzling gold yellow-brick road beneath his feet. He decided to follow it. Maybe it was the same one that led to the Wizard of Oz, in that story he enjoyed so much?

But before he knew it– although because it was a magic road, it could have been hundreds of miles– he had reached the end. And it had stopped just outside a town quite unlike any other Tommy had ever seen.

Every single bit of it was painted the same shade of dazzling red. Its appearance made Tommy think of something his mother had once said to him about a friend of hers, who went out one night determined to have lots of fun.

"She really painted the town red," Tommy's mother had laughed when she told him about it.

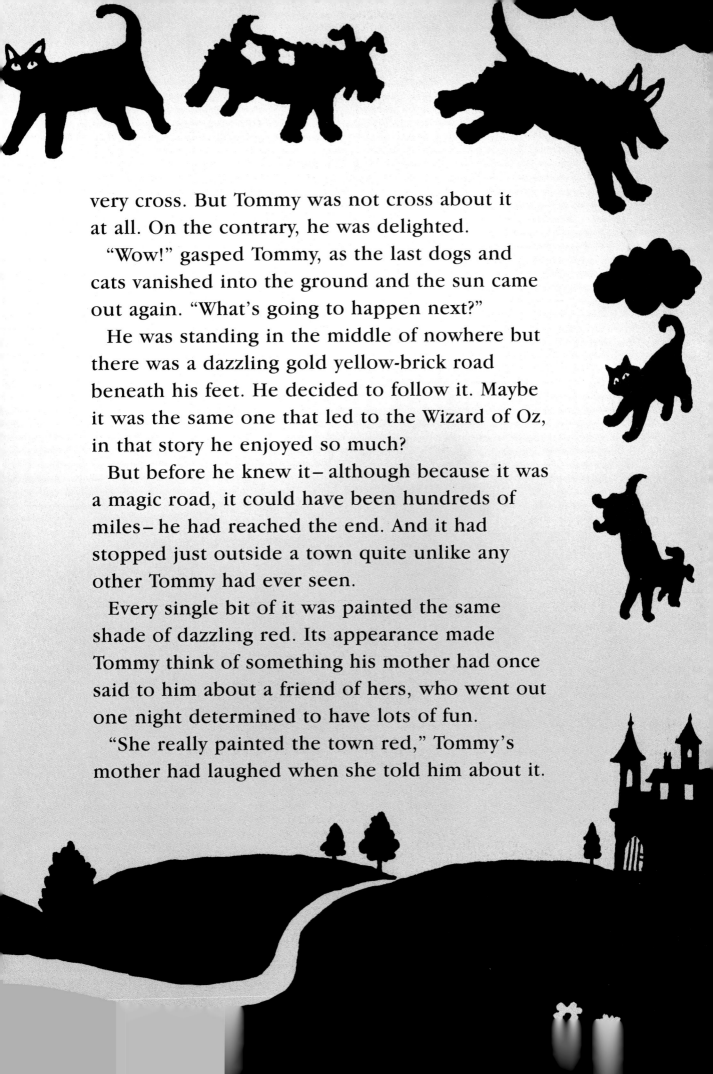

Tommy knew that meant she'd had a really good time, not that she'd spent the whole night with a paintbrush in her hand. That wouldn't have been much fun! Looking at this town, however, it looked as if someone had done precisely that.

The fact that absolutely everything, even the trees and flowers, were the same shade of red was not the only weird thing about the town. It also appeared to be completely deserted.

Or was it? Out of the corner of his eye, Tommy thought he saw moving figures. It was very spooky.

'This looks like a ghost town,' thought Tommy.

He was right. It was full of ghosts. But these ghosts were frightened of him!

"You're not going to haunt us, are you?" a friendly phantom plucked up courage to ask Tommy. "We've heard that humans go round wailing and clanking chains."

Tommy was about to reply, "No, that's what ghosts do!" but he realised that everything was back to front here. So he just smiled and said that of course he wouldn't.

However, Tommy was feeling a bit nervous himself and he was keen to explore the strange new world.

"I'm tired of seeing red," he told the phantom. "It's driving me up the wall."

His words came true. A moment later, Tommy found himself standing on the top of a great wall that went all around the town.

"I've been told that walls have ears," Tommy told it, jokingly. "Maybe you do! You are quite unlike any wall I've ever met."

"You needn't shout!" the wall retorted, proving that it did have excellent hearing.

Just then, a loud and very unexpected 'oink' sounded above Tommy's head, followed by a succession of noisy grunts. Tommy looked up and was amazed to see a herd of pigs flying towards him. They had made a V-shaped formation, like geese, but squealed rather than honked as they flew, propelling themselves along by flapping their huge pink ears.

"Well, if it can rain cats and dogs, there's no reason why pigs shouldn't fly!" Tommy laughed. "Maybe we could even hitch a ride on the back of one."

"Come on!" he shouted to the friendly ghost.

They both rose to the occasion – in the wonderful world of 'If', you really can – and floated upwards to join the flying pigs.

"You want to go the whole hog, do you?" squealed a large black-and-white sow with ten spotted piglets fluttering along behind her. "Well, jump aboard."

She flew them down to a beach and then took off again.

"I must keep up with the others," she grunted. "Or they'll have my bacon."

Tommy and the ghost made for the inviting blue sea. Curiously, it seemed to be singing. As Tommy got closer, he realised it was the sound of many different singsong voices, all talking at once but very softly. He couldn't hear what they were saying to him, but it all sounded very flattering.

"I think they must be whispering sweet nothings to me," Tommy laughed.

"Whhoo-oo, I love sweet nothings!" the ghost moaned with pleasure. "I'll sit here for a bit and fish for compliments."

He produced a fishing net out of thin air and dipped it into the ocean. But all he got for his pains, was a sackful of trouble.

This being 'If', however, it was not an imaginary sack full of imaginary troubles, it was the real thing.

"We're in for the high jump now,"
Tommy said anxiously, fearing the worst,
as the bulging bag was lifted out, dripping
with water and looking like a real load of
problems. He suddenly felt himself going
up in the world again. But this time it
was as if he was bouncing off an extra
springy trampoline.

"We're not 'in for the high jump', we are
in a high jump," Tommy called to the
phantom delightedly.

But when he finally came down to earth
again with a bump, there was no sign of
the friendly ghost. In fact, he was right
back where he had started – in bed.

And Tommy did wonder if he might not
have dreamed the whole thing. Just in case,
he quickly looked out of the window to see
if it was still raining cats and dogs – but
there was only a clear blue sky!

When Dreams Come True

There's a town called Corking, not far from here,
Where dreams come true every hundred years.
"That sounds terrific," I hear you cry,
But it isn't so great and I'll tell you why.

There was a girl called Mags with feet so large,
That people cried, "They're as big as a barge!"
She wished for little feet, small and round,
But when she got them, she kept falling down.

A man called Sam wanted a sea of beer,
And that's what he got– right up to his ears.
You'd think a sea of beer would satisfy him,
But the trouble was, he couldn't swim.

There was a girl called Lucy who climbed into trees,
Because she wanted to talk to the birds and bees,
But the sparrows and starlings all wanted a word,
And poor little Lucy couldn't make herself heard.

There was a boy called Arnie who wished he was strong.
His dream came true, but it didn't last long.
Everything he touched just snapped into two,
And in no time at all, he had run out of glue.

So you see what I'm getting at in this little rhyme,
It's easy to work out, if you give it some time.
Beware what you wish for– and I'm talking to you,
You never know, it might come true!

Follow the Leader

Sasha the sheep lived, as most sheep do, in a large field with a whole bunch of other sheep, carefully watched over by the farmer and his trusty sheepdogs. The farmer seemed to be a reasonable sort of chap, who made sure they had everything they needed, but the sheepdogs were a surly, miserable bunch, forever barking out their orders and expecting to be obeyed. This suited the other sheep quite well, as they were not good at thinking for themselves. But Sasha… well, Sasha was… different.

Ever since she was a tiny lamb her mother had known she would not grow up to be an ordinary sheep. While the other little lambs frolicked gaily in the meadow, chasing each other and gambolling nimbly, Sasha strode back and forth at the edge of the field, muttering fiercely under her breath. When she grew older she would sit for hours with her head buried in a book, or scribbling furiously on little pieces of paper which she hid in the bushes. Other times she went missing altogether, which sent her mother into a frenzy, convinced she had been carried off by a wolf. Then she would find her, propped upside down behind a tree. Meditating, Sasha called it. Getting in touch with her inner self. And it seemed that Sasha had an awful lot of self to get in touch with. The teenage years were the worst – she would stomp round the field, in one of her "moods," glowering at anyone who tried to follow her.

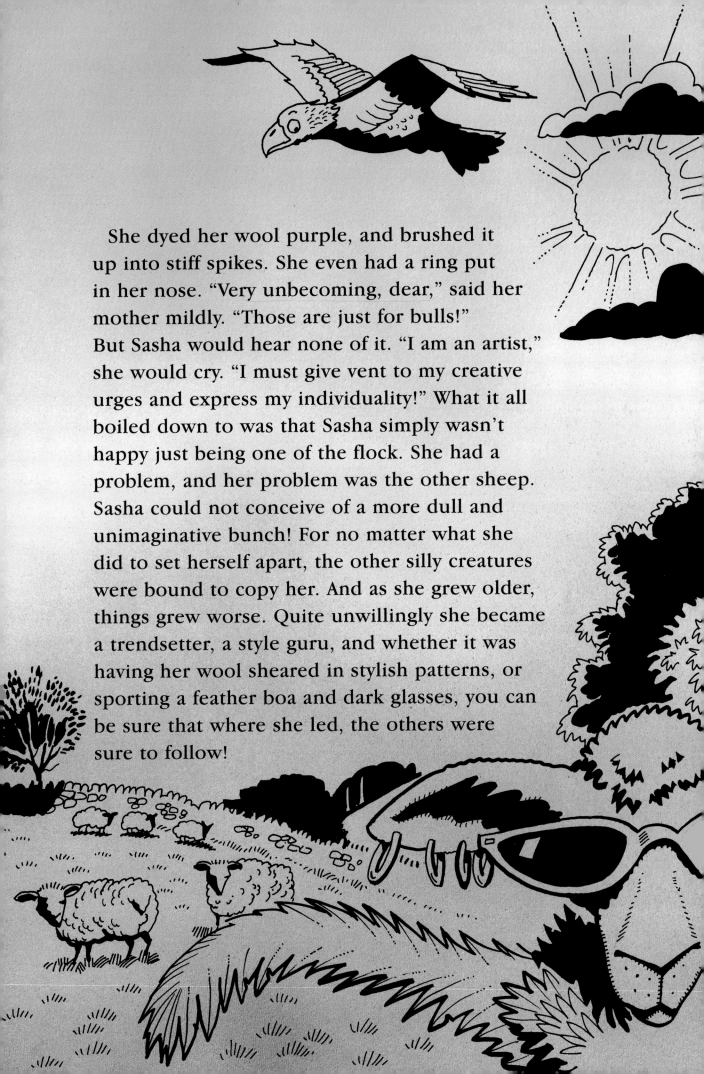

She dyed her wool purple, and brushed it up into stiff spikes. She even had a ring put in her nose. "Very unbecoming, dear," said her mother mildly. "Those are just for bulls!" But Sasha would hear none of it. "I am an artist," she would cry. "I must give vent to my creative urges and express my individuality!" What it all boiled down to was that Sasha simply wasn't happy just being one of the flock. She had a problem, and her problem was the other sheep. Sasha could not conceive of a more dull and unimaginative bunch! For no matter what she did to set herself apart, the other silly creatures were bound to copy her. And as she grew older, things grew worse. Quite unwillingly she became a trendsetter, a style guru, and whether it was having her wool sheared in stylish patterns, or sporting a feather boa and dark glasses, you can be sure that where she led, the others were sure to follow!

"It's the highest form of flattery, dear!" said her mother. "Baloney!" said Sasha.

And so it was one morning that Sasha woke in a particularly foul temper, having discovered all the other sheep copying her latest 'pirate' look– eyepatch and spotted headscarf– to find a handsome new sheepdog standing over her. "Get lost!" she growled, staring up at him.

"You must be Sasha," he smiled. "I've heard a lot about you from the other dogs– none of it good, mind you! I'm Sid. Do me a favour and come and lead this daft lot into the next field, will you? I want to make a good impression on my first day!" Now, as a rule, Sasha never did anything a dog asked her to. But there was something about Sid that made her sit up and take notice. He was different from the others. Pleasant, for a start. And then she noticed that his eyes were different colours– one blue, one brown!

'How brilliantly individual,' thought Sasha. The fact he thought the other sheep daft was just the icing on the cake! Sasha was smitten! The farmer could hardly believe his eyes when he saw Sasha jump up and do exactly as Sid directed. She had always been so very difficult before. Well, well, well – perhaps she'd finally met her match!

Which, of course, is exactly what had happened, although not in the way the farmer was thinking. From then on Sasha and Sid were inseparable. In fact, the farmer was so impressed by their teamwork that he decided to enter them in the individual sheepdog trials at the forthcoming county show. Dutifully they practised their routine every day, with Sid lying low in the grass listening attentively to the farmer's low whistles, and directing Sasha in a series of intricate manoeuvres. They were

magnificent, moving together as one,
in perfect harmony. The farmer felt sure
they would take the county show by storm.
Little did he know that is just what they
were planning to do – but again, not in the
way the farmer was thinking! For every night,
once the others were asleep, Sasha and Sid
had been hard at work secretly practising a
special routine of their own!

Well, the day of the sheepdog trials finally
dawned, and there was great excitement as
the sheepdogs rounded up the sheep and
herded them, led of course by Sasha, into the
farmer's truck. At the show, they sat dutifully
in their pen, and watched team after team of
dogs and sheep go through their manoeuvres.

"Mind-numbingly dull, isn't it!" Sasha
muttered to Sid. "Have they no imagination
at all?"

"Wait till it's our turn," smirked Sid. "We'll show them!"

But when it came to their turn, Sasha and Sid were nowhere to be found. "Would Sasha and Sid *please* take the field," said the announcer over the loudspeaker. "If there is any further delay, we may have to disqualify you!" There was pandemonium as everyone looked around frantically for the missing pair. But then, in a great burst of colour, Sasha and Sid emerged from the trailer and took to the field as the audience gasped in amazement. Sasha was dressed in a brilliant red flamenco dress, with a rose behind her ear, and Sid looked equally dashing in a dinner suit and dark glasses. As the loudspeakers crackled, then burst into life, and Latin

music boomed across the field, Sasha
and Sid sprang into action. They danced
the samba, lambada and salsa, moving
together in perfect harmony! The judges
were outraged and disqualified them at
once. Never had such a thing happened
at their show! But Sasha and Sid just kept
on dancing, as the crowd clapped and
cheered, putting on a show no-one would
ever forget, and securing Sasha's place in
the history books as a sheep quite unlike
any other! Even the farmer was pleased –
after all, it was great publicity!

As she snuggled down to sleep next to
Sid that night, Sasha felt truly happy.
She had made her mark at last. Funnily
enough though, salsa dancing has
become awfully popular these days…

The Sensible Tax

"The bridge is falling down," said the Minister
for Transport.

"We need more golf balls," said the Minister
for Sport.

The Prime Minister didn't look up from his
papers, but waved his hand wearily and said
with a sigh, "Go to the Treasury, and get what
you need."

"The Treasury is empty, Sir. There's not a single
penny left."

"I don't believe it," said the Prime Minister.
"It was full last week."

"I think we spent it all on that tunnel under
the sea, Sir," said the second minister. "You know,
the one we can't find the entrance to."

"Don't remind me!" said the Prime Minister.

Together, the three important gentlemen ran down to the Treasury. It was empty. Where once there were piles of gold and silver coins there was now nothing, just big balls of dust rolling across the bare floor.

The Prime Minister called a meeting.

"We need to come up with a new tax to raise some more money," he said. "What haven't we taxed yet?"

The ministers looked at him in silence.

"How about food?" said the Prime Minister.

"We've taxed that already," said someone.

"Roads?"

"Those too," said another.

"Windows? Pets? Water? Music? There must be something that the people do, or want, or can't help being that we could tax," said the Prime Minister.

One of his advisors coughed. "There is one thing," he said.

"Yes?" asked the Prime Minister.

"Well, we raise our children to be very sensible," said the man. "We teach them to wipe their feet when they enter the house, to

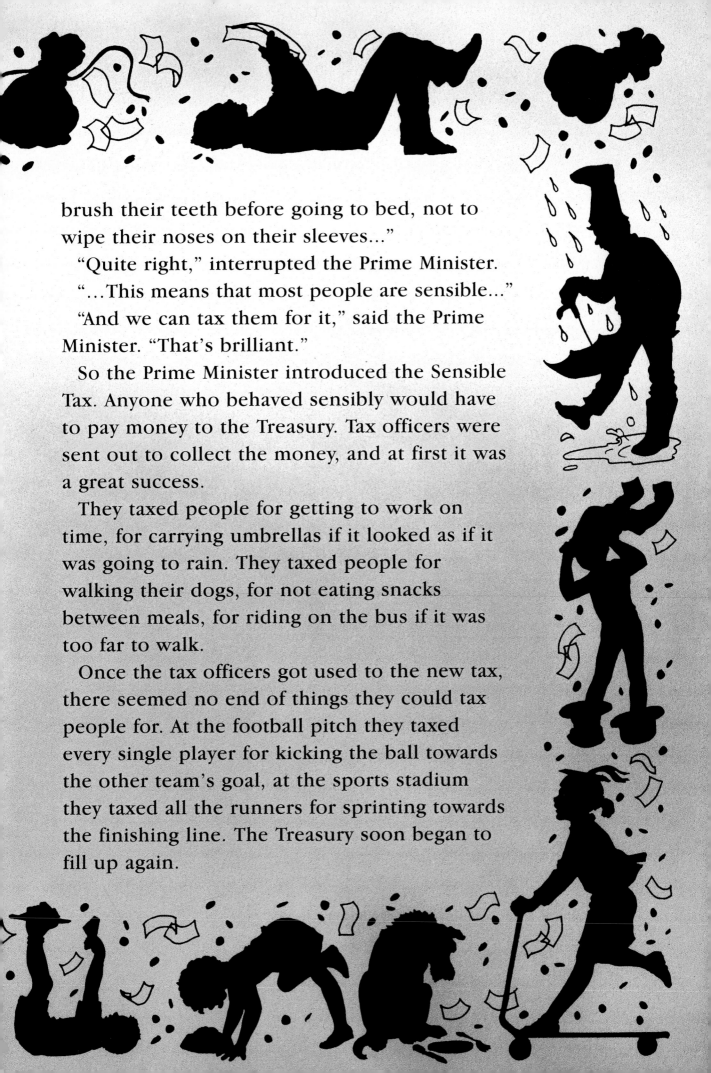

brush their teeth before going to bed, not to wipe their noses on their sleeves..."

"Quite right," interrupted the Prime Minister.

"...This means that most people are sensible..."

"And we can tax them for it," said the Prime Minister. "That's brilliant."

So the Prime Minister introduced the Sensible Tax. Anyone who behaved sensibly would have to pay money to the Treasury. Tax officers were sent out to collect the money, and at first it was a great success.

They taxed people for getting to work on time, for carrying umbrellas if it looked as if it was going to rain. They taxed people for walking their dogs, for not eating snacks between meals, for riding on the bus if it was too far to walk.

Once the tax officers got used to the new tax, there seemed no end of things they could tax people for. At the football pitch they taxed every single player for kicking the ball towards the other team's goal, at the sports stadium they taxed all the runners for sprinting towards the finishing line. The Treasury soon began to fill up again.

Of course, the new tax wasn't very popular with the people, and very soon they began to grumble.

"I've just been taxed for wearing my scarf," said Benjamin's dad when he came home from work one evening.

"Why were you wearing your scarf, George?" said his wife, Myrtle.

"Well, it's cold out," he asked.

"Yes, of course," she replied.

"This is ridiculous," said George. "All our lives we are told to be sensible and now they charge us for it. It's not a sensible tax, it's a completely stupid tax. The only people who never have to pay anything are those who are as daft as ducks."

Just then there was a knock at the door.

"I'm a tax officer," said the man at the door.

"This is just a random house check. Am I correct in thinking that you are about to eat dinner at dinner time, Madam?" said the man.

"Yes," said Myrtle.

"And is it piping hot and straight from the oven?" said the man.

"Yes," came the reply.

"And is it cooked all the way through? And will you be sitting at the dinner table to eat it, Madam? And is there pudding to follow?"

Myrtle answered 'yes' to all of these questions and the officer handed her a tax bill.

Just then Benjamin came wandering down the stairs wearing a wetsuit and a pair of flippers, and a top hat on his head.

"I don't want dinner," he said to his mum. "I've been eating chocolate all day. I'm off out now. I'll be back long after my bedtime."

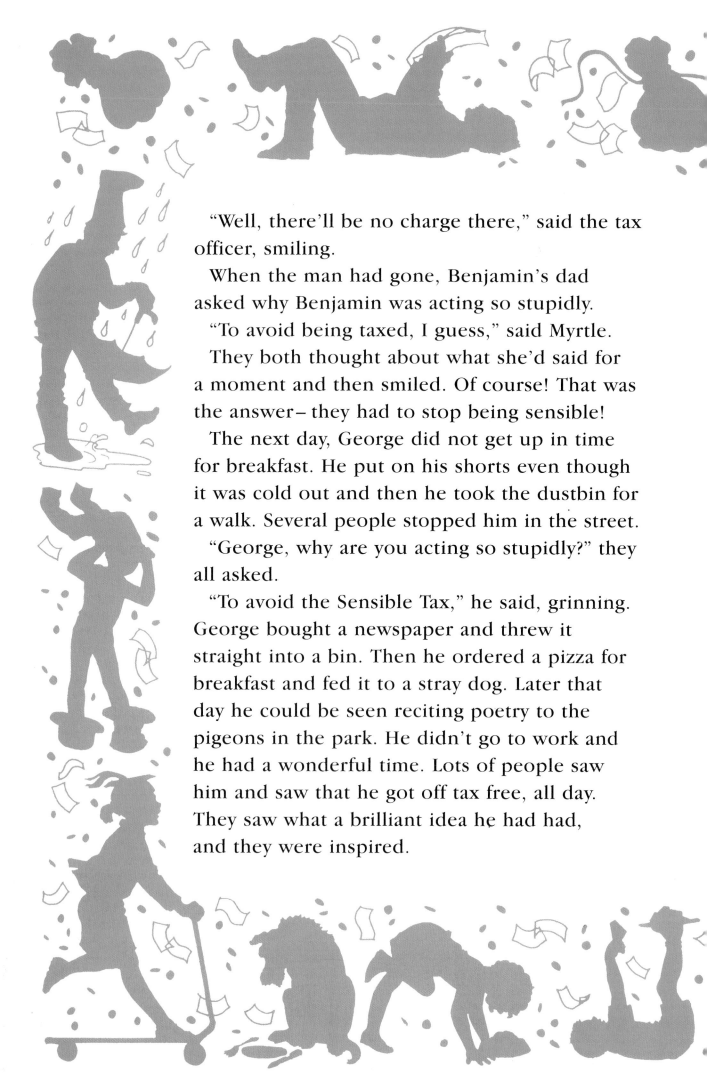

"Well, there'll be no charge there," said the tax officer, smiling.

When the man had gone, Benjamin's dad asked why Benjamin was acting so stupidly.

"To avoid being taxed, I guess," said Myrtle.

They both thought about what she'd said for a moment and then smiled. Of course! That was the answer – they had to stop being sensible!

The next day, George did not get up in time for breakfast. He put on his shorts even though it was cold out and then he took the dustbin for a walk. Several people stopped him in the street.

"George, why are you acting so stupidly?" they all asked.

"To avoid the Sensible Tax," he said, grinning. George bought a newspaper and threw it straight into a bin. Then he ordered a pizza for breakfast and fed it to a stray dog. Later that day he could be seen reciting poetry to the pigeons in the park. He didn't go to work and he had a wonderful time. Lots of people saw him and saw that he got off tax free, all day. They saw what a brilliant idea he had had, and they were inspired.

The next day, most people didn't go to work at all, and those who did didn't get there on time; some even went to the wrong jobs. They walked if it was too far to walk; if they had bicycles, they carried them. A lot of people went to the cinema in the afternoon dressed as pirates, but they didn't watch the film. No, that would have been too sensible. They faced the other way and sang football songs at the tops of their voices, instead.

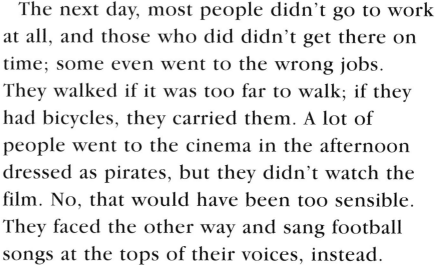

They all had a great day, and the next day they all got up late and did it all over again, only this time they found even more ways to be silly.

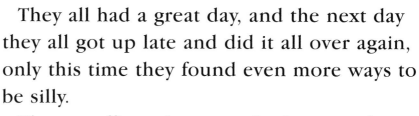

The tax officers began to look worried – the money had stopped coming in – and the ministers were even more worried. No-one was doing any work; the country was falling apart. They called an emergency meeting with the Prime Minister.

"Sorry I'm late," said the Prime Minister. "My train didn't leave on time and then it went off in the wrong direction. It's chaos out there. What's going on?"

"It's the Sensible Tax, Sir," said one of his ministers. "Everyone is acting stupidly so that they don't have to pay it."

"Well, this can't go on," said the Prime Minister. "The country's gone mad."

"We shall have to stop the tax," someone said.

The Prime Minister paused. He liked the Sensible Tax; it raised lots of money. Without it the Treasury would be empty again. But things were getting out of hand.

"Yes," he said, sadly. And then he smiled. "I've got it," he cried. "Why don't we tax people for wearing clothes?"

All the ministers threw up their hands in complete despair.

"Oh no!" they groaned.

It's Raining

I t's raining cats and dogs,
 And warty toads and frogs,
 And red-kneed bats and bowler hats.
 It's raining big fat hogs.

It's raining needles and pins,
And rusty cans and tins,
And things I don't like – such as bits of bike.
It's raining wheelie bins.

It's raining sugar and spice,
And sleek white rats and mice,
And currant buns and somebody's sons.
It's raining furry dice.

It's raining apples and pears,
And dolls and teddy bears,
And silly pigs in curly wigs.
It's raining plastic chairs.

It's raining shoes and socks,
And pebbles, stones and rocks,
And kipper ties and old pork pies.
It's raining party frocks.

It's raining bacon and eggs,
And washing lines and pegs,
And cowboy suits and exotic fruits.
It's raining hairy legs.

It's raining ducks and drakes,
And chocolate bars and cakes,
And glasses of milk and colourful silk.
It's raining garden rakes.

The Underwater Talent Show

Every morning for the past week, Prawn had woken up in a panic. Today was no different. 'What day is it?' he thought, treading water so frantically that he spun round in circles until his spindly legs got tangled up. He realised with a sinking heart that it was Saturday– the day of the Talent Show.

Prawn had never felt so talentless. All week he had tried to devise amazing feats to dazzle the talent show judges. He tried to lift ten sea slugs with his bare antennae but he couldn't even lift one! When he tried to pick one up he was horribly stung by the outraged sea slug, who thought he was being very cheeky.

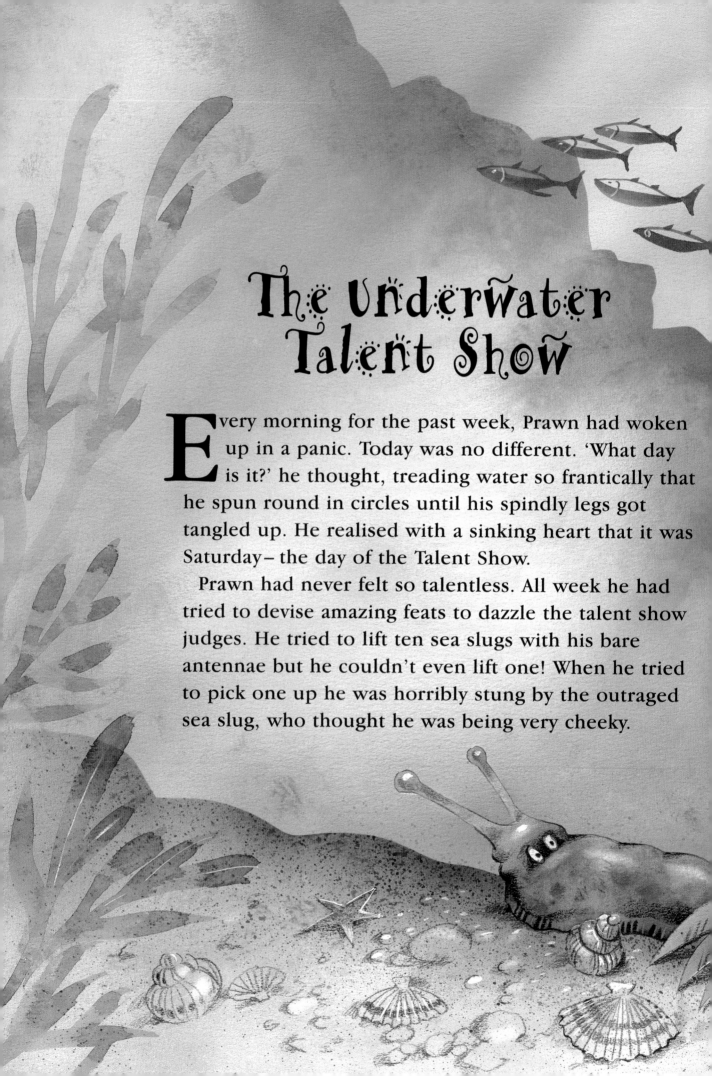

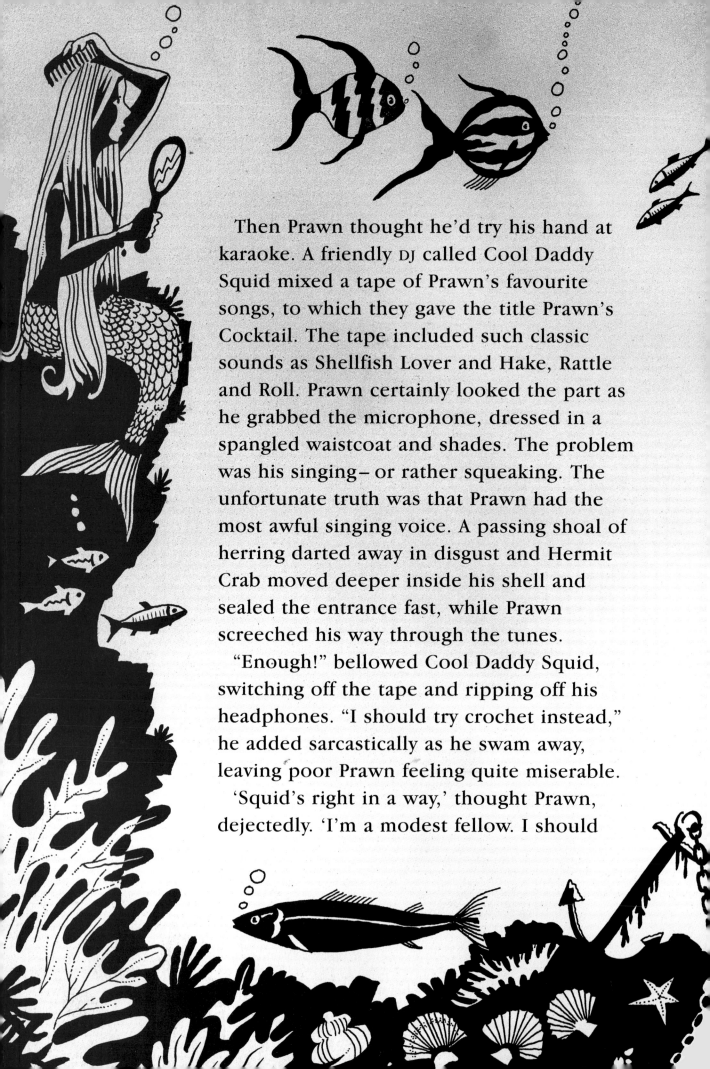

Then Prawn thought he'd try his hand at karaoke. A friendly DJ called Cool Daddy Squid mixed a tape of Prawn's favourite songs, to which they gave the title Prawn's Cocktail. The tape included such classic sounds as Shellfish Lover and Hake, Rattle and Roll. Prawn certainly looked the part as he grabbed the microphone, dressed in a spangled waistcoat and shades. The problem was his singing– or rather squeaking. The unfortunate truth was that Prawn had the most awful singing voice. A passing shoal of herring darted away in disgust and Hermit Crab moved deeper inside his shell and sealed the entrance fast, while Prawn screeched his way through the tunes.

"Enough!" bellowed Cool Daddy Squid, switching off the tape and ripping off his headphones. "I should try crochet instead," he added sarcastically as he swam away, leaving poor Prawn feeling quite miserable.

'Squid's right in a way,' thought Prawn, dejectedly. 'I'm a modest fellow. I should

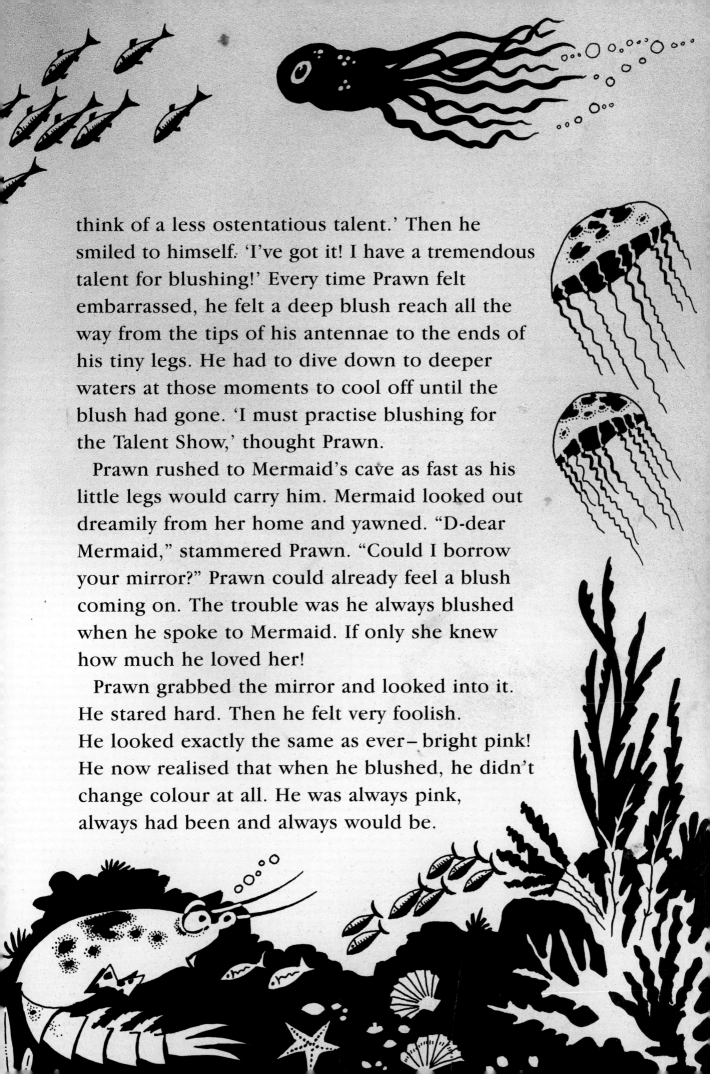

think of a less ostentatious talent.' Then he
smiled to himself. 'I've got it! I have a tremendous
talent for blushing!' Every time Prawn felt
embarrassed, he felt a deep blush reach all the
way from the tips of his antennae to the ends of
his tiny legs. He had to dive down to deeper
waters at those moments to cool off until the
blush had gone. 'I must practise blushing for
the Talent Show,' thought Prawn.

Prawn rushed to Mermaid's cave as fast as his
little legs would carry him. Mermaid looked out
dreamily from her home and yawned. "D-dear
Mermaid," stammered Prawn. "Could I borrow
your mirror?" Prawn could already feel a blush
coming on. The trouble was he always blushed
when he spoke to Mermaid. If only she knew
how much he loved her!

Prawn grabbed the mirror and looked into it.
He stared hard. Then he felt very foolish.
He looked exactly the same as ever – bright pink!
He now realised that when he blushed, he didn't
change colour at all. He was always pink,
always had been and always would be.

Mermaid gazed at Prawn from under her lovely lashes. "What's up, Prawn?" she drawled. "You look upset." "Oh, n-nothing," replied Prawn, as he handed her the mirror. She was looking at him with her clear, blue eyes and Prawn couldn't think of anything to say. "Must dash. Loads to do," he gulped as he paddled off. 'Ah, he is sweet,' thought Mermaid wistfully, as she went back into her cave.

Prawn was sad. The talent show would be starting soon, and he had nothing to offer. As Prawn peeped out through the weeds, he could see that the ocean was alive with excited and purposeful activity. A group of clams were practising opening and closing their shells in sequence. Anglerfish was unscrewing the light at the end of his fishing rod and changing it for a glitter ball. Then Prawn spotted Cool Daddy Squid with a nervous-looking young starfish at his side. "You're gonna be the greatest!" he heard Cool Daddy whisper to the starfish.

Prawn could also hear the sound of Mermaid singing scales, followed by much gargling. 'She's far too talented for me,' he thought, glumly. He was on the point of bursting into tears when Shark swam past with a jester's hat on his head. "Coming to the show, Prawnie?" he grinned. "It's going to be such marvellous fun!"

"See you there!" called Prawn. 'Yes,' he thought, 'I will go. Then I can admire Mermaid from afar.'

Prawn straightened his bow tie and set off for the show. "Hi, there!" called a familiar voice. It was Mermaid, wearing a dazzling ball gown and sporting pearls in her hair. Prawn started to blush. He felt hotter and hotter. "Wish me luck, Prawn,"

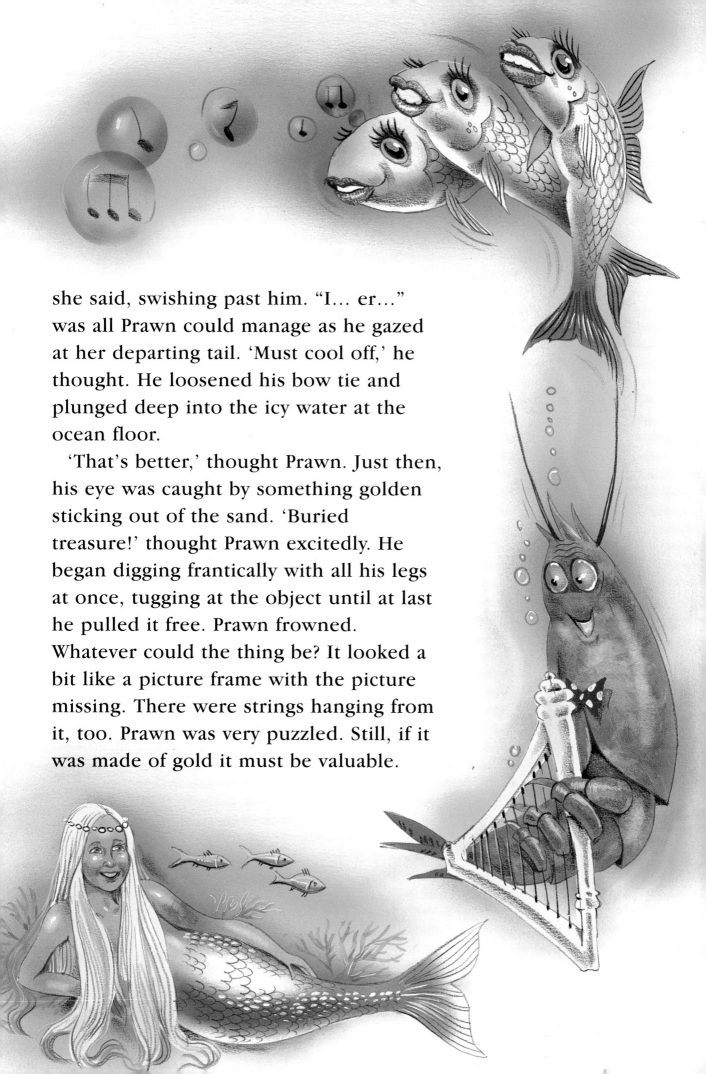

she said, swishing past him. "I... er..."
was all Prawn could manage as he gazed
at her departing tail. 'Must cool off,' he
thought. He loosened his bow tie and
plunged deep into the icy water at the
ocean floor.

‘That's better,' thought Prawn. Just then,
his eye was caught by something golden
sticking out of the sand. 'Buried
treasure!' thought Prawn excitedly. He
began digging frantically with all his legs
at once, tugging at the object until at last
he pulled it free. Prawn frowned.
Whatever could the thing be? It looked a
bit like a picture frame with the picture
missing. There were strings hanging from
it, too. Prawn was very puzzled. Still, if it
was made of gold it must be valuable.

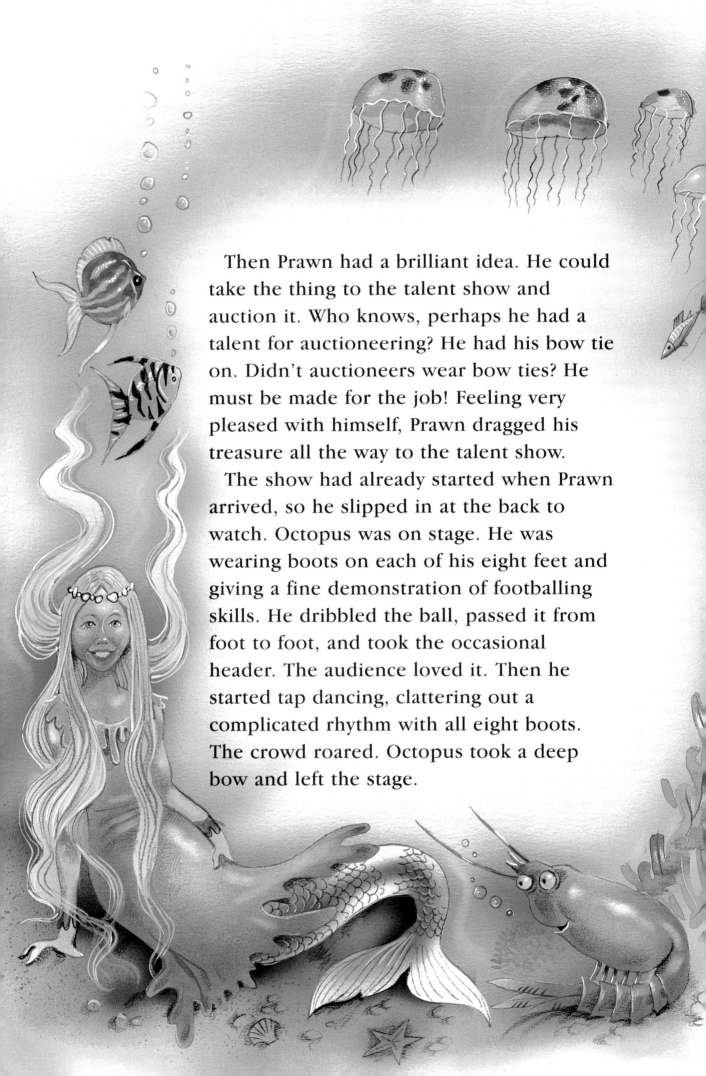

Then Prawn had a brilliant idea. He could take the thing to the talent show and auction it. Who knows, perhaps he had a talent for auctioneering? He had his bow tie on. Didn't auctioneers wear bow ties? He must be made for the job! Feeling very pleased with himself, Prawn dragged his treasure all the way to the talent show.

The show had already started when Prawn arrived, so he slipped in at the back to watch. Octopus was on stage. He was wearing boots on each of his eight feet and giving a fine demonstration of footballing skills. He dribbled the ball, passed it from foot to foot, and took the occasional header. The audience loved it. Then he started tap dancing, clattering out a complicated rhythm with all eight boots. The crowd roared. Octopus took a deep bow and left the stage.

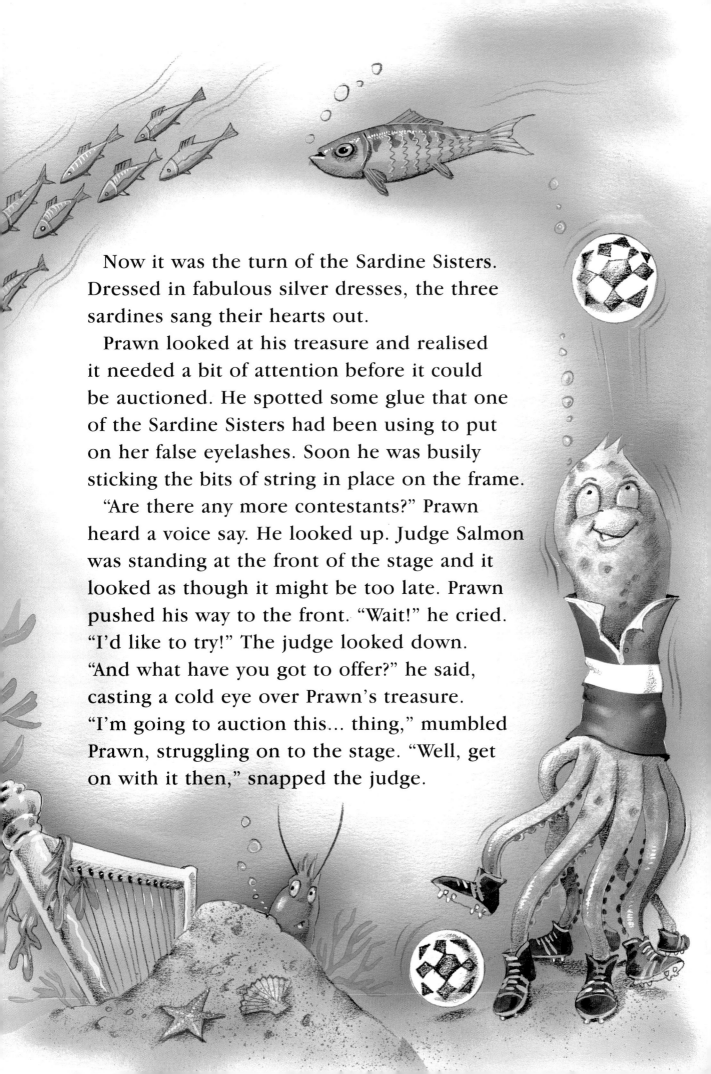

Now it was the turn of the Sardine Sisters. Dressed in fabulous silver dresses, the three sardines sang their hearts out.

Prawn looked at his treasure and realised it needed a bit of attention before it could be auctioned. He spotted some glue that one of the Sardine Sisters had been using to put on her false eyelashes. Soon he was busily sticking the bits of string in place on the frame.

"Are there any more contestants?" Prawn heard a voice say. He looked up. Judge Salmon was standing at the front of the stage and it looked as though it might be too late. Prawn pushed his way to the front. "Wait!" he cried. "I'd like to try!" The judge looked down. "And what have you got to offer?" he said, casting a cold eye over Prawn's treasure. "I'm going to auction this... thing," mumbled Prawn, struggling on to the stage. "Well, get on with it then," snapped the judge.

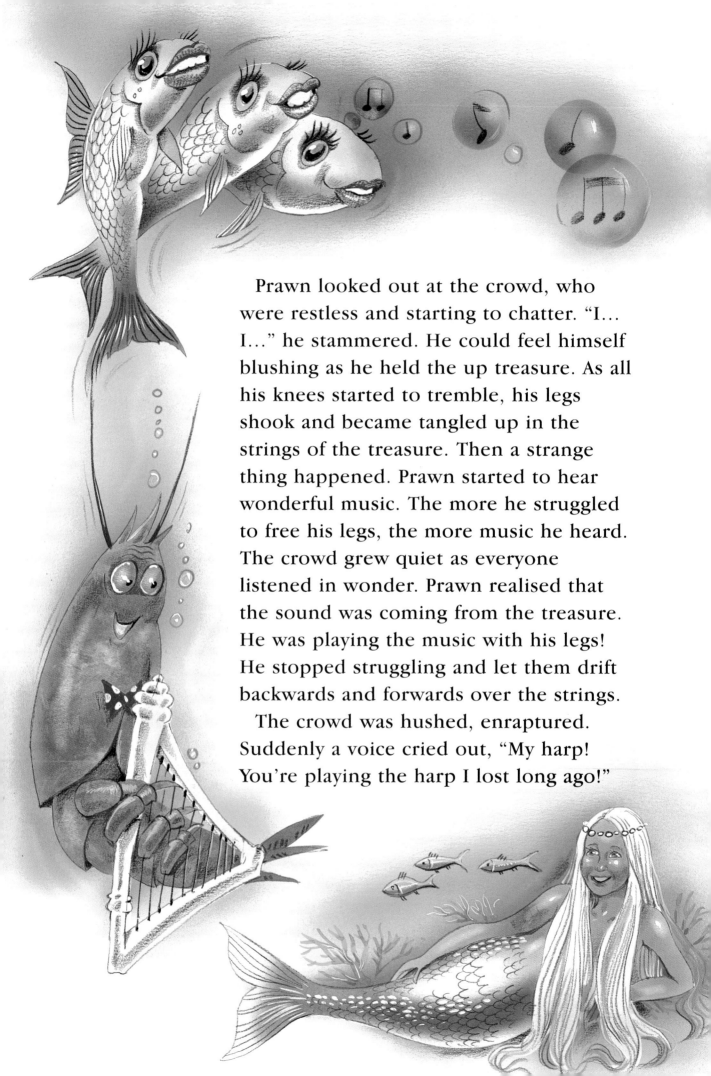

Prawn looked out at the crowd, who were restless and starting to chatter. "I… I…" he stammered. He could feel himself blushing as he held the up treasure. As all his knees started to tremble, his legs shook and became tangled up in the strings of the treasure. Then a strange thing happened. Prawn started to hear wonderful music. The more he struggled to free his legs, the more music he heard. The crowd grew quiet as everyone listened in wonder. Prawn realised that the sound was coming from the treasure. He was playing the music with his legs! He stopped struggling and let them drift backwards and forwards over the strings.

The crowd was hushed, enraptured. Suddenly a voice cried out, "My harp! You're playing the harp I lost long ago!"

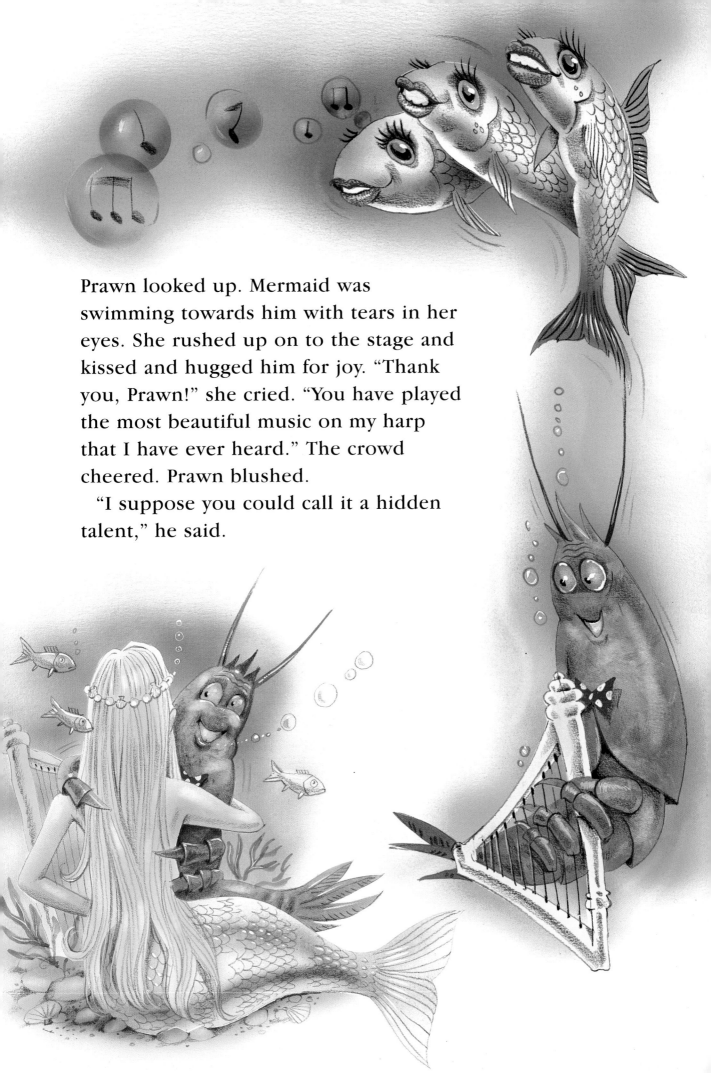

Prawn looked up. Mermaid was
swimming towards him with tears in her
eyes. She rushed up on to the stage and
kissed and hugged him for joy. "Thank
you, Prawn!" she cried. "You have played
the most beautiful music on my harp
that I have ever heard." The crowd
cheered. Prawn blushed.

"I suppose you could call it a hidden
talent," he said.

The Planet Where Time Goes Backwards

Far beyond our solar system,
In the outer reaches of space,
There's a planet where time goes backwards,
And it's the most peculiar place.

A place where birds climb into their shells,
And leaves flutter up to the trees,
Clouds suck rain from out of the ground,
And rivers flow out of the seas.

The cooks wash up at the start of the meal
And unpeel the spuds, I'm told.
Your dinner goes into the oven,
And comes out nice and cold.

On building sites, they start with a house
And take it apart brick by brick,
At lunchtime they spit out their sandwiches
(It looks like they're being sick!)

At petrol pumps they take fuel out of cars,
And football's not much of a laugh:
The match ends with both teams at zero,
And they start by having a bath.

You know something bad's going to happen,
Because someone will start to cry.
But the people get younger each day,
And they greet you by saying "goodbye".

Toby Finds a Job

Toby was honest, hard-working and really quite clever, but for some strange reason he could never find a job. He always seemed to get things wrong at interviews. So he stayed at home most days, painting his rooms, making new curtains, little nick-nacks to brighten up the place. He worked hard, and he liked his house, even if it was a bit unusual.

Toby's friends all knew that Toby was looking for a job and they were always on the lookout for things he could do. One day, his friend Suzie called to say that the office where she worked was looking for a 'spokesperson'.

'A 'spokesperson',' thought Toby. 'It's an odd sort of job, but I think I can do it.' He went to his shed and took the wheels off his bicycle. Then he went to all his friends and borrowed their bicycle wheels too. By lunchtime he had lots of wheels and hundreds of spokes. He went along to the company and said:

"I'm very good with spokes! See? I've got long ones, short ones, bent ones, but most of them are straight."

The interviewer scratched his head and laughed. "No, a 'spokesperson' is someone who talks to people – newspapers, radio and television. They tell them what the company does. It's got nothing to do with bicycle wheels."

"Oh," said Toby, and he went home again and made a new coffee table out of a big drainpipe.

The following day, Toby's friend Sam called to say that the school down the road was looking for

someone to help out. "The person they need,"
he said, "must be good with children." But Toby
didn't hear him right. He thought that Sam had
said 'chickens'.

'Chickens?' thought Toby. 'In a school? That's
most unusual, but perhaps they're learning
about farms or perhaps they have a pets corner.'

So he went to a nearby chicken farm and
borrowed as many chickens as he could fit into
his car. Then he went to the school.

"I've come about the job," said Toby, unloading
the chickens. The chickens ran all over the
classroom, squawking and clucking. Feathers
flew everywhere and the children screamed and
huddled into a corner.

"Get those chickens out of here," said the
teacher angrily.

It took Toby a long time to round up the
chickens and by that time the teacher looked so
cross that Toby thought it better not to ask for a
job. He went home and painted his kitchen
yellow with green spots.

A couple of days later, Toby's friend Jeremy telephoned to say that his company was looking for a fundraiser, did he want to do that?

'A fun dresser,' thought Toby afterwards. 'Now that's the job for me. I've always enjoyed dressing up in bright and unusual clothes, but I wonder what a fun dresser does at work. Perhaps he just goes around cheering everyone up.'

Toby went to his wardrobe. He had built it himself out of driftwood from the beach and old dustbin lids.

Toby chose his funniest clothes: a Viking helmet with horns sticking out of it, a shirt covered with frills and fancy trimmings, a pair of baggy trousers covered with bright patches, his flippers, a tie like a fish and, to complete the outfit, his wizard's cape, covered with stars and signs of the zodiac. He wasn't sure if others would think this was a fun thing to wear or not; it was the kind of thing he wore all the time.

When Toby got to the interview he leapt into the room with a loud, "Ta-daaa," and was greeted by stunned silence. The people in the office were very smartly dressed in white shirts and grey suits and just sat there with their mouths open.

"Is this not fun enough?" asked Toby, surprised by their silence.

"I beg your pardon," said a stiff-looking lady with a notepad.

"Is this the kind of fun dressing you had in mind?" asked Toby. "I've got more like this at home."

The ladies and gentlemen in their suits looked at each other with puzzled expressions and then one of them laughed. Then they all laughed.

"No," one of them said at last, gulping for air. "We're looking for a 'fundraiser,' you know, someone who raises money."

"Oh," said Toby, feeling very foolish indeed. "Not someone who dresses in funny clothes?"

"Not really," said the man, laughing so much his sides hurt.

Toby went home on the bus, trying not to worry about the funny looks he was getting from the other passengers.

A few days later, all of Toby's friends came to visit him. Sam was there, and Suzie and Jeremy.

They were worried about Toby. Would he ever find a job? Toby was excited to have all his friends round.

"You sit there, Suzie," he said. "It's my new inflatable chair. I made it myself out of car inner-tubes."

"Wow! It's great!" laughed Suzie. "It really is very comfortable."

"This chair is good, too," said Jeremy, sitting on one Toby had made out of old packing cases.

The friends chatted and laughed. They loved Toby, but they thought his job-hunting mistakes were really quite funny.

"What about that time you went for a job as a book-keeper," laughed Suzie, "with all those books under your arm."

"Well, I've got lots of books," said Toby, bashfully. "I'm very good at keeping them."

"Yes, but a book-keeper looks after money, not books," said Suzie.

"I know that now," said Toby.

"And that time you went for a job as a fencer," laughed Jeremy. "They meant putting up fences, not sword-fighting."

Toby blushed a bright pink colour.

When they had stopped laughing, the friends looked around Toby's room. The walls were painted in stripes of purple and green, the curtains were orange with little pink birds stitched onto them. It was a very unusual home, but they liked it. It was different, and it made their homes seem very dull.

"Could you make me some curtains like that?" said Suzie.

Toby looked at her with surprise. No-one had ever asked him to do anything like that before. "Of course," he said. "I'd like to make you some red ones with little blue boats on them."

"And can you make me a cupboard out

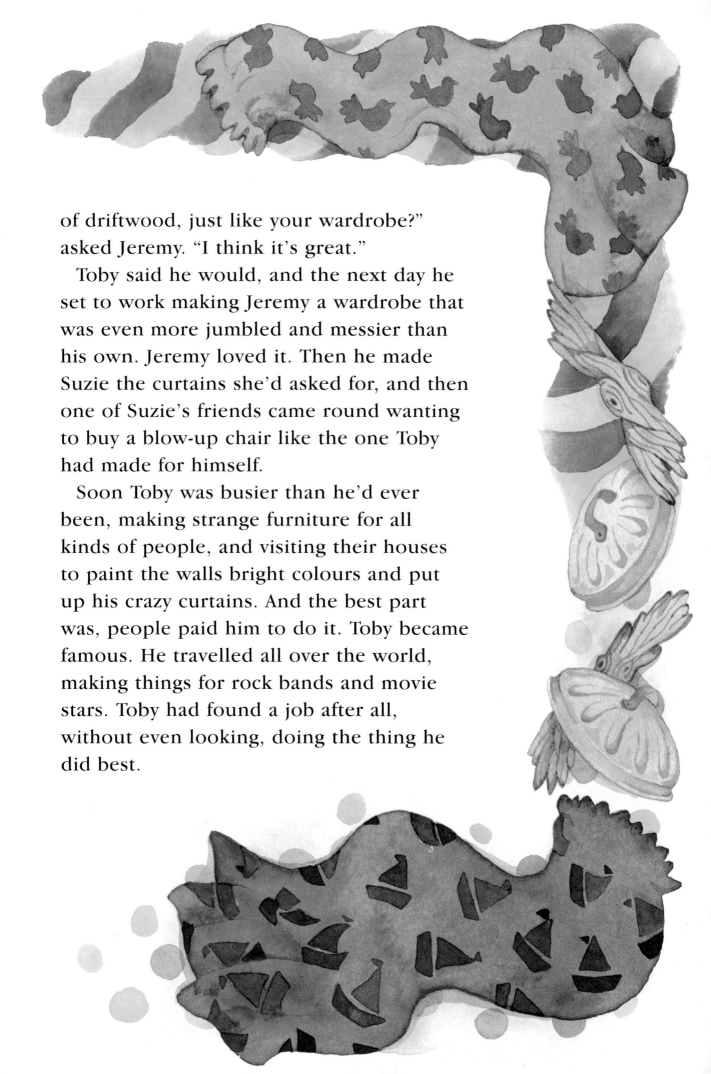

of driftwood, just like your wardrobe?" asked Jeremy. "I think it's great."

Toby said he would, and the next day he set to work making Jeremy a wardrobe that was even more jumbled and messier than his own. Jeremy loved it. Then he made Suzie the curtains she'd asked for, and then one of Suzie's friends came round wanting to buy a blow-up chair like the one Toby had made for himself.

Soon Toby was busier than he'd ever been, making strange furniture for all kinds of people, and visiting their houses to paint the walls bright colours and put up his crazy curtains. And the best part was, people paid him to do it. Toby became famous. He travelled all over the world, making things for rock bands and movie stars. Toby had found a job after all, without even looking, doing the thing he did best.

A Knight to Remember

Long, long ago, when kings ruled over kingdoms, fearsome dragons terrorised the lands and beautiful princesses swooned over dashing knights in shining armour, there lived a very worried man called Alfred Ramsbottom.

Alfred was a great big bear of a man, with an important job working as chief blacksmith to the king. He shod the king's horses, and equipped his knights with swords, shields and suits of armour.

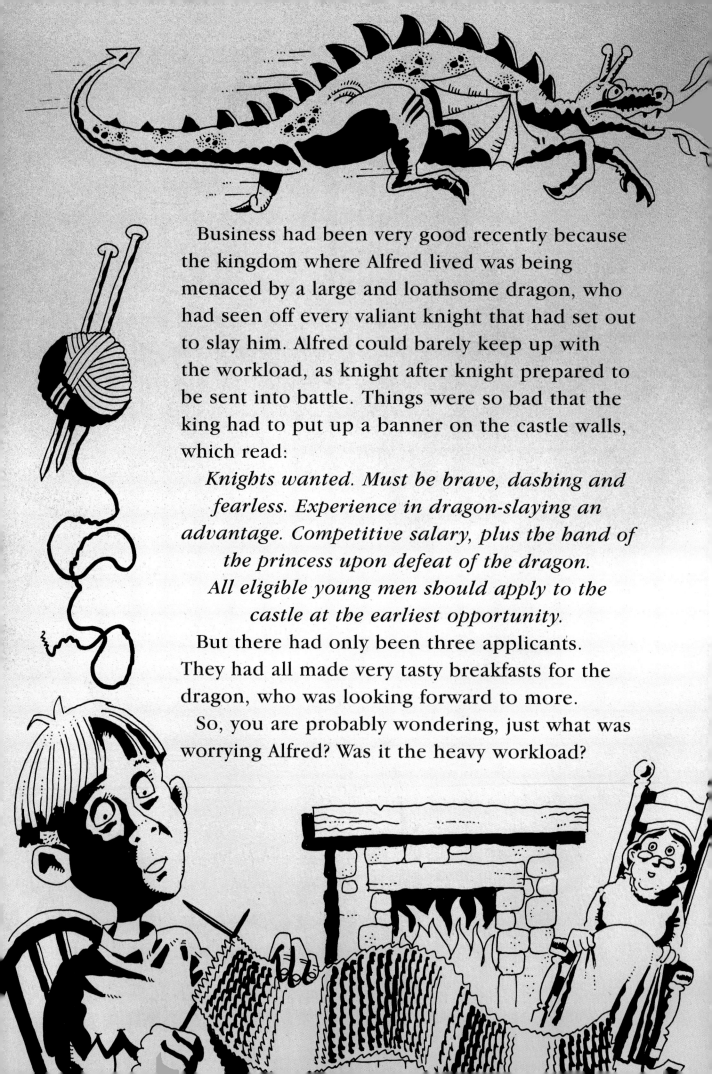

Business had been very good recently because the kingdom where Alfred lived was being menaced by a large and loathsome dragon, who had seen off every valiant knight that had set out to slay him. Alfred could barely keep up with the workload, as knight after knight prepared to be sent into battle. Things were so bad that the king had to put up a banner on the castle walls, which read:

Knights wanted. Must be brave, dashing and fearless. Experience in dragon-slaying an advantage. Competitive salary, plus the hand of the princess upon defeat of the dragon.
All eligible young men should apply to the castle at the earliest opportunity.

But there had only been three applicants. They had all made very tasty breakfasts for the dragon, who was looking forward to more.

So, you are probably wondering, just what was worrying Alfred? Was it the heavy workload?

Was it the dragon? Was he worried that the king would send him out to slay the dragon? Well, you won't be able to guess, so I'll tell you… it was his son, Nigel.

Now, Nigel was as different from his dad as it was possible to be. He was small, he was weedy, he had soft, smooth hands. Worse still, he liked music, and poetry and… knitting! He'd happily sit by the fire with his mother for hours on end, needles clicking away as he worked on a nice new tunic. There was no chance of him joining the family business— he couldn't even lift his father's hammers! Just the night before Nigel had overheard his parents talking:

"What will become of the boy?" groaned Alfred. "All he does is sit around the house all day singing and playing his lute. And as for the knitting— what good is that going to do him? How will he ever be able to make his way in the world?"

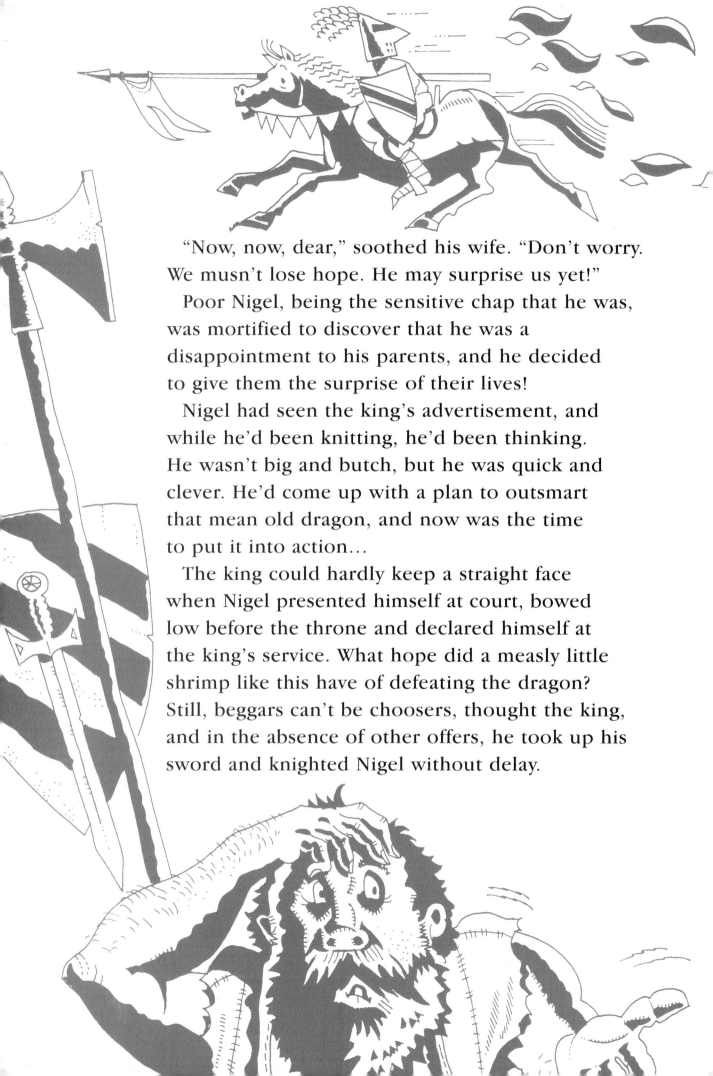

"Now, now, dear," soothed his wife. "Don't worry. We musn't lose hope. He may surprise us yet!"

Poor Nigel, being the sensitive chap that he was, was mortified to discover that he was a disappointment to his parents, and he decided to give them the surprise of their lives!

Nigel had seen the king's advertisement, and while he'd been knitting, he'd been thinking. He wasn't big and butch, but he was quick and clever. He'd come up with a plan to outsmart that mean old dragon, and now was the time to put it into action…

The king could hardly keep a straight face when Nigel presented himself at court, bowed low before the throne and declared himself at the king's service. What hope did a measly little shrimp like this have of defeating the dragon? Still, beggars can't be choosers, thought the king, and in the absence of other offers, he took up his sword and knighted Nigel without delay.

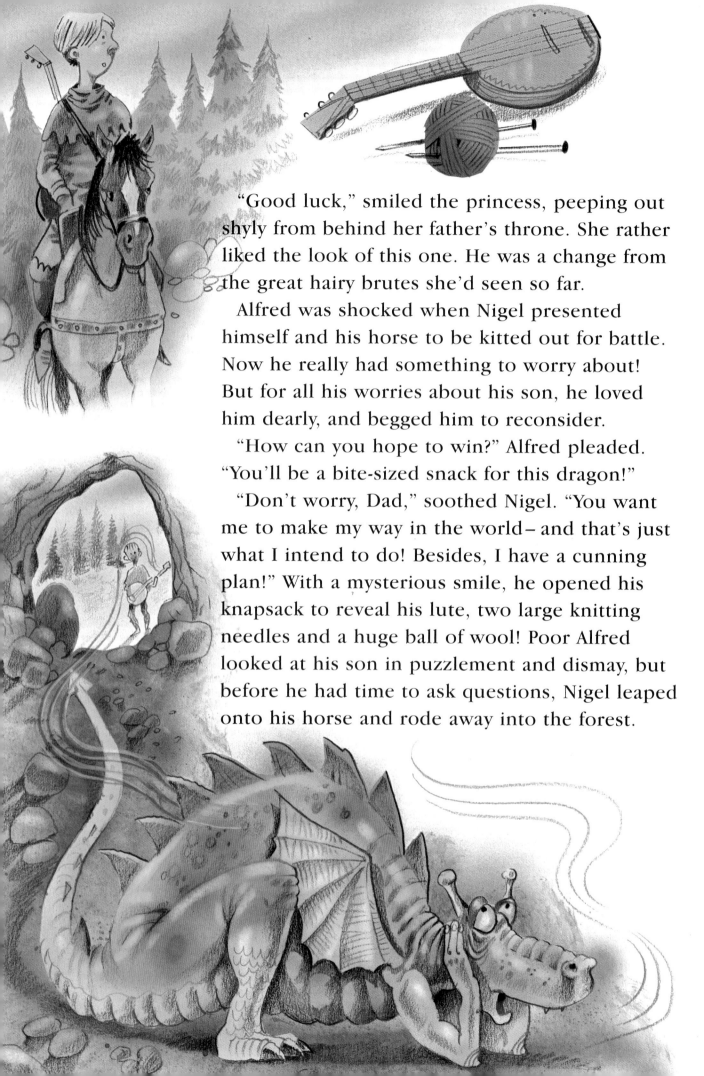

"Good luck," smiled the princess, peeping out shyly from behind her father's throne. She rather liked the look of this one. He was a change from the great hairy brutes she'd seen so far.

Alfred was shocked when Nigel presented himself and his horse to be kitted out for battle. Now he really had something to worry about! But for all his worries about his son, he loved him dearly, and begged him to reconsider.

"How can you hope to win?" Alfred pleaded. "You'll be a bite-sized snack for this dragon!"

"Don't worry, Dad," soothed Nigel. "You want me to make my way in the world– and that's just what I intend to do! Besides, I have a cunning plan!" With a mysterious smile, he opened his knapsack to reveal his lute, two large knitting needles and a huge ball of wool! Poor Alfred looked at his son in puzzlement and dismay, but before he had time to ask questions, Nigel leaped onto his horse and rode away into the forest.

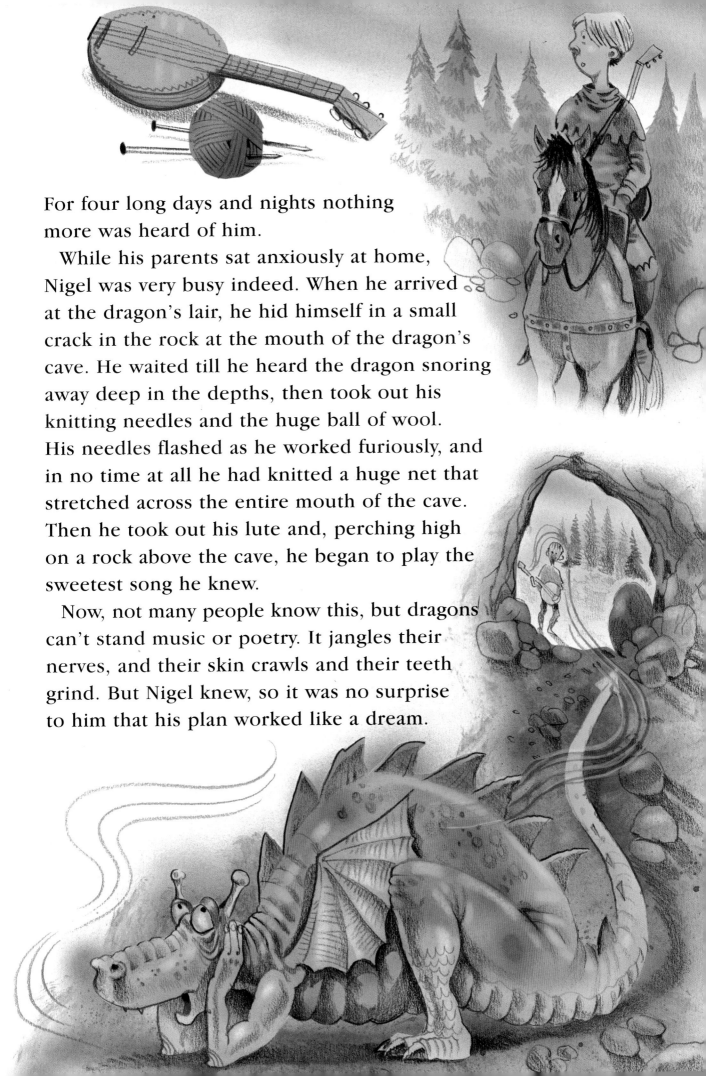

For four long days and nights nothing
more was heard of him.

While his parents sat anxiously at home,
Nigel was very busy indeed. When he arrived
at the dragon's lair, he hid himself in a small
crack in the rock at the mouth of the dragon's
cave. He waited till he heard the dragon snoring
away deep in the depths, then took out his
knitting needles and the huge ball of wool.
His needles flashed as he worked furiously, and
in no time at all he had knitted a huge net that
stretched across the entire mouth of the cave.
Then he took out his lute and, perching high
on a rock above the cave, he began to play the
sweetest song he knew.

Now, not many people know this, but dragons
can't stand music or poetry. It jangles their
nerves, and their skin crawls and their teeth
grind. But Nigel knew, so it was no surprise
to him that his plan worked like a dream.

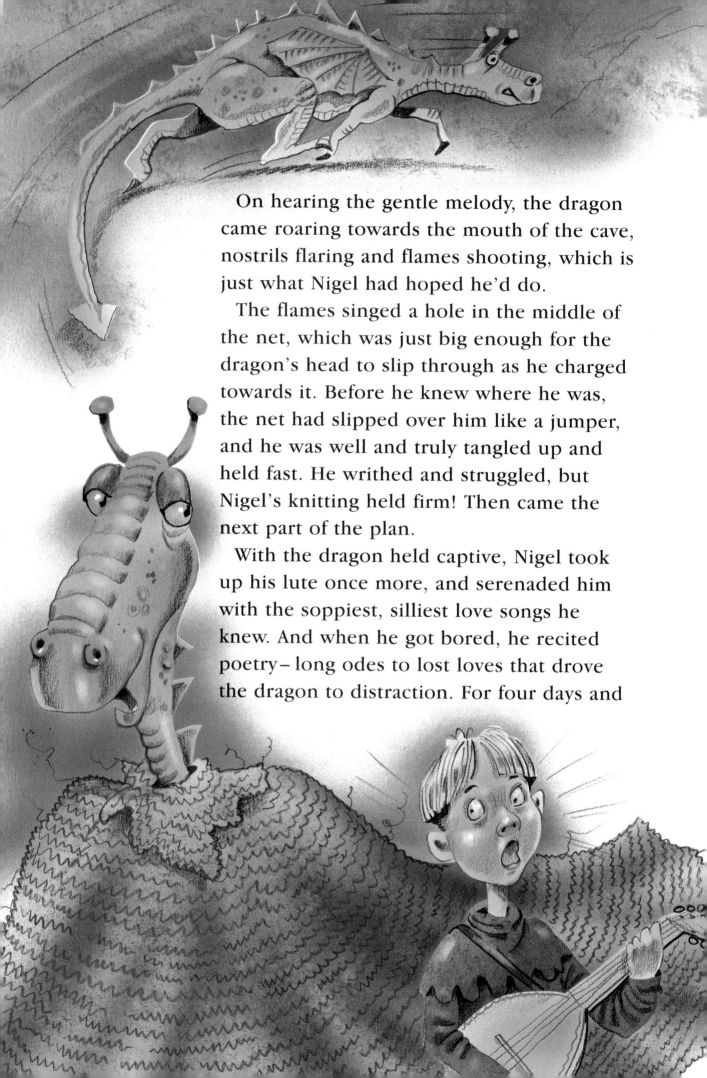

On hearing the gentle melody, the dragon came roaring towards the mouth of the cave, nostrils flaring and flames shooting, which is just what Nigel had hoped he'd do.

The flames singed a hole in the middle of the net, which was just big enough for the dragon's head to slip through as he charged towards it. Before he knew where he was, the net had slipped over him like a jumper, and he was well and truly tangled up and held fast. He writhed and struggled, but Nigel's knitting held firm! Then came the next part of the plan.

With the dragon held captive, Nigel took up his lute once more, and serenaded him with the soppiest, silliest love songs he knew. And when he got bored, he recited poetry – long odes to lost loves that drove the dragon to distraction. For four days and

nights Nigel kept up his performance, until the demented dragon could stand it no more, and begged Nigel to let him flee the kingdom to escape. Nigel kept on singing while he cut through the net, and the last time he saw the dragon, he was tearing across the distant hills, howling and holding his ears.

Nigel rode home triumphantly, and as you can imagine, the king was delighted. So was the princess, who whisked him up the aisle as fast as you can say knit one, purl one. As for Alfred, well, his worries were over at last. Nigel had made his mark as a knight to remember, and in the process had landed himself the perfect position in life, as a prince with nothing better to do than to spend his days singing, playing his lute and knitting. And he kept the princess in lovely jumpers. Perfect!

A Whale of a Time

Did you hear the story
   Of Wendy Bligh,
   The remarkable whale
Who loved to fly?

It happened like this:
She was sleeping one day
When a hot-air balloonist
Flew her way.

He looked down below
And spotted her hump,
"I'll land on that rock,"
Said he, with a thump.

He tied up his balloon
With a beautiful bow,
While Wendy slept on–
She just didn't know.

Then a big tornado
Whirled over the sea.
It blew Wendy upwards
As high as could be.

"What a wonderful feeling!"
The whale cried in glee.
"I am floating above
The sparkling blue sea."

The hot-air balloonist
Took her for a spin.
She chatted to sea birds
And waved her great fin.

He dropped her back home
At the end of the day.
"Oh thank you!" she smiled
And then swam away.

Good Homes Wanted

"**M**eow, meow!" A large black-and-white cat sat on the garden wall outside number three Cherry Tree Avenue, watching and waiting. At four o'clock precisely a schoolboy appeared at the corner of the road and the cat arched its back and purred excitedly as its friend approached.

"Hello puss," said the boy, whose name was Danny. "Been waiting long?"

"Meow, meow," replied the cat, which meant, 'since half past ten this morning.'

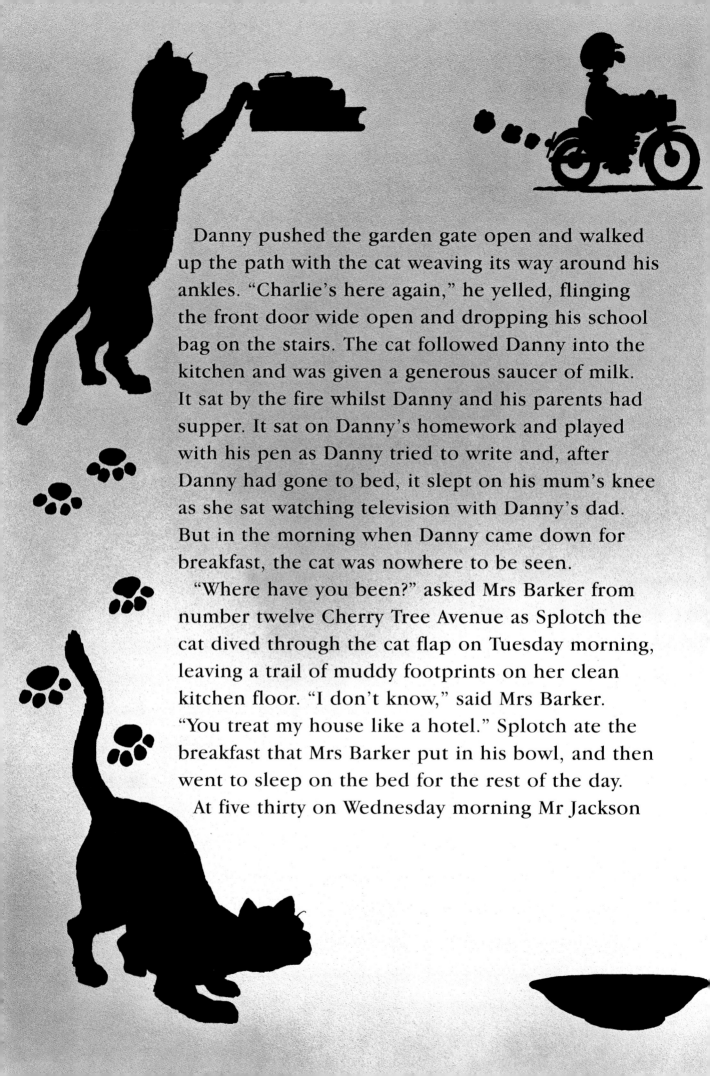

Danny pushed the garden gate open and walked up the path with the cat weaving its way around his ankles. "Charlie's here again," he yelled, flinging the front door wide open and dropping his school bag on the stairs. The cat followed Danny into the kitchen and was given a generous saucer of milk. It sat by the fire whilst Danny and his parents had supper. It sat on Danny's homework and played with his pen as Danny tried to write and, after Danny had gone to bed, it slept on his mum's knee as she sat watching television with Danny's dad. But in the morning when Danny came down for breakfast, the cat was nowhere to be seen.

"Where have you been?" asked Mrs Barker from number twelve Cherry Tree Avenue as Splotch the cat dived through the cat flap on Tuesday morning, leaving a trail of muddy footprints on her clean kitchen floor. "I don't know," said Mrs Barker. "You treat my house like a hotel." Splotch ate the breakfast that Mrs Barker put in his bowl, and then went to sleep on the bed for the rest of the day.

At five thirty on Wednesday morning Mr Jackson

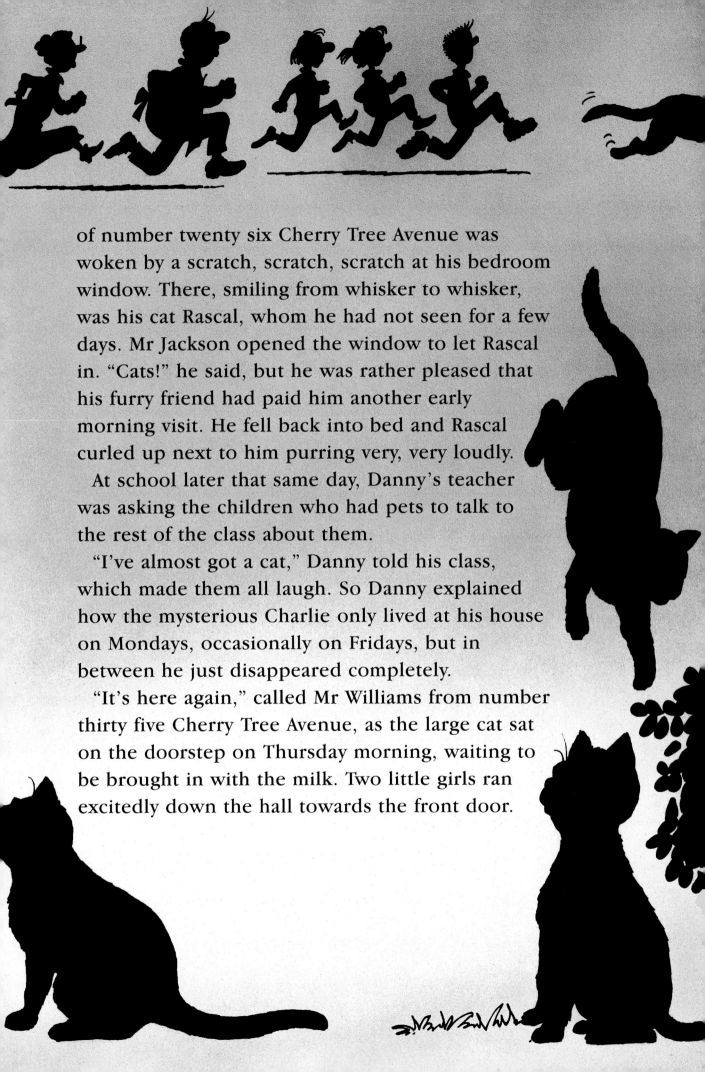

of number twenty six Cherry Tree Avenue was woken by a scratch, scratch, scratch at his bedroom window. There, smiling from whisker to whisker, was his cat Rascal, whom he had not seen for a few days. Mr Jackson opened the window to let Rascal in. "Cats!" he said, but he was rather pleased that his furry friend had paid him another early morning visit. He fell back into bed and Rascal curled up next to him purring very, very loudly.

At school later that same day, Danny's teacher was asking the children who had pets to talk to the rest of the class about them.

"I've almost got a cat," Danny told his class, which made them all laugh. So Danny explained how the mysterious Charlie only lived at his house on Mondays, occasionally on Fridays, but in between he just disappeared completely.

"It's here again," called Mr Williams from number thirty five Cherry Tree Avenue, as the large cat sat on the doorstep on Thursday morning, waiting to be brought in with the milk. Two little girls ran excitedly down the hall towards the front door.

"Oh please let him in, Daddy," cried Suzy, the older of the two girls.

"I want to hold him," said Jenny, pushing her sister aside. Mr Williams tucked his morning paper under one arm. "Now girls, no squabbling, or you'll frighten it," he said. But there was little chance of that. Mr Williams opened the door just a little and the cat rushed in rolling around on the rug enjoying the little girls' attention.

"Can we keep him?" asked Suzy.

"He could sleep on my bed," suggested Jenny helpfully.

"No, mine," insisted Suzy, and another argument broke out.

"Girls, girls," said Mrs Williams, appearing at the top of the stairs in her dressing gown. "Oh, look," she beamed as she spotted the cat. "He's come back. Do you think he'd like some bacon?" The cat rolled onto its back and pedalled an imaginary bicycle which meant,

'I'd love some.' Mr Williams shook his head in despair and retired to the lounge with his paper as his wife and daughters disappeared into the kitchen, closely followed by their very special breakfast guest.

"We could call him Socks," suggested Suzy, stroking the cat's two white front paws. "But I want to call him Patch," said Jenny, stroking the cat's broad black and white back.

"I think we should call him Chubby," suggested their mum tipping finely chopped bacon into a dish on the floor. "He certainly likes his food."

The next day was Friday. At exactly four o'clock Danny was delighted to see Charlie waiting in the usual place on the garden wall outside number three Cherry Tree Avenue.

But today, instead of following Danny up the path and inside for a saucer of milk, the cat meowed urgently and paced up and down on the wall as if it wanted Danny to follow.

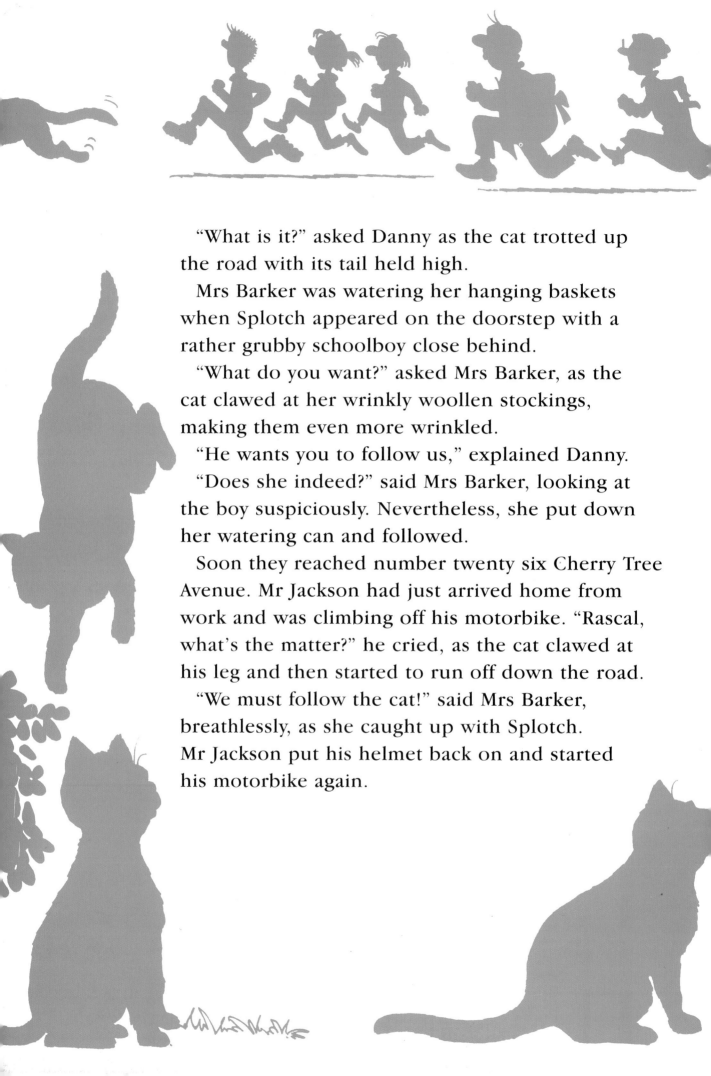

"What is it?" asked Danny as the cat trotted up the road with its tail held high.

Mrs Barker was watering her hanging baskets when Splotch appeared on the doorstep with a rather grubby schoolboy close behind.

"What do you want?" asked Mrs Barker, as the cat clawed at her wrinkly woollen stockings, making them even more wrinkled.

"He wants you to follow us," explained Danny.

"Does she indeed?" said Mrs Barker, looking at the boy suspiciously. Nevertheless, she put down her watering can and followed.

Soon they reached number twenty six Cherry Tree Avenue. Mr Jackson had just arrived home from work and was climbing off his motorbike. "Rascal, what's the matter?" he cried, as the cat clawed at his leg and then started to run off down the road.

"We must follow the cat!" said Mrs Barker, breathlessly, as she caught up with Splotch. Mr Jackson put his helmet back on and started his motorbike again.

He wobbled off after Rascal with Danny and Mrs Barker trying desperately to keep up.

"Nyawww," went the bike as it turned the corner into Market Street. "Meow, meow," said the cat as it spotted Mr Roe the Fishmonger.

"Well I never," said Mr Roe in surprise when he saw the strange line of people trying to keep up with a cat. Curiosity got the better of him, and he thought he had better join in—he might be missing out on something!

The cat then ran through the market closely followed by Mr Jackson and Mr Roe with Danny and poor old Mrs Barker bringing up the rear.

Stallholders gazed in amazement as the cat and its pursuers disappeared around the corner into the adventure playground.

Mrs Williams was pushing her two daughters on the swings.

"Look, it's Socks!" cried Suzy.

"No, it's Patch," corrected Jenny, and they both jumped off the swings and followed Mr Jackson, Mr Roe, Danny and Mrs Barker whose woollen stockings were now very very wrinkly indeed!

At last, and much to everyone's relief, the cat stopped. They all looked at each other, feeling rather awkward and embarrassed, and then they all looked down at the cat. She seemed to be smiling as with her nose she gently made a gap in the hedge to reveal six beautiful black and white kittens. Kittens all ready and waiting for their new owners to take them to their purrrrrfect new homes.

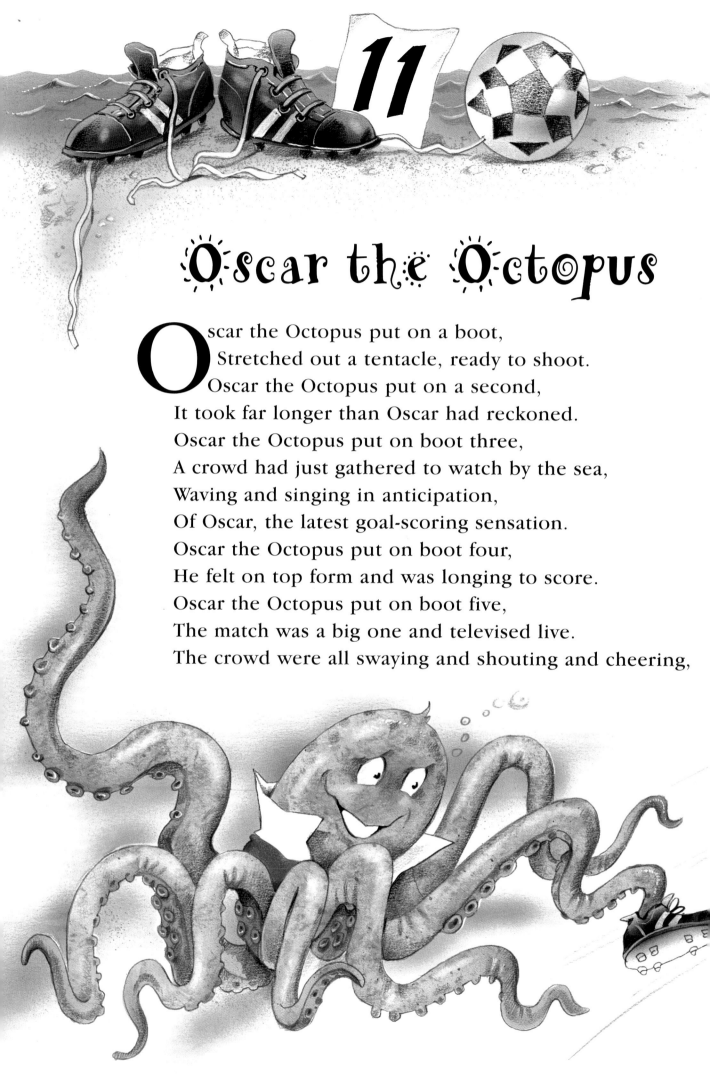

Oscar the Octopus

Oscar the Octopus put on a boot,
Stretched out a tentacle, ready to shoot.
Oscar the Octopus put on a second,
It took far longer than Oscar had reckoned.
Oscar the Octopus put on boot three,
A crowd had just gathered to watch by the sea,
Waving and singing in anticipation,
Of Oscar, the latest goal-scoring sensation.
Oscar the Octopus put on boot four,
He felt on top form and was longing to score.
Oscar the Octopus put on boot five,
The match was a big one and televised live.
The crowd were all swaying and shouting and cheering,

And hoping that Oscar would soon be appearing.
Oscar the Octopus put on boot six,
And stood on his head as he practised some kicks.
Oscar the Octopus put on boot seven,
And straightened his shirt – he was number eleven.
He gazed in the mirror and felt really proud,
It was time for his debut in front of the crowd.
Just one more boot – would he ever be ready?
The laces were fiddly, his nerves were unsteady.
Oscar the Octopus put on boot eight,
Walked on to the pitch but the Ref said, "Too late.
The game is all over, the whistle has blown,
Nobody scored and the crowd has gone home."

Steve and Stella

"Give that present to me!" Steve shouted at his sister Stella. "It's much better than my one!" He launched himself angrily at her and made a grab for the model dinosaur she had just been given by Father Christmas, who was sitting at the end of Santa's Grotto in a big department store. Stella stepped swiftly aside and Steve crashed straight into a model of Rudolph the Red Nosed Reindeer, complete with flashing nose. It swayed, then fell, bringing the Christmas tree down, too. Decorations went flying, and waiting children ran away, shrieking, for safety.

Steve and his sister Stella quarrelled all the time and it drove their parents mad.

Steve and Stella always felt hard done by. If one was given a present, the other would fly into a rage, either because he or she didn't have one or because they thought it was better than theirs. Often it ended in a fight and usually, the present got broken.

Their fight in Santa's Grotto was one of their worst battles. They had a severe telling off from their parents and had to clear up the mess they had made, paying for the damage out of their pocket money. But it made no difference. They still carried on quarrelling.

Then, one day, something so extraordinary happened to them that they never, ever quarrelled again.

It was a Saturday, and it started out like any other Saturday– with an argument.

Steve and Stella had decided go fishing. They had started to argue, however, about who would use the best fishing rod first. They were both standing by the stream at the bottom of their

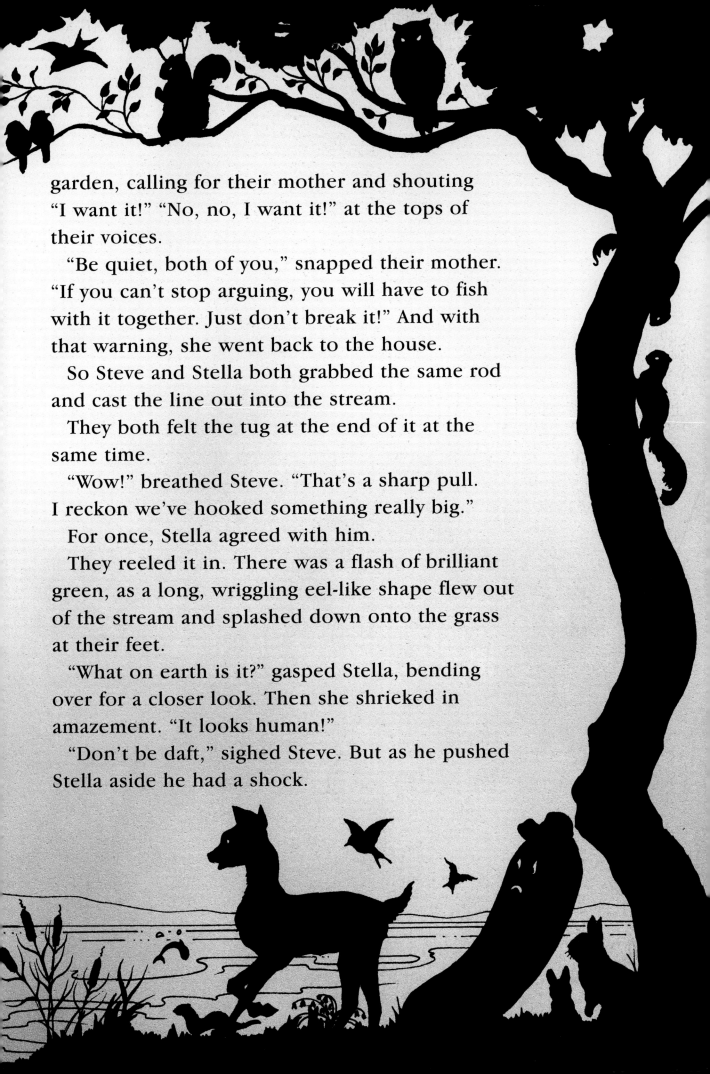

garden, calling for their mother and shouting
"I want it!" "No, no, I want it!" at the tops of
their voices.

"Be quiet, both of you," snapped their mother.
"If you can't stop arguing, you will have to fish
with it together. Just don't break it!" And with
that warning, she went back to the house.

So Steve and Stella both grabbed the same rod
and cast the line out into the stream.

They both felt the tug at the end of it at the
same time.

"Wow!" breathed Steve. "That's a sharp pull.
I reckon we've hooked something really big."

For once, Stella agreed with him.

They reeled it in. There was a flash of brilliant
green, as a long, wriggling eel-like shape flew out
of the stream and splashed down onto the grass
at their feet.

"What on earth is it?" gasped Stella, bending
over for a closer look. Then she shrieked in
amazement. "It looks human!"

"Don't be daft," sighed Steve. But as he pushed
Stella aside he had a shock.

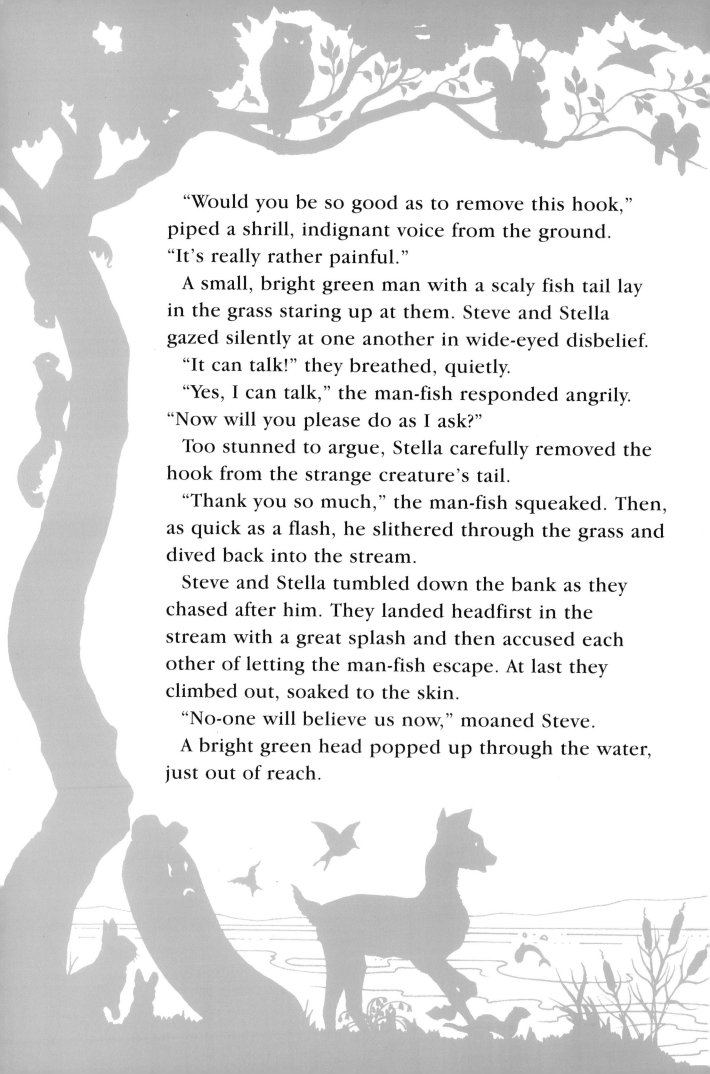

"Would you be so good as to remove this hook," piped a shrill, indignant voice from the ground. "It's really rather painful."

A small, bright green man with a scaly fish tail lay in the grass staring up at them. Steve and Stella gazed silently at one another in wide-eyed disbelief.

"It can talk!" they breathed, quietly.

"Yes, I can talk," the man-fish responded angrily. "Now will you please do as I ask?"

Too stunned to argue, Stella carefully removed the hook from the strange creature's tail.

"Thank you so much," the man-fish squeaked. Then, as quick as a flash, he slithered through the grass and dived back into the stream.

Steve and Stella tumbled down the bank as they chased after him. They landed headfirst in the stream with a great splash and then accused each other of letting the man-fish escape. At last they climbed out, soaked to the skin.

"No-one will believe us now," moaned Steve.

A bright green head popped up through the water, just out of reach.

"I almost forgot," the man-fish called to them. "I grant you three wishes for catching me and then letting me go."

He disappeared beneath the water and was never seen again.

Steve and Stella looked at one another. Were they dreaming? Had they really been granted three wishes?

"I've read about this kind of thing in fairy stories," said Steve doubtfully. "But everyone knows that's all make-believe."

"Well, it can't be make-believe, can it?" Stella retorted. "What about the little green man? He was a fairy tale creature alright."

Steve agreed that they had actually hooked a creature that could talk and was half man and half fish. "But I bet you're wrong about the wishes," he scoffed.

"That's fine by me, Mr Know-It-All," sneered Stella. "I'll have all three wishes. Now, what should I wish for first?"

"Oh no, you don't," said Steve, hurriedly putting a hand over her mouth to stop her.

Furious, Stella struggled away and tried to stop Steve from speaking. He pushed her away roughly, making her even more angry. The next moment, they had started fighting and the wishes went straight out of their heads.

Eventually, exhausted and feeling rather cold and hungry, Steve and Stella stopped fighting and flung themselves down on the grass.

"I'm starving!" complained Steve. "I wish I had a giant sausage to eat!"

There was a flash of bright green light and an enormous, delicious-smelling cooked sausage appeared, just beside him.

Steve and Stella stared at it, unable to believe their eyes and too amazed to speak.

Stella was the first to recover.

"You silly idiot! You've wasted a precious wish!" she screamed at her brother, beside herself with rage. "I wish you were that stupid sausage! That would teach you a lesson!"

Stella froze in horror, realising – too late – what she had just done. With a bright green flash, her brother turned into a giant sausage.

It was an astonishing sight, a sausage the size of a tree trunk lying on the grass beside her. The sausage was dressed in the tatters of Steve's clothes. His baseball cap was now perched on one end of the sausage, which made it look even more ridiculous.

Then it started moaning.

"Help me! I don't want to be a sausage!" came the faint sound of Steve's voice from deep down inside the sausage.

For the first time in her life, Stella felt sorry for her brother.

"I don't want you to be a sausage, either," she said. "I wish you were Steve again."

There was a bright green flash. The sausage vanished and Steve was lying on the grass next to her again.

"Oooh, that was really scary," he said. "Thanks for wishing me back."

"I missed you," Stella smiled.

"I missed you, too," grinned Steve.

And they really meant it. They started to enjoy each other's company and found that it was actually more fun *not* to fight. Their parents were so pleased that Steve and Stella had stopped quarrelling, they weren't cross about the state they were in when they came back from their fishing expedition– nor about the silly story they told about a little green man-fish and three wishes.

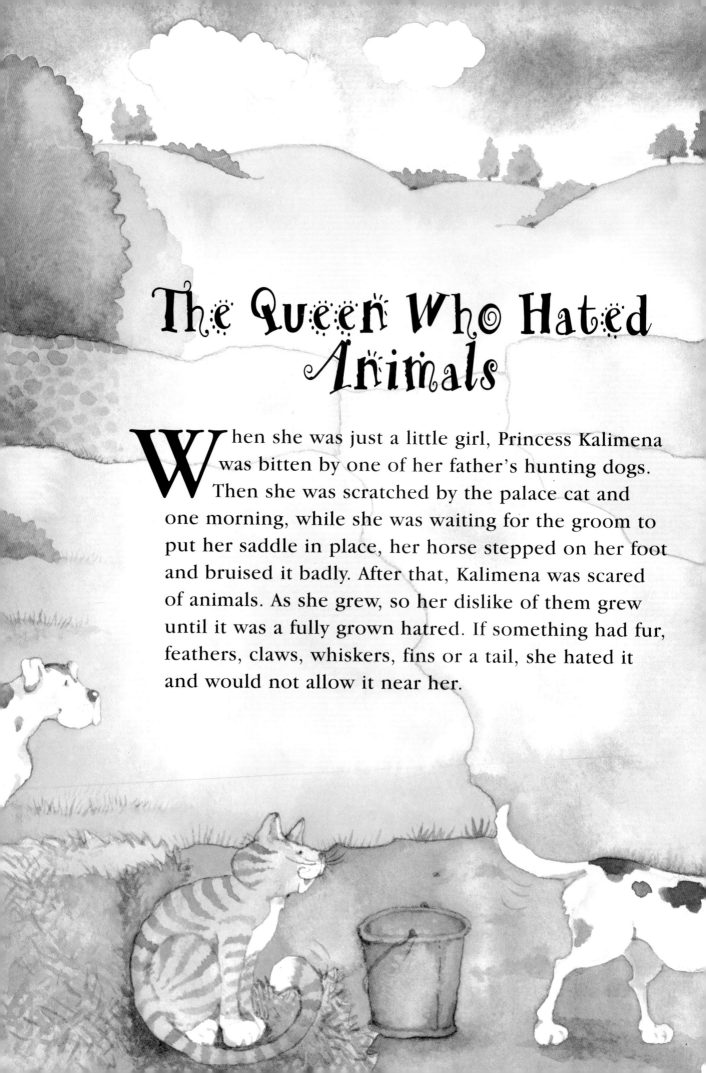

The Queen Who Hated Animals

When she was just a little girl, Princess Kalimena was bitten by one of her father's hunting dogs. Then she was scratched by the palace cat and one morning, while she was waiting for the groom to put her saddle in place, her horse stepped on her foot and bruised it badly. After that, Kalimena was scared of animals. As she grew, so her dislike of them grew until it was a fully grown hatred. If something had fur, feathers, claws, whiskers, fins or a tail, she hated it and would not allow it near her.

So when Princess Kalimena became Queen Kalimena, the first thing she did was pass a very unpopular new law.

"From this day forth, all animals are banned from the land," she declared.

Now this was not such a difficult thing to do in the palace grounds. The horses were removed from their stables, the dogs were taken out of their cosy kennels and the peacocks were banished from the gardens. But the servants in the palace had a terrible time. Spiders were brushed from the corners, shutters were closed against stray bees, but no matter what they did, woodlice always found a way in.

Out in the kingdom, it was even harder to banish the animals. The people needed their sheep and pigs, and their cows and chickens, and they loved their pets. What's more, how could they possibly banish the birds and snakes, butterflies and rabbits? It was a silly law made by a silly queen, they thought.

However, silly as she was, the Queen was very powerful and had to be obeyed. So the people found

a way round the problem. They kept the animals, but disguised them as other things so that the queen and her officials would never know they were still there.

One day, Queen Kalimena decided to take a tour of her land. She rumbled along the country lanes in her carriage, pulled very slowly by four very hot and tired guards.

"Can't you go any faster?" she yelled.

The queen waved to her subjects as they worked in the fields and she was pleased to see that there were no animals. However, some of the people did look very strange. Their clothes didn't fit them at all well and they didn't seem to be doing very much work. And once, when she was passing a hairy-looking scarecrow, she was convinced she heard it bleat like a goat.

When she became hungry, the queen stopped at the nearest house to have lunch. On this particular day, it was the house that belonged to Tasha and her family.

"The queen is coming," warned her father as he rushed into the house. "Are the animals hidden?"

"Yes," replied Tasha. "Just throw the tablecloth over the pig and we'll be ready."

"Now, stand very still," she said to the rabbits on the shelves who were pretending to be bookends. "And you two," she said to the cranes in the corner, "you're supposed to be lamps, remember, so no squawking."

The queen strode in haughtily.

"Your Majesty," said Tasha's mother, curtsying. "How lovely to see you."

"Oh, what a gorgeous shawl," said the queen, looking at two white swans that Tasha's father had hung on a peg with strict instructions not to flap their wings. The queen picked up the swans and draped them over her shoulders. "Oh, it fits me beautifully," she said. "So warm and surprisingly heavy."

She sat down.

Now, the chair that the queen sat in was really a kangaroo with a cloth thrown over him and when she sat down he did his best not to gasp or fidget. Tasha's mother put a wonderful display of food on the table, which was actually the pig, and the queen started to eat and drink.

Tasha and her mother and father watched nervously. Suddenly there was a bleating cry from outside and a thump. One of the sheep, which the farmers had put into the trees to make them look like low-lying clouds had fallen to the ground.

"What was that?" asked the queen, looking up from her meal.

"Oh, just the baby," said Tasha's mother. "He must have fallen out of his cot again. I'll go and put him back."

Just then, a hedgehog wandered out from under a chair and stopped in the middle of the floor.

"What is that?" asked the queen. "It looks like a hedge..."

"Oh, my brush," said Tasha. "I wondered where that had got to." And she picked up the hedgehog, turned it upside down and started brushing her hair with it. "I hate to have tangled hair, don't you, Your Majesty?"

"Indeed," said the queen, eyeing Tasha suspiciously. "Is there any pepper?" she asked.

"Here, Your Majesty," said Tasha, placing her pet hamster in front of the queen. Hammie was wearing a little hat full of pepper with holes in the top, and he was standing as still and upright as he could, with his eyes closed.

"What a strange-looking pepper pot," said the queen, picking up Hammie and shaking him vigorously. A cloud of pepper filled the room and Hammie sneezed.

"It sneezed!" cried the queen in alarm. "I am sure the pepper pot sneezed!"

Then one of the rabbits moved. It wasn't his fault; the heavy books were leaning against him. As books tumbled off the shelf the rabbit leapt out of the way to avoid being squashed.

The queen screamed and turned to Tasha, her face red with rage.

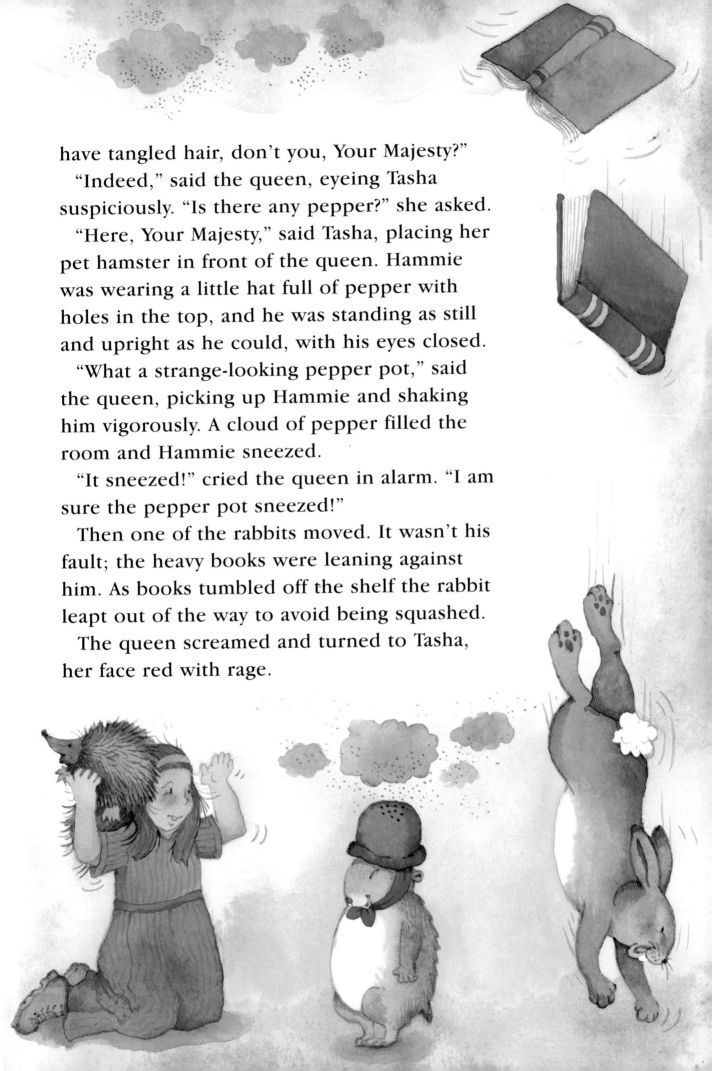

"You know I have banned animals!" she yelled, and stamped her foot hard, right on the kangaroo's foot. That was enough for the poor kangaroo. He started bounding around the room, with the queen clinging on for dear life. Squealing loudly, the pig ran off and the plates fell crashing to the floor. The cranes squawked and took off out of the window, the lampshades still on their heads. The cat cushions leapt from the chairs, the snake draught-excluders slithered out of the door and the kangaroo bounded out of the house and made for the open country, with Queen Kalimena still clinging on.

"Put me down!" screamed the queen, and finally the kangaroo did – but just then the swans decided it was time to get away.

They flapped their wings and took to the

air, taking the queen with them as they flew. Higher and higher they soared.

"OHHH!" screamed the queen. Then "Oohh," in a slightly different voice. She was flying, which was something she'd always wanted to do. The swans took her high over her kingdom, beating their great white wings and the queen laughed as she swooped low over the palace and the town. When the swans finally brought the queen gently down beside the lake, she was ecstatic with joy.

Her court officials ran outside.

"Shoot the swans," one of them shouted.

"No," cried the queen. "Let them live. Let all the animals live. They are wonderful."

So the swans returned to the lake, the rabbits went back to their burrows, the sheep climbed gratefully down from the trees, and they all lived properly ever after.

Ice Cool Duel

Angelino's Famous Ice Cream
Has a rival in the town,
A juggling ice cream man called Bob,
Who'll bring his business down.

Bob is quite a decent sort,
Saying, "Angelino, stick around,
We'll have a juggling contest,
The winner keeps the round."

Bob's talent is impressive,
Though his ice cream tastes like soap.
Poor Angelino, no performer,
Doesn't think he has a hope.

A crowd soon gathers on the pavement,
Two small children keep the scores.
Bob twirls a triple cornet,
To a ripple of applause.

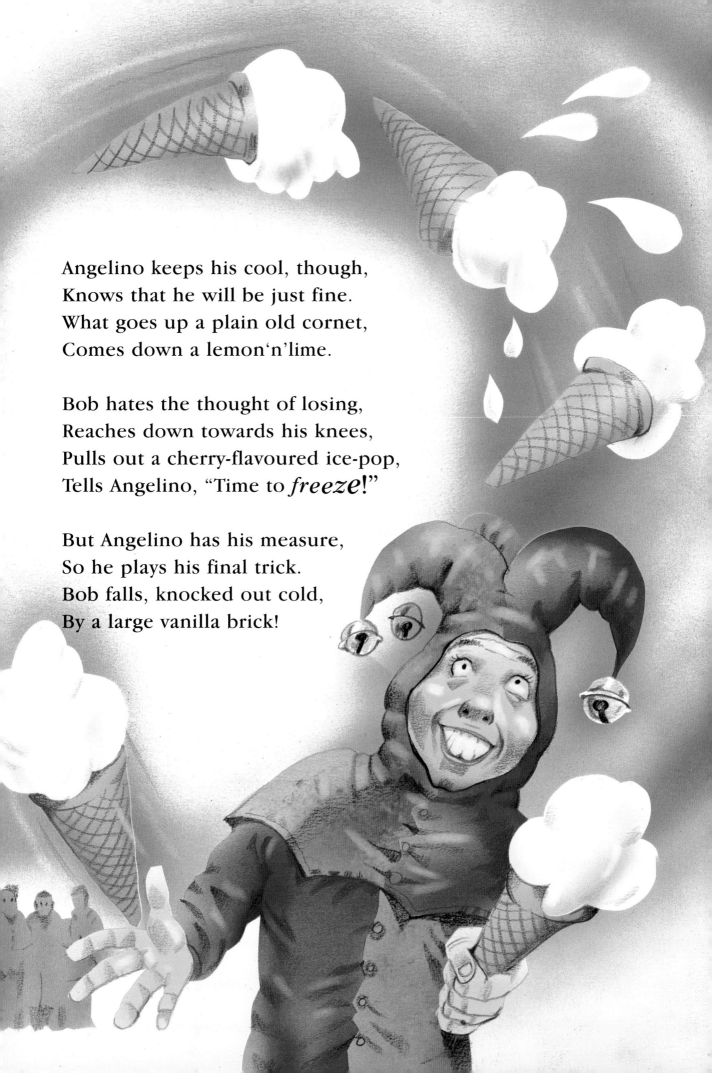

Angelino keeps his cool, though,
Knows that he will be just fine.
What goes up a plain old cornet,
Comes down a lemon'n'lime.

Bob hates the thought of losing,
Reaches down towards his knees,
Pulls out a cherry-flavoured ice-pop,
Tells Angelino, "Time to *freeze*!"

But Angelino has his measure,
So he plays his final trick.
Bob falls, knocked out cold,
By a large vanilla brick!

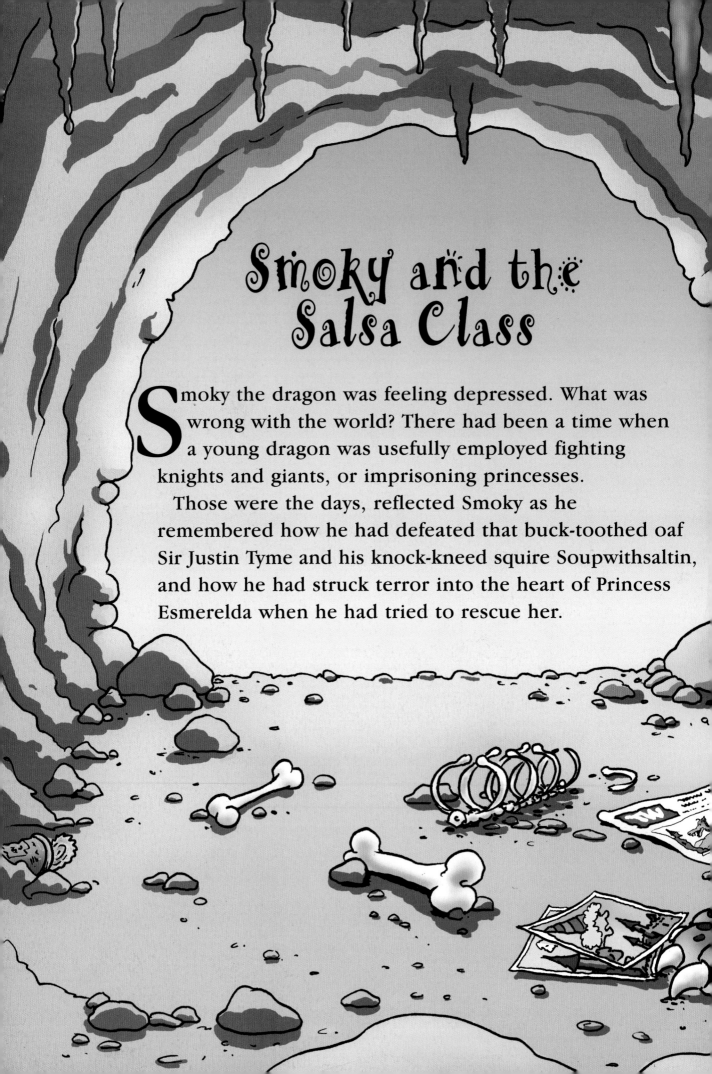

Smoky and the Salsa Class

Smoky the dragon was feeling depressed. What was wrong with the world? There had been a time when a young dragon was usefully employed fighting knights and giants, or imprisoning princesses.

Those were the days, reflected Smoky as he remembered how he had defeated that buck-toothed oaf Sir Justin Tyme and his knock-kneed squire Soupwithsaltin, and how he had struck terror into the heart of Princess Esmerelda when he had tried to rescue her.

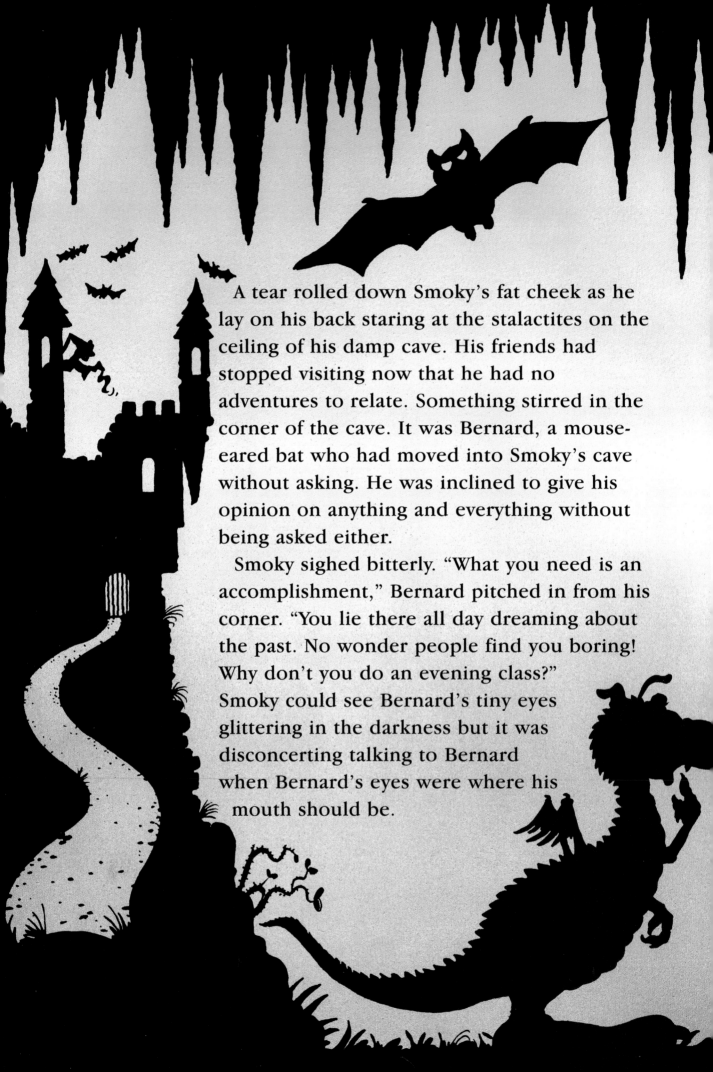

A tear rolled down Smoky's fat cheek as he lay on his back staring at the stalactites on the ceiling of his damp cave. His friends had stopped visiting now that he had no adventures to relate. Something stirred in the corner of the cave. It was Bernard, a mouse-eared bat who had moved into Smoky's cave without asking. He was inclined to give his opinion on anything and everything without being asked either.

Smoky sighed bitterly. "What you need is an accomplishment," Bernard pitched in from his corner. "You lie there all day dreaming about the past. No wonder people find you boring! Why don't you do an evening class?" Smoky could see Bernard's tiny eyes glittering in the darkness but it was disconcerting talking to Bernard when Bernard's eyes were where his mouth should be.

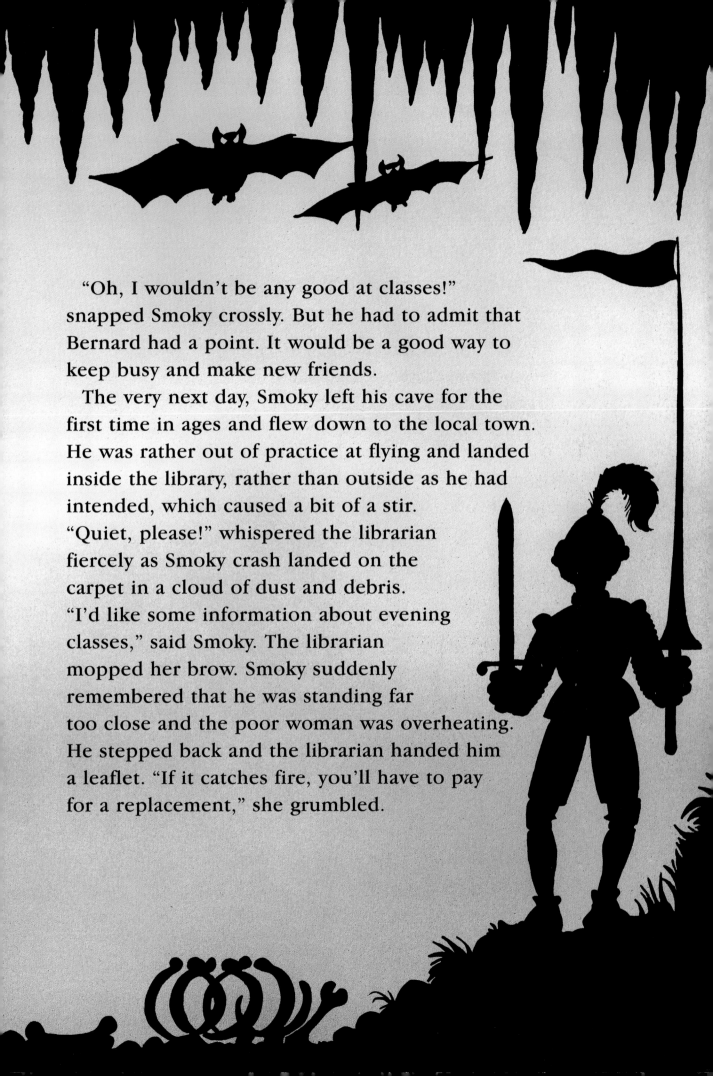

"Oh, I wouldn't be any good at classes!"
snapped Smoky crossly. But he had to admit that
Bernard had a point. It would be a good way to
keep busy and make new friends.

The very next day, Smoky left his cave for the
first time in ages and flew down to the local town.
He was rather out of practice at flying and landed
inside the library, rather than outside as he had
intended, which caused a bit of a stir.
"Quiet, please!" whispered the librarian
fiercely as Smoky crash landed on the
carpet in a cloud of dust and debris.
"I'd like some information about evening
classes," said Smoky. The librarian
mopped her brow. Smoky suddenly
remembered that he was standing far
too close and the poor woman was overheating.
He stepped back and the librarian handed him
a leaflet. "If it catches fire, you'll have to pay
for a replacement," she grumbled.

Smoky looked at the leaflet with amazement.

There were so many classes to choose from! Should he do Ballet or Cake Decoration, Beginner's Spanish or Motor Cycle Maintenance? Or Woodwork or Computer Studies? His head started to spin. Then he remembered what Bernard had said. He needed an accomplishment. Something to make him feel at ease and confident at parties, should he be invited to any, he thought wistfully.

Bernard was polishing off a fly sandwich when Smoky got back to the cave that evening. "I'm joining an evening class," he announced. "Oh, yes?" said Bernard between mouthfuls. "What's it to be?"

"Salsa dancing!" cried Smoky and gave a little twirl. "Salsa dancing?" squeaked Bernard. "Salsa dancing?" And he laughed so much a bit of sandwich went down (or maybe up) the wrong way and he nearly fell off the cave wall. When he'd finished coughing and spluttering, and had rearranged his wings, Bernard said in a rather serious tone, "Don't forget to buy some dance shoes," and promptly fell asleep. Smoky looked down at his large scaly feet and long sharp claws, and wondered where he might find shoes to fit.

The next day, Smoky flew down to the High Street in the hope of finding a shoe shop that specialised in footwear for dragons. After a fruitless search, he decided he would have to try an ordinary shoe shop and ventured into *Booted and Spurred*.

"I'd like a pair of dance shoes," Smoky said to the assistant. The man looked down at Smoky's huge feet and suppressed a giggle. "Exactly what sort of dancing did sir have in mind?" he asked. "Salsa dancing," replied Smoky. "Oh, that's alright sir! I think you'll find people wear all sorts of shoes for salsa dancing," explained the man. "What about bare feet?" asked Smoky anxiously. "Well," said the assistant, "I think you'll be fine as your feet are quite..." he hesitated, "erm...tough."

Before he knew it, it was time for
Smoky to make his way to the town hall
for his first class. He felt rather nervous as
he approached the hall. What would people
think of him? Would they mind dancing
with a bare-footed dragon? Perhaps they'd
all be scared and run away. He stepped into
the room and looked about him. Then his
jaw dropped in amazement. The room was
full of extraordinary folk all chattering away.
There was a witch in conversation with a
king, an ogre roaring with laughter and
slapping an elf on the back and a knight in
full armour chatting up a princess.

"Welcome, welcome!" said a voice. "You're
new aren't you?" Smoky turned round to see
the teacher approaching him with an
outstretched hand.

He knew it must be the teacher because he was the only ordinary human in the room. He was dressed in tight black trousers, a white shirt and the shiniest black shoes that Smoky had ever seen. "I'm Mr di Magico. What's your name?" asked the teacher. "Smoky," said Smoky.

"Well, Smoky" said Mr di Magico, "We'll be making a start in a minute, but do mingle first," and he was off to greet a timid-looking prince at the door.

Smoky heard a clattering noise as the knight struggled towards him. "Smoky, old mate!" boomed a pompous voice from under the visor. "Long time, no see!" Smoky was puzzled. He didn't recognise the voice. Then he caught sight of a pair of buck teeth. It was Sir Justin Tyme! Smoky felt rather abashed as he thought of how savagely

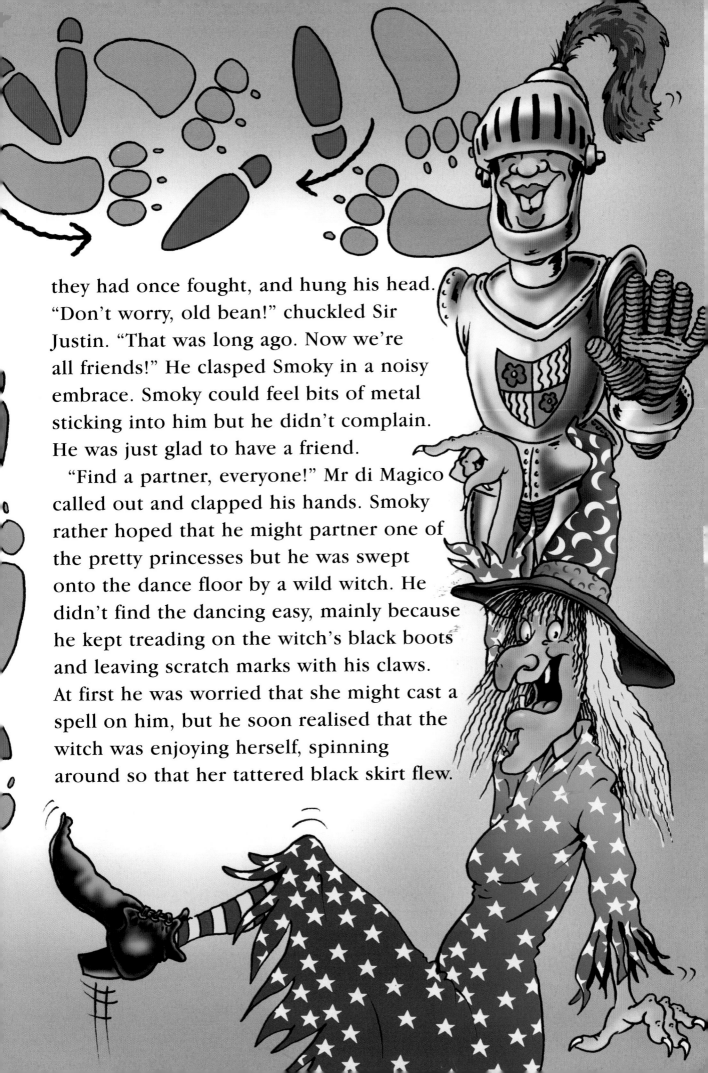

they had once fought, and hung his head.
"Don't worry, old bean!" chuckled Sir
Justin. "That was long ago. Now we're
all friends!" He clasped Smoky in a noisy
embrace. Smoky could feel bits of metal
sticking into him but he didn't complain.
He was just glad to have a friend.

"Find a partner, everyone!" Mr di Magico
called out and clapped his hands. Smoky
rather hoped that he might partner one of
the pretty princesses but he was swept
onto the dance floor by a wild witch. He
didn't find the dancing easy, mainly because
he kept treading on the witch's black boots
and leaving scratch marks with his claws.
At first he was worried that she might cast a
spell on him, but he soon realised that the
witch was enjoying herself, spinning
around so that her tattered black skirt flew.

"And change!" called Mr di Magico. Suddenly, there was confusion as everyone changed partners. There was plenty of "Sorry, old chap!" "May I...?" and "No, after you!" before Smoky found that he was now indeed dancing with one of the princesses. Not once did she look at Smoky. She kept her eyes fixed firmly on the floor and counted out the rhythm under her breath. Smoky decided that actually the witch was much more fun to dance with.

All too soon the class was over and Smoky flew back to his cave exhausted but happy. From the dark corner, Bernard opened one eye. "How did it go?" he enquired. "It was wonderful!" exclaimed Smoky. "I danced with three princesses, a queen and a witch.

I think I'm in love with the witch," he added.

"Yes, yes," snapped Bernard impatiently, "But what about the salsa dancing?"

"Oh the dancing," said Smoky sheepishly. "I wasn't very good at it. My big feet, you see. But they're having an end-of-term barbecue," he continued and started to grin. "And I'm certainly going to set that on fire!"

The Dotty Professor

"I've built my machine!" cried Professor Von Bean
"It's finished and ready to go!
The greatest invention I've had cause to mention!
It can trundle and suck and it blows!

"The wheels are half green – the wildest you've seen!
The levers all stick out at the side!
It takes just one flick of the switch on this stick
And you'll hear all the gears go inside!

"It's got stripy red panels and lovely blue flannels
And a huge great big pipe on the roof!
The coal goes in here and the smoke goes out there
And instead of a 'toot', it goes woof!

"The door's made of glass and the floor's made of grass!
There's flowers and plants on the back!
There's a cupboard inside that's really quite wide,
So there's somewhere to hang your wet mac!"

Von Bean was delighted and very excited
And happily burst into song.
But his assistant was flustered and suddenly blustered,
"I think that something is wrong!"

"I know I'm persistent!" cried Von Bean's young assistant
"And I love your machine through and through!
The lights flash on top when it spins and can't stop!
But tell me – what on earth does it DO?"

With a terrible cry and a long drawn-out sigh,
Von Bean said, "Oh what a fool!
I never once thought – I've really been caught
This machine does *nothing useful at all*!"

The Flying Contest

It was a hot day on the African savannah when the animals saw that a notice had been pinned to the trunk of a tree. They gathered around to read it.

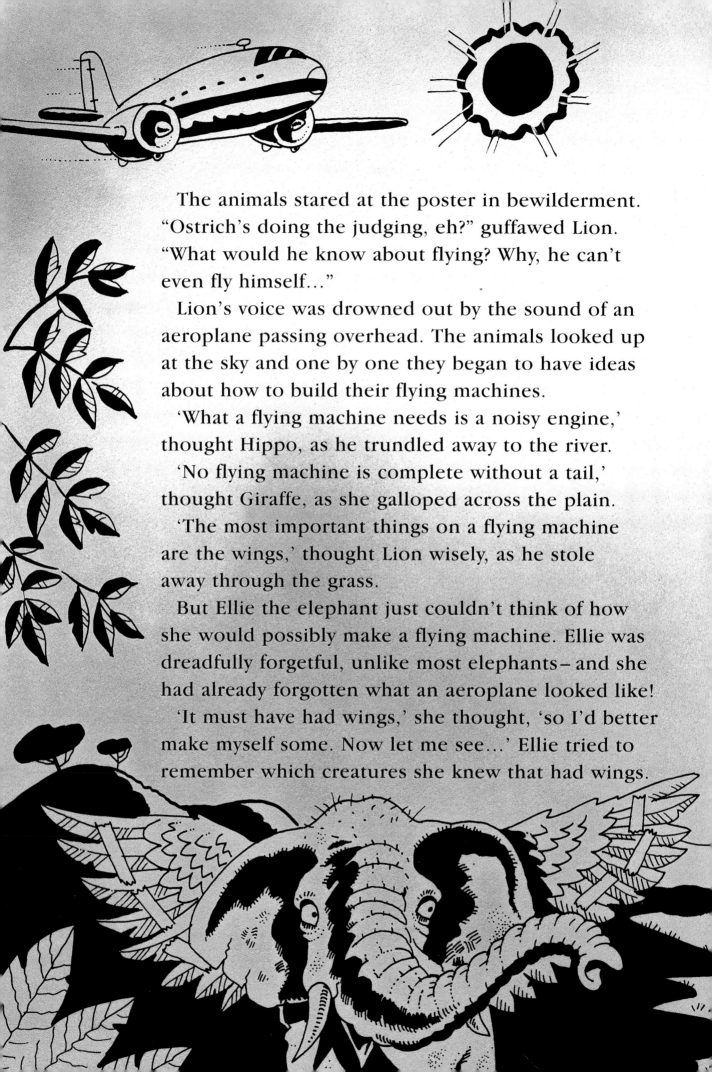

The animals stared at the poster in bewilderment. "Ostrich's doing the judging, eh?" guffawed Lion. "What would he know about flying? Why, he can't even fly himself..."

Lion's voice was drowned out by the sound of an aeroplane passing overhead. The animals looked up at the sky and one by one they began to have ideas about how to build their flying machines.

'What a flying machine needs is a noisy engine,' thought Hippo, as he trundled away to the river.

'No flying machine is complete without a tail,' thought Giraffe, as she galloped across the plain.

'The most important things on a flying machine are the wings,' thought Lion wisely, as he stole away through the grass.

But Ellie the elephant just couldn't think of how she would possibly make a flying machine. Ellie was dreadfully forgetful, unlike most elephants– and she had already forgotten what an aeroplane looked like!

'It must have had wings,' she thought, 'so I'd better make myself some. Now let me see...' Ellie tried to remember which creatures she knew that had wings.

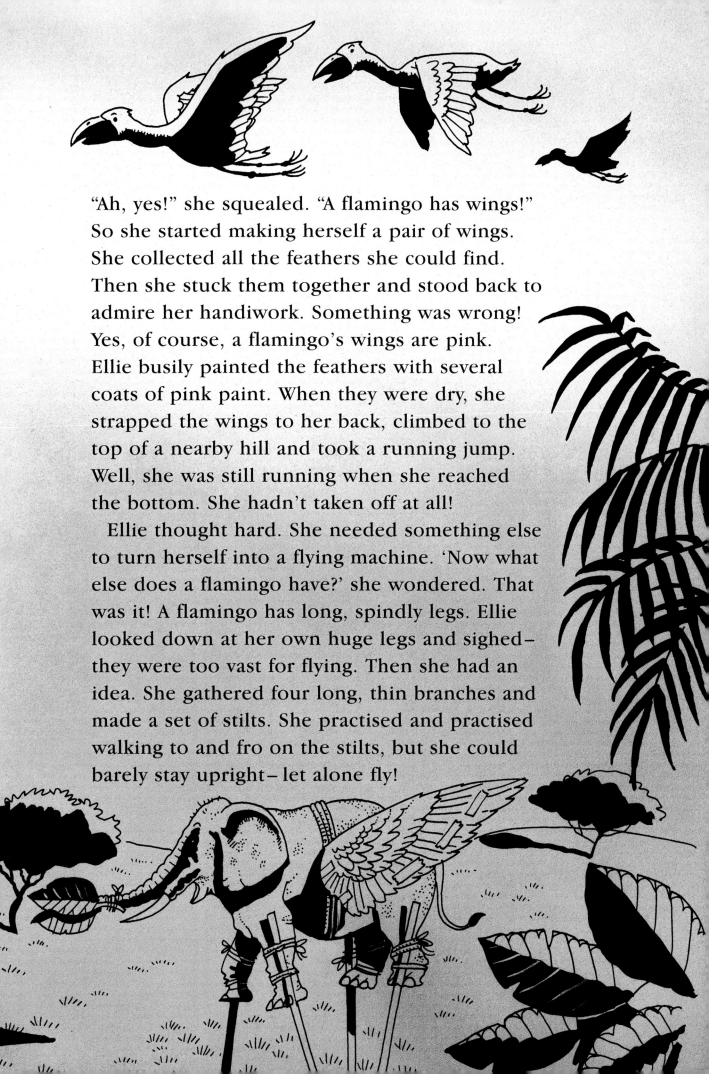

"Ah, yes!" she squealed. "A flamingo has wings!"
So she started making herself a pair of wings.
She collected all the feathers she could find.
Then she stuck them together and stood back to
admire her handiwork. Something was wrong!
Yes, of course, a flamingo's wings are pink.
Ellie busily painted the feathers with several
coats of pink paint. When they were dry, she
strapped the wings to her back, climbed to the
top of a nearby hill and took a running jump.
Well, she was still running when she reached
the bottom. She hadn't taken off at all!

   Ellie thought hard. She needed something else
to turn herself into a flying machine. 'Now what
else does a flamingo have?' she wondered. That
was it! A flamingo has long, spindly legs. Ellie
looked down at her own huge legs and sighed—
they were too vast for flying. Then she had an
idea. She gathered four long, thin branches and
made a set of stilts. She practised and practised
walking to and fro on the stilts, but she could
barely stay upright—let alone fly!

Something was still wrong. Then Ellie remembered. A flamingo has a curved beak. She found two large leaves and bent them into a curved shape. Then she painted them pink and fixed them onto the end of her trunk, like a beak. But she still could not fly.

'It's obvious,' thought Ellie unhappily, 'that I'm too heavy to take off. I'll have to lose some weight before Saturday.' So for the rest of the week, she gave up cream cakes and other fattening foods. 'It'll be worth it,' she thought, 'if I lose enough weight to fly.'

The day of the contest arrived and the animals brought their machines out onto the savannah to show off their flying skills to Ostrich. There was a great deal of tittering as Ellie emerged from behind a bush. She was an extraordinary sight as she teetered along on her stilts, with her pink wings and her flapping beak. She also looked rather unwell.

"Are you feeling alright, Ellie?" asked her friend Wildebeest, anxiously.

"Quite well, thank you dear," replied Ellie. "Just a little hungry."

"Let's begin!" snapped Ostrich. "Who's first?"

"I am!" cried Hippo, leaping into the seat of his machine. "What a flying machine needs is noise!" he shouted over the roar of the engine. It really was a magnificent machine. It looked a bit like a lawn mower with huge, shiny pistons.

"Isn't there something missing?" mused Cheetah with a smile.

But Hippo wasn't listening. "Here we go!" he cried, letting out the throttle as the machine shot off across the savannah in a cloud of black smoke. Faster and faster went the machine but it didn't take off, of course, because it had no wings.

"Ha, ha!" laughed the animals with glee, as it smashed into a tree and Hippo climbed out looking disgruntled.

"Who's next?" asked Ostrich.

"Oh, I am," said Giraffe. "What a flying machine really needs is a tail," she said, as she climbed into her machine. It was spectacular, with a gleaming metal tail standing proudly at the back. She cantered off across the savannah, four legs sticking out of the machine. Faster and faster she galloped, but she didn't take off, because it had no wings.

"Hee, hee!" giggled the animals, as Giraffe's legs got all tangled up and she collapsed in a dizzy heap.

"Who's next?" said Ostrich.

"Meee!" purred Lion smugly. "You foolish animals," he sneered. "What a flying machine needs is wings." And he leaped effortlessly into his machine. The animals gasped in awe. Lion's machine had a simply beautiful pair of silver wings stretching out on either side.

Faster and faster went Lion across the savannah and it looked as if his machine really might take off. He gave a great roar of triumph and a fly flew into his gaping mouth. He coughed, lost control and the machine careered off course and into a watering hole.

"Ha, ha, hee, hee!" bellowed the animals, as a very wet Lion crawled out of the water.

"Now, what about Ellie?" said Ostrich, wiping tears of mirth from his eyes. But Ellie was nowhere to be found. When she had seen the other animals' machines she had been so ashamed of her own efforts that she had crept away. Besides, she was feeling very hungry.

'I'll have a nice picnic on my own,' she thought. She wrapped all her favourite foods in a tablecloth, tied it with string and set off to find a quiet spot. She was munching a delicious jam doughnut when suddenly there was a tremendous gust of wind. Before she

could escape, she felt herself being lifted up in the tablecloth and carried high above the trees. She struggled to free herself and got all tangled up in the string.

Just then, the other animals felt the gust too. They looked up into the sky and stared in amazement. They couldn't believe their eyes! Ellie was floating down towards them with the tablecloth and string acting as a parachute!

"Ellie, you're the winner!" announced Ostrich, as she landed on the ground with a soft bump. The other animals cheered and cheered. "It's time to claim your prize – bring out the balloon basket!" called Ostrich. Ellie tried to squeeze her large frame into the basket, but it simply wouldn't fit.

"I'd miss you all anyway," she said. "Why don't we have a picnic together instead? I'm still hungry, as it happens!" So that is exactly what they all did.

The Singing Bank Robber

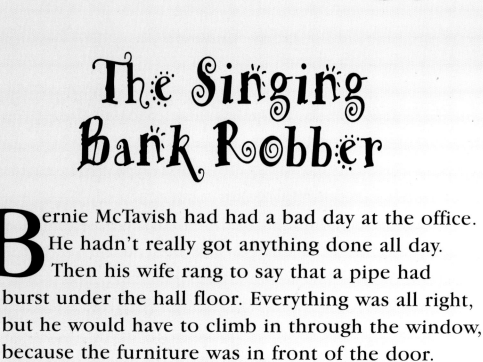

Bernie McTavish had had a bad day at the office. He hadn't really got anything done all day. Then his wife rang to say that a pipe had burst under the hall floor. Everything was all right, but he would have to climb in through the window, because the furniture was in front of the door.

Bernie put the telephone down with a sigh and put on his black leather motorcycle gear. He couldn't see the bag he usually put his office clothes in, so he found an empty cash bag in the safe and stuffed them into that instead.

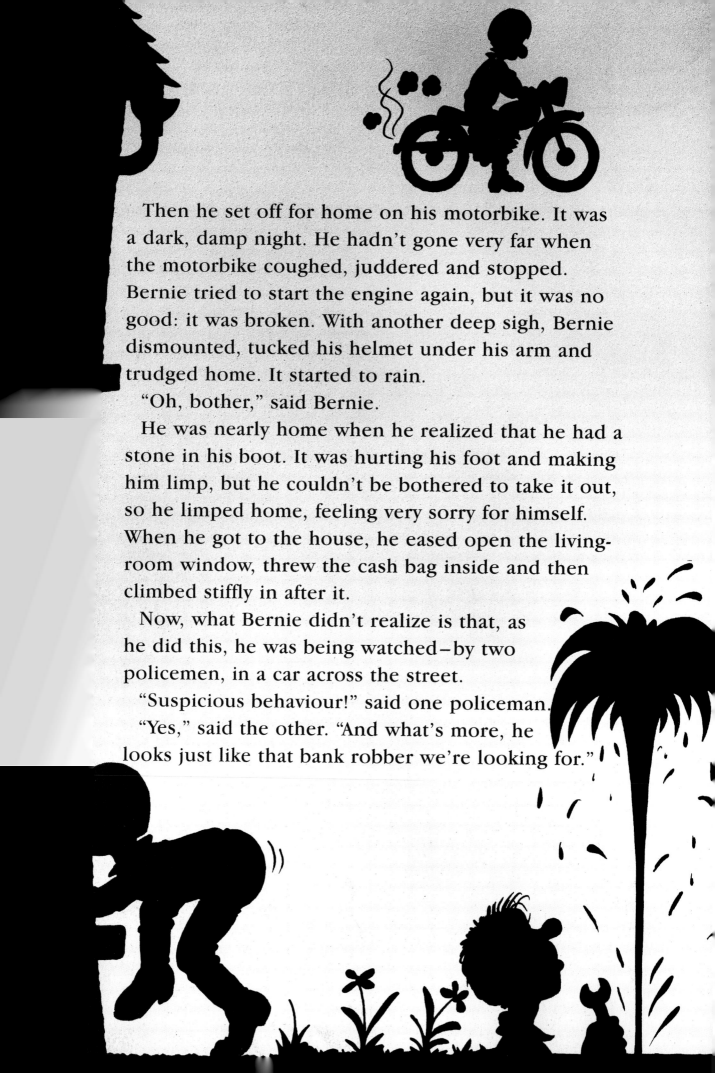

Then he set off for home on his motorbike. It was
a dark, damp night. He hadn't gone very far when
the motorbike coughed, juddered and stopped.
Bernie tried to start the engine again, but it was no
good: it was broken. With another deep sigh, Bernie
dismounted, tucked his helmet under his arm and
trudged home. It started to rain.

"Oh, bother," said Bernie.

He was nearly home when he realized that he had a
stone in his boot. It was hurting his foot and making
him limp, but he couldn't be bothered to take it out,
so he limped home, feeling very sorry for himself.
When he got to the house, he eased open the living-
room window, threw the cash bag inside and then
climbed stiffly in after it.

Now, what Bernie didn't realize is that, as
he did this, he was being watched – by two
policemen, in a car across the street.

"Suspicious behaviour!" said one policeman.

"Yes," said the other. "And what's more, he
looks just like that bank robber we're looking for."

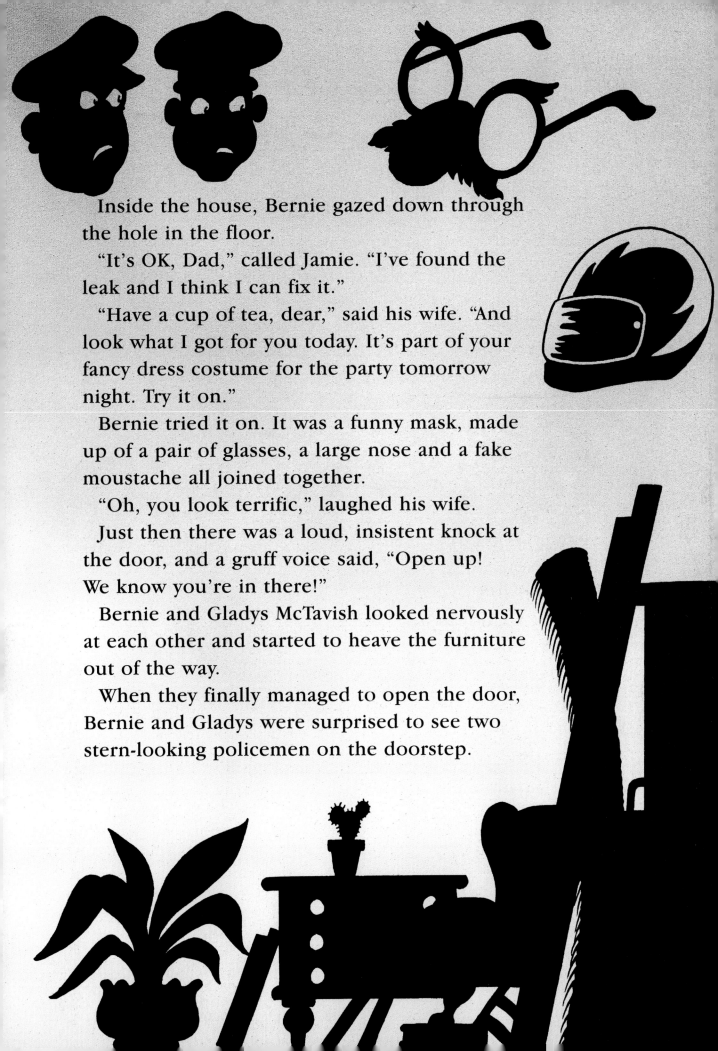

Inside the house, Bernie gazed down through the hole in the floor.

"It's OK, Dad," called Jamie. "I've found the leak and I think I can fix it."

"Have a cup of tea, dear," said his wife. "And look what I got for you today. It's part of your fancy dress costume for the party tomorrow night. Try it on."

Bernie tried it on. It was a funny mask, made up of a pair of glasses, a large nose and a fake moustache all joined together.

"Oh, you look terrific," laughed his wife.

Just then there was a loud, insistent knock at the door, and a gruff voice said, "Open up! We know you're in there!"

Bernie and Gladys McTavish looked nervously at each other and started to heave the furniture out of the way.

When they finally managed to open the door, Bernie and Gladys were surprised to see two stern-looking policemen on the doorstep.

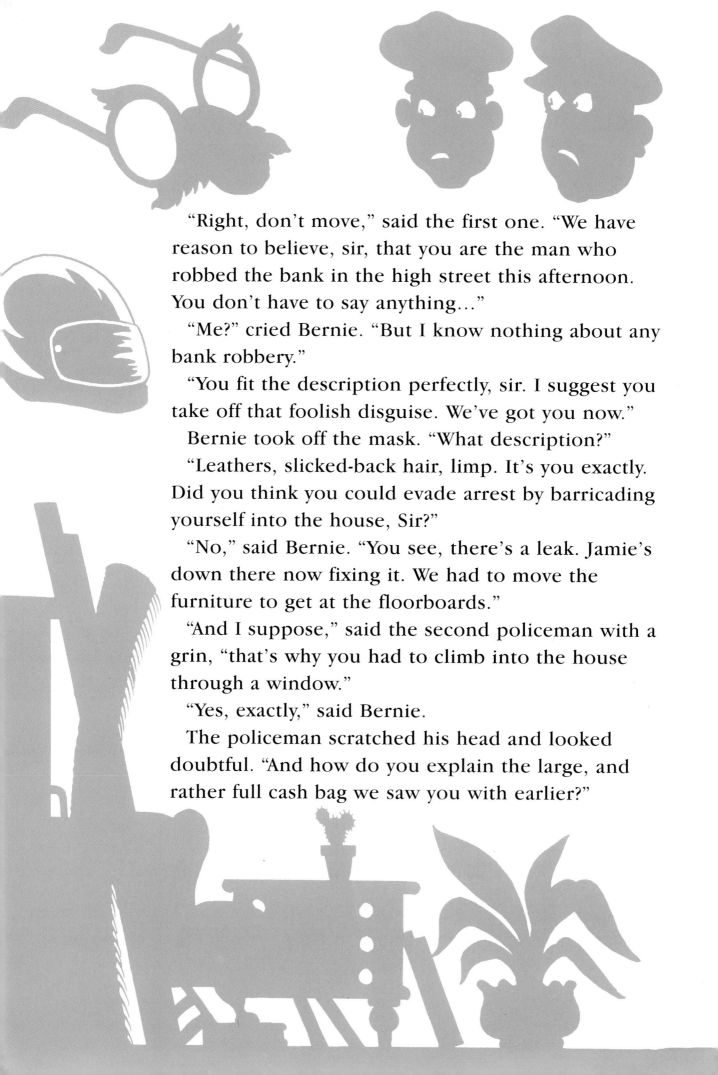

"Right, don't move," said the first one. "We have reason to believe, sir, that you are the man who robbed the bank in the high street this afternoon. You don't have to say anything…"

"Me?" cried Bernie. "But I know nothing about any bank robbery."

"You fit the description perfectly, sir. I suggest you take off that foolish disguise. We've got you now."

Bernie took off the mask. "What description?"

"Leathers, slicked-back hair, limp. It's you exactly. Did you think you could evade arrest by barricading yourself into the house, Sir?"

"No," said Bernie. "You see, there's a leak. Jamie's down there now fixing it. We had to move the furniture to get at the floorboards."

"And I suppose," said the second policeman with a grin, "that's why you had to climb into the house through a window."

"Yes, exactly," said Bernie.

The policeman scratched his head and looked doubtful. "And how do you explain the large, and rather full cash bag we saw you with earlier?"

"That was the suit that I wear in the office," said Bernie. "I always change before I come home. And my hair isn't slicked back, it's wet. I got caught in a large downpour."

"This all seems very unlikely, sir," said the first policeman. "How do you explain the bowling ball?"

"Bowling ball?"

"The robber threatened to knock over the bank staff with a bowling ball if they didn't hand over the cash. We clearly saw you with a bowling ball tucked under your arm, sir. You can't escape us."

For a moment Bernie didn't know what on earth they were talking about. Then his face brightened.

"Oh, no," he said. "That's not a bowling ball. That's my motorbike helmet." He showed them the helmet.

"Ah-ha," said the policeman, as if he'd finally found the flaw in Bernie's argument. "But you arrived on foot."

"Yes, my bike broke down," said Bernie. "You see, there's an explanation for everything."

"And the limp?" asked the second policeman, looking more and more puzzled.

"A stone. In my boot," said Bernie. He took off his boot and held it upside down, and a tiny stone tinkled out onto the floor.

The first policeman whispered something to the second policeman. The second policeman looked doubtful for a moment and then said, "Could you sing for us, sir?"

"Sing?" said Bernie.

"Yes, sing a song for us."

"Anything in particular, Officer?" asked Bernie. He was beginning to think these two policemen were completely mad.

"Something from an opera, sir."

"But I don't know anything from an opera."

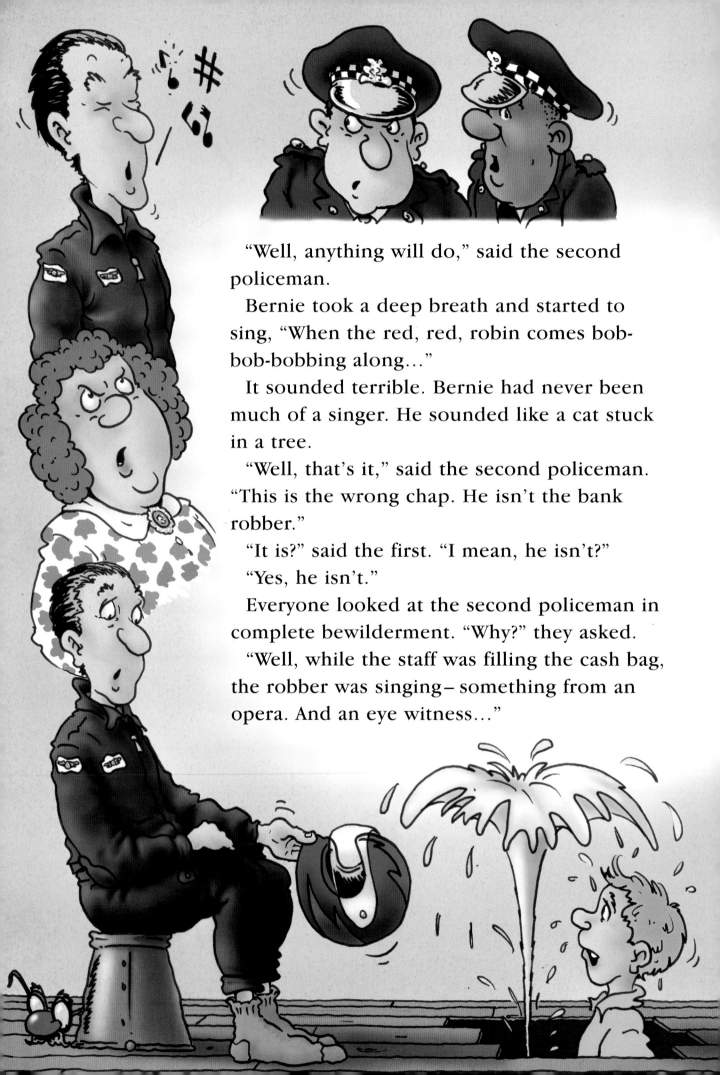

"Well, anything will do," said the second policeman.

Bernie took a deep breath and started to sing, "When the red, red, robin comes bob-bob-bobbing along…"

It sounded terrible. Bernie had never been much of a singer. He sounded like a cat stuck in a tree.

"Well, that's it," said the second policeman. "This is the wrong chap. He isn't the bank robber."

"It is?" said the first. "I mean, he isn't?"

"Yes, he isn't."

Everyone looked at the second policeman in complete bewilderment. "Why?" they asked.

"Well, while the staff was filling the cash bag, the robber was singing– something from an opera. And an eye witness…"

"Or an ear witness," suggested Gladys.

"...an ear witness said he sounded quite good. Very good, in fact. So this man, who fits the description in every way, but sings like a parrot with a stomachache, can't possibly be him."

"My singing's not that bad," said Bernie.

"We're sorry to have troubled you, madam," said the first policeman, and as they turned to leave, he added, "I'd get this mess sorted out if I were you."

Bernie sat down heavily on an upturned bucket and sighed. Could things possibly get worse? Just then Jamie appeared through the hole in the floor. He was dripping wet.

"I can't fix the leak, Dad," he said. "There's a lot of water coming in. Have you got a bucket?"

Bernie passed him his motorbike helmet. "Use this," he sighed.

Did You Ever See?

Did you ever see a jester juggling with ice creams,
Or a pair of giant hamsters, wrestling in your dreams?
If you've never seen a crocodile swallow twenty conkers,
Then you, my friend, are totally and utterly quite bonkers!

Did you ever see a puppy dancing with a brolly,
Or a pair of plump old ladies pushing bandits on a trolley?
If you've never seen an elephant sitting on a daisy,
Then you, my friend, are totally and utterly quite crazy!

Did you ever see a piglet all dressed in polka dots,
Or a princess on her wedding day break out in bright green spots?
If you've never been out walking with a pink giraffe named Sad,
Then you, my friend, are totally and utterly quite mad!

Did you ever see a colonel taking tea with a horse,
Or a three-legged mongoose – it's very rare, of course.
If you've never seen a witch's toad looking rather natty,
Then you, my friend, are totally and utterly quite batty!

Did you ever see a singing worm climbing up a wall,
Or a judge stand up in court and catch an orange cricket ball?
If you've never seen a kangaroo asleep in silk pyjamas,
Then you, my friend, are totally and utterly quite bananas!

Did you ever see a king and queen eating golden jelly,
Or a whale and several dolphins leaping straight out of your telly?
If you've never played the banjo with a very smelly cod,
Then you, my friend, are totally and utterly quite odd!

I know people think I'm mad– but here's my explanation–
I like to make up lots of stuff with my wild imagination!

The Dog who Couldn't Bark

Ben gazed into a pair of large brown eyes, and the large brown eyes gazed back. It was a good face, friendly and intelligent, the sort of face that promised fun. Ben liked it immediately. Even though there were seven puppies to choose from, Ben knew that the little brown-and-white one with the funny ears and the curly tail was the one for him.

The puppy began to chase round and round in circles; then he rolled over a couple of times as Ben looked on in amusement and admiration.

"I think I like this one best," announced Ben as the puppy grabbed the sleeve of his jacket and began to tug at it playfully. Ben's dad frowned. As well as being by far the smallest in the litter, the puppy had a floppy ear that fell over his eye whilst the other stuck straight up in the air. And his tail curled round and round, just like a pig's. "He's rather small," Ben's dad pointed out, and the little puppy doubled his height by standing on his back legs and springing around the kitchen as if he were on a pogo stick.

"Please..." said Ben, as the puppy jumped up and tried to nibble his nose.

"Oh very well," agreed Ben's dad, seeing that the two were already inseparable. "But he has to be a guard dog not just a pet."

The puppy bared his teeth and made the most fearsome and ferocious face he could.

"Oh look," said Ben, giggling. "He's smiling."

"Has he got a good bark?" asked Ben's dad,

Beware of the Dog

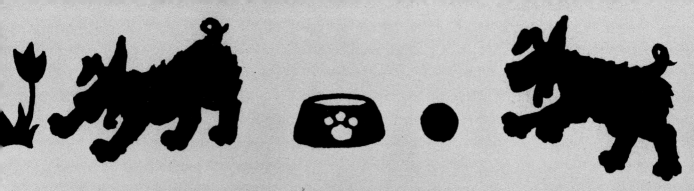

writing out a cheque and handing it over to Mrs Walker, the lady selling the pups. She smiled broadly. "Well that's the oddest thing, he doesn't bark at all. I don't think he can."

Ben's dad was still shaking his head by the time the three of them arrived home.

"A six-inch high guard dog, with a ridiculous tail, a floppy ear and no bark," he complained to Ben's mum as she watched Ben and his new best friend race around the garden.

"Well, Ben certainly seems to like him," she remarked. And Ben certainly did.

It didn't take long for the new puppy to settle in. Ben gave him the name Jake, which sort of suited him. Jake was having the time of his life, a splendid new basket, a smart tartan collar with his name on it, an enormous garden and a wonderful family. He tried very hard to please them all, in particular Ben's dad. He handed him the hammer when he was fixing the *Beware of the Dog* sign to the gate. He hadn't meant to drop it on his toe of course, but it was rather heavy for a small dog.

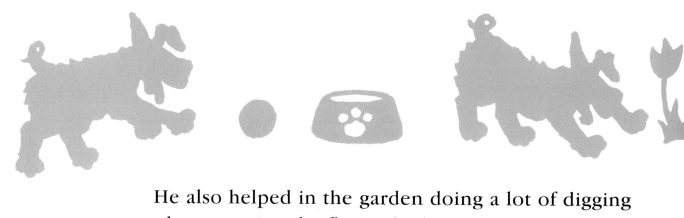

He also helped in the garden doing a lot of digging and rearranging the flower beds. After that Ben's dad had been so delighted that he had shut Jake in the back porch so he could have a lovely long rest in his basket– digging was hard work, especially when you only had short legs.

And Jake did so love his basket. But, as the weeks rolled by and winter approached, it occurred to him that he might be warmer and even more comfortable if he took his splendid grey blanket and laid it on the sofa in the lounge– after all Ben's dad spent many a happy hour there.

It wasn't easy dragging the heavy blanket down the hall but eventually he managed just in time to see two men climbing in through the lounge window.

"'Ere, they've got a dog," said the first man, whose name was Stan, as he shone a torch in Jake's bewildered face.

"That would explain the sign on the gate," replied the second man, whose name was Eric, as he tumbled headfirst through the window.

"What sign?" asked Stan, who could not read.

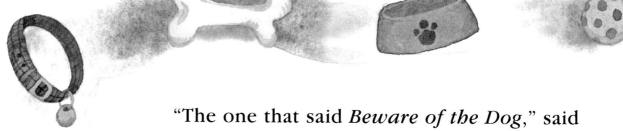

"The one that said *Beware of the Dog*," said Eric, putting his cap back on his head.

"Nice doggie, good doggie," began Stan. He approached Jake, who cocked his head to one side and wagged his tail.

"It's okay, he's friendly," said Stan. Eric tiptoed over, but didn't see Jake's blanket strewn across the middle of the floor and fell flat on his face. Jake licked his ear. "Geroff," said Eric, trying not to laugh even though he was rather ticklish.

"Shhh," Stan said, and then pointed to a cabinet in the corner of the room. "The family silver," he added, rubbing his gloved hands together. Jake stared inquisitively at the two men. They looked rather odd in their stripy jumpers and the peculiar masks that covered

their eyes. He wanted to bark, but of course he couldn't, so he just watched as both men began to fill a large sack with Ben's dad's golf trophies. Jake instinctively knew that this wasn't right, strangers tiptoeing about in the middle of the night helping themselves to whatever they fancied. He ran towards Stan and grabbed the seat of his trousers firmly in his teeth. "Get 'im off me," said Stan in a loud whisper, but Jake would not let go. Eric grabbed the dog by his back legs and pulled and pulled until there was a rrrrr**rrrrip**.

Stan's trousers tore to reveal a pair of red and white spotted boxer shorts. Eric landed with a loud thud on the floor.

"Shhhhh…" said Stan rather too loudly, but upstairs no-one stirred.

Jake ran round and round in circles. He knew he had to make a noise, so he opened his mouth to bark, but all that came out was a weak little whimper. Then everything went black as Stan threw the blanket over him.

Jake wriggled and squirmed and squirmed and wriggled until he saw a scrap of light appear. Then he wriggled towards it until his nose peeped out.

"Up there," said Stan pointing to the top of the piano. Just as Eric grasped the magnificent silver candelabra, Jake leapt onto the piano stool and then onto the piano trotting up and down the keys and creating the loudest and most terrible noise imaginable. Within seconds every light in the house seemed to be switched on and the sound of footsteps could be heard on the stairs.

"Run," shouted Eric, dropping the candelabra and the contents of the sack on the floor and

the two men fled through the open window.

When Ben's dad opened the lounge door, he couldn't believe his eyes. The sack lay discarded on the floor with all his prized golf trophies spilling out of it, while little Jake ran up and down the piano keys wagging his curly tail frantically.

Ben and his mum came into the room. "What on earth happened in here?" asked Ben's mum, looking worried.

"It seems we had intruders," explained Ben's dad. He walked over to Jake and scratched him behind his ears. "But our guard dog here raised the alarm." Ben and his mum ran over to congratulate the clever, courageous little puppy and Jake played an encore, dancing up and down the keys until everyone was laughing, holding onto their ears and begging him to stop.

"I think," began Ben's dad lifting Jake down, "I prefer Bach!"

1 Wish...

The Zoo

I wish I was an elephant,
'Cause it would make me laugh.
To use my nose like a garden hose
To rinse myself in the bath.

I wish I was a chameleon,
Chameleons are best.
I'd change my colour and life would be fuller,
For a change is as good as a rest.

I wish I was a hippo,
A hippo's life seems good.
They don't go to school, but keep nice and cool
Messing about in the mud.

I wish I was a dolphin,
A dolphin would be my wish.
Leaping and splashing, I'd be very dashing,
And swim along with the fish.

I wish I was an ostrich,
An ostrich would be grand.
But if I got scared, would I be prepared
To bury my head in the sand?

I wish I had more wishes,
But now my game is through,
I'm happy to be, quite simply me,
Enjoying a day at the zoo.

Madame Monocle's Magic Machine

It was the king's birthday, and Quentin the royal bard had spent days preparing a birthday poem of immense length for His Royal Highness. He had searched the royal library for the perfect rhyme, for the right adjective, for the words that were guaranteed to bring His Majesty pleasure.

At last the ink was dry and Quentin was ready to read his poem to the king. The court assembled, the king took his place upon his throne and Quentin cleared his throat and began.

"To you, dear Majesty, on the auspicious occasion of your birthday…"

He began to read his verse in a loud and pompous
voice. At first the king looked attentive. Then he
noticed that Quentin was holding a great many sheets
of paper – and was still only on page one! "Oh dear,"
thought the king. 'I wish I hadn't eaten so much.
I'm feeling rather sleepy.' His eyelids drooped.

"...my king so fair

with lustrous hair...." Quentin was saying.

Soon the king was asleep and snoring gently.
The queen was just wondering whether to wake her
husband, when there was a commotion outside the
throne room and in burst an old woman. She dragged
a brightly painted, clattering machine behind her that
made greasy black tyre prints on the marble floor as
she pushed her way through the throng towards the
royal throne.

"Wake up, Reggie!" hissed the queen, poking the
king in the ribs with a long, red fingernail. "You must
do something!"

"Eh? What? I'll teach that two-headed Martian a lesson!" shouted the king, who was dreaming that he'd been abducted by aliens. He sat bolt upright and stared at the old woman.

"Who...?" he began.

"How dare...?" started Quentin. But the old lady interrupted them both.

"I am Madame Monocle," she announced, "and this is my Magic Recycling Machine. Feed it your unwanted bits and bobs, your odds and ends, and watch them become transformed into fabulous, new and truly useful items before your very eyes!" She did a little pirouette before the king and ended with a curtsy.

The king was on the point of having Madame Monocle and her filthy machine thrown out, when he remembered how much Quentin's poem had bored him. This might be much more interesting!

The king didn't believe Madame Monocle for a minute, but he thought it would be amusing to see what happened next.

"Very well," he said. "What can your machine do?"

"What do you say we begin with a royal sock?" said Madame Monocle, reaching down to unbuckle the king's shoe. The court froze. What would the king do? Touching the royal foot was unthinkable! To everyone's utter amazement, the king sat quite meekly while Madame Monocle removed his sock, exposing five pink toes for all the world to see.

The court gasped as the old lady reached up and lifted a lid on top of the machine. In went the sock and up went a plume of purple smoke before she slammed the lid down again. Madame Monocle stood smiling sweetly as the machine began to make the most fearsome and embarrassing noises. It shook and steamed and gurgled and belched until finally out of a chute at one side slid a beautiful woollen scarf!

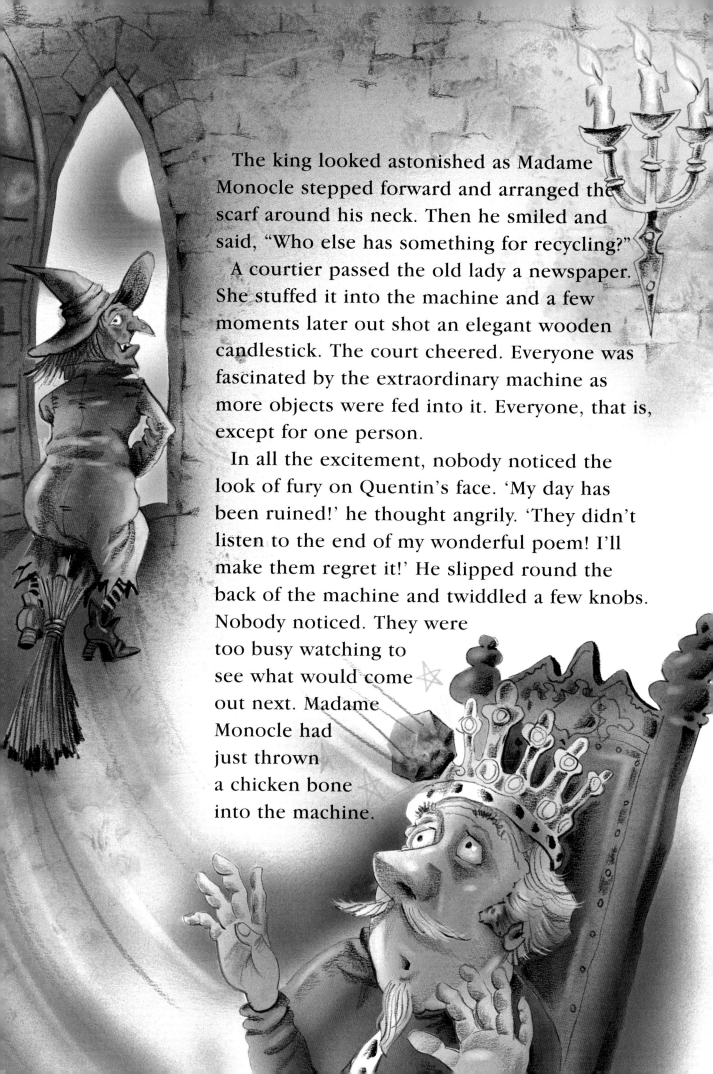

The king looked astonished as Madame Monocle stepped forward and arranged the scarf around his neck. Then he smiled and said, "Who else has something for recycling?"

A courtier passed the old lady a newspaper. She stuffed it into the machine and a few moments later out shot an elegant wooden candlestick. The court cheered. Everyone was fascinated by the extraordinary machine as more objects were fed into it. Everyone, that is, except for one person.

In all the excitement, nobody noticed the look of fury on Quentin's face. 'My day has been ruined!' he thought angrily. 'They didn't listen to the end of my wonderful poem! I'll make them regret it!' He slipped round the back of the machine and twiddled a few knobs. Nobody noticed. They were too busy watching to see what would come out next. Madame Monocle had just thrown a chicken bone into the machine.

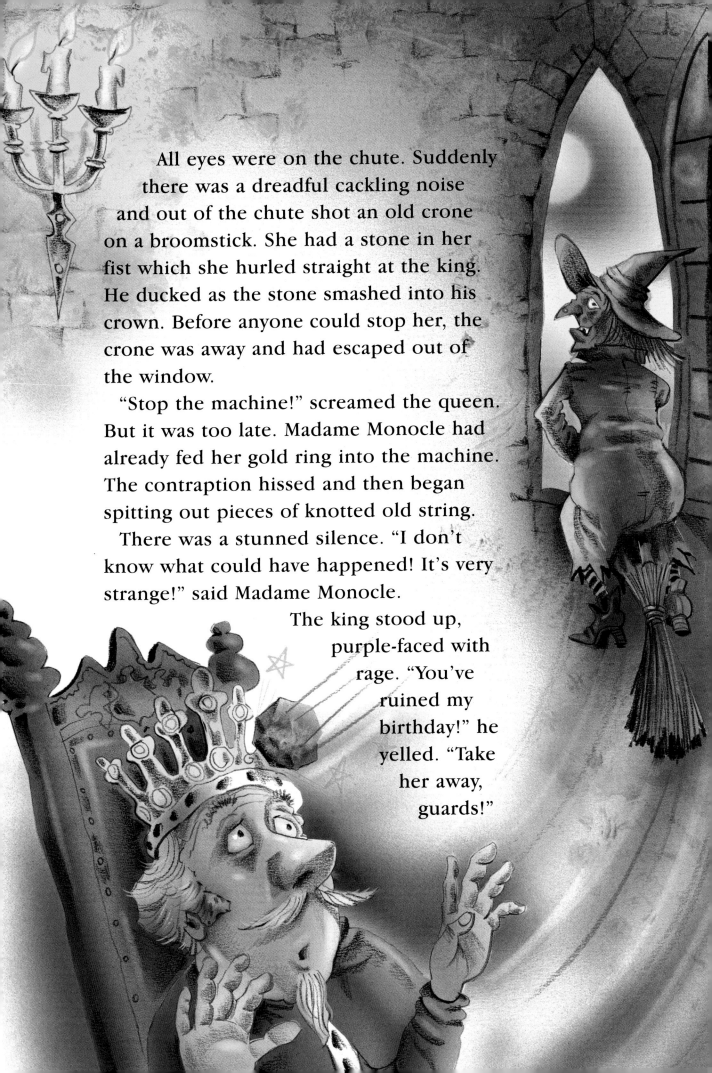

All eyes were on the chute. Suddenly there was a dreadful cackling noise and out of the chute shot an old crone on a broomstick. She had a stone in her fist which she hurled straight at the king. He ducked as the stone smashed into his crown. Before anyone could stop her, the crone was away and had escaped out of the window.

"Stop the machine!" screamed the queen. But it was too late. Madame Monocle had already fed her gold ring into the machine. The contraption hissed and then began spitting out pieces of knotted old string.

There was a stunned silence. "I don't know what could have happened! It's very strange!" said Madame Monocle.

The king stood up, purple-faced with rage. "You've ruined my birthday!" he yelled. "Take her away, guards!"

"Wait!" shouted the queen. "I know your game," she continued, pointing her finger at Quentin who was smirking in the corner. "Bone, crone, stone! Ring, string! Obviously our precious court poet has turned the machine into a ridiculous rhymer!"

"Bring him here!" commanded the king. The guards, who had Madame Monocle in a tight grip, dropped their hold. They surrounded Quentin and dragged him in front of the king.

"Well?" demanded the king.

At first Quentin denied everything. But in the end he had to admit that he had tampered with the machine. He told the king how hurt he was that no-one had wanted to listen to his poem.

The king looked thoughtful. He whispered something to the queen, who thought for a moment and then nodded. Finally, he said to Quentin "Although you have greatly displeased us, nevertheless the queen and I are forced to admire your skill at producing rhymes out of this machine. As punishment, you will feed it your own work and we'll see what comes out!"

Reluctantly, Quentin fed sheet after sheet of his poem into the machine. After much whirring, down the chute came a scrap of paper with a few lines of writing on it. Quentin picked it up.

"Well?" said the king.

"It's not quite what I would have liked…" said Quentin hesitantly.

"Let's hear it anyway!" retorted the king. Quentin arched his eyebrows and read:

There once was a young king named Reggie
Who liked cakes more than meat and two veggies
He declared, "It's a fluke
That greens make me puke,
And chops make me nervous and edgy!"

The king looked surprised. Then he burst out laughing and so did the entire court. "Brilliant!" he cried. "I love it! But talking of cakes – where's my birthday cake?"

There was an awkward silence in court.
Then Madame Monocle stepped forward.
"Perhaps I can help," she said, as she
fed a box of matches into the machine.
Hey presto – out came a chocolate cake
with candles blazing on it!
"My best birthday ever!" beamed the
king, as he blew out his candles.

There Was an Old Lady

T here was an old lady
Who lived down our street,
You wouldn't believe all
The things she could eat.

For breakfast each morning,
A full slap up meal
Of nuts and bolts served in
A bicycle wheel!

She always took care
To never miss lunch,
On brooms, mops and buckets
She'd nibble and crunch.

Trumpets and trombones were
Her favourite dinner,
But though always eating
She kept getting thinner.

For supper she'd snack on
Some bees in their hives,
All swiftly washed down with
The forks, spoons and knives!

What would finish her off
No-one could have known–
For that mad, old lady
Choked on a fish bone!